D1340047

RANDOM
HOUSE
LARGE
PRINT

Also by Lorna Landvik
available from Random House Large Print

Oh My Stars

The View from
MOUNT JOY

The View from
MOUNT JOY

— A NOVEL —

Lorna Landvik

RANDOM HOUSE
LARGE PRINT

Copyright © 2007 by Lorna Landvik

All rights reserved.
Published in the United States of America by Random House Large Print in association with Ballantine Books, New York.
Distributed by Random House, Inc., New York.

The Library of Congress has established a Cataloging-in-Publication record for this title.
Landvik, Lorna, 1954–
The view from Mount Joy / by Lorna Landvik.—
1st large print ed.
p. cm.
ISBN 978-0-7393-2750-0
1. Grocers--Fiction. 2. Radio broadcasters—Fiction.
3. Women in radio broadcasting—Fiction.
4. Minneapolis (Minn.)—Fiction. 5. Large type books.
I. Title.
PS3562.A4835V54 2007b
813'.54—dc22
2007030654

www.randomhouse.com/largeprint

FIRST LARGE PRINT EDITION

10 9 8 7 6 5 4 3 2 1

This Large Print edition published in accord with the standards of the N.A.V.H.

Jacket design: Royce Becker
Jacket photographs: © Ryan McVay/Getty Images

For Judy Heneghan, Kimberly Hoffer,
and Wendy Smith

For all the fun

Acknowledgments

A tip of the hat, a raise of the glass, and a rousing version of "Danke Schoen" as sung by ten thousand cowboys to:

Linda Marrow, dear editor and good listener; Suzanne Gluck, guiding agent and theater partner; everyone at Ballantine Books, including Gina Centrello, Kim Hovey, Cindy Murray, and Daniel Mallory; Sue Warga for her sharp copy-editing; WWW—my cabal and sorta secret society; Deborah Zwickey, who would like to honor her niece Mallory and granddaughter Hailey; the patient teachers and students at the Alliance Francaise; the congenial staff at the Riverview Theater (keep that real butter churning!); my friends at Lakselaget; the good mechanics at Flanery's; all the book clubs I've visited; the Bryant Lake Bowl for providing me a stage; Pete Staloch, Killian Hoffer, Dave Drentlaw, Jimmy

Martin, Drew Jansen, Barb Shelton, Renee Albert, Mary Jo Pehl, Sandy Thomas, Elizabeth Haas, Phyllis Wright, Wendy Knox, Beth Gilleland, and Dane Stauffer for the entertainment, friendship, and/or support; Mark Copenhaver for all the music; Peg Landin and Chris Oppegaard for providing generous lakeside hospitality; and always, Charles, Harleigh, and Kinga for being who you are in my life.

Prologue

Good evening, caller, you're on the air with God.

Wha? . . . I . . . I don't think that's funny.

Funny wasn't my intention.

But you're calling yourself God!

I don't know if you were listening carefully, caller. I said, "You're on the air with God." So am I. God is everywhere; therefore you're on the air with Him. You're also on the earth with God, in the kitchen with Him, in the tub with Him; you're everywhere with God!

Oh . . . oh, I get you.

I'm glad. Now, do you have a question or comment?

Well, you're a woman. What do you think of these feminist nuts who refer to God as "she"?

(Laughter) I think they're misguided. I think they're confused about their own identity and therefore about God's.

**Well, that makes sense, I guess. Best of luck with
your new show, and God bless!**

Oh, He has, caller. He has.

My groan was as reflexive as a burp after a burrito.
For the past week, a person couldn't listen to the
radio without hearing an archival clip from **On the
Air with God,** couldn't watch TV without an update
on "America's sexiest evangelist" trumping coverage
of slain baton twirlers or kidnapped flower girls.

Hello, caller, what can I do for you?

Have you ever read C. S. Lewis's Surprised by Joy?

Nope. Just the Narnia books.

**Well, if you get a chance, I really recommend it. The
title comes from Mr. Lewis's reaction to God in his
life. When God came into your life, were you surprised
by joy?**

**Hmmm . . . I guess I was. Am. Because joy's not
stagnant. It just keeps growing, kind of like a mutant
fruit—like one of those eight-hundred-pound pump-
kins you see at the state fair.**

"Oh, shut up," I said to the voice on the radio. "I've
heard just about enough of you."

There was a party going on downstairs, one I'd
happily return to (I'd better, I was the host) but I had
escaped to my office to take a long, slow, and very
necessary breather.

The lights were off and I didn't turn them on as I
sat down on my creaky swivel chair. Electric guitar
music jangled its way upstairs and on top of it, like
the descant part, laughter. Music and laughter; the
celestial choir as conducted by Bozo.

Sure, I had had a glass or two but I wasn't drunk on champagne so much as I was toasted, hammered, and plastered on the whole big wide world. I knew what it was like to be surprised by joy, and I also knew what it was like to be surprised by surprise. Hell, life is just one series of surprises when you think of it; some elicit a small "ooh" or a smile, and some knock the wind right out of you.

I myself have been breathless more times than I can count.

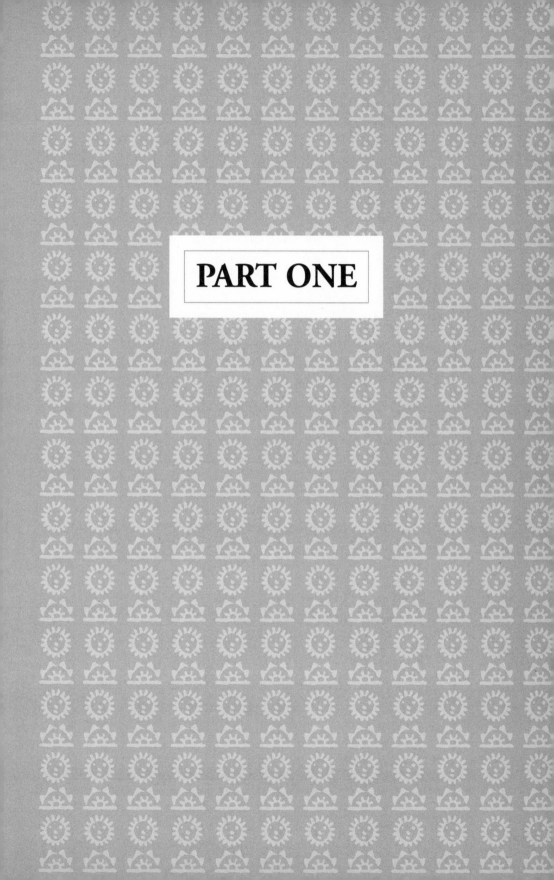

PART ONE

One

Standing at the urinal, I read the first graffiti to mar the freshly scrubbed wall of the school bathroom: **Viet Nam sucks** and **Kristi Casey is a stone fox.** In the fall of 1971, I was a senior new to Ole Bull High, and while I had formed judgments as to the former (I agreed, the war **did** suck), I had no idea who Kristi Casey was and whether or not she was a fox, stone or not. When I met her it only took a nanosecond to realize: **Man, is she ever.**

From my perch on the top row of the football bleachers, I used to watch her and the other cheerleaders, their short pleated skirts fanning out as they sprang into the air, screaming at the Bulls to "go, fight, win!" as if the continuation of human civilization depended on their victory. The late sixties still bled its influence into the early seventies, and many of us considered ourselves too hip in a mellow make-love-not-war way to look at those bouncing, pom-

pom-punching, red-faced girls without thinking, **Man, are they pathetic.** Except, of course, for Kristi. Every time she tossed her dark blond hair, cut in a shag like Jane Fonda's in **Klute,** every time she bent down to pull up a flagging crew sock, every time she offered up a sly dimpled smile, it was as if she'd handed us our own personal box of Cracker Jack, with a special surprise inside. She was the kind of girl who could do uncool things like act as secretary for the Future Farmers of America after-school club or solicit funds for Unicef during lunch hour (she told me having a wide range of interests looked good on college applications) and the consensus would still be: **Wow.**

Darva Pratt was not part of the consensus and, in fact, loathed Kristi Casey and all that she stood for.

"Look at her," said Darva, as if I needed prodding. It was during halftime, and as the marching band played the theme song to **Hawaii Five-O,** Kristi kept time on a bass drum she had strapped over her shoulders. "God forbid the band steal some of **her** spotlight."

After they played the bridge, the band quieted, playing two notes over and over as Kristi began a rhythmic duel with the band's official bass drummer. She pounded out an uncomplicated beat, which the bass drummer answered. The crowd cheered, and then it was the drummer's turn. His was a more complicated rhythm, which Kristi echoed, no problem. The crowd cheered again. This went on, the fans growing wilder as each drummer's challenge increased in speed and difficulty. Finally Kristi beat out a tempo so intricate, so tricky, that after a few beats her challenger threw down his mallets and bowed deeply, his long furry hat practically sweeping the ground. Flashing her bright, white smile, Kristi held up her arms in victory as the crowd exploded, the drum major signaled, and the band played the last measures of the song at full volume.

"Wow," I said after we had all sat down. "That girl can **drum**."

"Of course she can," said Darva. "She's our golden girl."

I laughed. "Jealous?"

Now it was Darva's turn to laugh. "Yes. It's my life-long desire to be the wet dream of hundreds of high school boys."

"Language, Darva," I said, putting a little gasp of shock in my voice. "**Language**."

The third quarter began, and we sat in the bleachers, warmed by the mild autumn sun, watching the game. Under a great bowlful of blue sky, the trees themselves cheered us on, waving their maroon and gold leaves in the breeze and dislodging a squad of crows who cawed their cheers; it was as if all of nature was throwing a pep rally for a bunch of high school kids. I shut my eyes and raised my face to that solar warmth, but my respite lasted only a moment before Darva's sharp elbow found purchase in my lower ribs.

"Look at what your girlfriend's doing now."

Some schools are named after presidents or astronauts. Ours honored a nineteenth-century Norwegian violinist and our mascot was a furry bull. I opened my eyes to see Kristi, chasing it along the sidelines.

Darva made a tsking sound. "When it comes to high school girls, I thought the bar was set pretty low, but man, she knocks it over."

"**You're** a high school girl."

"A status that will be changed tomorrow, when I hop a train to Sandusky, Ohio."

"What's in Sandusky?"

Darva's eyes squinted behind her lavender-tinted glasses. "Oh, sand. Some dusk."

Every day Darva made plans to escape to "anywhere but here," sometimes to great and faraway cities and other times to Podunk and its many counterparts. She claimed every hour spent in high school caused the death of a million innocent brain cells and that she could no longer be a participant in their slaughter.

"Write me when you get there, okay?" I said, nudging her shoulder with my own, and we watched as the Washburn Millers trounced the Bulls 37–6.

A transfer student, I was grateful that Darva had be-friended me the first day of school.

"What have you got?" she asked, sliding her lunch tray onto the table as she sat across from me. "An infectious disease?"

Looking around the empty table, I scratched my head. "Yeah, malaria. I picked it up on leave in Da Nang."

The girl laughed. "I personally like boys who've seen war before they've graduated high school. Gives them a certain maturity."

She pressed the edges of her milk carton apart and then forward, opening up a little spout.

"By the way, malaria's not contagious."

"What are you, Albert Schweitzer?"

"Darva Pratt," she said, holding up her milk carton.

"Joe Andreson," I said, and clinked her carton with my own, toasting my first friend at Ole Bull High.

It was a friendship that would have consequences.

"What're you hanging around with **that** freak for?" asked Todd Randolph, whose locker was next to mine.

I spun the dial of my combination lock. "What freak?"

"**That** freak," said Todd, gesturing at Darva, who, with her dangly earrings and ropes of love beads and bracelets, fairly jingled as she continued walking down the hallway to her own locker. "That hippie chick. She doesn't even wear a bra, man."

I didn't say anything but looked pointedly at the chubby-girl breasts revealed underneath his snagged Ban Lon shirt.

Todd Randolph flushed. "Fuck you."

"Todd, buddy," I said, clapping him on the back, "I'm flattered, but really—no thanks."

Like any other high school, Ole Bull High had a tightly controlled clique system, but I just couldn't be bothered with it. This is not to say I was above all that crap; not only had I had a fair amount of prestige at my old school, I'd **enjoyed** it. I was not the king, like Steve Alquist, whose letter jacket sleeves barely had room for all his award insignias, but I was at least in the court, and I took pleasure in all its privileges. I was a part of everything that mattered— but everything that mattered was now two hundred miles away.

"No," I said when my mother told me we were moving. "No, I'm not going. No way. Forget about it."

"Joe," said my mother, her eyes tearing up, which never failed to make me cave in just to stop them. "Joe, I know all your friends are here, and your team . . . but I need you. I can't make it here anymore, and I can't make it in Minneapolis without you."

She wouldn't have had to "make it" anywhere had my father not gone off and gotten himself killed in the stupid Cessna of stupid Miles Milnar, who was Granite Creek's big-shot developer ("We're going to turn this hick town into a resort haven!") and my dad's best friend. Their last view of anything was probably the soybean field they were about to crash into; Miles Milnar never got to see Granite Creek become "the next Aspen" (the jerk—didn't he consider our lack of mountains a slight **disadvantage**?), and my dad never got to see me graduate from the eighth grade. I suppose it's lousy to lose your dad at any age, but to lose him at fourteen seemed especially cruel; here I was on the cusp of manhood (my voice cracking like spring ice, the rogue hair sprouting on my chin) with no man to pull me up, clap me on the back, and welcome me into the club. For a while there, I really thought I was going to die from the pain of it. Or the anger.

Things never got back to the way they had been, but eventually my mom stopped crying all the time, I stopped thinking I was going to explode, and a new normalcy crept into the house I'd grown up in. And now she was willing to throw away that normalcy we'd worked so hard to cobble together.

"Just tell her you're not going!" said Steve Alquist at the kegger that was my going-away party.

"Yeah, you could stay at my house," said Gary Conroy, who'd played D with me since we were pee wees. "She can't break up the team like that!"

"You could come to my house for supper," said Jamie Jensen, my might-be girlfriend. ("Might-be" because she'd just broken up with Dan Powers and we'd been hovering around each other, waiting for someone to make a move.) "I've got to cook two dinners a week for my 4-H project . . . and my lasagna's pretty good."

"I'll bet it is," I said, and because I was a little drunk, I reacted to the internal voice that hollered, **It's now or never, stupid!** by leaning over and kissing her. That she kissed me back almost made me feel worse than I already did.

But as bummed out as I was about leaving Granite Creek, I couldn't **not** go. It was a close call, but I figured in the scheme of things, my mother needed me to go with her more than I needed to stay.

"You owe me **big-time**," I said as we loaded up the rental truck a week after school got out.

"I know I do, Joe. And I'll figure out a way to make it up to you; I promise I will."

"You don't have to make anything up to me," I said, the gruffness in my voice a fence holding back my emotions.

She sniffed. "I love you, Joey."

It seems there's been a shift in the family hierarchy; nowadays parents do everything for their kids. If junior's an athlete, his parents enroll him in expensive clinics and traveling teams and easily transfer him to a different school to give him a better playing opportunity. Hell, when we played, lots of parents didn't even come to regular games, saving their appearances for tournaments or playoffs. Not that we minded—our parents weren't on us the way parents are on kids now. But conversely, it was understood that in the family's decision making, the adults were the captains and the kids were second string, if they were even allowed on the team.

But all I knew as we drove through our shady neighborhood was: **My life as I know it is ending!**

My mother must have picked up my telepathically transmitted howl, because when she spoke again, her voice was bright and cheery. It was that sort of bright and cheery that reeks of fakeness, but when it came to my mom, I'd take fakeness over tears any day.

"You'll see, Joey—it's going to be great living in a city! It'll be one adventure after another!"

"Sure it will, Ma," I said, and just as we turned off Main Street toward the freeway, I looked at the marquis of the Paramount movie theater. **Play Misty for Me** was showing, and I could imagine the crowd—my crowd—that would see it that night; could imagine the insults they'd yell at the screen if the dialogue was lame; could imagine the perturbed "shh!" they'd get from other patrons as they passed Hot Tamales and jujubes down the row, rattling the boxes like maracas; could imagine how I might kiss Jamie Jensen and how she would taste like buttered popcorn.

It wasn't until we were on the freeway, heading south, that I realized how much my jaw hurt, how I was clenching my teeth so hard that I thought they might crumble in their sockets. How could "one adventure after another" even **compare** to **Play Misty for Me** showing at the Paramount?

My aunt Beth lived in a house by Lake Nokomis, and my bedroom had a window the morning sun blared into, slapping me in the face and shouting, **Wake up!**

"Well, honey, just pull the shade," advised my mother when I told her how I couldn't sleep past dawn in that room.

"As long as you're getting up so early, why don't you go down to Haugland's?" said my aunt Beth, refilling my coffee cup. (She had assumed without asking that I liked coffee, and to my surprise, I found I did.) "I know they're hiring down there."

"Maybe I will," I said, heaping a spoonful of jam on my toast. My aunt had a pantry full of fancy stuff she ordered from specialty catalogs—cylinders of German cookies, imported tins of fish, French pâtés, Swedish candies, and jars of fancy English curds and jams that emptied a lot faster now that we were living with her. But that was the cool thing—well, one of the cool things—about my aunt Beth: she never made me or my mother feel like we were slumming. To her we were guests she couldn't believe it was her good fortune to host. I knew she wanted me to work so I'd get out of the house—but in a good way.

"It's the best way to meet people," she said. "Haugland's is right by the lake, and it's swarming with kids in the summer."

I did get the job, although the cashiers and bag boys saw far more of the swarming kids than I did as a stock boy. But I didn't care; I was content to be alone in the back room, slapping prices on cases of Rice-A-Roni with a little sticker gun, wondering what my friends up in Granite Creek were doing. I didn't allow myself to brood in front of my mother—she had enough problems without me to worry about—but I wasn't ready to transfer my loyalties to new kids here and liked my solitude, liked punctuating every thought of Jamie Jensen with a little **blat** of the sticker gun, liked feeling my muscles strain as I lifted crates and boxes off the trucks, liked sitting on a ladder, having my lunches of Slim Jims and Dr Pepper late in the afternoon, after everyone else had had their break. But after a week or so, my self-imposed social moratorium got boring, and I found myself wandering up to the front of the store during breaks to chat with the cashiers—three college girls and a young housewife—and the bag boys, gangly junior high kids full of zits and braces.

"So you're goin' to Ole Bull, huh?" asked Kirk, the gangliest and zittiest one, and when I nodded, he said, "My sister goes there."

"Is she cute?" I asked, figuring if there was any family resemblance between the two, it was a moot question.

"She's a bitch is what she is," he said, but before I could ask for further details, the store owner appeared and Kirk suddenly busied himself straightening out the stack of paper bags.

"The dairy truck's here," said Mr. Haugland, as if announcing a losing score. He was a guy in his late thirties who had inherited his grandfather's store—but none of the old man's enthusiasm or love of the grocery business.

"I wanted to be a professional musician," he had complained to me my first day on the job. "I had a band—the Courtmen—in college. We did covers—Buddy Holly, Chuck Berry—but some original stuff too. Damn, I had it made."

"What happened?" I asked, taken aback when I saw a glitter of tears in his eyes.

"Life," the balding grocer said stiffly, handing me a roll of toilet paper to shelve.

Now, following Mr. Haugland to help him check the dairy inventory, I rolled my eyes at Kirk, as if to ask, **Can you believe I'm supposed to** work? and he rolled his in sympathy.

August staggered by in its hot and humid way, but in the air-conditioned cool of Haugland Foods, with its piped-in music and coupon specials, I never broke a sweat, and it didn't take long before I was feeling my old optimistic self. My mom—whose optimism had taken a beating the last couple of years—was feeling pretty good herself, having several weeks earlier gotten the letter that welcomed her into the Minneapolis school system as a music teacher at Nokomis Junior High. "Look at us, both getting ready for our first day of school!" she said, nudging me away from the bathroom mirror, where I'd been gargling with Listerine until my tonsils were numb. She looked pretty, in a motherly way, but what gladdened my seventeen-year-old heart was an excitement I hadn't seen in her since my dad died. It was the same look she used to have on her face when they were going out on a date ("It's dinner and dancing in Grand Rapids, honey!" she'd tell me, doing a little cha-cha step as my dad draped her coat around her shoulders), the same look she'd have when Dad came home from a two-day business trip, always bearing presents: a bouquet of flowers for her and an **Archie** comic book or an issue of **Mad** magazine for me.

I set down the bottle of mouthwash and, at the same time, we reached out to hug each other, and it didn't feel weird or dorky or anything.

"I love you, Joe."

"Love you back," I said, and then before the sap really started to ooze, I hustled out of that tiny little bathroom, reminding her that this year I'd get the donuts.

After my first day of kindergarten, I'd come home to find my mom and dad sitting on the porch with a platter of chocolate-covered donuts and a pitcher of milk, and since then it had been a tradition in our family to welcome the beginning of the school year with donuts.

"Glazed for me!" shouted my mother in a high, excited voice that made me feel grown-up and a little sad too.

In homeroom I found a prime seat in the back, and as Miss Cullen read the roll, I scoped out the action. You can find the same types in any school: there was Todd, the fat kid masking his insecurity by being loud and, in his estimation, funny; Blake Erlandsson, jock king à la Steve Alquist; Sharon Winters, who by her heavy use of black eyeliner and white lipstick fell into the girl-most-likely-to-say-yes category; and Leonard Doerr, wearer of glasses, high-water pants, and a brush cut that clearly announced his status as class nerd. My tendency to feel sorry for the guy vanished when, responding to Miss Cullen's recitation of his name, he called, "**Hier, danke!**" and then, as if we couldn't figure it out, explained, "**Das ist Deutsch, mein Freunden!** And if you'd like to participate in the fun and fellowship of the German club, just talk to me because I'm **Herr Präsident!**"

"Herr Simpleton's more like it," said someone under her breath.

Miss Cullen didn't scold the name-caller; in fact, she pinched her lips together to stop her smile.

"Thank you for that announcement, Leonard," she said, raising her eyebrows as she adjusted her glasses. "And if any of you have any questions about available clubs and after-school activities, don't forget to check out the bulletin board." She nodded toward it and then looked down at the roll. "Dykstra, Gwen?"

I think it was the size of Ole Bull High more than anything that made it seem a less friendly place than Granite Creek High; its senior class (so enamored of itself that every morning our slogan, "Of O-lee Bull, we are so true, we're the Class of '72!" was sung by a designated student over the PA system) was bigger than my old school's entire student body. How could you welcome a new kid when there were so many kids you didn't even know from last year?

Still, obeying evolutionary law, I was adapting to my new environment. By Wednesday, I knew where each of my classrooms were and wasn't wandering around like a dork trying to match the number on my schedule to the one painted next to the classroom door; by Thursday, Greg Hoppe, who sat next to me in English, had joined Darva and me at our lunch table. I knew I'd found a kindred spirit when our English teacher paired us up for an assignment.

"One of you gets to choose a character from your favorite novel," said Mrs. Regan, so excited her voice quivered almost as much as the wattle hanging from her chin. "And the other chooses a scene from your favorite novel in which this character will enter!"

"I choose Portnoy from **Portnoy's Complaint**," said my new partner.

Having read the book myself, I smiled and tried to think of a suitable heroine to insert into the pages with Portnoy.

"And I choose **Rebecca of Sunnybrook Farm**."

Greg rubbed his hands together. "This is going to be **good**."

He was the editor of the **Ole Bulletin** and invited me to join the newspaper. On Friday, I attended the first staff meeting.

On Tuesday of the following week, Mr. Teschler asked me to stay after class. This wouldn't be big news if the request had been related to history, the class he perfunctorily taught; what excited me was that Mr. Teschler wanted to talk to me about his real passion, which was coaching the hockey team.

"I saw you play up in Alexandria," he said, his thumb strolling through the thicket that was his sideburn.

"You did?" My heart skipped like a girl's.

"Sure. Last year at the sectionals. You played for Granite Creek, right?"

I nodded.

"Great hockey program they've got up there. Anyway, you played some good D. Look forward to having you on our team." His thumb wandered around his jawbone and then back again. "You are planning to play, aren't you?"

My head bounced in a nod.

"Careful, kid, I don't want you to throw your neck out," said the history teacher, giving his sideburns one last scratch. "Now why don't you get an eraser and wipe off the blackboard? Then give me twenty push-ups."

Seeing the expression on my face, he laughed. "Kidding. Just kidding. At least about the push-ups."

My stock got a real boost when word got around that I was a hockey player. Blake Erlandsson asked me to join some other players at his house, "to talk about taking the Bulls to state this year."

My mother couldn't have been more excited if I'd won a National Merit Scholarship.

"The team captain, huh? What's he like? Would you like me to bake some of my brownies to bring over? Or maybe some Rice Krispies bars? Or maybe we should—"

"Ma, relax. It's no big deal. I'm just getting together with some guys to talk hockey."

My offhandedness did not erase the flush on my mother's face or her smile, and she stood on her tiptoes to kiss my cheek.

"I'm just glad you're making friends is all," she said.

"Making friends?" I said. "Ma, I can't **not** make friends. Everyone wants a piece of Joe Andreson."

When Blake Erlandsson's mother opened the door, a blast of perfume and hairspray singed my nasal hairs.

"Hi," she said, in a voice that sounded like we were meeting at a bar rather than at the threshold of a door whose welcome mat was in the shape of a sunflower. Her face was sparkly with makeup: her eyes were ringed in blue iridescence, her lips were a frosted pink, and even her rouge glimmered. Her platinum-blond hair was piled up on top of her head in loopy curls, and she wore a lime-green minidress with fishnet stockings and white boots.

Hey, baby, I wanted to say, but stuck with a safer greeting.

"Hi, I'm Joe."

"Of course you are," she said, taking me by the arm and pulling me into the house. "And I'm Mrs. Erlandsson, although I like Blake's friends to call me Mimi."

"And I'm Bob," said a voice, interrupting my fantasy of being led up the stairs and into a bedroom by the wild, frosty-faced Mimi. "Blake's father."

The man who stuck out his hand had the same bright Partridge Family/Brady Bunch fashion sense as his wife; he wore plaid flares and a polyester shirt and combed his longish hair the way his son did—parted on the side with a big swoop of bangs.

"Uh . . . pleased to meet you," I said, shaking the man's hand.

"So you're going to give the Bulls a little more—" He didn't say so much as grunt what I was going to give the Bulls, punching a fist in the air.

"Bob's a big hockey fan," explained Mimi. Having

abandoned my arm, she took her husband's, and he turned his face to hers and they kissed.

"Joe," said Blake, bounding into the entryway. "You're here."

I held out my hands as if to say, **Ta-da!**

"Come on downstairs. We've been waiting for you, man."

"Nice to meet you," I said to the real live TV sitcom couple, following Blake down the shag-carpeted stairs and into the rec room.

There were a half dozen guys sitting on Naugahyde bar stools and beanbag chairs. Blake pointed to each one with his can of pop as he said his name.

"That's Jeff Lindaner, Brad Wilkerson, Charlie Olsen, Garret Mays, Tom Zebriski, and Phil Lamereau." He nodded at the smallest guy. "Roll the film, will you, Wilkey?"

The lights went out, and everyone faced the small screen set up in front of the fireplace. Not having a place to sit, I leaned against the paneled wall.

"This is our game against Roosevelt for the city championship— Well, to get to the city championship," said Blake as a grainy black-and-white film began to roll.

"Fuckers beat us five to two," said someone else, adding with pride, "And I almost got a game misconduct."

"You almost always get a game misconduct," said Blake. "Olsen here thinks the game's about scoring penalties and not goals."

"I'm the enforcer," said Olsen. "Just doing my job."

It didn't matter that the quality of the Super 8 film

was poor; when the first puck was dropped, we were all rapt, hypnotized by the grainy figures zigzagging across the screen. There were cheers when the Bulls scored, cries of frustration when they didn't, and boos when the Teddies put one in.

"So what do you think, Joe?" asked Blake, turning on the lights after the movie had flickered to a stop.

"You guys looked pretty good," I said, Mr. Diplomat.

"Come on, what'd you really think?"

"Hey," said Olsen, whose thin voice didn't go with his big, bulky body, "why argue with him? He says we looked good."

"We'll look even better this year with all those crappy seniors gone," said Wilkey.

"Hey, Kellog made all-state," said Blake, "and Reese—"

Before he could finished his defense of the graduated players, there was a stampede of footsteps and giggles on the staircase, and suddenly the testosterone in the room bobbed under a wave of estrogen. We hockey players sat there like we'd been collectively back-checked into the boards, stunned by the force of the cheerleading squad that stood before us.

"Hey, guys!" said the girl in front, by looks and attitude obviously the ringleader. "It's party time!"

"Kristi!"

I should have figured it was Blake Erlandsson who'd hold his arms open for the little fox to jump into, giving all of us a sweet peek at the backs of her thighs as her short pleated skirt flipped up.

They kissed each other, a long tonguey kiss, and

I felt like a perv watching them, but I couldn't look away.

Olsen leaned in toward me, whispering, "Now you can see how she got mono."

"That's right," said the girl, pulling away. "The kissing disease. Something **you'll** never get, Olsen."

The other girls, who stood in a semicircle by the staircase, tittered.

"Yeah, Olsen," concurred one of them.

The biting insults were defused by Mr. and Mrs. Erlandsson, who came down the stairs bearing white boxes.

"Pizza time!" warbled Mrs. Erlandsson in a sing-song voice, and soon the guys were shoving folded slices into their mouths as the girls primly pinched off pieces of pepperoni or corners of crust.

"So Kristi, this is Joe Andreson, our new defender."

"What is it you like to defend?" she asked, raising one carefully plucked eyebrow.

"Whatever needs defending," I answered, resisting the urge to look away.

"Kristi missed the first week of school because of mono," said Blake, either unaware of or unconcerned about our sexy little exchange.

"It really screwed up my summer," said Kristi. "And then on top of everything, I missed cheering for the first game."

"And we missed you, Kristi," said one of her cheerleading minions, and the others murmured their assent.

"Anyway, I'll be back on the field tomorrow, and I'm going to lean to the left, lean to the right—"

The Pavlovian cheerleaders couldn't help themselves, getting into formation and chorusing, "Stand
up, sit down, fight, fight, fight!"

They jumped in the air before landing on the floor
in splits, and because we couldn't do anything with
the hard-ons all of that exposed jumping flesh had
given us, we cheered and whistled.

"All right, girls," said Kristi, flipping the ends of
her shag with her fingers, "time to go!"

"But you just got here," whined Blake.

"I've got a week's worth of French to make up,"
said Kristi. She put her arms around Blake and kissed
him, smiling to her audience before kissing him
again. "When I'm done with my verb conjugations,
I'll come over here to practice more of that."

Olsen articulated what we were all thinking when
he whispered, "Ooh la la."

Two

FROM THE Ole Bulletin SEPTEMBER 1971

Fall means football, and at Ole Bull High, **football rules**! At least, so say the big red-and-black signs posted throughout the school. But our Roving Reporter wonders, in these trying times of Nixon and napalm, are football and its frantic fandom anachronistic? And so to those brave souls who've allowed us to put their views on record, RR asked: Do you think school spirit is passé?

Shannon Saxon, Ole Bull cheerleading mascot: "No! School spirit will never be passé! School spirit is what drives the student body! School spirit brings us all together—united we stand, divided we fall! Ole Bull is number one because of our school spirit!"

Mike Oxenfire, senior: "What's **passé** mean, man?"
(Note from RR: Mr. Oxenfire is hopeful that this is

the year he graduates, seeing as he'll celebrate his twenty-seventh birthday in January.)

Darva Pratt, senior: "Are you serious? With all that's going on in the world, this is the best question you can come up with?"

Sam McGinness, phys ed teacher: "If it is, you ought to find a way to get it back. Everyone works better when they feel a sense of community, an esprit de corps if you will. Get involved, people! Support one another, your teams, your teachers, your fellow students! Everybody wins when you're all on the same side!"

The **Ole Bulletin** was put together by a staff of twelve students who met three days a week at seven o'clock in the morning.

"They don't call it zero hour for nothing," said Mr. Lutz, who had been advisor to the paper for more than ten years. "But for those of you yawning and grumbling about missing your beauty sleep, remember: The news waits for no one."

"The news doesn't have to wait," said Greg Hoppe. "It's asleep too."

Mr. Lutz smiled as he unscrewed the cap of his plaid Thermos.

"Tell that to I. F. Stone," he said, pouring coffee into a cup that read, **Newsmen deliver.** "Tell that to Nelly Bly. To H. L. Mencken. To Ernie Pyle."

A girl raised her hand.

"Who are you talking about?"

Mr. Lutz narrowed his eyes as he sipped his coffee.

"Let me tell you something, O'Grady," he said.

"While I do believe there is no such thing as a stupid question, I also believe there are those that come awfully close. So with that in mind, your assignment, O'Grady, will be to write a three-hundred-word column on influential journalists of the modern age."

"Dang!" said the girl. "I **thought** they were probably reporters."

"A reporter's job isn't to think, O'Grady. It's to **find out**."

Mr. Lutz did something close to the impossible: He made it easy to get out of bed and get to school an hour before everyone else did. He joked and allowed you to joke back, and yet he made you want to work hard, made you think that gathering whatever was newsworthy in the halls of Ole Bull High was important.

"But," he would remind us, "there is a wider world out there, as hard as it is to imagine."

As editor in chief, Greg Hoppe was in charge of the assignment desk, which meant fielding and then okaying story ideas.

"I want to write about Doug Benson," said a girl. "Did you know he got a perfect score on his SAT?"

"You wrote about your boyfriend last year, Pritchett. When he got a perfect score on the PSAT."

"I'd like to write a piece about girls' sports and how we always get the shaft," said another girl. "I mean, it's so unfair it's unreal!"

"Sounds like it might work better as a commentary," said Hoppe.

"How about a story about Gisela Brunhoffer, the new exchange student?"

"Go ahead, Myers. But don't try to wangle a date out of it."

I can't remember if I volunteered to do the first "Roving Reporter" column or if Hoppe couldn't get any other takers; either way I wound up asking students and teachers a pressing, probing, or totally inane question once a week for the rest of the school year. It was fun—it didn't take a lot of thought on my part, plus it was a good way to introduce myself to cute girls. Shannon Saxon wasn't in Kristi's category, but she was cute enough.

"Thanks for putting me in your 'Roving Reporter' piece," she said as we sat in a booth at Marty's a few days later. "I didn't come off stupid, though, did I?"

I shook my head even though I didn't think she'd come across as **smart.**

"I thought it was a good question to ask right before homecoming," she said. "I mean, this is one game we need to get fired up for."

Our homecoming game was against Southwest, and Shannon, who was the Ole Bull mascot, was nervous.

"Southwest's the **worst**," she complained. "Everyone in the stands pretends they're playing a violin and makes this really obnoxious noise." Making a face, Shannon mimed playing a violin and made a screeching sound loud enough to be heard over the Troggs on the jukebox.

"You're right," I said. "That is obnoxious."

"Then they shout, 'Tora! Tora! Tora!' " She shook her head, disgust puckering her soft features. "Of all the dumb mascots in the world, I think ours has to be the dumbest."

"Isn't Roosevelt's a teddy bear? That's pretty dumb."

Her lower lip jutted out in a pout, and if she thought the gesture was cute, we were poles apart in our opinions as to what constituted cute.

"The teddy bear is **cuddly**. A violin-playing bull is just stupid."

"Okay, Shannon," I sighed. "A violin-playing bull **is** stupid."

She kicked me under the table, hard. "Thanks a lot, Joe. I thought you were on my side."

As my shin throbbed, I stifled the urge to kick her back.

"I am on your side; I just agreed with you that a violin-playing bull is stupid. But what kind of mascot is a school named after an obscure Norwegian fiddle player **supposed** to have?"

Tears welled in Shannon's cow-brown eyes. "I never even wanted to be the mascot—I wanted to be a regular cheerleader, but Kristi said I wasn't the right body type. I guess she thinks I look better covered up in brown fur and horns."

I laughed, but the glare Shannon returned showed me she wasn't trying to be funny.

A couple of days earlier, Blake Erlandsson had pulled me aside after history class.

"I got a favor to ask you," he'd said, and when I told him to fire away, he said, "Kristi wants you to ask Shannon Saxon to homecoming and then double-date with us."

Somebody from the jostling herd that filled the hallways between bells bumped into me.

"Shannon Saxon? I interviewed her for the paper. Well, I asked her a question."

"She's a good friend of Kristi's," Blake had said "I think you'd like her."

"Why not?" I'd said, shrugging.

"You're a good man, Andreson," Blake had said, clapping me on the shoulder. "I'll give you the details as they come in."

Shannon and I had both slid into the restaurant booth with the semi-high expectations anyone brings to a first date, but after I delivered the seventh or eighth joke to the same blank face, I realized that Shannon didn't have a sense of humor. She also had a worldview limited to Ole Bull sports and cheer-leading, which sort of limited conversational oppor-tunities.

The fog of boredom lifted, however, when Shan-non mentioned Kristi and her views as to what con-stituted a cheerleader's body.

"Why would she think you're not the right body type?"

"Well, geez, everyone knows a cheerleader has to be just about perfect." Shannon leaned over the table, the pillows of her big chest threatening to knock over her malt glass. "You know how Nancy Hasberg stays so thin?" Opening her mouth wide, she pretended to stick her finger down her throat.

Clueless, I held up my hands. "What, she's sick a lot?"

Shannon smiled the smile of the old Cheshire cat. "She **makes** herself sick a lot."

I knew Rod Westby, Granite Creek's top wrestler, often made himself puke before a match.

"Cheerleaders have to make weight?"

"Well, not formally," said Shannon, and with her

straw she jabbed at the last inch of butterscotch malt in her glass before sucking it down. "But **informally**—well, that's why girls like me can be a mascot but not a cheerleader."

It wasn't that Shannon Saxon was fat. She did have big boobs—always a plus, I figure, no matter what your weight—and her ass would be more comfortably positioned in a Buick than a Jaguar, but still, she had the kind of curves guys like and girls seem determined to Tab-and-hard-boiled-egg away. (How I knew this bit of feminine arcana was because Shannon had told me the butterscotch malt she inhaled was a reward for sticking to a three-day diet of nothing but Tab and hard-boiled eggs. My turtle sundae, judging from the way she helped herself to it, was part of her rewards system too.)

"So Kristi makes the rules for the cheerleading squad, huh?"

Shannon shrugged, eying the melted puddle at the bottom of my dish.

"You **are** new, aren't you, Joe?" With a half twirl of her long spoon, she scooped up what remained of my sundae and swallowed it, as quick as a salamander downs a gnat. "Kristi Casey runs **everything**."

After our trial run at Marty's, I knew that in the malt-guzzling, whining Ole Bull mascot, I had not found my heart's desire. Not by a light-year. It wasn't that I was looking—but still, dread is not something you want to feel when corsage-shopping for your date.

"Why didn't you say yes to me, Darva?" I asked as we walked the narrow aisle through the refrigerated, perfumy air of the florist shop.

"Joe, you know I can't lower myself to barbaric so-cial rituals like a homecoming dance."

"But it wouldn't be barbaric with me. It'd be fun."

Darva put her arm around a tall vase and leaned in to the lilies it held, closing her eyes as she breathed in their scent. She was wearing a gauzy Indian tunic thing under a leather vest and earrings that jangled, and I was seized with the urge to take her arms and put them around me.

"Hey," said the store clerk, a thin woman with a brown cloud of hair. "Don't touch the flowers."

"I wasn't holding them," said Darva evenly. "I was holding the vase."

"Same diff," said the clerk, and she snapped her gum so loudly I flinched.

"Where are your corsages?" I asked.

"For homecoming?"

She offered a sour smile as I nodded.

"You've got to order your corsage," she said, pro-nouncing every syllable as if English wasn't anywhere near my native language. "Then we can make them up with your school colors or to match your date's dress."

I looked at Darva, who rubbed one index finger on top of the other, as if scolding me for being naughty.

"Gee, Joe," she said, "Don't you know anything about barbaric social rituals?"

Leveling her gaze first at Darva and then at me, the clerk jangled some change in her smock pocket and said, "There might be some left in the case over there." She nodded toward the back of the store, her shellacked hair unmoving.

The pickings were slim in the refrigerator case:

There was a red-and-gold carnation corsage, a white one made from roses whose edges were turning brown, and a grouping of daisies and small yellow roses on an elastic band.

"Take the wrist corsage," said Darva, opening up the refrigerator, "and let's get out of here. This place gives me the creeps."

Snapping her gum all the while, the cashier gave me change and handed me the corsage in a clear plastic box.

"Aren't you going to get him a boutonnière?" she asked Darva, her voice still coated with hostility.

Pulling out the Tootsie Pop she'd just put in her mouth and using it as a pointer, Darva gestured to me.

"You think I'm going to the homecoming dance with **him**? What would my lesbian lover think?"

The cashier's mouth dropped open, revealing the pink gum wadded up on top of her molars. "Your lesbian lover . . . ," she began, as if by repeating the words she'd better understand them.

"Well, he hasn't had the operation yet," said Darva as I hustled her toward the door. "In fact, he wanted to quarterback the homecoming game before he starts his hormone treatment."

As I opened the door, the cashier's gum popped so loudly it sounded as if she had fired a gun at us.

"Say cheese!" said my mother again, throwing us into yet another half-second state of blindness.

She had been invited by Blake's parents to come and record the happy couples before we skipped off to the homecoming dance.

"There's no reason the girls' families should get to take all the pictures," said Mimi, Blake's mother, who was wearing a hot-pink miniskirt and a black-and-white op-art shirt so swirly I could barely look at it. "I mean, we like our memories too!"

"Twelve scrapbooks of them," said Blake in an aside to me. "One for every school year." He was dressed in a well-cut suit that made the one I'd gotten at Granite Creek's Dapper Duke for last year's hockey banquet **look** like a suit I'd gotten at Granite Creek's Dapper Duke for last year's hockey banquet.

Shannon was wearing a green dress whose many tiers of ruffles didn't do her any favors; really, she sort of looked like an upside-down artichoke.

But Kristi—well, as usual, Kristi was something else.

She wore knee-high black boots under a long red and black dress slit up the front to reveal a very short pair of red hot pants. It was scooped in the front, just low enough to advertise, **Hey, boys, this way to Breast World!** Her hair had been pinned up on top of her head, except for two little ringlets that zigzagged in front of her ears, and I thought having to deal with Shannon's sullen mood (we'd lost the homecoming game that afternoon, 21–7, and she was rah-rah enough to still be carrying the burden of defeat) was a small price to pay for being in the presence of the gorgeous vision that was Kristi.

"Okay, you kids better get going," said Mimi. "We don't want to make the cutest couples late for the big dance!"

My mother had been willing to obey protocol, but when Mimi opened her arms to hug us all and wish us "a magical night," my mother felt free to do the same. She was always hugging and kissing me at home, but I had long ago given her orders "not to make a public spectacle, Ma. I'm not kidding."

Touching their triceps, she dipped herself politely toward each of my friends, saving her big embrace for me.

"Have a wonderful time, honey," she whispered in my ear. "I love you!"

"You too," I whispered, worming my way out of her arms and her suffocating momness.

As school mascot, Shannon had been given the honor of announcing the homecoming court. The rest of us serfs stood on the edges of the gym, watching the royal procession.

"I voted for you," I whispered to Kristi, who didn't seem to be clapping as enthusiastically as the rest of the onlookers.

"You don't know how many people have told me that," she said as she watched Blake, who'd been crowned king at an assembly earlier in the week, escort the queen up a paper walkway that was supposed to signify the red carpet. "If you ask me, the whole thing is rigged." She offered Blake a sour smile and a slight wave as he passed, and then, taking my hand, said, "Come on, Joe."

A surprised thrill—on the whole, not a bad feeling—zipped through me.

We cut behind the crowd of people and out a side door.

"Where're we going?" I asked as Kristi pulled me down the hallway.

"To the car," she said. "To get this party in gear."

Opening the driver's door of Mr. Erlandsson's Lincoln Continental ("You can't take those pretty girls in your dinky little Maverick!" he had said, throwing Blake his keys), she nodded at me to get in on the passenger side.

"Reach under your seat and give me that purse, will you?"

Obediently I did as I was told and watched as she took a joint out of the black satin bag and punched in the dashboard's cigarette lighter.

"Sometimes they do random checks at the door," she explained, lighting the joint. She took a long inhale and passed it to me.

"Are you sure this is okay?" I said, regretting my words as soon I'd said them.

"Oh man, don't tell me you're a wuss too?"

"No, not at all," I said, taking a toke from the joint. I tried to hold in the smoke, but it tumbled out of my throat in a cough.

Kristi laughed. "Yeah, you're a pro." She took the joint and drew in a deep inhale. "But at least you're a little open-minded." Her voice strained through her clenched throat. "Blake's so straight he won't even try it. He says he doesn't want to break team rules. Not like it's even hockey season yet." She exhaled and waved the rush of smoke out the open window. "God, he'll be pissed if he smells dope in his dad's car."

"Maybe we should leave," I suggested.

"We will, when we finish this," said Kristi, handing me the joint.

The fact that I could count on one hand the times

I'd smoked dope wasn't because of ideology but availability; beer was the preferred party favor in Granite Creek, and weed was available only when Dan Powers's brother was home from Iowa State.

"I mean, really," said Kristi. "Colleen Whitley? Colleen 'I've-got-a-mustache' Whitley? Come on! I wouldn't say she's a dog, but I hear she enjoys a nice bowl of Alpo for breakfast."

Proud of myself for not coughing, I exhaled out the window and turned to her.

"I have no idea what you're talking about."

"The homecoming queen! There's no way I didn't get enough votes to at least be a lousy **princess,** let alone the queen! It's all rigged, I'm telling you—that skanky Miss Rudd is in charge of the vote counting, and she hasn't liked me since I put too much food coloring in the Christmas cookies in her stupid home ec class."

I looked at her fingernails as she took the joint; they were painted the color of pink you see inside seashells.

"I wonder if I could hear the ocean if I listened to your fingernails," I said.

Kristi laughed. "Oh man, you're **stoned.**" She took another deep toke, and after she exhaled, I took her hand and held it up to my ear.

I made a slow shushing sound.

"I was right," I said. "It is the ocean!"

I made the shushing sound again.

"The secrets of the Caribbean—all inside your fingernails!"

Laughing, Kristi pulled her hand away. "Not only are you stoned, you're **weird.**"

When we got back to the gym, the band was doing a serviceable cover of America's "Ventura Highway" and Kristi untied Blake from his knot of friends and dragged him onto the dance floor.

The phrase **What am I—chopped liver?** came into my head followed by a wave of marijuana-induced reflections: **How did chopped liver get such a bad rap? Why doesn't someone say, "What am I— minced beef tongue?" or "What am I—diced giz- zards?" Or how about sliced head cheese? Wouldn't sliced head cheese be the wallflower of the butcher case?**

"So **there** you are," said my date. I had heard friendlier voices.

"Shannon!" I said. "Tora! Tora! Tora!"

Her forehead crimped. "Is that supposed to be funny?"

"It's supposed to be, but if you don't agree, I won't hold it against you," I said in a fair Cary Grant im- personation. "I will, however, hold **me** against you. Come on, let's dance."

Shannon gave me the kind of look stoned blather like that deserved but let me take her hand, and sur- prise, surprise, we started to have fun.

She was a good dancer and, thanks to my mother's lessons, so was I. When the band played "Colour My World," she followed my lead, and we glided through the clumps of couples who thought hugging one another and swaying constituted slow dancing.

"The last time I got to dance like this was my cousin's wedding," said Shannon. "Not many boys know how to **dance** dance."

I dipped her backward, and the green ruffles of her dress fluttered like leaves in a spring breeze.

"But you are forgetting, I am not a boy," I said, now Maurice Chevalier. I pulled her back up. "I am a man."

During the band's break, we gathered around a table where a few teachers and parents were dispensing punch and cookies.

"Hope you move just as good on the ice rink as you do on the dance floor," said Mr. Teschler, handing me a Styrofoam cup of punch.

"Well, I **can** do a nice little rumba while I'm backchecking," I said to the hockey coach.

He laughed, thank God, even as I screamed to myself: **"Rumba while I'm back-checking?" Not only is he going to think you're stoned, he's going to think you're a homo!**

After the band played "Cherish" and the lights came on, Shannon said, surprise in her voice, "That was **really** fun."

"It was," I said, just as surprised. I felt a mellowness that was either residue from the pot (the fun-and-wonder rush had long since burned off) or from all the dancing.

In the backseat, I put my arm around Shannon, and before Blake had driven out of the parking lot, we were making out.

I put my hand inside her coat and my hands made little swishing sounds as they made their way up and down those slippery ruffles. Shannon had pressed herself into me, and the weight of her breasts against my chest and her tongue in my mouth made me breathless, yet I thought this kind of suffocation might not be such a bad way to go.

"Hey, are you lovebirds coming in?" asked Kristi, leaning over the front seat to slap my knee.

Shannon turned her face away from mine. "Where are we?"

"The Coliseum," said Blake. "We're gonna get some pizza."

Shannon looked at me. "Are you hungry?"

"Yeah," I said, kissing her.

We steamed up the windows good, but kissing was all Shannon was willing to do, batting my hands away anytime they wandered south or north.

When we finally dragged ourselves out of the car, Shannon stumbled and I grabbed her arm so she wouldn't fall.

"Oh my gosh," she said, "I feel like I'm drunk or something!"

Holding her face in my hands, I kissed her, pleased that she had found me intoxicating.

The dim, candlelit restaurant was packed with Ole Bull kids, and Crosby, Stills, Nash and Young's "Love the One You're With" was playing on the jukebox.

"Over here, you guys!" shouted Kristi, waving from a crowded table, and as we sat down on two chairs at the end, she gestured toward the half-eaten pizzas in the middle of the table.

"While you guys were out in the car losing your virginity, we took the liberty of ordering."

"We were not losing our virginity!" sputtered Shannon, to the amusement of everyone at the table, and with a sudden urge to practice chivalry, I decided to defend her honor.

"Yeah," I said, helping myself to a piece of pepperoni. "We were just looking for yours. We heard you gave it to the busboy out in the back alley years ago."

There were a few whoops of laughter, but they were quickly swallowed in deference to Kristi. A cloud of silence floated over the table.

"Hey," I said, shrugging at the girl whose eyes were throwing daggers, swords, and scythes at me. "It was just a joke."

"Well, **duh**," said Kristi finally. "I'd never give my virginity to a busboy. Maybe a cook, but never a busboy." Flashing her dimples, she laughed, and as the whole table laughed with her, I had the distinct impression that I had just sidestepped a land mine.

A confetti of daisy petals fell as I walked Shannon to her door.

"My poor corsage," said Shannon, cupping what remained of the flowers bunched together on her wrist.

"Oh well," she said, looking up at me with a smile. "Thanks for a great time."

"It **was** a great time," I said, trying to keep the surprise out of my voice. "I'll call you, okay?"

Shannon nodded, and as she leaned against the door, I leaned against her, topping off an evening of good kisses with one final tongue-intensive one.

I could have stood there all night, melding into the warmth of her green-ruffled body, but then the porch light came on, and if that isn't a signal to leave, I don't know what is.

"Did you have a good time?" asked my mother, who was curled up on the couch, reading.

"Sure," I said, sitting next to her. "Whatcha reading?"

She held up the book so I could read the title.

"**Jane Eyre**? Again?"

My mother smiled. "I don't know if you can ever read **Jane Eyre** too many times."

"I feel that way about **Mad** magazine."

She pushed some hair off my forehead with her fingers; she'd been trying to rearrange my hair since I was a kid. When I reflexively tossed my head back out of her reach, she took my hand instead. I didn't pull it away. I don't know of many guys who'd sit holding hands with their mother, or at least any that would admit it, but hey, it wasn't as if there were cameras in the room. My mind was all over the place, flashing on Shannon and the way her pillowy breasts felt pressed against my chest; on getting high with Kristi and how dope smoke tastes so raw in your throat, like a wet weed burning; on the lyrics to Paul McCartney's "Uncle Albert/Admiral Halsey" which was all over the radio; on wondering if he ever thought, **What am I doing in Wings, man? I used to be a** Beatle!; on wondering how much my paycheck from Haugland's would be because of working overtime last Saturday.

We sat on my aunt's corduroy couch for a long time, both of us staring into the fireplace, and our clasped hands were like our little anchor, holding us down as we flew off with our own crazy thoughts.

Three

A LETTER TO THE EDITOR IN THE Ole Bulletin, NOVEMBER 17, 1971:

I have seen rudeness and immaturity before in school assemblies (who can forget the less than welcoming response to "Up with People!") but never to the extent that was exhibited during Officer Jeffrey O'Conner's "Drugs Are Dumb" program.

We are seniors in high school! Is there any need to interrupt an interesting, informative program with comments like "Do you know where I can score a nickel bag?" or "Hi—I wish I was"? Those hecklers thought they were pretty funny to disrupt, but their bravado was nowhere to be found when Mr. Brietmayer asked them to stand and identify themselves!

Let's not let some drug-infatuated hoodlums taint others' perception of our wonderful school.

To those hoodlums who are bent on disruption and, more so, on tainting the good name of our school, I repeat Officer O'Conner's lecture title: Drugs are dumb! And you're the evidence!

Katherine Bleursten

A LETTER TO THE EDITOR IN THE Ole Bulletin, NOVEMBER 24, 1971:

Regarding K. Bleursten's rant in last week's paper: who died and made her our parents? I for one did not find the narc's program to be interesting or informative, but rather a dull and uninformed lecture that in no way addressed the reality of marijuana use. When is our government going to see that on the list of societal problems, the occasional use of pot is not one of them? We all need a little something to lighten our load; when Officer O'Conner pushes aside his after-hours beer or rum and Coke, I'll ash my after-hours joint. Until then, I'll be lighting up if for nothing else than to help myself forget that in my generation there are people like Katherine Bleursten.

For obvious reasons I remain,

Anonymous

Memo to: Floyd Lutz, advisor to the Ole Bulletin
From: Robert Brietmayer, principal

Dear Floyd,
I've been fielding a couple of calls regarding the editorial page of last week's paper and I've got to say, while I believe in freedom of the press and all,

I can see where a parent's nose might get out of joint. That is to say, we don't want to paint a picture of Ole Bull as a haven for drug users!

I admire the tireless work you've done as advisor to the paper for the past ten years, but there are lines we don't want to cross, Floyd, and this may be one of them.

If you have any questions as to what constitutes a letter that inspires good debate versus a letter that inspires unnecessary agitation and grief, let me know and I'll be glad to help you edit!

Along with my Roving Reporter duties, I had gravitated to the op-ed page and had forged a partnership with Greg Hoppe, writing commentary together. Mr. Lutz didn't seem to think it a breach of journalistic ethics if we occasionally wrote an anonymous rebuttal to a particularly stupid letter, particularly ones written by a certain Katherine Bleursten, who as student council president had lobbied for student uniforms and addressing teachers as "sir" and "ma'am."

"Sorry about that," I said, after reading the memo Mr. Brietmayer had sent to Mr. Lutz. "We didn't want to get you into trouble."

Mr. Lutz took the paper from my hand and crumpled it up.

"Don't worry about it," he said, tossing it into the round file. "Brietmayer sends me about a dozen of these a year. It's when he doesn't respond to an issue that I think we've failed in our duty."

"What's our duty again, boss?" asked Hoppe, squinting at the copy he'd just written on the typewriter.

"To cause a little brain activity."

Mr. Lutz poured the last of his coffee into his cup—by the end of zero hour he'd always emptied his big plaid Thermos, but other than tapping his pencil a little faster, he gave no signs that he was overcaffeinated. "So keep writing those hard-hitting letters, boys. Keep answering back to those people whose imaginations aren't big enough to question authority."

Hoppe and I looked at each other. It was great having a teacher who told us, in so many words, that it was okay to give the finger.

"Does Shannon ever wear that fur costume when you're getting it on?"

I sighed, pretending not to hear.

"I said, does Shannon ever—"

Shaking my head, I leveled my most withering glance at Darva. "You're interrupting my muse."

"Joe, if your muse is responsible for that, I'm doing you a favor by interrupting it."

We were in art class, working on our soap sculptures, and Darva was right—mine looked more like a dropped ice cream cone than a reclining nude, which had been my intention.

"Not all of us have your talent, Ms. Nevelson."

Darva laughed and smooched the air with her lips. "I love that you know who Louise Nevelson is. I love that you said 'Ms.' "

"Whatever floats your boat." Examining my sculpture, I wondered if I should whittle away what I'd intended to be arms, and claim defeat: **Yeah, I meant it to be an ice cream cone.**

"Joseph, you look frustrated," said Mr. Eggert, our art teacher. In his suit and tie, he looked like an accounting teacher, but I didn't know of many accounting teachers who'd play Sly and the Family Stone along with Emerson, Lake & Palmer and the Mothers of Invention during class time.

"Music is not only a stand-alone art," he told us the first time he put **Plastic Ono Band** on the stereo. "It's a helper art too. It unleashes those receptors in your brain that spark creativity."

"I already had a name for it," I said, holding out my palm, showing him my sad little blob of soap. "**Limpid Nude.** But now I think I've got to call it **Limpid Rocky Road.**"

Cocking his head, Mr. Eggert pressed together his narrow lips, which were bordered in the bluish stubble of his five o'clock shadow. After a moment of appraisal, he said, "I believe the second title more accurately explains the work."

He had kinder words for Darva, who'd carved the insides of a broken watch.

"Once again, Miss Pratt, you amaze me."

Darva beamed. She'd told me she had wanted to be an artist from the first time she held a crayon and added her own flowers to the violets already existing on her bedroom wallpaper. She was Mr. Eggert's pet, but understandably so; her work was leagues ahead of the rest of ours.

As the art teacher walked around the tables, offering encouragement and advice, I went back to work, paring away at my nude and turning her into a dairy product.

"Hey, you're not going to have anything left," said

Darva, watching me as shavings of soap fell to the table.

"Maybe I don't want to have anything left," I said, cutting deeper into the soap. "Maybe I want to create nothingness."

"Existential art," said Darva. She flicked the drapery of her long black hair behind her shoulders and laughed. "Cool."

She waited for a moment—I think for my response—and when I didn't offer one, she asked, "So you're coming tonight, right?"

"Coming where?"

"To the planning meeting."

My mind thumbed through pages of my mental calendar and came up with only one thing: my date with Shannon. We were going to the library to study—code for parking by the river.

"Uh, sorry, Darv, I've got plans."

Anytime something bothered her, she flexed the little muscles at her jaw hinges, and I didn't need to look at her to know that they were getting a workout now. I would have been happy if she'd spent the rest of the hour engaged in her jaw isometrics, but she was not concerned with making me happy.

"I thought these were your plans. At least they were when I asked you last week, remember? 'Yeah, sure I'll come,'" she said, and with her impersonation she made me sound both retarded and dishonest.

"Well, something came up," I said, trying to keep the defensiveness out of my voice. "Sorry to disappoint you."

Darva sighed. "The world disappoints me, Joe. It just hurts a little more when a friend does."

I smiled then, thinking that if she was back to making her world-weary jokes, I was in the clear. Only I could see by the hurt on her face that she wasn't joking, and I felt bad.

But guilt always buckled under the tonnage of lust, and so later that night, while Darva sat in a booth at the Canteen with her band of believers who thought whatever protest they planned could somehow have an effect on stopping the war in Viet Nam, I was in the backseat of Shannon's Delta 88, using my powers of persuasion for an entirely different cause.

"Come on, Shannon," I said, trying to wiggle my hands free of her iron grasp. "Pretend I'm Columbus and you're Queen Isabella, and you've hired me to explore the unknown."

I thought if I could get her laughing, her defenses might drop a little. I was half right; she did laugh, but held fast to her no-hands-below-the-waist rule.

"You can beg all you want, Joe," she said, moving my hands up under her sweater to her bare breasts. "If you can't be happy with what I'm willing to give you, well, then, let's just go home."

"I'm happy, I'm happy," I said; who wouldn't be with his hands around such sweet round nippled melons? And as much I would have loved to travel south, Shannon's rigorous patrol of the borders kept not only her safe but me too. I would have loved the sweet thrill of having my hands—or Lord, my dick— in her pants, but it sure made things a lot easier knowing I couldn't. I wasn't ready to have a girlfriend I actually got it on with; whatever responsibilities went along with that seemed too big and complicated for me to deal with. As long as Shannon's mouth, her tongue, and especially those luscious breasts were available to me, I wasn't going to complain. Too loudly.

The fact was, I loved to kiss, and the more I kissed Shannon, the less we had to talk. Shannon might have had an expansive mind, but if she did, a large part of it had been fenced off and was being used as grassland. If our conversation had to do with something other than who was going out with whom or a recounting of everything she had eaten that day, well, she wasn't interested.

Once I'd asked her if she thought Nixon's opening up of relations with China was a good idea, and she said, "Joe, why don't we just go back to my house and you can sit around the living room and talk to my parents about that."

Now she sat up, looking at the dashboard clock.

"Oh, geez, Joe, look at the time. I've got to go."

Just like that, I was yanked out of our body-to-body bliss.

"Come on," I said, trying to pull her back down. "It's still early."

Elbowing me away, Shannon corralled her breasts into the confines of her bra. "The library closes at eight. I told my parents I'd be home right after."

Considering how cautiously she drove—braking at every corner to look to her left, her right, and her left again—I was home in no time, deposited on the curb in front of my aunt Beth's house like a piece of furniture the Salvation Army was slated to pick up.

I stood there in the cool autumn evening, thinking of the excitement that awaited me inside the house—a game of Monopoly with the family (whoopee!), a review of my math homework (yee-haw!)—and then I remembered my mom and aunt had gone to a piano recital. My options of thrills and chills having decreased by half, I trudged toward the house and the yawning abyss that was my calculus book when a lightbulb blinked on in my head.

The antiwar meeting. I still had time to get to the Canteen and help save the world and my friendship with Darva.

Hopping on my bike, I pedaled as if I was being timed, nearly wiping out twice on the mats of wet leaves that lay wrinkled against the curb. By the time I got to the coffee shop, my thigh muscles were re-minding me I had a week or two worth of drills be-fore I'd be in prime hockey-playing shape.

There were two sections to the Canteen: the coffee shop, in which diners sat salting their fries at a horse-shoe counter or plugging quarters into the little juke-boxes with which every booth was equipped, and the "dining room" to the left, boasting a fancier atmo-sphere, thanks to carpeting and wall sconces.

"Joe, over here!"

Tracking Darva's voice, I saw her in the last booth of the coffee shop.

"Hey, you made it—great!" she said, patting my back as I slid into the booth. "Joe, this is Sheila and Ellen and Wes."

I recognized the girls from school but had never seen the guy, who wore a scrawny goatee and "Mc-Govern for President" and "ERA Now!" pins all over his jean jacket.

"Sorry I'm late," I said, "but I was on the phone with an underground Weatherman, and you know how long those underground Weathermen can talk."

Darva laughed, but the others looked at me with blank faces.

"Are you making fun of what we're trying to accomplish here?" asked Ellen, whose slightly pink nose and large front teeth made me think her favorite food might be carrots.

"Relax, Ellen—he showed up, didn't he?" Darva rolled her eyes and smiled at me. "We're just a little frustrated; we were hoping for a much bigger turnout."

"I warned her," said Wes, he of the weak-willed goatee. "There's no one more resistant to change than the average high-schooler—even if he might be called upon to fight a war."

"I don't think we have to worry about being drafted anymore," I said.

"Well, I did. I graduated from high school two years ago, and I had a really low draft number."

"Did you go?" I asked.

"Wes is a conscientious objector," said Darva proudly, leaning into him, and it was at that moment I realized they had a thing going. It was at the same moment that I realized it bothered me.

"Cool," I said, when what I wanted to say was, "Chickenshit!" It wasn't as if I was pro-war or anything—if the draft had affected me, I'd be crossing the border into Canada before you could say "deserter"—but I didn't like this guy and his smug goateed face and the way he put his arm around Darva and stroked her neck with his pointer finger. What an **asshole**!

"So what else do you do?" I asked as a waitress finally noticed my existence and slapped a laminated
menu on the table in front of me.

"A Coke," I said to her, handing back the menu,
and to Wes I said, "Besides conscientiously object."

"I go to the U," said Wes, "if that's all right
with you."

"Hmmm," I said, considering this. "I'd prefer if
you went out of state."

"What is the matter with you guys?" asked Darva,
impatience sharpening her voice. "Are you trying to
waste all our time or just some of it?"

Smirking as if she was scolding only me, Mr. Goat
Man stroked her neck with his finger again, a finger
I now wanted to break at the knuckle.

Instead, I crossed my arms, leaned forward in a
posture of great interest, and said, "So what have you
got planned?"

A look of relief passed over Darva's face, and I saw
in her smile an acknowledgment that I was the better man.

"We're going to have a sit-in," she said. "Next Friday, during the pep rally."

"During the pep rally? How do you have a sit-in
during a pep rally?"

"You know how the cheerleaders always run into
the gym and try to get everyone all fired up right
when the football players come out?" said Sheila,
widening her eyes as she pushed her glasses up the
bridge of her nose. "We'll come in right after them—
when everyone's standing up and cheering."

"Yeah," said the rabbity Ellen. "Imagine the statement we'll make."

My stomach suddenly felt as if something cold and clammy was passing through it. **The statement we'll make?**

"So who—" I cleared my throat and any remaining soprano notes that might come out of it. "So who do you expect to be a part of this sit-in?"

"Why, there's us, of course," said Sheila, "and anyone else who wants to join us."

"Our dream is that the whole school'll rise up," said Ellen.

"Rise up?" I said. "Doesn't that defeat the purpose of a sit-in?"

I got no response, but that was okay—I didn't feel like laughing either.

There were those jocks for whom a pep rally was something evangelical, but most of us were just glad for the excuse to get out of class. Still, there was something about this pep rally—it was the last game of the season and our football team had surprised everyone by **winning** lately, so much so that we had climbed out of second-to-last place and into second-to-first. The whole school was jazzed—even the freaks and stoners who usually skipped assemblies to get high outside in the parking lot.

The plan was that after Mr. Brietmayer gave his little speech (the principal seized every opportunity to remind us that he had been an all-conference running back in college) and after the football players raced into the gym to the rousing accompaniment of bounding cheerleaders and the school band playing the Ole Bull fight song, our Gang of Four (Wuss—I mean Wes—had only accompanied Darva to the planning meeting and was not a participant) was to enter the gym through different doors and walk ("Solemnly, guys," said Ellen. "Remember—**solemnly**") to the little stage that had been constructed, where we would sit down and unroll the "Stop the War!" banner Darva had shoved in her waistband.

"I'm a little nervous," Sheila had admitted earlier that morning when we rendezvoused in the parking lot. "What do you think'll happen?"

"**Anything,**" said Darva. "But whatever happens, remember: We're on the right side."

The hallways emptied, and after the last of the students straggled in, I left my post by the bathroom and stood by the gym door, waiting for my cue. From my vantage point, I could see a section of bleachers, filled with the laughing, jostling students who would soon become either my hecklers or my supporters. I saw Mr. Brietmayer sitting on a chair on the stage, palming the sides of his Brylcreemed hair. He sat with his legs spread wide apart, the fabric of his brown suit pants stretched tight across his thighs, and I wondered if a guy who sat like that—as if to remind everyone not to worry, his testosterone level was still up there even if he didn't throw a pigskin ball around anymore—would take a sympathetic view toward matters of free speech when practiced by his students.

"What's the matter—wouldn't they let you in?"

I spun around, as if in the vortex of a hot wind.

"Kristi!" I said with the same guilty surprise a kid says, "Mom!" when caught with his hand in whatever cookie jar he wasn't supposed to have his hand in.

With the big bass drum strapped around her, Kristi stood there, hands on hips, shaking her head.

"Shouldn't you go in there?" I asked.

"Shouldn't you?"

We stood looking at each other for a moment, me trying too hard to look as if I had every right to be standing in the hallway and she looking as if I did not.

"Don't tell me," she said, slowly swinging one mallet back and forth, "you're with those antiwar dorks."

"Antiwar dorks?" I said, my face flushing.

"Listen, Joe," she said impatiently. "People care about the war, but they don't care about the war in a pep rally. Don't let those saps play you for a sucker."

I was about to ask her which Jimmy Cagney movie playing on the late show she'd stolen that line from, but a whistle blew and suddenly she was off, banging on her drum as the band started playing the school song.

The thunder of more than two thousand pairs of feet stomping the bleachers rose to my ears, and then I watched as Ole Bull's football team burst through the main doors.

A roar went up and the team, escorted by the frantically jumping cheerleaders and Kristi's driving beat, ran around the gym, their faces grim, their fists held clenched to their sides, as if their business was as serious as gladiators facing a pride of lions.

The roar and the school song both got louder. I saw Leonard Doerr rush out to join the team, and then I saw Jim Klatz shove him aside.

Jim Klatz was a tackle who had a full scholarship to Nebraska, and if All-Around Nerd was a prize given,

Leonard Doerr would win by a wide margin; these facts were givens. Still, you didn't have to see Leonard's apologetic shrug to know this sort of thing happened to him all the time. Never mind that he was dressed head to toe in school colors; never mind that he took meticulous play-by-play notes of every game the Bulls played; never mind that he was the student manager of the team, for Christ's sake.

Even though I wasn't the most gung-ho participant in this protest, that Kristi thought it was a bad idea had made me want to do it, had made me want to show her that, unlike the rest of the world, my reason for being wasn't to serve her. But seeing the ultimate football groupie getting shoved by the ultimate football player made me tired and made the pointlessness of an antiwar protest in the midst of a pep rally seem like a big bottle of NyQuil. To stop the fatigue, I turned around and walked down the hallway and, checking to make sure no one was around to witness my illegal act, I took the little hammer out of its box and broke the glass of the fire alarm with it.

In the minuscule pause between the noise and the recognition of what the noise meant, I raced into the john, only to emerge seconds later in the crowd that filled the hallway.

"We could do the sit-in here," said Darva later that afternoon as we watched the Polar Bears score their third touchdown of the game.

"Not much point to a sit-in when everybody's already sitting," I said, and shoved another handful of booster-club popcorn into my mouth.

The October air was cold and sharp, and seeing

her chin tremble in a shiver, I leaned into her, warming her.

"You better cut that out or that bull of yours is going to charge up the stands after me."

"Funny," I said, looking down at Shannon, who was pawing at the ground with her leg as Kristi brandished an invisible red cape.

"The Bulls are gonna hit, the bulls are gonna gore," screamed the cheerleaders, "and then the Bulls are gonna get out there and score, score, score O-lee, O-lee, O-lee Bull!"

"So how long have you and Wes been going out?" I asked, and from my tone of voice you would have thought I'd asked her how long she'd been dating Spiro Agnew.

Darva laughed. "What do you care?"

I shoved another handful of popcorn into my mouth, trying to think of a reasonable answer.

When I couldn't think of one, I swallowed and said, "I'm who set off the fire alarm."

"**What?**"

I shushed her, letting her know I didn't think it was necessary that the kids in front of us hear my private confession.

She looked at me for a long moment, hooking behind her ear a strand of hair the wind had blown across her face. A play on the field caused some attention from the stands, but we ignored it.

"Why?" she finally said. "Why'd you blow a chance for us to do **something**?"

"Give me a break, Darva. It's not like four kids sitting down during the middle of a pep rally was going to change the world or anything."

"And doing nothing is?"

"It just seemed so . . . I don't know, so high school."

"So it wasn't a march on Washington," said Darva, her voice a cold, fast whisper. "We've got to work where we're at."

"Pithy slogan. Did that guy Wes teach it to you?"

Darva smiled at me as if she didn't immediately understand what I said and wanted to be polite until she did.

"Excuse me," she said finally, and as she stood up I leaned back to let her pass. I stayed sitting like that for a long time, too disgusted with myself, with everything, to follow her through the crowd, which collectively moaned as the Polar Bears scored another touchdown.

Four

From the Ole Bulletin, November 1971:

Barring some unforseen reescalation, it looks as if the Class of '72 is not going to be drafted to Viet Nam. That is, the Bulls aren't going, but what about the Cows? In this age of equality, what are women's obligations during war time? Your Roving Reporter thought he'd find out by asking, "Should women be drafted?"

Donna Shelton, junior: "I'd go in a second—I mean, how hard would it be to be surrounded by cute young guys in uniform?"

Mrs. Wanda Meegan, English teacher: "I would move to Canada if they initiated a draft for girls; of course, I would move to Canada if I were a boy and was drafted. You'd think we would have figured out by now that war creates more problems than it solves and that we do not achieve peace through strength. We achieve peace through peace. Drafting women would be an abomination, but it's my opinion that drafting men is an abomination too."

Sean Knutsen, sophomore: "No way! What kind of war could we win if girls were fighting alongside us? It's like these girls who think they should be able to play basketball or baseball with the guys—what are they, nuts? They can't throw for *$!*—they probably couldn't even lift a gun, let alone shoot it!"

Charlie Olsen, senior: "Bring 'em on! I wouldn't mind being in a foxhole with a bunch of foxes! I'm all for making love, not war, but if girls were let into the army, I could do both things at the same time. . . ."

Hockey was a big sport at Ole Bull High, and it is not an overstatement to say that after scoring twice and assisting the game-winning goal during my first game, my life changed.

Kids I didn't know congratulated me in the hallways.

"Great game, Joe!"

"Keep it up and this time we'll get to state!"

"Nice slap shot!"

Mr. Eggert compared my back-checking to art.

"You might think of dancers when you hear the word **choreography**," he told the class at the beginning of the period, "but there's poetry in motion in a sport well played, as evidenced by our Mr. Andreson."

He raised the chalk eraser as if it was a glass of wine he was toasting me with, and I ducked my head in embarrassment and pleasure.

During our next game, against Southwest, my line was able to hold off Darryl Sobota, who, last season, had been the third-highest scorer in the state. I also intercepted a rebound and took the puck up the rink and shot into the top shelf of the net. It was to be the only goal of the game, and after the Bull fans counted down the last ten seconds on the clock, they went nuts.

My teammates circled around me.

"Fuckin' Bobby Orr, man," said Wilkerson, smacking my helmeted head with his own.

"Glad you left fuckin' Hooterville for the big time," said Olsen, smacking my pads with his stick.

"Great game, Joe," said Blake Erlandsson, smacking my back with his hands as he bear-hugged me.

The next day during morning announcements, Mr. Brietmayer congratulated the team and me in particular, and when everyone in my homeroom erupted in applause, I thought, **I could get used to this.**

We won the next four games and I was pretty convinced that the world was my oyster, especially one night after practice when Kristi Casey stopped by.

We were all at the piano when the doorbell rang.

"Collection," I said. As a former paperboy, I recognized a certain persistence to the ring.

Beth sighed as she got up. "I'm going to call his mother and tell him she shouldn't allow him to collect after dark."

As she wondered aloud where she left her purse, my mother and I got back to singing "Till There Was You."

We sang every verse, and when we were done, I assumed the applause I heard behind me was my aunt's.

"Come on, Miss Channing," I said, riffing a little on the introduction to "Before the Parade Passes By." "We're ready for your solo."

The laugh I heard was not my aunt's, and as I turned toward its source, a wave of heat torched my face, singeing my hairline and blistering my ears.

"Hey, Joe," said Kristi, baring her crocodile smile.

"Hey, Kristi," I answered, the thrill I felt from her standing in my living room (why was she standing in my living room?) slapped down by the mortification I felt knowing she had seen me sitting around the piano with my mother, playing Broadway show tunes, for Christ's sake.

"I didn't know you played piano."

"Well, my mom **is** a music teacher," I said, as if apologizing. "She sort of made me."

"Nonsense," said my mom, nudging me in an isn't-he-silly gesture. "We couldn't keep him away from the piano—even as a toddler, he'd climb up on the piano bench and try to pick out tunes with his chubby little fingers."

Everyone laughed at this little item of interest while I, way past mortification now, brayed, "**Maaaa.**"

"So you guys sit around and sing together?" said Kristi, her smile not going anywhere. "Like in **The Sound of Music?**"

"Sure!" said my aunt. "In fact, I'll bet Joe would be happy to put on his lederhosen if you asked him nicely."

She held up her hands as if to fend off the look I gave her.

"Beth," said my mother, getting off the piano bench, "why don't we scrounge around the kitchen and see if we can find something to eat for these kids?" She patted Kristi's shoulder before taking my aunt's arm. "Take off your coat, dear, and make yourself comfortable."

"Thank you," said Kristi. "I'll do that."

I watched as she unbuttoned her pea coat and laid it on the couch, watched as she took off her wool hat and fluffed her hair, and I tried to breathe normally.

"So what brings you here?" I said, the suaveness I tried to project undermined by a little squeak in my voice.

"I was in the neighborhood," she said lightly, and as she came toward me, I braced myself. For what, I didn't know.

She sat next to me and I smelled Love's Baby Soft, the baby-powderish perfume all the girls were wearing. She flipped the songbook to its cover and read, **Best of Broadway.**

"It . . . it's not that I like—"

"Play this one," said Kristi, and because it didn't occur to me to do anything different, I did.

The song was "Try to Remember" from **The Fantasticks,** and I had only played a couple of measures when she said, "Sing too."

And so I sang, because whatever Kristi wanted, you were happy to give it.

"That was so pretty," she said softly, and as she pressed her shoulder against mine, the baby-powder smell got stronger. "Play it again."

I did, singing all the verses. It's a nice ballad, and I knew I had a nice enough voice—nothing flashy, but nice—and after my voice faded away, riding the last note, and after the vibrations of the piano strings slowed to a stop, Kristi Casey leaned even closer and kissed me.

The surprise factor surprised me—well, **stunned** me—so much so that I was immobilized, and it wasn't until she drew back her head and smiled that I realized she had stopped and that I wanted more.

"Thanks for the concert," she said, stopping too abruptly the slow delicious slide her hand made down my thigh by patting my knee. "But I gotta get going. My squirrely brother's waiting for me out in the car."

I was discombobulated from that kiss, from that hand on my thigh, and didn't quite understand what she was saying. "Kirk . . . Kirk's out in the car?" I had worked with the bag boy for more than a month before figuring out his sister was Kristi.

She was already shrugging into her pea coat. "Yeah, like I said, I was in the neighborhood. I had to pick him up at work."

"It's cold out there." It seemed I was vying for the lame conversationalist award.

"Well, **duh.** That's why I'm leaving. My mother would be **p-i-s-s** pissed if I brought him home frozen." She wiggled her fingers at me. "**Mañana,** Jose."

I wasn't a greedy bastard—the fact that Kristi's mouth had been on mine for one moment in time was enough for me, and besides, I was practical.

What were the odds of that happening again? Pretty damn good, and **beyond,** it turned out.

One day after lunch, I was getting my books for my afternoon classes when I saw a folded square of paper on my locker floor.

Meet me in the audiovisual office at 2:00, it read, and was signed, **K.**

I stood staring at the pile of books on the shelf above my jacket, my mind playing badminton with two thoughts: **K's gotta be Kristi. K can't be Kristi.**

"You trippin', man?" asked Todd Randolph, nudging me as he opened his combination lock.

"Huh?" **K's gotta be Kristi. K can't be Kristi.**

"You look like a zombie standing there."

"Nah," I said, grabbing my history and English books and shutting my locker. "Zombies look like this." I opened my mouth, letting my tongue push out my lower lip, and rolled my eyes back.

"No," said the guy who considered himself the funniest kid in our class. "Zombies look like that." He pointed at Terry Seagren, a kid whose navigation down the hallways was a little harder than most, considering the leg braces he wore.

"Asshole," I said, shaking my head.

Todd Randolph gave me one of the many smirks he passed out all day. "Takes one to know one."

The bell rang at two o'clock, and seconds later, I knocked on the door of the audiovisual office. To say I was relieved when Kristi opened the door is to understate my emotions—I was thrilled, excited, and mystified. Apparently I looked the way I felt, and she laughed, pulling me into the small room as she closed the door and turned the skeleton key in the lock.

"I'm glad you made it."

"So what—" I began, but Kristi shut me up good by pushing me onto the padded chair behind the desk and climbing on top of me and laying a kiss on me so sweet I thought that if I'd died and gone to heaven, I didn't mind dying and heaven was even better than advertised.

"Wow," I said when she pulled her face away from mine, allowing me to finally inhale.

She smiled, and when it was sincere, there was no smile prettier than Kristi Casey's.

"You ain't seen nothin' yet," she said, and delivering on her promise, she lowered herself to her knees. As I screamed to myself, **Is she doing what I think she's doing?** she unzipped my fly, answering yes.

"Oh my, you're all ready," she said, freeing my boner from its cotton gate.

"Kristi, I—" I didn't know what I was going to say, but it didn't matter; any words, any coherence was literally swallowed up when Kristi took me in her mouth.

Every single sensor in my body was on high alert: **Kristi Casey's giving me a blow job!**

I leaned back in the chair, my eyes rolled back so far in my head I wouldn't be surprised if I could read the advertisement for Bell and Howell projectors pinned to the wall behind me. **Kristi Casey's giving me a blow job!** Could anything in the known world feel as good as those lips around my dick? It was as if all of me was submerged in velvet, in wet velvet, and my pelvis rose off the chair and back down again, wanting to plunge itself in that deep wet fabric.

"Oh God!" I shouted as her tongue darted along the tip of my cock. "**Oh, God!**"

"Shh!" said Kristi, and immediately I obeyed; her mouth was needed for far better things than scolding.

My fingers were laced through her hair and when I came, my grip must have been pretty tight because the second thing she said to me was, "Ow! Next time don't pull my hair, Joe." The first thing she said, after sitting back on her haunches and wiping her mouth with the back of her hand, was, "I sure hope that stuff's not fattening."

I laughed; I could have just as easily cried, sang, whistled, or yodeled, but laughter seemed the safest response to the unbelievable, fantastic, and glorious thing that had happened to me: **Kristi Casey just gave me a blow job!**

"I'll write you out a pass, Joe," she said, standing up and brushing the knees of her bell-bottom jeans.

I laughed again; there was no language for what I was feeling, so laughter would have to do.

When I stood up, my legs felt as wobbly as if I'd been out on the rink all day and had just taken off my skates.

"What'll you say?" I said, zipping up my pants. " 'Please excuse Joe from Calculus. Kristi Casey was giving him a blow job'?"

"If that's what you want," she said, scribbling something on a pink pad. She tore the small square off and handed it to me. It read: **Pls. xcuse J. A.— busy w/b.j.**

Laughing—I was on top of the world; how could I not laugh?—I folded the paper and stuffed it in my back pocket as she wrote out another pass.

"Who do you have anyway?"

"Uh . . . Mrs. Gleason."

"Well, if she asks—which she won't—tell her you were helping Mrs. Moriarty for the book drive."

"Where'd you get these?" I asked as she finished writing and handed me the new pass, which was marked only with a time and signature.

"They're in every teacher's desk," she said, putting the remaining passes in her shoulder bag. She fluffed her hair with her hands. "How do I look?"

"How do you **look**?" I reached for her, wanting to answer her with a kiss, but she sidestepped me and opened the door.

"Hey, Joe—can you help me move a dresser tomorrow? Blake was going to help me, but he's got to go straight to work after hockey practice."

Although I'd preferred her to ask me to pledge my undying love (which I would have), I said sure. After what she'd done for me, I'd have moved a dresser, a refrigerator, and a sectional couch, all in one trip.

"Great! I'll pick you up at seven, then." She poked her head out and looked down the hallway.

"Coast is clear," she said, and although she didn't wink, her smile made it seem as if she had. "See you later, Joe."

"Innt ma Krissi the preesing eur seen?"

I shrugged helplessly.

"Innt ma Krissi the pressing eur seen?"

"Thank you, Grandma," said Kristi to the old woman whose bed we stood around. To me she said, "She's asking you if you don't think I'm the prettiest thing you've ever seen."

I gave a big, enthusiastic Boy Scout nod. "I do, Mrs. Swenson. I sure do."

Kristi laughed.

"Way to force a compliment out of him, Grandma." She went to the dresser I had helped her move, and rummaged through the top drawer.

"I'm going to brush your hair, Grandma," she said, finding a brush. "It looks kind of wild."

"Ese ays zas a ashon."

"She says that's the fashion these days." Kristi laughed again, a laugh I hadn't heard from her before, sweet and light.

Very gently, she swabbed the woman's thin white hair with the brush she found in the drawer. "I can come right after school tomorrow, so I'll wash it for you then."

A semblance of a smile lifted one side of the twisted grimace that was Mrs. Swenson's mouth.

"Ill eu iv e a ehicur too?"

"A pedicure, a manicure, anything you want, Grandma."

The old woman looked at me, her blue eyes full of the life the rest of her body seemed to have given up on.

I smiled at her, and instead of smiling back, she winked.

Kristi pretended to swat her with the brush.

"Stop flirting, Grandma. Joe's too young for you."

"I ike eh yeh."

"Well, he's **too** young. You'd be corrupting a minor."

The old woman's laugh was more a cackle, and

drool spilled out of the side of her mouth that couldn't move.

"But I'll turn eighteen in February," I said, because even though the drool was a little gross, I liked hearing that laughter.

"E sti ey art," said Mrs. Swenson, her good hand patting the left side of her chest.

Kristi didn't have to translate that for me.

"Yes, be still," I said, pretending to calm my own rapid heartbeat by patting my chest and a moment later, a nurse's aide came into the room, asking what all the merriment was about.

"She's only sixty-nine," said Kristi as we stood in a jerky elevator that smelled like one of those casseroles—maybe tuna noodle—that stinks a little like vomit. "I know she seems a lot older, but that's because of the stroke." The elevator groaned as if the cables were overstretched. "You should have seen what she was like before it."

"When . . . when did it happen?" I said, almost unsure of how to talk to Kristi when she was so un-Kristi-like.

"Last year. She was having coffee at the bakery when her friend said all of a sudden—bang!—'the donut flies out of her hand and she drops to the floor.' " She pressed her frosted lips together and shook her head. "I used to spend nearly every weekend with her when I was little. She was so much fun—we'd make popcorn balls and watch Lawrence Welk together. I know that doesn't sound like much fun, but it was."

The elevator bounced to a stop and the doors opened with a quiet groan.

"What about your grandpa?" I asked as we stepped into the overheated lobby, which smelled even more strongly of that casserole with questionable ingredients.

"Oh, he died when I was seven. And I never even knew my dad's parents. Grandma Dorothy's all I've got left."

Her voice was so sad, so lonely, that I had to put my arm around her. She rested her head on my shoulder for a moment, and even though I might have looked like a concerned and caring guy, the only thought jumping around like a monkey in my head was: **Did I earn another blow job? Huh? Huh? Did I? Did I?**

Five

From the Ole Bulletin, **December 1971:**

Christmas vacation, and the livin' is easy. Our Roving Reporter merrily roamed the halls, asking a handful of Bulls how they planned to spend two sweet weeks of wintry freedom.

Leonard Doerr, senior: "Well, the German club is having their big **Weinachten** party—I'm making apple strudel for it!—and then there's our big church concerts (come on down, everyone—I'm in the handbell choir) and of course I'll be writing a lot of my college applications. I've got my fingers crossed for Northwestern, but I wouldn't say no to Oberlin, either!"

Heywood Jablome, senior: "I'll probably spend the holidays with my parole officer."

Babs Johnson, junior: "I'm going skiing with my family in Colorado."

Janet Vromann, junior: "I'm going skiing with Babs' family in Colorado, 'cause my parents don't ski. My dad said he tried it once, but he couldn't stop and he ran into his instructor. Fortunately he was only going down the bunny hill, so he wasn't going all that fast. Still, fast enough to break his wrist. And fast enough to break the instructor's tailbone. I hope I don't break anything of mine or the Johnsons'."

Mr. Frank Lutz, Ole Bull **advisor:** "I'm going get my fireplace going and sit in my favorite chair and read until I'm cross-eyed."

Laurie Stein, junior: "I'm collecting toys for kids who might not get anything for Christmas. It's kind of funny, 'cause I'm Jewish and we don't celebrate Christmas, but this is more about Santa Claus than Jesus—no offense to anyone. What I mean is, I do a lot of volunteer work and this is one of the annual projects, and I think it's neat when a kid who's not expecting anything under her Christmas tree—if she even **has** a Christmas tree—finds a doll or a sled or something. It's just kind of a neat thing."

Despite the fact that I'd be spending time with my own grandmother, whose company didn't thrill me the way Mrs. Swenson's company thrilled Kristi, it was a big relief to go back to Granite Creek for Christmas. I didn't care that the skies held a big surprise clearance sale, dumping its overstock of snow on us for the entire ride and throwing in a bonus of winds that rendered visibility to about two inches;

didn't care that a four-hour drive took us seven; didn't care that tow trucks and highway patrol cars trolled the highway like vultures, ready to feast upon another inevitable spin-out.

"I think I aged ten years," said my mother when we finally pulled into my grandma's driveway.

"Well, then I aged twenty," said my aunt Beth, who had shared driving duties with me. "And she'll add on another five." She nodded toward the front door, which Grandma had opened and now stood in front of, arms crossed.

My mother fixed her lipstick in the visor mirror. "We're all going to get along this Christmas, remember, Beth?"

My aunt sighed. "Sure, Carole. Whatever you say. Santy Claus is going to come and the turkey won't be tough and we'll all get along."

It didn't take long to see that the magic of Christmas wasn't about to cast its spell on this house. We had barely sat down in the small living room with our coffee and cookies before Grandma started complaining.

"My goodness, you said you'd be here by four—I've been worried sick about you. Would it have been so hard to call?"

"Mom, we only stopped once, at the Dutch Girl in Alexandria, but the line to the phone was too long and we figured we'd lose even more time if we waited."

"Big café like the Dutch Girl is bound to have more than one phone," she said with a sniff. "And I was going to have a nice warm dinner waiting for you."

"Mom, I told you not to have dinner ready, that we were going to stop at the Dutch Girl."

"Well, it's a good thing that I didn't, because it would have been ruined."

"At least we get to enjoy these delicious cookies and coffee together," said Aunt Beth, and if sarcasm was venom, hers would be lethal.

"You expect me to brew a pot at ten o'clock in the evening?" said Grandma, not about to apologize for serving instant. "Just like you expected me to slave the day away making homemade cookies?"

"Mama, we didn't expect anything," said my mom, putting her arm around the thin ridge of Grandma's shoulders. "We're just glad to be here."

"Some people have a funny way of showing it," said Grandma, looking at my aunt as if she had tracked something in on her carpet, even though it was a house rule you had to take your shoes off the second you stepped inside.

We all tried, but the small talk was just that: small. And I was glad when my mom yawned and said we were pretty tired from the long drive and it was time to hit the hay.

"Well, I washed both the kitchen **and** the bathroom floors this morning," said Grandma, as if we weren't the only ones who had a reason to be tired. "And don't forget **I've** got to get up early to put the turkey in."

"I'll help you." Aunt Beth's offer came just a beat before mine and my mother's, but Grandma wasn't interested in any of them.

"At five A.M.?" Her snort substituted for a laugh. "I get you up at five A.M. and the one thing I can count on is a bunch of crabapples for Christmas dinner. **No thanks.**" She stood up then, pulling her sweater around her, as if the wind had just blown in, and told everybody good night. Both my mother and aunt stood, and maybe it was because I didn't like the way she acted—as if her cheek barely had room for their kisses—that made me envelop my grandma in a bear hug and lift her off her bootie-slippered feet.

"Oh my!" she said in a strangled voice, as if I'd punched her instead of hugged her, but I held on, held on until I felt a twinge of pressure that let me know she was hugging me back.

I was assigned, as usual, my uncle Roger's twin bed, with its bedposts carved up with initials and spotted and scarred in the places where his chewing gum had been pried off. The last time I had seen him was a couple of months after my dad's funeral, watching him pack his duffel back on the very same bed.

"You come and spend the summer with me, mate," he said, rolling his underwear into little cylinders. "I'll be in either Tahiti or Bora Bora, and what they say about Polynesian women is true."

"What do they say about Polynesian woman?" I asked.

Roger looked at me. It's not often a person has eyes the colors of gemstones, but his were a true turquoise, a color so pretty and jewel-like, you could imagine another kind of man getting in trouble for them, getting beat up for them. But anyone picking a fight with Roger over his eye color or anything else was going to pick a fight they were bound to lose; my uncle was wiry but strong, his arms banded tight with muscles made from crewing on boats that sailed the seven seas and scything through jungle forests and hoisting hundred-pound sacks of grain on his shoulder to be delivered to tribal chieftans. My uncle had been one of the first to sign up for the Peace Corps, and after his stint in Ethiopia, he'd decided adventure's call was louder than the peeps coming from Granite Creek and had been traveling the world ever since. As a kid, I thought he was Jack London, Long John Silver, and John Glenn rolled into one, far and away the most romantic figure of my boyhood.

It didn't matter to my grandmother that he loved his life, only that he wasn't spending it near her, just as she didn't mourn my grandfather so much as resent him for leaving her. Those were some of the conclusions my mom and Beth had come up with in their many discussions of our family. Another one was that they never wanted to wind up like Grandma. In fact, the Christmas before last, they both counseled me to "always keep an open heart."

"An open heart meaning . . . ?"

"Meaning be glad for someone else's happiness," Aunt Beth had said.

That Christmas Eve, Grandma had handed Beth her present and before she could even open it, Grandma had said, "Now, I know it's nothing special for someone who's got a big-shot job down in Minneapolis, but I thought it was cute." The gift was a straw purse with a little wooden apple for its knob, and even I could tell that Grandma's idea of cute was not in step with her daughter's, yet Beth's thanks were profuse and genuine-sounding.

"Also meaning letting someone love what he or she wants to love," continued my aunt. "Even though it would be easier for you if they loved something else."

It was a tradition to read Roger's Christmas let-ter—this one had been postmarked from the Gala-pagos Islands—after we opened presents, and it had also become a tradition for Grandma to say some-thing like "You'd think he could manage a visit home once in a while, all the world traveling he does" or "Seems he likes to spend the holidays with those na-tives more than his own family."

"Above all," said my mom, wrapping up the tuto-rial in what constituted an open heart, "don't let what happens in your life make you bitter. No mat-ter **what** happens."

I thought that was pretty brave advice coming from a woman who had been widowed at age thirty-eight; pretty brave advice from both daughters of a woman who was pickled in a brine of hurt and bit-terness.

Lying back in Roger's old bed, I stared at the ceil-ing, upon which he had painted the solar system (earning another Boy Scouts badge), thinking of the promises and advice I had been given in this room. I didn't know about the promises, but I sure could have used the advice, although considering the topic on which I needed counsel, I wasn't about to solicit any from my aunt, let alone my mom.

But what **was** a guy supposed to do when the finest girl in school was using him as her own personal sex toy and in particular, what was a guy supposed to do when he was more than happy to be that sex toy?

"Are we going steady?" I'd asked Kristi after the second blow job, this one given in her car parked in a secluded spot by Minnehaha Falls.

She was putting on lip gloss and didn't look away

from the rearview mirror, but nodded slightly to let me know she appreciated that I'd made a joke, only she didn't find it very funny.

"Joe," she said after she'd blotted her lips, "if you think I'm gonna drop Blake for you, think again."

"So," I said, making my voice sound high and wounded, "this is just about the sex?"

Raising one eyebrow, Kristi looked at me, then turned the ignition key. "You want the facts, Joe?"

I let my voice stay high. "Yes, please."

She slid the lever of the heater and a blast of warm arm huffed out of the vents.

"Joe, I don't mean to brag, but I'm Kristi Casey, okay?"

I nodded; this much I understood.

"And my boyfriend's Blake Erlandsson, and come on, wouldn't you say we're **the** couple at Ole Bull?"

My head continued its steady bob.

"And I'm never gonna jeopardize that, okay?"

"So why," I said, truly trying to understand, "are you giving me blow jobs?"

"For the practice."

"You can't get enough practice with Blake?" I had to laugh. "Seriously, I think he'd be happy to practice as much as you'd like."

Kristi tossed her head and looked at me for a long moment, as if trying to figure out how much she could tell me.

"I'd never think to give Blake a blow job," she said. "All it would take is for him to tell one person—he's so tight with Olsen, and you know what a big mouth Olsen has—and then I've got some slutty reputation like Sharon Winters, and what do I need that for?"

I shook my head, not quite believing what I'd just heard.

"What makes you think I might not tell anyone?"

The usual calm, cool look of superiority disappeared from her face.

"'Cause I trust you," she said, a little wheedling note of panic in her voice. "'Cause I think this is a . . . a mutually beneficial situation, wouldn't you say? And why would you want to endanger a mutually beneficial situation?"

"You're right, I wouldn't. But I know what I'm getting out of it. What are you?"

"Like I said, Joe, practice. I . . . I want to know how to do things, to be good at things."

"Like sex," I said, more as a statement than a question.

"Exactly. And not that I'm just thinking about my reputation—I mean, God, how outdated is that? Then again, the reality is, if you're a girl, it **does** matter. And Blake . . . well, Blake's not exactly the horniest guy I've ever met."

"He's not?" I had never gotten this good a scoop as the Roving Reporter.

Kristi shook her head and turned the radio on low. Creedence Clearwater was singing "Bad Moon Rising," and we listened to it for a while.

"I mean, you can't have everything—and come on, Blake's got just **about** everything. Captain of the hockey team **and** the baseball team. Two Division One scholarship offers. Homecoming king—although we know the whole thing was rigged. And I don't think anyone would think he's **not** the cutest guy in the whole school."

I shrugged; on this subject I really didn't have an opinion.

"Plus he's smart and I couldn't ask for a sweeter guy; God, the presents he gives me! So it's not like I'm complaining. . . . It's just that, well, I guess I have a more developed sex drive than he does. And whether we wind up together for good or not, when I go away to college I plan to do my share of sexual experimentation—I mean, that's what college is for, isn't it?"

"I sure hope so."

Kristi took a box of Marlboros out of her purse and offered me one.

Shaking my head, I said, "I didn't know you smoked. Cigarettes, that is."

Her eyes lit up. "You got some dope?"

"No."

"Bummer. And I don't. Smoke cigarettes, that is. At least not habitually. It's against cheerleading rules." She offered me a conspiratorial smile. "But you know what I think about rules."

"I know you like to break some of them. But there are other rules I'm not so sure about."

"Like which ones?" she asked, opening her window. As winter air skated into the front seat, the car lighter popped out and she lit her cigarette.

"Well," I said, touching her hair, "shouldn't there be a rule about me having to, well, having to return your very generous favors?"

Shaking her head to dislodge my hand, she took a long drag, and the smoke she exhaled drifted into the icy air.

"You mean like go down on me?"

Like a Labrador retriever begging his master to throw the stick, I nodded wildly.

Kristi laughed and inhaled again. "I don't think so." She released an oblong smoke ring and we both watched as it wafted toward the open window before disintegrating. "I mean, no offense, but that would just seem too boyfriendy-girlfriendy."

Boyfriendy-girlfriendy?

"So for now it's just blow jobs?"

"If you're lucky," she said, shifting the gear stick into drive. The old Ford LTD fishtailed as she pulled out onto the snow-packed road, and she chuckled while I sat with my hands on my lap, feeling as powerless and hopeful as a girl.

I lay there contemplating the deep yellow rings of Saturn and the bright red Mars my uncle had painted on the ceiling. I was beat from the long treacherous ride, but my mind was too busy to relax, let alone sleep. For weeks now I'd been on the losing side of a battle for sleep. I don't use the word **battle** indiscriminately; from Kristi's first ambush, I had been excited, unsettled, and on watch, like a soldier waiting for the next encounter and what the ramifications of that encounter might be.

It wasn't as if I was in a slump, but I wasn't scoring like I had been in those first couple prove-myself games. To make things worse, Blake was the sort of team captain who believed in positive reinforcement and never failed to mention the nice plays I'd made each game, to which I would think: **If you only knew.** I did feel guilty—I mean, I liked the guy—but hell, could I help it if he wasn't satisfying his girlfriend on a certain level? And Shannon—our back-seat play seemed just that: **play.** And now that I'd sampled a bit of the serious stuff, play was sorta boring. And if we weren't making out, Shannon was talking, and that's where she and my interest parted company.

"Are you seeing someone else?" she asked one evening after I declined her invitation to go to the "library."

The telephone receiver slipped from my grip.

"Seeing someone else? What makes you think I'm seeing someone else?" My voice, high and wounded, reeked of guilt, but apparently Shannon didn't pick up on this because she quickly offered me an apology.

. "I'm sorry, Joe. It's just that we seem to be drifting and that's the last thing I want to do with you . . . drift, I mean."

I rolled my eyes and offered that I didn't want to drift either. **More like paddle away as fast as I can!** But I didn't say that either because in truth, I really didn't know what I wanted or what I wanted to do.

Darva sensed I was going through some weird shit; I could see it in her frank, squint-eyed assessment of me every time I sat down at our art table. But the break in our friendship hadn't healed yet, at least not enough to bear the weight of a confession. Not that I really wanted to make one.

My life was snarled up enough for me to think that even Christmas spent with a grandma who could scald your skin with her bitterness was a reprieve. At least I knew what to expect here; tomorrow at dinner I, like my aunt and mother, would gnaw through the turkey my grandmother seemed to dehydrate rather than roast, and I would strain to come up with a sincere thanks for whatever personal hygiene product she had ordered from her favorite mail-order catalog (usually soaps tethered by rope or dimpled to look like golf balls and one stellar year, a shoe shine kit housed in a vinyl container shaped like a boot).

I could also expect the tension that would hail Aunt Beth's reading of my uncle Roger's letter. Grandma would shake her head and purse her mouth, her lips wrinkling, as if they'd been pulled tight by a drawstring, scowling over the letter's every description, as if labyrinthine bazaars, lava-spewing mountains, or coconut-throwing monkeys might be of interest to someone, but they sure weren't to her.

On this three-day trip, I also knew my mom and aunt would clean out the laundry room that Grandma used as an all-purpose storage bin; I knew they would give her a permanent wave to the accompaniment of Dean Martin and Perry Como's Christmas albums; I knew they would bake and freeze enough casseroles to keep her going until spring thaw; I knew they would bend over backward to make an old woman be something she wasn't genetically capable of being: happy.

And so to help everyone out, I tried extrahard to be the king of cheer, Mr. Entertainment, the comedian—sometimes even to the point of raising Grandma's frown into a semi-smile. No sense letting out the real miserable what-the-hell-is-going-on Joe and bumming everyone out.

Six

FROM THE Ole Bulletin, JANUARY 1972:

ANNUAL "BEAT THE WINTER BLUES" SHOW SCHEDULED

by Alison O'Grady

"In 1964 we had the entire football team doing a pas de deux from **Swan Lake**," chuckles Mrs. Holbrook, advisor to the drama club. "In 1968 Paulette Renfrow sang a medley from **Seven Brides for Seven Brothers.** As you know, our Paulette went on to become first runner-up in the Miss Minnesota contest just last year."

Are there any burgeoning beauty queens who can sing in this year's lineup? Any macho football players willing to don tutus for a laugh?

We'll find out on February 21, when the annual "Beat the Winter Blues" will be put on by the most talented—or brave—students of Ole Bull High.

"We're looking for all kinds of acts," says Mrs. Holbrook. "We pride ourselves on the diversity of our lineup—so whatever your talent is, be sure to come and try out!"

**Tryouts are the fifteenth and sixteenth of this month at three-thirty in room 304.
Mrs. Holbrook advises singers to bring their own sheet music.**

"Did you hear Debbie Teague's p.g.?"

"Who's Debbie Teague?"

Kristi rolled her eyes, one of her favorite gestures.

"Only little Miss Perfect—or tried to be. Ha! I guess she didn't try hard enough!"

I had been told to meet Kristi in the empty audio-visual office, and I was impatient with the social commentary, anxious to get down to the wonderful business of fellatio.

"Shouldn't we get started?" I asked, unbuttoning my fly.

"My, my, don't we have a sense of entitlement," said Kristi, fanning out her fingers to admire her pink frosted fingernails.

"No," I said quickly, feeling a rush of panic, as if I was an alcoholic who'd been cut off by the bartender before I even sat down at the bar. "No, I was just . . . uh, so what happed to this Debbie girl?"

"She's pregnant! Her parents shipped her off to some home for wayward girls to wait out the blessed event. **Debbie Teague!** I've gone to school with her since kindergarten and I don't know that there's an honor roll she hasn't been on, a brownie point she hasn't tried to earn . . . **Debbie Teague!** She was the straightest girl I know!"

"I bet she's bummed," I said, when what I wanted to say was, **Come on, come on, come on!**

"Yeah, bummed that for being so smart, she couldn't figure out how to use a little birth control!"

Leave it to Kristi to make gloating look attractive. Her moral superiority and cheer over someone else's misfortune brought a flush to her cheeks and a glitter to her green eyes that left me, well, attracted. Still, I decided a risky move might be the only way to get things started.

"I'm sorry to hear about your friend," I said, standing up, "but I guess I should get to class."

Smiling, Kristi pushed me back into the swivel chair.

"Don't you want what you came here for?"

Do you even have to ask such a stupid question?

"Well, sure," I said, all nonchalance. "I mean, if you want to."

Kristi laughed. Sitting on the desk facing me, she put her feet on the chair and pushed them so the chair moved side to side.

"Debbie Teague's not my friend. But she was the accompanist for the Beat the Winter Blues show. And since she's now **indisposed,** and Mrs. Holbrook is having a hard time finding a replacement, I told her I'd ask you."

I planted my feet on the floor to stop the slow rocking back and forth.

"Nah." I could play stuff like "Till There Was You" and "Send in the Clowns" at home, but I sure wasn't going to do it onstage. "Thanks but no thanks."

"Come on," said Kristi. "Mrs. Holbrook's my favorite teacher and she doesn't ask just any lame-o to student-direct. She asked me because she has confidence that I can get done what needs to get done. Besides, you're such a good player, Joe."

"Nope. Not interested."

Kristi feigned a big, shoulder-lifting sigh and folded her hands in her lap.

"Well, if that's the way you want it," she said, her voice sweet. She pivoted and pushed herself off the side of the desk. "Only you might as well know: If you can't do this one simple favor for me, consider all future favors from me over."

I gulped. "By favors you mean . . . ?"

"Uh-huh," said Kristi, smiling as sweetly as a candy striper asked by her first patient to tell him a little about herself.

"You mean now?"

"Now and who knows how many more times?" said Kristi, and before she finished her sentence, I had agreed to the trade by unbuttoning my jeans.

I wound up having an okay time at the talent show. Because of hockey, I only made it to one rehearsal, but it's not like I needed more. I mean, it wasn't like I was a beginning piano student.

"Wow, you're good," said a girl named Holly after I'd accompanied her while she sang the Carpenters' "Close to You."

"You are," agreed Miss Holbrook. "In fact, if you'd like to vamp at all between acts, feel free."

And so I did. Kristi, as the student-director, had cast herself as emcee, and on the night of the performance, she walked out onto the stage in a black sparkly evening gown, basking in the enthusiastic applause and whistles the male half of the audience gave her.

She pushed down the air with her hands and finally the crowd quieted.

"All right, then, without further ado, let's move on with the show. Ladies and gentlemen—Pete and Petey!"

A skinny little ventriloquist came out carrying a dummy. I played "Me and My Shadow." The audience laughed, and as Pete settled himself on the stool, the dummy looked in my direction and said, "Oh, so we got a wise guy at the piano, huh?"

None of the soloists I played for had bad voices, but none of them had great ones either; the fun for me came in the music I'd play in between acts, or to introduce them.

Before Sharon Winters came onstage in her leotard (a costume that nearly upstaged Kristi's) to do a gymnastic routine, I played "Ain't She Sweet." Before the identical twin brothers who juggled came out, I played "All Shook Up." To introduce Leonard Doerr, I played "He's So Fine." It could have been a pricky thing to do—Leonard Doerr, after all, was probably the antithesis of the kind of guy the Chiffons were singing about—but he laughed when he heard it, and then surprised everyone by his act, which was a series of impressions. He did Johnny Carson and Rod Serling and then Johnny Carson as Carnac the Magnificent doing Rod Serling.

"**The Twilight Zone**," he said, holding up an imaginary envelope to his head. After a moment, he pretended to open the envelope and read what was inside.

"What do students call Mr. Lehman's advanced geometry class?"

The joke was a C− but the impression was an A+, and he followed that with a Mick Jagger impression and then Richard Nixon doing Mick Jagger.

"Pat—I just can't get no satisfaction," he said in Nixon's gravelly, jowl-shaking voice, and the audience howled.

He got wild applause, and after he took a bow, Kristi came out from the wings and kissed him on the cheek.

"Pat," he said, flashing the peace sign to the crowd, "let's spend the night together."

The show should have ended there, but there was enough talent at Ole Bull High for another half hour of entertainment before Kristi wrapped the show up by sitting behind a drum kit and blasting out a version of "Wipe Out." My impulse was to jump in by playing the guitar part on piano. It was just backup stuff, because this was entirely Kristi's show. Man, could that girl **drum.** The drumsticks in her hands were a blur as they battered the snare drum and the toms, and when she crashed the cymbals at the end, the whole audience erupted in a wild ovation. From the smile she threw at me, you knew she would have accepted nothing less.

After the show, the cast members received their fans out in the hallway.

"Whoa," said Coach Teschler, slapping me on the back. "Quite the piano man, Andreson!"

"Sharon—nice moves!" said Charlie Olsen, his voice like a wolf whistle.

"**Du bist sehr gut!** " said one of Leonard Doerr's fellow German club members, who swarmed around him.

My mom and aunt found me in the crowd.

"For the maestro!" said my aunt Beth, handing me a cellophane-covered cone of roses.

"What's this? You never give me flowers after a hockey game."

"You'd never forgive me."

"You're right," I said.

My mother had sidled up to me, sneaking in a sideways hug.

"You were so good," she said, and the happiness on her face made me think of something Jay Mitvedt said upon hearing that our sixth-grade class had won the school paper drive. As captain, Jay had been urging us for weeks to "collect as many newspapers as you can" and the day of the drive, he nervously watched each classroom add to their piles of paper, paying particular attention to room 307, who had one kid whose mother emptied out an entire station wagon of twine-tied newspaper bundles. When the announcement of our victory came over the PA system, Jay had shouted, "This is a cherry-on-top-of-a-whole-hot-fudge-sundae kind of day!" and at the time I remember thinking, **Geez, it's only a paper drive,** but right now, looking from my mother's face to Kristi's, I could understand the sentiment.

"Joe, what pretty flowers," she said, and reflexively I stuck out my hand, presenting them to her.

"Well, thanks!" said Kristi. She held them in the

crook of her arm, like a beauty queen, and said hello to my mom and Beth.

"He plays piano like Elton John **and** gives me flowers!"

"He **is** thoughtful," said my aunt Beth, smiling. "And you—my gosh, what a great drummer!"

"And a wonderful emcee," added my mother. "And just look at you—what a beautiful dress."

"I dug it out of the costume bin. Mrs. Holbrook said the last time someone wore it was when they put on **Dinner at Eight** back in the sixties."

"Well, you certainly do look lovely," agreed my aunt.

"I second that emotion," said Blake Erlandsson, and it suddenly seemed we were besieged by people—Mays and Lamereau from the hockey team, Greg Hoppe and some other kids from the paper, and Shannon.

"Joe, I felt like I was watching Liberace or something!" she said, and I thought, **Gee, thanks,** and then she kissed me and what I thought was: **No thanks.**

Seven

Hey Joe—

I'm in my government class, which means I'm bored out of my gourd (if Mr. Hasselback's lectures were pills, they'd be a narcotic strong enough to knock out an elephant), but being bored out of your gourd can be helpful in that it forces you find something to do. So I thought I'd finally write you the note I've been thinking about writing for a long time, my I-miss-you note. I know I was mad at you for too long about that peace assembly. I'm not usually a grudge holder—but sometimes I just feel so apart from high school life and when someone like you comes along, someone I feel such a kinship with, well, I guess I take any betrayals (real or imagined) pretty hard.

But I'm tired of carrying this heavy old grudge, so wait a second . . . (Long pause as I throw it out the window.) Whew! That feels so liberating!

So are we friends again, Giuseppe? I know we've been civil, but I think it's time to move past civility and back into friendship.

If you're in agreement, give me a sign at lunch—arrange your Tater Tots in a peace sign or something and I'll rejoin you at the table.

Darva

"Miss Casey, what are you doing?"

It took a lot for Kristi to lose her cool, but being caught in a home ec classroom just as she was about to go down on me qualified as **a lot**.

Kristi slid her hands off my kneecaps and patted the floor in front of her.

"I, uh, I lost my contact. Joe here was helping me find it."

Miss Rudd practically spat out the words. "You lost your contact." Her head bobbed as fast as her foot tapped the wooden floor. "Well, I believe you're about to lose much more."

My mind was a record stuck in a groove: **Ohshitohshitohshitohshitohshit.**

I could tell by Kristi's startled, wide-eyed expression that her inner record was playing the same tune, but as she stood up, her features smoothed out into a look of bland contempt. Flaring her nostrils, she asked Miss Rudd, "What's that supposed to mean?"

Two spots of color rose on the home ec teacher's cheeks, as if she'd been slapped on both sides of her face. Her fingers fluttered up to her throat, as if she was checking for a pulse.

"That means that your days as cheerleading captain could possibly be coming to an end. I'm sure

Mr. Brietmayer will think that using a classroom—how'd you get in here, by the way?—for salacious purposes is reason enough for a suspension, let alone a demotion in cheerleading rank."

I had gotten off the polished chrome worktable I'd been sitting on (the size of the relief I felt that I still had my pants on, that they were still zipped when Miss Rudd had crashed our little party, was incalculable) and I crossed my arms in front of my chest, trying to look like I wasn't quaking in my boots, trying to look as cool, in fact, as Kristi.

"I don't think that's going to happen, Miss Rudd," said Kristi, hoisting her big leather purse onto her shoulder. "Because whatever warped, **untrue** story you plan to tell Mr. Brietmayer can't compare with the warped, **true** story I could tell him about you and Mr. 'I'm Married' Carmody."

All the blood vessels under the teacher's face constricted, erasing the red spots on her cheeks. She opened her mouth, but Kristi wasn't done talking. And not only was she not done talking, she was mimicking Miss Rudd's high and breathy voice.

"I'm sure that Mr. Brietmayer will think that using the teachers' lounge for salacious purposes is reason enough for a suspension, if not a demotion in teaching rank."

The home ec teacher stared at Kristi, her pale face frozen in shock. It looked as if she wanted to speak, but words could not slip past the tight O that was her lips.

"You're just better hope you don't get pregnant," said Kristi, sauntering past the inert teacher. "Because how would you explain **that**?"

Following Kristi out of the room, I stopped myself from reaching out to pat Miss Rudd's shoulder, to offer some comfort to the poor woman. Instead, I stared at the floor, my eyes looking at nothing higher than the toes of my shoes.

"What was that all about?" I said, catching up to Kristi in the empty hallway.

"Everyone knows Miss Rudd has a crush on Mr. Carmody," said Kristi. "I'm just assuming they've acted on her crush."

Holding the railing, I frog-jumped down the staircase after her. "You mean you said that thing about using the teachers' lounge for salacious purposes without knowing if they really did?"

"Well, they probably did. And it shut her up, didn't it?"

"Yeah, but for how long?"

She didn't answer, and when we reached the first floor, Kristi looked at her watch.

"Well, I suppose I should get to that stupid Frost Fling meeting. I am decorating co-chair, after all."

"Kristi, what about Miss Rudd? What makes you think she won't go to Mr. Brietmayer's office right now?"

"First, of all, Brietmayer never stays after school." Half of her face was full of white teeth and dimples, a cheerleader's grin offering twinkly encouragement and good old team spirit, but her eyes were as cold as her smile was warm. "Second, Miss Rudd knows what she's up against."

After imitating Miss Rudd's fluttery fingers running up her throat, Kristi turned and headed toward a half hour of arguing over crepe paper colors, and I turned toward the nearest exit, almost—but not quite—running.

For the next few days, anytime the phone buzzed in the classroom, any time a student aide brought a note to the teacher, I was sure both were delivering the same message: **Please send Joe Andreson to Mr. Brietmayer's office.** But then Mr. Pedley would hang up the old-fashioned receiver and say, "Jill Foth, you're wanted in the library," or Miss Westrum would unfold the note and ask Bill Brendal to please report to the attendance office.

Only after I expelled a gush of air would I realize I'd been holding my breath.

When it became clear that there would be no consequences paid for getting caught nearly in flagrante delicto, I wondered, **How does she do it?** She told me Gray Billings, the president of the audiovisual club (also president of the **Lost in Space** fan club, a fact advertised on a T-shirt he wore nearly every day), had given her a spare key to the projection room office, scene of several of our trysts, but Kristi seemed to have access to every room in the school.

"Did you ever hear of juice?"

"Juice?"

"Not the kind you drink. **Juice** juice. Connections. The power of persuasion. You know—muscle."

"What are you, a mafioso?"

"I wish," said Kristi. "but the simple truth is if I want something, I figure out a way to get it."

Our last game of the season was the best game I ever played, but we still lost 4–3, slamming our hopes of getting to the state championship right into the boards. I've never been in a prison visiting room, but I have been in a locker room after a big loss, and imagine the grimness factor is about the same.

There were no jokes, no cut-downs from Olsen—the guy had his face buried in a towel that wasn't entirely successful in muffling his sobs. Wilkerson was crying too, but soundlessly, his face an integrated sprinkler system of snot and tears. Lamereau was swearing like he had a bad case of Tourette's syndrome, and Mays was sitting on the bench, stunned, rubbing the hand he had unwisely used to hit his locker door.

Coach Teschler had stood in the corner like a prison guard, glaring at the lowlifes he had the misfortune to supervise. Finally he turned his attention to the ceiling and, pulling in the middle of his upper lip with his bottom teeth, he stared at a flickering fluorescent light, as if its inability to keep a steady light going disgusted him too.

"Hey, you can't say we didn't try," said Blake Erlandsson. "Wilkie, that pass to Olsen in the first period—**beautiful**." He smiled at Wilkerson before directing his proud-parent smile toward me. "And Andreson—man, a hat trick! That deke you put on the goalie for the first one—could it have been prettier?"

The pleasure I felt over the compliment was neutered by embarrassment and awkwardness. Now was **not** the time for pep talks, but apparently Blake was blind to the glares the rest of the team leveled at him.

"We don't have anything to be ashamed of," he said, taking off his elbow pads. "In fact, it was an honor to be your captain and to play for the Bulls!"

It was so pathetic, I had to clap; if ever there was an obvious plea for a demonstration of support, this was it. Two or three other guys joined me, but even the clog dancers who had entertained us at our last school assembly had gotten a better response than this.

The usual clot of cheerleaders and girlfriends and a few parents were waiting out in the hallway. Kristi gave me a world-weary shrug as she stood behind Mr. Erlandsson, waiting for her turn to comfort Blake.

I watched her for a moment; she was fiddling with her cheerleader necklace, draping the chain over her bottom lip and then pulling the little gold megaphone back and forth across her mouth, as if she was zipping it shut. You could tell she wasn't used to standing in line and didn't like it a bit.

"Oh, **Joe!**"

I staggered under Shannon's hug, thinking briefly that it was too bad football wasn't a girls' sport because she would have made a hell of a linebacker.

"Oh **Joe!**" she said again, pressing her cheek against mine. "Joe, I am so sorry!"

"It's okay," I offered lamely as she dissolved into tears.

She clung to me, and because I had my hockey bag slung over my shoulder, I stumbled, off balance, and silently yelled at her to let go.

"Shannon," I said, trying to shift my bag behind me, "let's get out of here."

She pulled away from me, a look of hopefulness breaking through her cloudy face.

"Okay, Joe," she said, a little hiccup punctuating her words. "My car's outside."

I broke up with her that night. I figured my timing could be considered either cruel (she was already so bummed out from our hockey loss that I further added to her misery) or kind (why spread out the pain?).

It turns out Shannon wasn't as crushed as I'd thought she'd be.

"What do you mean, you think we should see other people?" she asked, pushing me—hard— against the back door. "You feel me up for more than an hour and then you suddenly decide **we should see other people?**"

It's true, we had been steaming up the car windows of her Delta; just because I didn't want her to be my girlfriend didn't mean I still didn't want to squeeze her tits one last time.

"Well, I—"

"Oh, just shut up," she said, reaching behind her to fasten the dangling ends of her bra. "Just shut up and get out of my car."

I smiled with what I thought was compassion and apology, but maybe it was too dark for Shannon to see.

"And wipe that smirk off your face!" She jabbed a button through a buttonhole of her shirt. "Wipe that stupid smirk off your face and get out of my car!"

"But, Shannon, it's cold outside."

"I don't care!" And just to show how much, she leaned over me and opened the back door, pushing me to ensure my exit.

"Hey!" I said, tumbling out into the snow. "Hey, give me my jacket!"

She wadded up my down-filled jacket and threw it at me, as if it was trash on top of garbage, and then slammed the door before climbing over to the front seat. I grabbed my jacket and scrambled away from the car, not convinced as she revved the engine that she might not further decide to make a point by running over me.

The car lurched forward, and she drove a few yards before the brake lights blinked on and the trunk popped open.

"Get your stupid hockey stuff!" she yelled, sticking her head out of the open window.

I ran toward the car, sliding on the ice-hard street, and after I grabbed my bag and stick, I slammed the trunk as hard as I could.

"Loser!" shouted Shannon, and as I watched the lights of her car get smaller, my teeth chattering like wooden chimes in a windstorm, I found I really couldn't disagree with her.

It was a wet and rainy spring. A sense of boredom crept into classes that only the teachers with bigger imaginations were able to fend off. Clusters of kids gathered in homeroom, wondering who had heard from their college of choice, a certain desperation coloring their voices as they compared SAT scores and grade point averages. Tryouts were held for the baseball team, and I joined dozens of guys playing catch in the gym because it was too rainy to go out in the field.

In art class, Mr. Eggert was battling the general

ennui by cranking up the Led Zeppelin and Procol Harum. Our assignment all week had been to work on self-portraits of ourselves at the age of fifty.

Darva had a stack of magazines in front of her, but instead of cutting out pictures that captured what she might be like in thirty-plus years, she was mumbling as she scraped a hardened pellet of rice off her embroidered shirt.

"What's the matter?" I said. "Food fights a little too immature for you?"

"**You** didn't have a chow mein bomb explode on you," she said, licking her finger to rub at the palm-sized stain just under her collar bone.

Earlier, someone (I'm pretty sure it was Olsen) cut the power to the basement cafeteria so we were all submerged in darkness long enough to hurl at invisible targets whatever it was we had on our lunch trays.

Darva regarded my unstained shirt.

"How did you came out so unscathed?"

"I'm tricky," I said, weaving and bobbing in my seat like I was trying to avoid a punch. "But did you see Todd Randolph? He got hit with a carton of chocolate milk."

We both laughed; Todd Randolph was usually on the giving end of a joke—practical, mean, or otherwise—and so it was especially gratifying to see him on the receiving end, especially considering he'd been wearing a white sweatshirt.

The arm of the record player clicked as it dropped an album, and when the needle found its first groove, the voice of Maria Callas filled the art room. In Mr. Eggert's class, we listened mostly to rock, but every now and then he liked to demonstrate "passion expressed a little differently."

Darva got back to her magazines; her self-portrait as a fifty-year-old was a collage of motion. On a big piece of posterboard, she'd pasted hundreds of birds, from pretty little canaries to condors, along with butterflies, airplanes, and spaceships.

With the side of my little finger, I brushed the droppings of my eraser off the paper. I had originally started sketching my face but, copying Darva (she was just so **good**), had decided instead to portray my fifty-year-old self as an idea. But it seemed my muse was taking a nap from which she didn't want to wake, and so I decided I would sketch a tree. I can't say that it represented a depth of character I hoped to attain by then, or any kind of strength or new growth, but I was smart enough to realize that other people might interpret it as such.

"So I got my ticket," said Darva, cutting out the face of a loon from a **National Geographic.**

Darkening the side of a branch with my pencil, I tried to answer in my head the question Mr. Eggert often asked: **Where's your light source?** I looked past Darva out the window, trying to see how the light played on the row of linden trees lined up along the boulevard.

"My ticket to Europe, as long as you're asking," said Darva. "But please, your enthusiasm is embarrassing."

I let my eyes settle on Darva. "Sorry. I was in the moment."

It was an expression Mr. Eggert used; his goal, he had told us, was to teach us "to be in the moment" and "to let your art be all that exists while you're in my classroom."

She smiled, and because it was one of those smiles with so much invitation in it, I smiled back.

"So you got your ticket and you're going to Europe," I said, showing her that my moment hadn't been completely pure.

"Yep. I'm going to work the whole summer and save every dime so I can leave in September."

"Still going by yourself?"

Darva lowered her head and looked at me over her tinted glasses. "Why, are you finally ready to throw away convention and come join me?"

"You'd ditch me for the first Frenchman you met."

"Well, I'm landing in Amsterdam. So I'd probably ditch you for the first Dutchman."

"If you hadn't already made plans with the guy who sits next to you on the plane."

She dabbed glue on the loon's mouth, explaining that he was foaming at the mouth.

"How does a loon represent you at fifty?" I asked.

"I don't know," she said. "Don't you think we'll all have gone a little crazy by then?"

I looked at Darva and was seized with a desire to lean across the table and kiss her on her strawberry-scented lips.

"Seriously, Joe. Off in the great wide world—we'd have fun! And I know it'd make my mother feel a lot better if I went with someone."

Darva's parents were old—her siblings had been out of the house before she was born—and I knew that as much as she wanted to get out of the house and away from her parents, she worried about them.

"I'll take a rain check," I said, not about to give up my own dream of going to the U of M in the fall and playing hockey for the Golden Gophers.

Maria Callas's voice ran up a ladder not many voices climb and then raced down it, and as the orchestra swelled beneath Callas, Darva got back to her picture of flight and I got back to my tree.

Heavy rain kept customers away from the store that night, and Ed—he had long ago told me to call him by his first name instead of Mr. Haugland—had let two-thirds of his employees punch out and go home. The rest of us were all in a goofy everybody's-gone-but-us mood.

Up at the cash registers, Kirk the bag boy was reading the **National Enquirer** out loud, his voice as deep and dramatic as an actor reciting Shakespeare.

"Who **was** that man Ann-Margret was seen with?" He looked up, his face twisted with concern. "I implore you, who was it?"

Wendy, the cute college junior whose miniskirts, much to the delight of all males on the premises, were almost as short as her work smock, laughed and told him to shut up, didn't he know she had a biology test to study for?

"I could teach you something about biology you wouldn't find in that book," I said, to which the cashier folded her arms across her chest and said, "In your dreams, Joe."

Kirk licked his finger and hissed—teenage lingo for **She burned you good.**

"But you," she said to Kirk, "I wouldn't mind

going over Chapter Three with you." She lowered her head and blinked her eyelashes. "It's all about reproduction."

"Won't I need a note from my parents?" asked Kirk, his voice rising an octave. "Or from my pediatrician?"

A voice came over the in-store PA system.

"I hate to break up the laughs, kids, but, Joe, I need you in my office, ASAP."

I bowed to Ed, looking out the little sliding glass window in his office that overlooked the store.

"And bring me an RC while you're at it."

Ed was sitting behind his desk, an electric guitar in his lap.

"Wow," I said, setting the bottle of pop on his desk. "Nice Telecaster."

Ed smiled proudly and strummed the strings. "Thanks. I thought this might be the perfect thing for slow nights like this."

"You mean you're going to play it?"

A blush washed over the store owner's face and into the deep recession of his hairline.

"Figure it's about time."

This was big news; Ed had told me he'd been so disconsolate about the breakup of his band and taking over the running of the store, he'd stopped playing the guitar altogether.

"Well, that's great, Ed. Too bad I don't have an electric keyboard. We could sit up here and jam."

"That's right," said Ed, a rare look of excitement replacing his usual expression of boredom and regret. "Let someone else remind Mrs. Emery she can't use

expired coupons! Let someone else bust Mr. Snowbeck when he shoplifts Twinkies! Let someone else
clean up spilled milk in aisle two!"

"Take it easy, Ed—you can't throw the store into
anarchy just because you got a new guitar!"

Laughing, Ed held the Telecaster like a rifle and
pretended to shoot from it.

"Anarchy," he said when he was done firing his
imaginary bullets. "Do you realize how long it's been
since I've done anything that even **vaguely** resembles
anarchy?"

He didn't wait to let me venture a guess.

"Too long. From now on, I'm not just Ed Haugland,
grocery store owner; I'm Ed Haugland, gui-Tarzan."
He looked at me, his pale blue eyes brimming with intensity. "You really play the keyboard?"

I shrugged. "Ed, you came to the talent show, remember?"

"Oh yeah—you were good!"

His hand splayed out, he held the guitar against his
chest and leaned toward me, the expression on his
face racheted up a notch, from excitement to glee.

"Hey, you know what? I've got a keyboard! It belonged to Des Gunderson, and when our band broke
up, he sold it to me for five bucks. Poor old Des is
selling washers and dryers down at Sears now. Not
that he was Jerry Lee Lewis or anything—but man, I
didn't think he'd end up at Sears, selling washers and
dryers." I could see him settling back, making room
for his usual moroseness, but then, like a rogue elf,
he cackled. "I'll bring it in tomorrow, okay? Oh wait,
you don't work tomorrow, do you? Well, it'll be here
on Monday."

"Great," I said, not knowing if it would be or not, but I was not the kind of guy to rain on the rare parade that Ed Haugland was finally riding in.

Ed strummed the strings, his fingers moving from a C chord to a G minor. He hadn't plugged in his guitar, so it made a tinny, faraway sound. I got up, figuring I'd been dismissed.

"Hey, look who came out in the rain," I said, seeing out the window the hunched figure of old Mr. Snowbeck. He stood in the snacks, crackers, and cookie aisle, and after one furtive glance to his left and another to his right, his gnarled, liver-spotted hand darted out of his pocket, grabbed a box of Twinkies, and shoved them into his open coat.

"I'll go shake him down, boss," I said in my best Bowery Boys voice.

The grocer shook his head. "Nah, let him be. Poor old geezer's gotta think he can get away with something once in a while."

It was still raining hard at closing time, and we raced like star sprinters to the car.

"Fuckin' A!" said Kirk, slamming the passenger-side door. "What is this, monsoon season?"

"I think you get torrential rains during monsoon season. This is a **deluge**."

"Thanks for giving me a ride. I'd be waiting here all night—I'd **drown** before my sister picked me up."

"What's she doing tonight?" I asked, keeping my voice casual. It had been three weeks and two days (you better believe I counted) since I'd last been serviced, and Lord knows I was desperate for one of Kristi's very special lube jobs.

"Who knows?" Kyle turned on the radio and twirled the knob until he got to KQ. "Oh man, Jethro Tull. Cool."

I turned on the defroster and backed out of the lot. We lived close enough to Haugland's that I usually walked or rode my bike to work, but it was raining so hard that my aunt had offered me the keys to her new Mustang.

"I mean, listen to this part," said Kyle, turning up the volume. "Who'da thought a **flute** could sound so cool?"

To me, the guy played the flute like he was on speed, but to each his own.

We drove down the parkway, the rain hammering the car, obscuring the view in between each swish of the windshield wipers. Even though the heat was on, I was shivering my ass off and I imagined Kirk was too, although the violent head bobbing he was doing to the music was probably warming him up some.

"You mind if I sit here till the song—or the rain—is over?" asked Kirk when I pulled up in front of his house.

"How about the song? This rain's gonna last all night."

"Cool."

I turned off the ignition and then turned the key so that the radio came back on. Kirk turned up the volume and sang along to "Aqualung," his hands crabbed as he played a mini air guitar. The rain, like thousands of dropped nails, banged on the car roof, and the tires of a car passing by splashed through the water.

As the song faded out and the silky knowing voice of the DJ came on, Kirk leaned toward the windshield, squinting his eyes.

"Is that Heinz?"

"Who?"

"Shit," he said, opening the door, "it **is** Heinz!"

He tore out of the car, slamming the door, and I watched him, a blur racing through the rain.

I sat there for a moment, but there was no way I could drive off without finding out who this Heinz guy was—some East German refugee who brewed homemade beer and cobbled the Casey family's shoes while waiting to see if he'd been granted political asylum? Figuring I was already wet, I got out of the car and ran after Kirk. I chased him up onto a lawn and near a row of shrubbery.

"Come on, Heinzy, don't be scared. Come on, boy."

My shoes squishing in the wet grass, I knelt by Kirk.

"**Oh**," I said. "Heinz is a **dog**."

"A puppy, actually. We just got him a week ago." He whistled softly. "Come on, boy."

The dog was cowering under the bush, and nudging its branches aside with his shoulder, Kirk stretched his arm until he finally got hold of the puppy's collar.

"There you go, buddy," he said, and after tucking the whimpering dog into his open jacket. He took off, running across several lawns to his house. Hunched over in the driving rain, I ran behind him, and when he shoved open the back door, I followed him inside.

"Mom!" he hollered. "Mom—who let Heinz out?"

He took a shriveled towel off the stove handle and, holding the dog on the kitchen counter, began rubbing him dry. The puppy's body vibrated with shivers.

"Poor little Heinzy," murmured Kirk, rubbing the spaniel's long ears.

A door swung wide open and banged against the kitchen counter.

"Made it," said a woman, dodging the door as it swung back, but when her drink sloshed out of her glass, the triumph faded from her voice.

"Shit." She looked at us and giggled. "I mean, shoot."

"Mom, why'd you let Heinz out without his leash?" said Kirk. "You know he's too little to be outside without his leash—and it's pouring outside, did you know that?"

"From the looks of you, I can make that deduction," she said, saying each word with a strained precision. "You should get out of those wet clothes, Kirk, and you"—she waved her hand at me, and the smoke from her cigarette zigzagged—"whoever you are, should get out of those wet clothes too."

"That's Joe, Mom. And Joe, that's my mom."

"How do you do, Mrs. Casey?"

The woman's face brightened, and the smile she offered was a worn-down, blurry version of Kristi's.

"Well, I do very well, young man." She held up her glass in a salute. "Thank you so much for asking."

She sat down at the uncleared kitchen table, ashing her cigarette in a saucer.

"And for your information, I did not let little Heinzy out—your father did. **After** he crapped on the rug." She smiled again, pointing her cigarette at Kirk. "The dog, that is, not your father."

"Come on, Joe," said Kirk, bundling the puppy under his arm, "let's go to my room."

"Nice to have met you," I said.

Nodding, her eyes half-closed, Mrs. Casey inhaled her cigarette. "I mean it, Kirk—give him some dry clothes and put his in the dryer." She exhaled a long stream of smoke. "I will not have this polite young man catch his death in my house."

On the television, Mary Tyler Moore was yukking it up with Mr. Grant, but there was no one in the living room appreciating whatever joke had just been told, at least no one conscious.

"And that's my dad," said Kirk, pushing aside a metal walker as we passed a man sprawled out on the couch, snoring. One arm hung limply, its hand open, as if reaching for the empty glass that lay on its side on the carpet.

As a paperboy in junior high, I always liked collection days, standing inside entryways, waiting for the man or woman of the house to find their wallet or coin purse to pay me. I always liked the surprise glimpses inside households: the paintings and sculptures of nudes filling the school librarian's parlor, the Edith Piaf records that were always blasting in the motorcycle mechanic's little rambler, the smells of chocolate chip cookies or baking bread that filled the house of Mrs. Tompkins, a crabby lady who never tipped me once. There were two parish houses on my route and both of them smelled like medicine, the Lutheran one like Pepto-Bismol and the Catholic one like cough syrup; if I thought about it,

Pastor Johnson always did look like he had a stomachache and Father Frank was always hacking away, the phlegm gurgling in his throat like rainwater through a gutter.

The Casey house smelled of cigarettes and liquor and the kind of couches you see for sale at the Goodwill. It was not what I expected from the house Kristi Casey burst out of into the world every morning.

I felt kind of stupid, but less stupid than cold, so I changed into a bathrobe that Kirk gave me. His bedroom was in the basement, right next to the laundry room, and I could hear my tennis shoes banging around in the dryer with the rest of our clothes.

Kirk put a couple of 45s on an old record player. His room was much more organized than the rest of the house: his **Mad** magazines and **Archie** comic books and issues of **Amazing Stories** in neat piles on a shelf, his bed made, the linoleum-tiled floor relatively free of clothes. We sat around on two taped-up beanbag chairs, throwing the dog a rolled-up pair of socks Kirk got out of his dresser.

"Sorry about my parents. They're not always like that."

I shrugged, and while I tried to think of something not completely lame to say, Kirk added, "Usually they're a lot worse."

I laughed, and then, thinking maybe he wasn't joking, I stopped. That made Kirk laugh—the kid was nothing if not astute—and then I had to laugh a little more and we settled back, tossing Heinz his sock ball while we listened to 45s.

After a while the puppy lost interest in the socks

and settled into Kirk's lap, and I thumbed through the little boxes with handles the records were stored in.

"Man, you've got a lot of these."

"I collect them. I've got everyone from Anka to Zimmerman."

"Zimmerman?"

"Bob Dylan. I wanted to impress you with the breadth of my collection—you know, A to Z—but I couldn't think of any Z's except Dylan's real name."

"But Anka?" I asked the kid who had been playing air guitar to Jethro Tull. "You listen to Paul Anka?"

"A collector doesn't have to listen to everything he collects."

"Hey," I said, pulling out a record in a paper sleeve. " 'Red Rubber Ball.' The summer I was going into ninth grade this song was playing on the radio all the time. I used have a little transistor that hung from the bars of my banana bike—I'd have to change the batteries about every other day 'cause I played it so much.

"And look at this—'Cherish'! That song reminds me of my friend Steve's older sister, Dee Ann Alquist. She ratted her hair about this high"—I held my hand a half foot above my head—"and she had a little heart necklace that would disappear deep in the vee of her V-neck sweaters."

" 'Deep in the vee of her V-neck sweaters,' " said Kirk. "You said that the way the people of Metropolis say, 'It's Superman.' "

"And look at this one," I said, pulling another record in a paper sleeve out of the box. " 'Michelle.'

There was a girl named Michelle in my sixth-grade class and I'd—"

"Joe, please," said Kirk, and the puppy opened an eye to look at his master and then closed it again. "Give me a break. If you've got a story for each of my records, we'll be here all night."

"Sorry," I said, rifling through the box but silencing my commentary.

I don't know how many 45s we listened to, but when the record player clicked off after playing the Byrds' "Turn, Turn, Turn," I realized I didn't hear the dryer anymore.

"I better get my clothes," I said.

After I changed in the tiny mildewy-smelling closet that was the basement bathroom, Kirk met me at the stairs.

"Hey, are those Kristi's drums?" I asked, seeing a drum set on the other side of the furnace.

"Well, they're officially mine. I got them the Christmas I turned eight, but they're the ones Kristi learned on."

"She's a great drummer."

"I will give her that," said Kirk, nodding. "It's kind of an idiot-savant thing, I think. She grabbed the sticks out of my hands one day, sat down, and started playing like Keith Moon."

The puppy, sleeping in Kirk's arms, stretched out a paw. "Come on, I'll walk you out. Just in case my parents wake up and think you're a burglar or something."

His mom had joined his dad in the living room, echoing his snore with one of her own. She was half sitting, half lying on an easy chair; he was in the same position on the couch, his hand still reaching for that spilled drink.

As we walked softly past them, Kirk shrugged, a what-are-you-going-to-do gesture, before pulling the afghan up over his mother's shoulder.

"Thanks again for the ride," he said, opening the front door for me.

"Anytime. Thanks for the laundry service. And for playing all those records. I don't know when I last heard 'Monster Mash.' "

"A true classic."

As I closed the front door behind me, a car door slammed and suddenly, as I was walking down the walkway, Kristi was running up it.

"Joe?" she said, surprise stretching her voice thin. "What are you doing here?"

"Hi, Kristi," I said, breathing in the fresh, rain-washed night.

She stood inches away from me, looking at me with, I don't know, sort of a panic in her eyes.

"Were you out with Blake?" I asked conversationally.

"Joe, I asked you a question: **What are you doing here?**"

"I gave Kirk a ride home from work," I said, nodding toward the house. "Then Heinz was loose and I helped—"

"You were inside?" she asked, her voice matching the look in her eyes.

"Yeah, Kirk played me a bunch of his records and—"

"That asshole," she said, marching past me.

"Hey, he's a nice kid."

She whirled around.

"Listen, Joe, not everyone's family sits around the piano singing show tunes."

"Kristi, I don't know what you're—"

"All I can say is, if you open your big mouth about anything you saw in there, well . . . well, then I'll tell everyone about your aunt being a dyke."

Staring at me for a split second, she wore the same look of cold triumph I'd seen on her face in Miss Rudd's classroom.

She had raced up the cement stairs and into the house before I even had time to formulate a simple **What's that supposed to mean?**

I stood there like an idiot, staring at the door and trying to figure out what and who had just gone inside it.

Eight

My mom and aunt were in the kitchen, playing Scrabble. As usual, the coffeepot was on—they knocked back caffeine any time of the day or night, with no visible side effects that I could see—and while my mom studied her tiles, my aunt dug at something in a cake pan.

"Hey, Joe," said Beth as I shut the back door. "Sit down and have a brownie with us."

"Maybe you'd better not," said my mother. "We've got lousy dental insurance."

Beth laughed and set down the spatula. "It's the first time we ever made these. They've got caramel in them, and the caramel sort of hardened."

"Eighteen," said my mom, laying down the word **retire.** "Not much for a triple word score."

She wrote down her score and reached over to touch my arm. "How was work?"

I shrugged, watching as my aunt laid chunks of

the excavated brownie on a napkin and pushed it toward me.

"No thanks," I said, holding up my hand.

My aunt looked at me, and I could see in her face that she saw something in my own.

"Are you all right?" she asked.

"Joe," said my mother, "you didn't do anything to Beth's car, did you?"

I almost laughed; would that things were as simple as putting a dent in my aunt's Mustang!

"Do you like women?" I asked, knocking over decorum and censorship at the same time.

I watched the color fade from Beth's face as I heard my mother ask, "What did you just say?"

Feeling reckless and angry and tired, I turned to her and said, "I asked Aunt Beth if she likes women. I want to know if she's a homo."

My mother's eyebrows and jaw dropped, and then she began to recite my name, a timeworn signal that I was in deep trouble.

"Joseph Rolf Andreson—"

"It's okay, Carole," said my aunt, offering up the kind of smile the clowns in those velvet paintings wore. She looked into her coffee cup for a long moment before meeting my eyes.

"Well, since you asked, Joe," she began, "yes, I do like women. So I guess that makes me homosexual— although we prefer to use the word **lesbian**."

She couldn't even muster up a sad clown smile now, and I wondered if the lump in my throat was going to dissolve or if I was going to be asphyxiated right there at the kitchen table. I thought of our request nights, how her living room would turn into a little piano bar, with me playing songs she and my mother asked for. Just the other night, my aunt had stood behind me, her hand on my shoulder, singing "Let It Be." My mother's and aunt's musical tastes hadn't ossified in their youth; they both loved the Rolling Stones and the Beatles, especially their ballads, and a request night inevitably included "Lady Jane," "Norwegian Wood," "Angie," or "Hey Jude." I thought of the presents Beth liked to surprise me with: the book—**Cat's Cradle, The Moviegoer, The Electric Kool-Aid Acid Test**—she'd wrap in gold paper and leave on the dining room table; the sports coat from Dayton's she'd draped over the hallway chair, the note pinned to the plastic garment bag reading, **You'll look sharp in this!** (and she was right, I did); the imported wafer cookies from Germany she kept buying because I liked them so much.

She was funny and kind and had welcomed us in with open arms, but as I met her stare, sharp little pieces of disgust and betrayal pierced the lining of my stomach and worked their way up to my throat as I realized I hardly knew her.

"Joe!" said my mom as I jumped out of my chair and raced across the kitchen.

"Joe!" she called again as I ran up the stairs two at a time and I heard her call my name a third time as I slammed the door to my bedroom.

Two weeks after my dad's funeral, my uncle Roger took me camping at Lake Superior. Our little fire, a ragged triangle of red and orange, was the only color in the dark nightscape, and I remember the unease I felt that I couldn't tell where the black lake left off and the black sky began. I was cold, but I didn't know that I was shivering until my uncle put his arm around me.

"It's okay to cry, you know," he said.

"Why do you say that?" I snapped, angry that he was giving me permission to do something I was desperate to do and just as desperate not to do.

"Because I'm concerned about you."

"Did my mom tell you to say that?" I said, leaning forward to poke at the fire with a stick, but my intent was to shrug off his arm. "Because really, she's crying enough for the both of us."

"She's sad."

"Well, **duh.**" The fire snapped, and I was surprised at the thought that jumped into my head: **I hate you as much as that fire is hot.**

"Would you rather she didn't cry?"

I prodded the fire with my stick.

"I just don't like to see her so sad," I said finally.

"She'd be just as sad if she didn't cry. But she knows it hurts even more."

"What does?" I said, jabbing at a chunk of red-hot wood until it spit back sparks.

"Not crying. Crying's turning a valve, Joe. Turning a valve to release the pressure."

"In that case, my mom should call in a plumber, 'cause she doesn't know how to turn it off."

He didn't say anything, and I crouched there, my chin resting on my knees, attacking the fire with my stick and feeling a lot younger than fourteen.

After a while my uncle said, "Well, I for one could go for a s'more," and for a few minutes I did nothing but concentrate on toasting my speared marshmallows to a perfect golden brown, but the bottom marshmallow caught fire, and even though I tried to blow the flame out, it burned black, and I remembered all the campfires I'd sat around with my dad, all the marshmallows he'd purposely stuck right in the fire to be charred black—**Don't ask me why, but it seems the more burnt the outside, the better it is on the inside**—and at first I thought I could swallow that gasp, that great big mournful hiccup, but as the rest of the marshmallows caught fire I dropped the stick and cradled my head in my arms.

And man, did I cry. My uncle made his s'more sandwich, and it was only when he was done eating it that he brushed the graham cracker crumbs off his jeans and moved close to me.

I stayed in that little nest his arms made, stayed with my face against his chest and cried, my loneliness and grief as big and black as the lake and the night sky around me.

Hey, Joe, the creek's frozen. Get your skates and we'll go shoot a few pucks.

Hey, Joe, come with me to Grudem's and help me pick out a birthday present for your mom.

Hey, Joe, come sit and look at the stars with me.

Hey, Joe, didn't I tell you to rake up those leaves?

I'm not telling you again, Joe—get to bed now!

How many invitations both bad and good had my dad extended to me, how many questions had he asked me, how many orders had he given? I sat there, my thoughts turning into a math class, trying to remember everything he'd said, trying to count the sentences, the words. Trying to count the times we'd played catch, the number of episodes of **The Dean**

Martin Show and **Bonanza** and **I Dream of Jeannie**
we'd watched together, the canoe trips we'd taken,
how many of his "famous Hawaiian" hamburgers (a
simple recipe—a hamburger topped with onions and
pineapple) he'd grilled in the summer, how many
times after I'd cried out as a little kid in the middle of
the night, he'd stumbled into my bedroom with a
squirt gun to shoot the boogey man who hid under
my bed. How many, how many, how many?

"I'm scared I'm going crazy," I said, trying to catch
my ragged breath. I explained to my uncle how I
tried to count things I'd never be able to count. "Like
how many times he said my name. How could I ever
count that—and why would I want to?"

"You're just trying to find a way to hold on," said
my uncle.

"I don't know how long I can hold on."

"I'll help you. And your mom'll help you."

Nodding, I wiped my nose with my palm and
moved away from him, not so much because I
wanted to but because I felt like I should. I was fourteen, after all, not four.

"If counting things helps you," said my uncle, spear-
ing a couple of marshmallows on a stick, "keep counting." He handed me the stick. "But if you're counting
just to keep from crying, hell, I'd try crying."

I did, and it did. Help, that is. I started crying myself
to sleep, and even though it drained me, it didn't
drain me **and** make me nervous, the way the counting had. I didn't become a big crybaby like poor
Laird Pitoski, who sealed his fate as **the** kid to pick
on when, in the third grade, he sat sprinkling his

desk with tears because he spelled the word **write** wrong. It wasn't in my nature to cry in public like that, but in the privacy of my bedroom—man, I could let loose.

That night, in my room at my aunt's house, it didn't take long at all before I had to turn over the soggy bog my pillow had become. I hated the picture I had in my head of Beth's face when I asked her if she liked women. I hated making her feel bad—but why hadn't she and my mom told me her big secret? It's not like I had anything against queers—I just never suspected my own aunt was one. Why had Kristi known, and why would she tell me the way she had?

In school, I didn't go out of my way to run into Kristi and she didn't go out of hers to run into me. I knew the golden age of blow jobs was over, but I was glad, not wanting to sully myself with a mean, snaky girl like Kristi. Ha! The truth was, as much as I mourned the loss of those blow jobs, I missed Kristi. Yeah, she could be mean and snaky, sure, but being with her was like sledding down an icy hill on a thin piece of cardboard—fast and danger-ous and wildly **fun.**

Once I saw her studying in the library, and until I drew the flint-eyed attention of the librarian, I hid behind the stacks for a while watching her.

One of Kristi's hands was splayed through her streaky blond hair, the other tapping a pencil on the table in one of her elaborate rhythm schemes. Sur-rounded by books, her face was scrunched up in concentration, and it gave me a little thrill to see that she was struggling.

I'd see her waltzing through the hallways, the queen on a walking tour, greeting the serfs with a halfhearted wave, a little smile. And I couldn't **not** see her at pep rallies, punching her pom-poms in the air in an attempt to force the student body to believe that the upcoming golf tournament or track meet was just as exciting as a football game.

But while it was easy to avoid someone in the halls of a big school, I did not have the same success in my aunt's house.

"What do you think you are, a burglar?"

"Oh, hi!" I said, startled. I had been so absorbed in closing the door as quietly as possible, in tiptoeing across the floor, that I hadn't seen my mother on the chair by the fireplace. "Well . . . see ya!"

"Don't even think about leaving this room until I'm done talking to you." My mother's voice was quiet, but in the way Marlon Brando's voice as Don Corleone was quiet. "Now sit."

I sat.

"Have you apologized to your aunt yet?"

I shook my head. "I haven't seen her."

"I'm not surprised, the way you've been sneaking in and out of the house."

"Mam, I—"

"Well, you'll have a chance to apologize tonight. Now go and change into some nice clothes—Beth'll meet us at the concert."

"What concert?"

"**My** concert," said my mother, and her smile had the bite of a raw onion. "Remember? I'm a music teacher? At a junior high school? And tonight's our big spring concert. Now hurry up—go get dressed!"

It didn't matter what I screamed at myself: **Tell her no, man! What are you, a mama's boy? Don't be such a pussy!** Ultimately I knew that in the annals of what my mother considered important, her spring concert **and** an attempt at conciliation with my aunt were important. And despite any evidence to the contrary, I did not like disappointing my mother.

Spring had sprung and the world was giddy with it. Tulips splashed color all over the neighborhood, and the tight shiny buds dotting the branches had burst open into leaves. The air was sweet with the cologne of lilacs and crab apple blossoms.

After we got out of the car in front of the school, my mom jumped over a muddy part of the boulevard she just as easily could have walked around and then tagged me, shouting, "You're it!" and I chased her into school, both of us laughing like dorks.

In the auditorium, behind the curtain, I helped her arrange with more precision the chairs the janitors had placed onstage, and the giddiness factor rose as the junior high kids rushed in, grabbing at the music stands their instrument cases bumped into, shouting at one another and at my mom.

"Hey, Mrs. A., do you have an extra reed?"

"Hey, Mrs. A., I can't find my **Love Story** music!"

"Hey, Mrs. A., you look nice!"

She did too—all flush-faced and excited, unable **not** to smile, borrowing a reed from one clarinetist to give to another, finding the missing sheet music, thanking her complimenter, a pimply trumpeter.

"Joe, my man!"

I turned around to see who belonged to the hand

that clapped my back with a little too much enthusiasm.

It was Kirk Casey.

"Please don't tell me my mom gave you a solo."

He had been drumming at our jam sessions, but he played the trumpet in the school band.

"Didn't she tell you? This whole thing"—he swept the air with his trumpet—"is just accompaniment. To me. I'm going to be playing the entire Jethro Tull oeuvre."

"**Oeuvre,**" I said, laughing. "Looking forward to it."

I could have pretended I didn't see my aunt wave, but I did.

"I should have saved us seats up front," I said, sitting next to her. "I didn't think there'd be this many people."

"Carole's reputation has preceded her," said my aunt, looking around at the auditorium filling up with people.

She had come straight from work and was wearing her corporate attorney clothes and looked, well, nice. I mean, you'd never guess she was a lesbian, not that I ever did. I was ready to get all mad at her again for her secret little life that she thought she had to hide from me, but I was distracted by the two people getting into—or trying to get into—the row across from ours.

They looked a little lost, a little tentative, like a trailer park couple checking into the Ritz, and as the man parked his walker at the end of the row, the woman helped him ease into the seat on the end. She looked at me right before sitting down and stared at me the way a clerk in a convenience store stares at a guy coming in at 2:00 A.M.: **Is he coming in for cigarettes or a stickup?** Finally recognizing me, she offered a little wave and a smile, and it was Kristi's smile, once removed and aged a couple decades. I nodded back at Mrs. Casey before looking around for her daughter—seeing that smile had made me want to see the real one, the full-beam this-can-get-me-whatever-I-want smile of Kristi's. But if she was at the concert, she wasn't sitting with her parents.

The house lights dimmed at seven o'clock sharp and then the center of the curtain flapped open and a spotlight found my mom.

She stood with her arms behind her back, looking like she'd just been surprised by a group of people jumping out at her and shouting, "Happy birthday!"

"Welcome," she said finally, her smile both shy and thrilled. There was a squeal of feedback from the microphone.

She waited a moment and tried again.

"I promise that's the most discordant note you'll hear all evening," she said, and then, tilting her head and cupping her hand to the side of her mouth, she said, "Right, kids?"

"Yes, Mrs. A.," chimed a bunch of voices from behind the curtain.

The audience laughed, and then my mother said, "Well, then, without further ado, let the music begin."

The house lights dimmed and the pulleys squeaked as the curtain opened and my mom strode to the music stand that served as her podium and tapped it with her baton. Within seconds, she was conducting the orchestra in the theme from **Romeo and Juliet,** followed by the theme from **The Pink Panther,** followed by the theme from **The Days of Wine and Roses.**

It was after all, a spring concert that was "saluting the magic of movie music."

I can't say I have any basis of comparison, but for a junior high school concert, this one was pretty good. In Granite Creek, one of her piano students had given my mom a framed poster on which, in cramped and irregular calligraphy, she had written, **Fluency in music means you can communicate any-where in the world.**

I was recruited to hang it above the piano, besides several other of her favorite sayings immortalized by her students in various handwritten signs and needlepoint wall hangings: **The wrong note you played in one piece will be the right note in the next. Musicianship is next to godliness. Do you speak music here?**

Watching her onstage, it was easy to see she be-lieved in all those slogans and easy to see she had made her students believe; they played with enthusi-asm and care, and when they played "Lara's Theme" from **Doctor Zhivago,** I saw a couple of women dab at their eyes with a tissue. One of the women was my aunt.

Noticing me noticing her, she shrugged and whis-pered, "It's such a pretty song."

I rolled my eyes, and she stuck her tongue out at me.

After hearty applause, the band played a soft

accompaniment as a flutist in a miniskirt began her solo.

She was what my mother would call "a real musician," and playing the theme song from **Alfie,** she filled the auditorium with notes as full and pure as a northern sky full of stars.

Why hire magicians when there are musicians? was another one of my mom's sayings, and I looked in my program to read the name of the cute flute player who was imitating Merlin up there onstage. Jenny Baldacci was the ninth-grade alchemist turning music into something that not just the ears heard. When her solo was finished I'm sure I wasn't the only one who wanted to personally thank her for taking me into a dream when I was still awake, for the assurance that for a few moments it was possible to be drunk on clear 200 proof beauty.

When the band started playing "Raindrops Keep Falling on My Head," I felt a tiny little tick go off inside me, like the tick a combination lock makes just before it's ready to drop open, and I realized that something had been released in me too and that I didn't hate my aunt anymore. Or wasn't mad at her. Whatever it was I felt, it was stupid; my aunt Beth was always going to be my aunt Beth, whether she wore her fancy work clothes or bib overalls, whether she cried at a junior high school band playing "Lara's Theme" or at John Lennon singing "Imagine."

I couldn't help the laugh that escaped me, knowing my aunt Beth was always going to be my aunt Beth, even if she didn't think Paul Newman **or** Robert Redford was the cutest in **Butch Cassidy and the Sundance Kid,** but Katharine Ross.

Beth shot me a look that asked, **What's so funny?** and instead of telling her, I took her hand and squeezed it.

Man, if you were to look at me, you would have thought I was class nerd of '72, sitting there in a darkened auditorium, bobbing my head as the first measures of the theme from **Shaft** began its sneaky climb, patting the hand my lesbian aunt had tucked in the crook of my elbow.

Nine

FROM THE Ole Bulletin, JUNE 1972:

This is the last time the Roving Reporter will take his pen to paper, asking the questions everyone wants answers to. The last time the voices of the mighty Bulls, Class of '72, will be recorded. And so your Roving Reporter, standing with his classmates on the precipice of a whole new world, asked seniors to look beyond the near future of college and/or work, and answer the question, "Where do you hope to be in ten years?"

Darva Pratt: "Through the doors of perception and into the Outer Limits."

Blake Erlandsson: "Playing center for the North Stars would be nice."

Leonard Doerr: "Boy, that's a good question. Maybe I'll earn a degree in German and be living in

Bavaria with **mein e Frau**! As some of you may know, I've placed in the top five of the Minnesota Youth Chess Tournament for the past three years, so maybe I'll step up my game and take on some of those Russians! Or maybe I'll be pursuing a doctorate in one of my many fields of interest—electrical engineering, chemical engineering, or Germanic languages! Or . . ." (**Ed. note: Mr. Doerr has many plans for the future, but because of space limitations, we must end his soliloquy here.**)

Sharon Winters: "I hope to either be a Rockette or a mom."

Hugh Jorgan: "If I'm not in jail, I'll be happy."

Kristi Casey: "On the front page."

The bell rang and as the staff of the paper filed out of our zero-hour class, Mr. Lutz motioned Greg Hoppe and I to his desk.

"Hugh Jorgan," he said, drumming his fingers on a copy of our final issue of **The Ole Bulletin.**

Greg and I exchanged the kind of look people do when they're busted.

"And don't think I wasn't aware of those other charming sobriquets you used throughout the year. Mike Oxenfire . . . Heywood Jablome." He shook his head.

"Sorry, Mr. Lutz, we were just—"

"You're lucky no one ever called in to complain."

I stammered out an apology over Greg's. Mr. Lutz waved his hand, dismissing us, and as we raced toward the door, he muttered, "Hugh Jorgan," and laughed.

My senior year at Ole Bull High didn't end in any great crescendo; in fact, it was sort of anticlimactic in the way it petered out.

Since that rainy night in front of her house, Kristi hadn't spoken to me, and pretty soon I stopped making overtures. She wasn't the only one with pride. I became just another member of her public, grateful to get my glimpses of her in the hallway, in pep rallies, and finally in the commencement program.

It was tradition at Ole Bull that two seniors give speeches: the valedictorian and one that the entire class nominated. And so, on a hot June evening, the class of '72 sat on the football field, sweating in our caps and gowns, as we got a lesson in public speaking. The example of what **not** to do was given by Marcy Greblach, a girl so shy she acted like a simple hello was an assault rather than a greeting. Her speech was so quiet and breathy and hard to understand that the principal had to get up twice to adjust her microphone.

"Did she just say to 'give ourselves to Satan's power'?"

Sitting next to me, Darva chuckled softly. "I think she said 'we can never sate our potential to' . . ."

"To what?"

Darva shrugged. "I couldn't hear."

At least Marcy was smart enough (she should be; after all, she **was** the valedictorian) to understand the importance of brevity and ended her mumbling before we all fell unconscious in a collective bout of narcolepsy.

The next speaker on the program was the antidote to dozing off, one Miss Kristi Casey, who couldn't, of course, merely **stride** to the podium; nope, she had to stride with a bass drum strapped to her chest. She banged out the beginning of our school song and then stood with one hand behind her ear, our cue to clap back the rhythm. We did, thunderously, after which Kristi beat out another tattoo, followed by our rhythmic clapping. The frenzy grew until it seemed more a rally than a graduation ceremony, until Kristi belted out an intricate cadence and as we clapped back our answer, she pounded on the drums, going faster and faster until we could do nothing but stand up and cheer, clapping our hands until they stung.

She took off her drum in the middle of all this applause, offering us one of her famous sly and glimmery smiles, and motioned us to sit. We obeyed and I added my sigh to the hundreds issued by all members of the male population in the audience.

"Good God," said Darva. "I bet if she gave the **sieg heil** sign everyone would give it right back."

Kristi's speech was full of the usual rah-rah maxims ("Let's go out and show the world what the Class of '72 is all about!") and reminiscences ("Can it only be three years ago when we were wide-eyed sophomores stumbling through the hallways, studying our class schedules like treasure maps?"), but what she didn't give us in substance, she more than made up for in style, and when she was done she grabbed her drum again and beat out a rhythm to her chant, "Free at last! Free at last! Free at last!"

We all stood—even Darva—raising our fists and shouting the same declaration. My mom told me later that my grandmother, who'd come down from Granite Creek, had leaned toward her to say that in all her born days, she'd never seen such a radical assemblage that was my graduation ceremony.

That summer after graduation, I worked a lot at Haugland's. Sometimes while I was shelving boxes of macaroni and cheese or cleaning up a spill on aisle seven, a couple of girls might wander by, their rubber flip-flops slapping the bottoms of their feet, beach towels tied low on their hips, their perfume a blend of coconut suntan lotion and cigarette smoke and, inexplicably, orange pop, and I'd hold my breath because I didn't want to do anything to interfere with my appreciation of the passing parade.

"Hey, Joe," the ones who knew me would say, and I'd draw in breath again and say something that would make them all laugh; everyone seemed to laugh more easily in the summer.

"You realize I personally search shoplifters," I said once to a trio of girls whose bikini tops were skimpy geometrics of fabric straining to hold back their luscious, lotion-slathered breasts. "So please, **shoplift.**"

It became one of my standard lines—especially after a tall, dark-eyed girl scanned the shelf of groceries behind her and grabbed a packet of birthday candles, which she shoved under one of the strings of her string bikini.

"So search me," she said, and as her friends tittered, she took my hand and placed it on the crocheted triangle that covered her left breast.

"Well, yes, here it is," I said, moving my hand to pull out the little cardboard packet. I was wearing a long white work apron that I hoped was hiding my excitement because honest to God, I'd sprouted a woody big enough to knock over the pyramid of Duncan Hines cake mix I'd been setting up.

"You want to play more hide-and-seek later?" asked the tall brunette.

"Sure," I said, in a voice that sounded more amphibian than human.

The girl smiled at my croaking. "Well, good. What time do you get off work?"

"Nine," I said, my head going crazy in a spasmodic nod.

"We'll be waiting for you outside," she said, and I watched as she and her friends slunk down the aisle, the globes of their butts moving under their beach towel sarongs.

The tall brunette hide-and-seeker never showed up. It was that kind of summer—nothing ever really got off the ground. Shannon Saxon came in once or twice but always with a purpose that had everything to do with groceries—"Where's the peanut butter, Joe? A bunch of us are going on a picnic tomorrow"—and nothing to do with me. Too bad; she looked pretty cute in a sunburnt, nose-peeling way, and the overflow of her bikini top was something to behold.

Darva and I took in a movie now and then, but she was working practically all the time to pay for her trip to Europe. I never saw Kristi.

"Oh, she's gone for the whole summer," said Kirk when I casually asked why she never gave him a ride to or from work. "Lucky for me."

A flare of disappointment ignited in my chest—

my fantasies of seeing Kristi walk through the store in a beach towel sarong weren't going to come true?

"Where'd she go?"

Kirk rolled his eyes. "She's a camp counselor, if you can believe it. Imagine how messed up the kids in her cabin are gonna be."

I hung out with Greg Hoppe and some of my hockey teammates, but as far as social lives go, mine was as slow to start as the used Dodge van for which I had just forked over two hundred bucks. (The low price had something to do with the balky ignition and, I was convinced, the fact that it smelled of feet.)

What turned out to be the high point of that whole summer were the jam sessions we had in Ed Haugland's. Every Tuesday and Thursday night after closing we played covers from Ed's glory days in the Courtmen—Buddy Holly, Chuck Berry, Little Richard, and Elvis. We also played more current stuff—the Beatles, the Rolling Stones, the Who, the Beach Boys, Santana, Led Zeppelin, Small Faces, and in deference to Kirk, the occasional Jethro Tull. A three-piece band composed of a balding supermarket owner on guitar, a stockboy on keyboards, and a pimply cashier on drums wouldn't be a groupie's dream come true, but trust me, we rocked. It sounds dumb, but it was true: We were brothers and the blood we shared was our music. We just understood one another—a riff on Ed's guitar would set off one on my keyboard, and Kirk in his sunglasses ("I drum better in them") would bring us all together with the steady anchor of his beat.

The store closed at nine, but we didn't get out of there until one or two in the morning, and then only because Ed had to be back at the store a couple of hours later for the deliveries.

"Your parents don't care when you get home so late?" I once asked Kirk as I drove him home.

"The good thing about having your bedroom in the basement is that you don't wake anyone up when you come home. Plus the fact that it's hard to wake up someone who's in an alcoholic stupor."

This he said matter-of-factly and, as far as I could hear, with no bitterness.

"How long . . . how long have they been that way?"

"Since my dad's accident."

"When was that?"

"Uh, I'd just started fifth grade, so—" He fanned his fingers on his thigh. "So four years ago. Well, almost five."

"What happened to him?"

"I vant to suck your blood."

I looked at Kirk, wondering if he had a freaky side he just now felt comfortable enough to share with me, but seeing his finger pointing upward, I ducked to see better over the steering wheel and spotted three bats swooping around in the halo of light cast from the street lamp.

"They spook me out, man," said Kirk, shuddering. "I feel like I could get rabies just by looking at them."

I eased the van over the curb, shifted into park, and turned off the ignition, staring up at the bats. After a long moment, Kirk said, "You okay, Joe?"

I nodded, even though I'd just been sledgehammered by sadness.

When I spoke, my voice broke. I cleared my throat.

"Once on my paper route I threw a paper at old lady Rumdahl's house. She was kind of the town witch—you know, she had this long gray hair and she'd yell at kids for walking on her lawn. Anyway, I threw the paper and all of a sudden a whole bunch of bats flew out of the chimney. I burned rubber riding home, man, 'cause I was sure those bats were chasing me. I got a bunch of calls from people who didn't get their paper that day. I was still scared the next day, so my dad got on my mom's bike—it was a blue Schwinn with a basket **and** handlebar tassels, no less; I guess he didn't have his own bike—and anyway, for a whole week he rode along with me. At five-thirty in the morning. Until I wasn't afraid anymore."

"That was cool," said Kirk, nodding. "Nice of him to do."

"It was."

I watched as one of the bats dove to the right and another to the left, leaving one to circle above the street lamp before zigzagging off in a third direction. Embarrassed, I pulled my fingers under my eyes to wipe away the tears.

"He turned those rides into little nature lessons," I said. "Telling me how much bats contribute to the ecosystem, how they can pollinate night-blooming flowers, stuff like that. After all the papers were delivered, he'd take me to Kit's Kaboodle for breakfast."

Kirk laughed. "What the hell is a Kit's Kaboodle?"

"Granite Creek's premier dining institution. Well, that and Wally's Casa de Spaghetti. Only Wally's wasn't open for breakfast." I sighed, my ribs rising slowly under the ache in my chest. "We'd have blueberry pancakes and a side of bacon, and we'd sit by the window and watch the sun come up behind the old courthouse."

I rarely talked about my dad—it just hurt too much—but now I found myself telling Kirk how thrilled he'd been when I taught him the trick all paperboys learn pretty early on: how to grab the rolled-up paper out of your shoulder sack and throw it onto the porch or steps, all while riding no-handed.

"At least he pretended he didn't know how to ride no-handed," I said. "For all I know, he was just humoring me."

I told Kirk how he'd always had my mother cut his hair and how he'd pretend to cry when she was finished.

"It sounds stupid," I said, remembering how he'd flutter his hands and say he'd have to wear a hat until it grew out. "But it was really funny. My mom and I would crack up."

I told him how my dad had flooded the backyard so I could practice my slap shot even though the pond we skated on was only two blocks away; I told him how he'd lie on the couch while my mom was at the piano, saying "Beautiful" or "Lovely" after every song she played.

"He loved Gershwin and Irving Berlin."

"I've heard of the first guy, but who's Irving Berlin?"

"He wrote 'White Christmas.' "

"Oh."

I told him how we'd watch **Bonanza** every Sunday night and how I thought it was so cool I had the same name as my favorite character. My dad knew this and during commercials he would say things like, "Little Joe, I'm riding over to Cheyenne tomorrow—you want to come with?"

"One night he told me to ask Hoss if she'd make us some popcorn."

" 'I'm not Hoss,' my mom said. 'Hoss is a two-hundred-fifty-pound man!'

" 'Then you can be Hop Sing, the houseboy.'

" 'Hop Sing yourself,' said my mom. 'Go make your own popcorn.' "

I honestly couldn't remember if I'd told anyone these stories; it had always seemed safer not to talk about my dad at all. But sitting in that stinky Dodge van while vampires disguised as bats roamed the night sky, I felt a rare peace.

"How old were you when he died?" Kirk asked.

"Fourteen."

"Shit. That's how old I am now." Biting his lip, he picked at a hangnail on his thumb. "I know my dad's messed up, but it'd sure be a bummer if he died."

I nodded. "**Bummer**'s the word."

It was Kirk's turn to talk then, and he had good stories of his dad too.

"We used to shoot baskets a lot and play horse—only if I was winning, he'd change the word to **rhinoceros** or **elephant**, some animal whose name had more letters, so he could catch up. And he was on a bowling league and he'd bring me to the bowling alley every Thursday night. I was the team water boy."

I had to admit it was hard for me to imagine the guy I'd seen passed out on the couch and shuffling into the auditorium with a walker as the playful, funny man Kirk was describing.

"What happened to him?" I asked.

"Look at us sitting in the dark in this van, man. Like we're on a date or something." He yawned and tipped his head, resting it against my shoulder.

Laughing, I pushed him off.

"He was at work one day and he fell off a loading dock. It really screwed up his back."

"How do he and Kristi get along?" I asked.

Kirk shrugged. "Well, Kristi's always acted like she was born into the wrong family—like she's a princess or something forced to live with the servants—but when he messed up his back . . . well, she acted like it was his fault. I mean, I guess it is his fault he drinks too much, but he can't work anymore and . . ." He shook his head. "My sister's the biggest bitch in the world, man." He shook his head and then yawned so big it looked like he was trying to take a bite out of a grapefruit. "I'm beat. Take me home, Jeeves."

The biggest bitch in the world, aka Kristi Casey, came back into my life during my second semester at the U of M, the day after my femur fractured and I was almost blinded. She burst into my room, her smile still dazzling, still dimpled, and in my druggy, one-eyed haze I thought I must be seeing an apparition.

"Kristi?" I said, wondering if the ghost could talk. "Kristi Casey, is that you?"

"The one and only," she said, and as she leaned over me to kiss my cheek, I smelled an unfamiliar perfume.

"You don't smell like baby powder anymore," I said, disappointed. Was it asking too much of this ghost, who'd gone to all the trouble of manifesting

herself into human form, to have gotten Kristi's
smell right too?

The spirit laughed, and I had to admit that even
though she had screwed up on the scent, she had the
laugh down to a T.

"I left that perfume back in high school," said
ghost Kristi. "I'm into more sophisticated fragrances
now." She held her wrist under my nose. "This is
Wind Song. Like it?"

I nodded. It was pretty. I closed my eyes, happy to
fall back onto the soft pillow of my narcotics while I
breathed in the beautiful song of the wind.

"Wait a second," I said, pushing aside the arms of
Morpheus, intent as I was to make a joke, to make
this faux Kristi laugh the way I had made the real one
laugh. "Why would anyone call a perfume Wind
Song? I mean, wouldn't you say that farting is a **wind
song**?"

The apparition put her hand on my forehead.

"Maybe you shouldn't try to talk, Joe."

I wasn't about to argue humor with a ghost, and
besides, I was already asleep.

In eight games with the Gophers I had scored eleven
points: eight assists and three goals. A reporter from
the **Minnesota Daily,** after writing a story about me,
invited me to her sorority dance. Another girl sent
packages of cookies to my dorm room with notes
that said while she hoped I enjoyed the gingersnaps,
she was the sweeter cookie. And when Eric Wilner,
the team captain, couldn't use two tickets he had to
the North Stars, he gave them to me. I had been liv-

ing a life better than the one I dreamt, only now, thanks to an unbelievably stupid—and embarrassing—move, it was over.

"I was at the game," said Kristi when I woke up. I wondered why she was still at my bedside; after all, hadn't I been sleeping for a month? Or had it been seconds?

"I was home on break," she continued as I tried to focus my good eye on her face. "And I was hoping to get together with you, but geez, I sure didn't think it'd be in a hospital room."

"I think I messed up my eye," I said, touching the convex bandage over my left eye. "Oh yeah," I said, nodding at my leg in traction. "I broke my leg."

"You got **mangled,** Joe," said Kristi, and her voice somehow balanced glee and concern.

"I did?" I thought for a moment, but my mind seemed as cloudy as the winter sky framed by the square hospital window.

"You can remember that I used to wear Love's Baby Soft perfume but you can't remember you got creamed on the ice? Well, you did have a concussion—maybe that explains things."

"I **did**?"

As she began the play-by-play of what happened, a nausea that had nothing to do with my injuries began curdling inside me.

Hockey's not exactly badminton—with all the checking and tripping, with sticks, pucks, and often fists flying, it's not a huge surprise when a player finds himself taking a little field trip to the emergency room. I myself had been there twice, once as a bantam when I got a high stick to the forehead and had to get six stitches just below my hairline and once as a squirt when I took a nice backward dive on the unforgiving surface of the rink and knocked myself out. It's understood that in a fast, physical game, played on ice no less, there is a possibility of getting hurt; still, I never in a million years imagined the **way** I'd get hurt that would put me in the hospital.

"I saw **everything**," said Kristi. Sitting on my bed, she practically squirmed with excitement. "Mark and I had **great** seats—we were in the third row right on the center line and—"

"Who's Mark?" As drugged and in pain as I was, I still was curious about Kristi's social life.

"Oh, just this friend of mine from college. Anyway, we were basically right across from the benches and I saw you fall when you were changing up."

I remembered that. Geez, I had felt so stupid; I couldn't believe it. I had gotten off the bench and was ready to hop back onto the ice when the blade of one of my skates got caught on something—a water bottle? The bench leg? Someone's discarded mouth guard?—and I felt myself stumble forward over the boards. That was as far as my memory took me.

"It was kind of funny at first," said Kristi. "You know, it just looked like some clumsy move that you and your teammates would laugh over. But suddenly there's a Badger trying to catch a pass and he slams into you and your leg is still caught up in whatever it was that it was caught up in and you're hanging off the boards—your front half lying there on the ice and your leg bent really funny up behind you. And then, **bam**—the puck flies in and smacks you right in the face just as you fall to the ice. Really, Joe, I've never seen anything like it. You're lucky you didn't get brain-damaged." She leaned close to me, her beautiful face inches from mine. "You're not brain-damaged, are you, Joe?"

"Agghhhhhhh," I said, squirting spit out of the side of my mouth and rolling my eyes back in my head.

"Whew. No more than usual."

"Ha ha ha."

Kristi leaned even closer and kissed my cheek. "Well, listen, Joe, it's great to see you again—I'm just sorry it's under these circumstances."

She stood up and wound a scarf around her neck before putting on her coat, and I figured out she was leaving.

"Do you have to go?" I asked.

She wiggled her fingers as she drew on a glove. "I do—but I'll come back tomorrow. What can I bring you?"

"How about a Kristi Special?"

She laughed as if I'd just told her a great joke. "I was thinking more along the lines of magazines or candy."

"There's no candy sweeter than a Kristi Special."

She said something, but it wasn't loud enough to hear over the fatigue that suddenly roared in, as dense and thick as a blizzard.

A compound fracture of the femur. A separated shoulder. A puck to the eye. A concussion. And worst of all, the sad dark knowledge that I was out for the rest of the season. Kristi hadn't been the first to categorize all of the injuries and their inevitable consequence, but she'd been the first one I'd understood through the vapor of the pain and drugs. And because she was Kristi, I couldn't hate the messenger—I was just so glad to have the messenger back in my life.

I had been loving the whole college experience: my classes were engaging even if they were **huge**, the girls were cute, and my roommate, a turkey farmer's son from Worthington, was nice enough when he wasn't sleeping, which he mostly was.

But it was when I laced up my skates as a Golden Gopher that I knew Fate had winked at me, singling me out for not just dessert but whipped cream too. And then all of a sudden I was lying on a hospital bed, looking at everything with one eye while nurses checked the lines of stitches that climbed up my leg like thin black bugs.

I don't recommend slogging across campus on crutches in the middle of a Minnesota winter. My leg ached—I swear the pins they implanted were mini-icicles—and having those crutches' pads shoved up under my arms did not make my still-sore shoulder feel any better. Plus snow and ice isn't the easiest surface to get around on for an able-bodied person. . . . Plus I still had waves where I'd see everything double. Yeah, I was in a funk.

"Joe, honey, you got some mail," said my mother one gray afternoon that perfectly matched my prevailing mood.

I had regressed; not only had I left my dorm and my sleeping roommate to move back to my aunt's house, but I was driven to and from school. I assured everyone it was just until I could get around better, but I sure didn't mind the ease and convenience. Okay, the babying. My mom and aunt treated me like I was the Great Poobah and they felt honored to wait on me, serving me my meals on a tray as I reclined on the couch (it felt better to have my leg up), typing my papers, and one night playing three hours' worth of whist just because I was the mood for it.

"It's not from Kelly, is it?" I had just broken up with a girl who was less a nice home ec major and more an obsessive weirdo, and she—via letters and phone calls—liked to remind me what a jerk I was.

She looked at the envelope. "No, fortunately—it's from Madison. Isn't that where Kristi goes to school?"

I might have actually smiled.

"Yeah, it is," I said, reaching for the letter.

"And there's a postcard too."

Wow. Pay dirt. I looked at the front of the postcard, a picture of a cow in a meadow, before flipping it over.

Bonjour mon ami—
  I heard through the international grapevine that you broke your leg. Je suis desolée. As you may have been smart enough to figure out, I'm in France right now. In the town of Limoges— famous for porcelain and tasty beef cattle. I just got a job (I like everything about being an artist but the starving part). I'm an au pair, taking care of two little boys named Benoît and Pascal. We have mandatory finger painting and I'm teaching

them how to sing "Chelsea Morning." How do
you like them pommes? Get better!

Darva

I smiled for the second time that day and laid the
postcard on my chest, imagining little French boys in
berets singing Joni Mitchell. Then, on a roll, I smiled
again as I opened Kristi's letter.

Hey Joe,
   I'm supposed to be listening to my boring
astronomy professor's lecture on supernovas, but I
think they probably have more exciting lectures
on Uranus . . . ha ha.
   So how're you doing, Joe? I can still picture you
falling so weird on the ice—yikes! I suppose
you're not having fun sitting out all those games
either . . . but wait, I'm not writing to depress
you, I'm writing to cheer you up!
   So get a load of this—I tried mushrooms for the
very first time. Have you ever? It was wild! My
friend Brian (he's from Santa Fe and says this
Hopi Indian kid in high school turned him on to
mescaline) and I and another couple took them
and went to the movies—oh my God, we saw
Serpico—that Al Pacino is cute! (That's how I
judge all movies—on how cute the leading man is,
ha ha.) Next weekend we're going to go camping
and take them—Brian says being out in nature on
mushrooms will blow my mind! I can't wait!
   Other than expanding my universe, it's the
same old same old. My roommate's kind of a
jerk—a big fat load who eats in bed when she
thinks I'm sleeping. She sounds like a big rat,

gnawing through her potato chips and malted milk balls. I am cheerleading, but for the JV basketball team, which is kind of b-o-r-i-n-g. I'm thinking maybe cheerleading is more of a high school thing. . . .

So I hope you're feeling better and getting stronger and life's treating you better because YOU DESERVE IT!

Write me when you have time.

Love,
Kristi

I stared at the word **love** for a long time. Breaking all recent records, I smiled again.

Ten

I didn't—couldn't—suit up for games, but when I hobbled into the stands, the crowd gave me a standing ovation. The next time they cheered, and the game after that they clapped. Well, some of them. I didn't think I liked getting attention for being the spaz who fell over the boards, but when the applause stopped I felt—and this is going to sound pathetic— a little abandoned. Then I got pissed off, resenting the fans for watching the players on the ice instead of me and then resenting them for taking my attention away from the game. To tell you the truth, it was a relief when the season ended.

But then just when life seemed to be getting back to something I might enjoy again—I was off my crutches and back in my dorm—my mom told me she had a boyfriend.

She said this during what had been a perfectly nice dinner. Beth had been telling us about a new cheesecake cookie that her company's test kitchen had developed.

"This was not one of their better efforts," she said. "They had these hard red chunks in them that were supposed to be the strawberry flavoring. Hal Lawson was in my office—he's in charge of R&D—and he bites into one.

" 'Guess we're going to have to research a better strawberry substitute,' he says, and pulls out a piece of the tooth he just broke!"

My mother laughed for about a half second and then started clearing the table.

"Speaking of dessert," she said, "we're going to have company for ours."

She looked frazzled, as if she'd run up a bunch of flights of stairs and still couldn't find the room she was looking for; there were pink spots high on her cheeks and she was sort of breathless.

"Who's coming, Carole?" asked my aunt, a tease in her voice.

"His name is Len, Joe," she said, looking at me. "He teaches civics at my school."

She blew at a curlicue of hair that was spiraling down from her forehead and grabbed my plate, even though I wasn't quite done, and stacked it on her own.

I glared at my aunt. "Did you know about this?" I was suddenly mad at her, mad that my mother would confide in her before me. As usual, I was the last to know about anything.

"I didn't tell you about him," said my mother quickly, "because I didn't know if there was anything to tell. We've only just . . . well, started going out."

"Great," I said, with a big oily phony smile. "I can't wait to meet the guy."

"Joe—"

"No, really, Mom. I mean it." And it was true, despite the sour sarcasm in my voice, I had a great curiosity to meet the guy whose sudden appearance in my life made me want to run to my room and bawl like a baby.

He was bigger than me, which made me immediately defensive, and rumpled-looking in a frayed-collar, snagged-knit-tie, bad haircut kind of way. That I noticed all this made me feel like a big fruit and made me resent him all the more.

We both watched my mom shake the aerosol can and swirl pyramids of whipped cream on slabs of pie. I found myself smirking when she handed me the piece with the most whipped cream, but then I caught my aunt Beth's look, which asked, **What is your problem?**

"Len played hockey too, Joe," said my mother after she had finished serving us.

"Well, in high school," said the big guy. "I wasn't good enough to play in college." He spooned some of his whipped cream into his coffee. "I sure was sorry to hear about your accident, Joe. How're you feeling?"

"Fine," I said, and as my ears grew hot, I attacked the dessert in front of me as if I were an entrant in a pie-eating contest. My fork had turned into a shovel, and after I wolfed it down, I expected a bell to ring with a judge announcing, **Winner!**

"Whoa," said Beth. "You were hungry."

I dragged a napkin across my chin. "Well, I just realized I've got this thing . . . this study group thing. We just started it and—" I looked at my watch with great urgency. "Man, I'm supposed to be at the library now."

Len stood and shook my hand, and my aunt offered me her cheek to kiss.

"I'm glad to see how seriously you're taking your studies," she said with a saccharine smile.

My mom walked me to the door. As she watched me put on my gloves and jacket, she asked, "You think he's nice, don't you?"

Her voice begged me to answer yes, and so I did.

"Oh, Joe." She reached out, wrapping her arms around me, and like a little baby, I held on too long, too hard.

Eventually you get over your mother's betrayal. Especially when you realize that it'd be pretty psycho to think that your mother had betrayed you in the first place just by liking some guy. I mean, my dad'd been dead for five years; it wasn't like she hadn't put in her time mourning. I came to the brilliant conclusion that big, soft-spoken Len Rusk made my mom what I'd wanted her to be for years—happy—and it'd be sort of twisted of me to begrudge him for that.

Besides, I was not one to make good judgments about relationships, considering the one I'd just gotten out of.

Kelly was a devoted hockey fan who, when hockey practice began, hung around the hallway outside the locker room, greeting me with a big "Hi, Joe!" She was cute enough that I found her attention flatter-

ing, but during our first date—burgers at Stub &
Herb's—she confessed to me that **Love Story** was her
all-time favorite movie and wouldn't it be great if she
and I became like Jenny and Oliver?

"People have actually said I look like Ali Mc-
Graw—she plays Jenny—especially around the
mouth." Wagging her head, she offered a big smile so
I could see the resemblance. I didn't. "And Oliver—
Ryan O'Neal—plays hockey too, except for Har-
vard. So I guess that means you're Ryan and I'm Ali!"

I ignored the blinking read warning that screamed:
Nut alert! Nut alert! and slept with her that night.

"Joe," she whispered as we lay sweating and spent,
"I think we're making our own **Love Story**."

The thrill I felt after **finally** losing my virginity was
tempered by the thought, **She's losing her mind.**

The idea of personal space was one that held no interest to her. Anytime I came home, there were notes
posted by the dorm phone: "Joe, call Kelly." A home
economics major, she brought pans of brownies and
seven-layer bars for me to share with the team—a
nice enough gesture, except she did this before every
practice, and every home game. I wondered when
she found time to go to her own classes, what with all
the baking and following me around—I couldn't
walk across the campus without her suddenly ap-
pearing from behind a corner. I'd be studying in
Coffman Union and there she was, looming in front
of me, her shadow falling across my books. Walking
across the bridge that spans the West Bank and the
East, I'd hear, "Joe! Joe! Wait up!" and have to resist
the urge to run.

But like I said, she was cute and the sex was

good—any sex at that point in my life couldn't help but be good—and so I put up with her and her strange behavior, trying to convince myself it was cute and quirky and not nutty and obsessive.

She was hurt when I moved back home after my injury, asking why I wouldn't let her nurse me back to health.

"Because you're not a nurse," I said.

"But I'm your fiancée."

I cannot tell you the drop in temperature my blood took; suffice it to say I was chilled by her words.

"No you're not," I said, and because I couldn't help it, I added, "Not even close."

"What's that supposed to mean?"

I shrugged. "It means I sure as hell never asked you to marry me."

"Well, maybe not in so many words."

"Not in so many words, not in so many actions, not in so many **anything**." I tried to look authoritarian, not an easy thing to do when you're lying on your aunt's couch underneath a quilt appliquéd with butterflies. "Now look, Kelly, I think you're a . . . you're a very nice person, but—"

"But you don't love me the way I love you." Hot spots of pink rose on her cheeks and her eyes darkened.

"I guess not," I said.

"Well, that's just fine," she lied, and I knew it was a lie, because as she said it, she shoved the lamp that was on the end table next to the couch and it fell to the floor. Fortunately the floor was carpeted.

"**Just fine!**" she said, and picked up a photograph of my mother, my aunt, and me and flung it against the wall, where the glass shattered. This seemed to please her, and she looked around for something else to throw.

I don't need to elaborate on how a guy feels seeing his aunt wrestle a candy dish out of his crazy girlfriend's hands and then wrestle the crazy girlfriend out of the door. Let's just say **humiliation** was pretty high up there on the list.

There was a spate of hang-up calls and a delivery of burnt brownies (with a note that read, "These are black like your heart!"), but fortunately for me (and unfortunately for him) some basketball player responded to the cute girl bearing chocolate chip cookies and is now starring in Kelly's **Love Story** fantasy.

The rest of my freshman year passed without any drama, which was good because it gave me a little respite before the excitement of summer.

"Joe? Hey, it's Kristi! Listen, a couple of us are going up to Taylor's Falls—we've got a big tent, so pack up your stuff and I'll pick you up Friday morning!"

"Kristi? When did . . . Friday? When did you get home?"

"So I'll see you Friday morning, okay?"

"I think I'm working."

"Get it off. I'll be by about eight!"

It would have been stupid for me to protest any longer because she'd already hung up.

"I heard from your sister," I told Kirk as I tuned my guitar at our jam that evening. Ed had bought me a black Telecaster for Christmas (talk about feeling chintzy—I'd gotten him a Neil Young album), and although I still occasionally sat behind the keyboard, I was having more fun with the guitar.

"She's in town?"

"Well, yeah. I think so. I mean, she didn't sound long-distance or anything." Turning the E string peg, I tried to look nonchalant. "Doesn't she stay at your house when she comes home from school?"

Kirk shrugged. "I guess not."

He stomped the bass pedal twice and played a jazzy little riff on the snare drum.

"So," I said as I tuned the E string, still nonchalant, "you think I could have the weekend off, Ed?"

Ed looked up from his own fretboard and clenched and unclenched his fist.

"Man, my hand's bugging me again. Forty-two years old and I'm already getting arthritic."

"You're an old man," said Kirk. Like a nightclub drummer accenting a joke, he played a quick **ba-dum-dum.**

"So you think I could?" I asked.

But it was Kirk who answered first. "First of all, Joe, why would you want to spend a weekend with my sister, and second, **why would you want to spend a weekend with my sister?**"

"Ben-Gay doesn't even help," said Ed, massaging his hand.

"Well, she invited me to go camping with her and a bunch of people," I said, "and I . . . well, I used to go camping all the time. And I haven't been in a long time, so I thought this would be really fun."

"Tim Gjerke always wants more hours. . . . Kirk, you want to pick up an extra shift or two?"

Kirk shrugged and twirled a drumstick. "I could."

"I guess you've got a weekend off," said Ed, and he played the heavy rift that begins "In-A-Gadda-Da-Vida."

The brook was babbling. Literally.

"Can't you guys hear it?" I asked as we sat on the narrow strip of stony sand that lined the creek.

Kristi laughed. "What's it saying, Joe?"

Gesturing for everyone to keep quiet, I cocked my head, one hand held behind my ear. I listened for a while, nodding.

" 'By the shores of Gitche Gumee,' " I translated, " 'by the shining Big-Sea-Water, stood the wigwam of Nokomis, daughter of the Moon, Nokomis.' "

The five people around me hooted and hollered.

"Wow," said a girl named Pam, "that's a poetic creek!"

"Shh!" said Kristi. "I want to hear that tree over there. It's reciting Shakespeare!"

Thrilled at our collective wit, our laughter pushed us until we were couldn't stand upright. It was my first acid trip, and like everyone else, I was one awestruck tourist.

A trap door had been opened to my mind and large truths jostled against one another in their haste to get through. I lay on my stomach, pressed against a million tender blades of grass who hummed a chant so primordial that I knew every living thing could be heard if I just understood how to listen. I listened closely, realizing that the grass with its greenness, its scent, its dandelions, its hidden clovers, was but the top layer, a ceiling covering Mother Nature's rec room below. And who knew—maybe she was down there, underneath us all, **right now,** her hair long strands of the silver and gold men dug out of mines, her beating heart the slow pulse of volcanic lava . . . and what's above? Quickly, I rolled over and looked up at the sky—the blue celestial roof of this crazy funhouse— just in time to watch angels wearing clouds do-si-do with one another. Birds who were magnified in size waved their wings in greeting and whistled the theme song of **The Andy Griffith Show.** The trees shook the maracas of their magic leaves as the wind blew by.

On the grass, I could feel every single bone in my body, and then it was as if my eyes turned inward and I could see my own skeleton, and all the activity that took place within it. "Oh, man," I said, "I didn't know there were little elves inside my leg who helped my broken bone to heal."

"Nice elves," said Pam.

"I'm wondering why my hand is strung with Christmas lights," said a guy named Paul, fluttering his fingers in front of his face.

"They're not Christmas lights," said Kristi. "They're dewdrops that crystallized."

"Dewdrops that crystallized," I said. "That's the most beautiful thing I ever heard in my life."

"But you're not done ever hearing," said a guy named Rob.

"I hope not," I said. "Because I plan on hearing things that I never knew I could hear."

"Right on," said Pam.

"I plan on seeing things I never knew I could see," said Kristi.

"Wow," said Rob. "That's the second most beautiful thing I ever heard."

"Have you ever heard elephants cry?" I asked.

Kristi laughed. "Or bees yodel?"

"I would **love** to hear bees yodel," said Pam. "I'm half Swiss."

"Which half?" asked a guy named Steve. "The half that has the crystallized dewdrops around it?"

Pam patted her chest and thighs. "I don't see any crystallized dewdrops." She pushed herself up and looked across the creek. "I do see Elton John sitting on a buffalo, though."

"Ask him to sing 'Rocket Man,'" said Steve. "I love that song."

And so it went. The day offered up one Technicolor, multi-orchestrated, perfume-saturated, light-showered, mind-blowing, high-flying moment after another, and when we had finally come down and were all in our sleeping bags under a balmy summer sky, I said that I was as wiped out as I'd ever been in my life.

Except for the sounds of deep breathing and light snoring, there was no response.

Finally Kristi giggled. "Me too," she said. "Like a newborn baby who's just worked her way out into the world."

I thought for a moment, my fingers laced behind my head, looking up at the uncountable twinkle of stars.

"Exactly," I whispered. "That's it exactly."

I saw Kristi only two more times that summer, and both times involved group camping and mind-altering drugs.

The first time was a pot-infused trip to the Apple

River in Wisconsin, where we rode inner tubes down the rapids and laughed like we were on a day pass from the funny farm, and on the second we camped at Gooseberry Falls, where we took a nice trip aboard a mushroom train, a speedy, slightly psychedelic little dash that included glimpses of fir trees that appeared to be dancing the Pony, and a jumping frog who I was sure was the fifth Beatle.

"Isn't Pete Best the fifth Beatle?" asked Steve, who again was part of this drug-taking, camping cabal. He had watched with me the frog's leap across the path and into the grass and heard my pronouncement as to the frog's true identity.

"If he is, he's a pretender to the throne," I said. "That little leaping amphibian knows more about Paul and John and George and Ringo than anyone."

"We should have caught him, then," said Steve. "That little bugger's probably worth a lot of money."

Everyone else decided to stay another day at the campsite—Steve was intent on finding that frog and seeing if it would harmonize to "Eleanor Rigby" with him—but Kristi and I had to head back.

"Stupid work," she said.

"Yeah," I said, disappointment darkening my voice, while inside I thanked Ed Haugland for scheduling me to work the evening shift, handing me the gift of a three-hour drive with Kristi.

She pushed in a Long John Baldry tape as soon as we got into the van, and turned it up loud enough to wipe out the possibility of conversation. As we drove for an hour listening to tapes of her choice, at the volume of her choice, I felt little jabs of resentment, remembering how things were in Kristi World.

When a Jefferson Airplane tape finished and before she put in another one, I remarked, half under my breath, "She reminds me of you."

"Who?" said Kristi, her antennae always out for any mention of herself.

"Grace Slick."

Kristi looked at me, interested. "Why?"

I shrugged. "She always sounds so bossy when she sings."

There was a pause and then, tipping her head back, she let out a big laugh.

"How do you know I sound bossy when I sing?"

"You sound bossy when you **breathe**," I said, and she laughed again.

She didn't put another cassette in for the rest of the ride, and we had a long conversation that covered a dozen topics, including why Kristi hadn't continued her relationship with Blake once she got into college. "What attracts you in high school isn't necessarily what attracts you in college. Plus you wouldn't believe what dud letters he wrote! I thought, Who is this boring dork who sends me football and hockey scores? Like I care!"

"Well, maybe because you were a cheerleader he thought you were still interested in sports."

Kristi rolled her eyes. "Yeah, **right**."

She talked about her roommate. "I told you about her, Joe—she's the one who eats in bed. I mean, forget about the freshman fifteen—she put on the freshman forty! Her name is Betsy, but it should really be Buttsy—I'm not kidding, her ass is getting so big her parents are going to have to pay double tuition!"

"Nice," I said, shaking my head.

"What's the matter with you?"

I changed lanes to give the Camaro that was practically kissing my fender the whole lane to itself.

"Nothing's the matter with me. I just wonder what's the matter with you sometimes."

"Geez, Joe—when Buttsy makes her bed, it rains **crumbs**! I've got to dodge orange Cheetos crumbs!"

I switched back to the lane the Camaro was flying down, and wished a speeding ticket on a guy I'd never even met before.

"So are you mad at me?" asked Kristi.

"The more you talk I am," I said, bugged by her baiting tone of voice.

"When did you lose your sense of humor?"

"Oh, so now it's my fault that I don't think you're funny."

"Most people think I'm extremely funny."

"You can be very funny," I agreed. "You can also be very mean."

Kristi blew out a dismissive burst of air. "You sound just like a girl."

"Better than sounding like an asshole."

She breathed in a quick gasp of air and turned, looking out the window. Silence filled the van like a bad gas, and I was about to break it by pushing in the **Exile on Main Street** tape when Kristi spoke again.

"Sorry."

This—Kristi apologizing—was big. Still, I wasn't in the mood to let her off the hook.

"It's not me you should apologize to, it's your roommate."

"Ha! That girl wouldn't accept an apology unless she could eat it!"

I shoved the tape in then and cranked up the volume, letting Mick Jagger sing "Tumbling Dice." We didn't speak for the rest of the ride home, although occasionally Kristi offered commentary by leaning forward to beat out an angry rhythm on the glove compartment, and after I dropped her off, she disappeared off my radar for the rest of the summer.

I still get a hollow feeling in my stomach, like I've missed dinner by a couple hours, when I think of my second hockey game as a sophomore. I had been training hard in the preseason, lifting weights and running sprints, and physically I knew I was in as good shape as I'd ever been. I got the assist on the game-winning goal in our opening game against Duluth, and I was gearing up for another great season when in the second period of game two a goon high-sticked me and I fell to the ice. When I got up, blood splattered on the rink, and I realized that the vision in my right eye was blurred. The captain skated over and escorted me off the ice, and for the second time in my Gopher hockey career, I took a little field trip to the emergency room.

My doctor looked just like James Arness from **Gunsmoke,** only he wore a stethescope around his neck instead of a bolo tie.

"You're a lucky kid," he said. "An eighth of an inch closer, and you could have lost your eye."

"But I'll see all right?"

He nodded. "Fine enough to see the scar."

And that should have been the end of that—I mean, I had ten stitches, but I easily could have suited up and played the next game. But I just . . . couldn't.

"My leg doesn't feel right," I said in Coach Deight's office. "I get out there and I feel like it's going to break."

Mr. Deight sat back in his chair, his folded hands on his belly, twiddling his thumbs.

"What does the doctor say?"

I shrugged, feeling my face grow hot.

The coach sat there for a while, his office chair creaking as he rocked back and forth in it.

"It's not really about the leg, is it, Joe?"

I lowered my head until I was staring at my lap.

"Is it about the eye?"

I sat there, the big wall clock like a fussy old lady, tsking each second.

"I think it's about both," I said finally, raising my head. As much as I didn't want to admit to my cowardice, I knew the sooner I offered an explanation, the sooner I could bolt out of the office.

"So you want to take a couple games off?"

I nodded.

The coach sniffed and picked up a pen, clicking it a couple of times before scribbling something on a pad of paper.

"We'll just say that you need a little time off the ice to recuperate from your injuries."

"Thanks," I said, getting up. I was nearer to tears than I'd ever want to show a hockey coach.

It wasn't official, but I knew: my hockey career was over and I think the depression I fell into was deeper than the one I'd tumbled into after my dad died. That's not to say I loved hockey more than my father, but after his death, I had my mother to worry about and I knew I couldn't shine any light on the darkness that surrounded her if I stayed in my own black pit. This time there was no one I had to be strong for, and I mourned the loss of my hockey career as if it was a real person. And in a way it was, I guess, because playing hockey had defined me. It had been my constant companion since I was a little kid waiting for the ice on the creek to freeze. I loved everything about the game, loved it with all my senses: the metallic scrape of blades against the ice, the clatter of sticks tapping against it and the cracking sound a slap shot makes; the sensation of flying down the rink, dodging opponents, the passing, shooting, and deking out the goalie; getting to the bench out of breath and grabbing the water bottle, squirting a slug of cold water down my throat. I even loved the Zamboni and watching the wet trails it made as it cleaned the ice. And now a big part of my life was gone—by my own choice—and you better believe I mourned it and the wuss I had become. I don't know what had snapped, but something had, and I just couldn't face going out on the ice anymore.

It was a depression I kept close, like a girl I was especially protective of, and yet in front of people, the girl suddenly became ugly and I told her to beat it, so that no one would know the mighty Joe Andreson would consort with such a loser. I sure couldn't introduce her to my mom—she was happy and in love with Len Rusk, and I didn't want to throw a wet blanket on that particular party.

I was in my dorm room one Friday night, my sleepy roommate having roused himself enough to invite me to a sorority party whose hostesses, he claimed, always had good pot ("Man, they should change their name to Delta **High!**"). Sitting at my desk, I was mindlessly throwing a tennis ball against the wall and catching it, back and forth, back and forth, the small thumping noise it made accenting the first syllable of the word that pounded in my head: loser, loser, loser.

Eleven

"Whaddya mean, **crap?** These are good!"

Ed Haugland shook his head as Kirk shoved a spoonful of Blue Barties into his mouth. "Cereal's not supposed to turn milk purple."

"It's not purple," I said, dipping my spoon in my bowl. "It's blue. And you should try these—they **are** good."

"I predict they'll last as long as CinnaBombs," said Ed.

"CinnaBombs were the **best**," said Kirk. "I can't believe they took those off the market."

"They had to," said Ed, "when all those people started dying of acute sugar poisoning."

"Cereal's supposed to be sweet!"

"No, those had a nasty aftertaste," I said, remembering. "The cinnamon flavoring had a real bite to it."

Often before our jam sessions, we'd sit in the break room and fortify ourselves with some new product from the grocery store aisles. Ed said our opinions were invaluable; we had the undeveloped palates of children, and whatever we liked, he knew not to recommend to anyone over the age of eight.

"Of course it's a sad commentary on the state of our food," said the professional grocer. "When in doubt, they put in either more sugar, more salt, or more chemicals."

"Yes," said Kirk in the quavery voice of an old man, "in my day, we didn't have refined sugar! We just sucked on beets whenever we got a craving for sweets!"

"You'll see," said Ed, laughing. "There's going to be a big counterrevolution against all this crap they put in foods."

"Well, don't sign me up," said Kirk. "It's the crap they put in that makes it taste good."

After draining the half inch of purplish/blue milk left in my bowl, I let out a long and sustained burp, shaping the belch into words, which was a particular talent of mine.

"Are we going to sit around talking about food all night or are we going to play?"

Kirk, who was working hard to bring his skill level in burp-talking up to mine, opened his mouth wide, and on top of a deep bass belch rode his "Play."

We hadn't even jammed a half hour when Ed sat back in his chair, his hand falling to his side.

"I can't hold on to the pick anymore," he said. "My hand's all numb."

Kirk lifted his sunglasses and rested them on top of his head, and the two of us exchanged looks that telegraphed a little worry, frustration, some impatience. You had to have been deaf not to hear the wrong notes Ed had been playing, blind not to have seen how his hand fumbled against the strings like a paw, but as we had in the past, we all, including Ed—**especially** Ed—tried to ignore it. Some nights he played like Jimmy Page and we'd be lulled into thinking that everything was fine, but more often than not, he'd have to end the jam session early because of numbness, pain, or what he complained was "my hand's inability to do what I tell it to do."

Kirk drummed his sticks against the rim of the snare—his nervous tic.

"Have you seen a doctor yet, man?"

Ed bowed his head and shook it.

"Well, make an appointment," said Kirk.

"We'll go with you," I said, to soften the sharpness of Kirk's order.

We sat in the waiting room, amusing ourselves by finding the hidden pictures in a **Highlights** magazine feature.

"There's the shoe," I said, pointing to the sneaker camouflaged in tree bark.

"And there's the dick."

I laughed and then shushed him, nodding toward the receptionist, a gray-haired woman who wore a silk rose pinned on her smock lapel.

"You can't talk about dicks around her," I said, my voice low.

"Well, I wouldn't be if they didn't hide one here in the picture."

"You moron," I said, looking carefully where he pointed. "That's a rocket."

Wiggling his head, Kirk smiled. "That's what the ladies call mine."

"In your dreams."

"No, in **theirs**." After giving me one of his signature smirks, he leaned toward me and pulled a letter out of his jeans pocket. "I don't think we're going to find any more hidden pornography in there, so if you want to see something **really** good, take a look at this."

I unfolded the paper, which bore the University of Florida letterhead.

"Hey, you got in."

He nodded, his face composed into a cool nonchalance. It was a composure he couldn't hold.

"Can you believe it? I was going to wait until Ed got out"—he glanced at the door behind which patients disappeared—"but I couldn't! **Florida!** I'm going to school in fucking Florida!"

"Congratulations," I said, slapping him on the back. "That's just great."

And it wasn't as if I was lying. I knew how much he had wanted to go away to a school near the ocean. He had applied to schools in California and Florida with the goal of studying marine biology (I'll bet there are thousands of others who like Kirk were inspired to go into their field by watching Jacques Costeau on TV), and practically every check he'd gotten from Haugland Foods had gone into his college fund. I was truly happy for him, although I couldn't deny the presence of the little gnarled troll who sat inside me, arms folded, pouting. **What about me? What about our jam sessions? You've al-**

ready got a life of adventure planned, and I don't know what the hell I'm doing with mine!

My junior year was almost over and my declared major was in journalism—certainly a romantic enough field—but the trouble was, any pictures of myself shouting out questions to Gerald Ford ("What's the real truth behind the Warren Commission, Mr. President?") or wending my way through the maze of a Moroccan bazaar to meet with a CIA operative for a handoff of top-secret documents or tracking down the MIA soldier whose name a college girl had worn on a copper bracelet faded under the troll's sneer: **As if that's going to happen.**

When I dropped out of hockey, I seriously considered dropping out of school; what kept me going to classes was that I had no idea what else to do. I was still on the **Minnesota Daily** staff but worked more as an editor than a reporter; it took a lot less energy to change the words of someone else's story than to come up with the story myself. I was in a funk—not a serious, where's-the-revolver funk, but I did sigh a lot.

When it came to my own future, my imagination was like the balky old van I drove, not taking me very far before it sputtered to a stop, whereas Kirk's was a sleek Corvette with a V-8 engine and a full tank of gas. I admired and envied him for it, wondering how a kid like that got the confidence to get his hands on a set of keys like those.

But everything **is** relative, and when Ed got a diagnosis of multiple sclerosis, the weight of my own problems didn't seem so heavy.

One day I found Ed behind a pallet of canned goods in the storeroom, sobbing.

"God!" he wailed, practically slapping the tears off his face. "I hate this! I hate how one day I can feel great and the next day I don't have any sensation in my legs!"

He spent his energy on running the store, and if there was extra left over, a jam session **might** happen, but it was the rare one that lasted over an hour.

"I'm just so **weak**! I'm as weak as a little old lady!"

"You're as **fucking** weak as a **fucking** old lady," reminded Kirk, who advised Ed to swear more because it was one small thing he could do to make himself feel better.

As the summer went by, I spent more and more time in the grocery store, doing the schedules, taking care of the orders, making the deposits, trying to ease Ed's load as much as possible. Kirk helped as much as he could, but he had a second job busing tables at a local diner to sock away as much money as possible for school. **Not** playing until two in the morning had to be a relief for him; I mean, the guy had to sleep **sometimes.**

It was a strange summer. Some nights I crawled into bed feeling bruised and battered, as if I'd been the target of a 350-pound Hell's Angel whose precious hog I'd accidentally leaned on. In reality, I was being pushed by responsibility and pulled by resentment, but what really roughed me up—brought me to tears a few times—was guilt. How could I complain about working so hard in the store after watching Ed try to reach for a box of borax with fingers that refused to close around it? How could I resent Kirk's happiness? As possibility exploded around him like fireworks, how could I stand off to the side, muttering, **Yeah, sure. Great show, but how about some of that for me?**

By nature, trolls are small, but when mine decreased in size it meant not that his strength was waning but that he was becoming more potent, more concentrated, and I didn't like it one bit. I hated this puny, petty side of me, yet when I tried to strangle the troll, he just grew tougher and wilier. The fight was exhausting.

It's something to walk your own mother down the aisle to meet her husband.

"It's a pretty old-fashioned tradition," said my mother, straightening my bow tie as we stood in the little church office before the ceremony. "I mean, the idea of being **given away**—like property—is sort of sexist."

"Do you want me not to do it?" I asked, hopeful.

My mom brushed the lapels of my tux. "I'm not letting you off that easily." She laughed and kissed my cheek. "Besides, I want to show you off. Look how handsome you are."

"Ma, no one's going to be looking at **me**."

I turned away then and looked in the mirror, frantically blinking back tears as I adjusted the tie she'd just tied. Really, my one big fear of the whole day was that everyone was going to be nudging one another, whispering about the bride's crybaby son who couldn't stop blubbering.

As my mother and I stood at the back of the church, ready to begin our processional down the papered aisle, all the solid material, bone, ligaments, and muscle, that composed my knees liquefied when the organist began playing the wedding march.

Oh man, I'm gonna pass out!

My mom squeezed my biceps and her smile said a thousand things, preeminent among them. **Hey, look at us, what we've been through. You'll always be my Joe. You can do this. I love you.**

Bone marrow began to set, ligaments and muscles were fused, and I took a step, confident that my knees had jelled—if not all the way, at least enough to hold me up.

At the reception, I had three reasons to celebrate: (1) my mother got married to the guy she loved, (2) I hadn't passed out while she was doing it, and (3) my uncle Roger had traveled across three continents to make it to the wedding, and while he hadn't exactly made it to the ceremony, he did make it to the reception.

"I had no idea he was coming!" I said as I danced with my grandmother.

"Oh, I didn't believe he would until I saw him." My grandma pursed her lips and then, throwing all caution to the wind, let her mouth relax into a smile. "I guess he didn't have time to get a haircut."

"Come on," I said as my grandmother dipped under my arm. "You know he looks dashing."

"Well, he should," she said, dipping back out in a nice little spin. "He's my son, isn't he?"

Another miracle of the day was that my grandma was in a good mood, laughing and joking and showing off her moves on the dance floor. When a silver-haired guy cut in, I was sad to leave.

"Will you save me a waltz?"

"Oh, Joey," she said, letting go of my hand to take her new partner's. "I'm not going to make any promises I can't keep."

I joined the group thronged around my uncle.

"The last wedding I was at, there was a fight because the cow the bride's family gave the bridegroom's was said to give sour milk."

"No kidding," said Miss Johnson, a math teacher, twirling her necklace around her finger.

"Is that right," said Miss Remington, and if I didn't know her as a no-nonsense geography teacher, I could have sworn she was batting her eyelashes.

"Yeah, things were getting a little hairy, until the bride's brother pulled in a mangy old goat and said the family had suddenly remembered the second half of the dowry."

"No kidding," said the math teacher.

"Is that right," said the geography teacher.

"Tell me more," I said, mimicking their breathless voices.

"Joe," said my uncle, clapping me on the back, "let's go find us a brew, eh?" He bowed to the circle of women. "I shall return."

Steering me toward the bar, he thanked me. "I was afraid that math teacher was about to ask me to dance again, and not only does she have two left feet, but she has two left feet that like to step on mine."

He ordered two beers from the bartender, and we clinked bottles. "God, it's good to see you, Joe." He took a draw of his beer, and as we both leaned against the bar, surveying the crowd, he made a sweeping motion with his hand. "Good to see Carole with a good man again, good to see my mother having a good time—she moves pretty well for an old bag, doesn't she?"

"Real nice," I said, laughing.

The band, composed entirely of former students of my mother's, was playing "The Look of Love," and my grandma and the silver-haired guy were dancing as if they'd been doing the cha-cha together for years; she not only followed his every step but seemed to anticipate it.

"She should dance every day," said Roger. "She could have avoided a whole lot of unhappiness if she just danced every day."

I took a long pull of beer, feeling like I had to defend her. "It's kind of hard to dance without a partner."

My uncle shrugged. "I'm not saying she had to re-marry. Hell, it takes resiliency—and hope—to marry again, and God knows Ma does not have a lot of re-siliency or hope in her makeup. Not like Carole." He gestured with his bottle at my mother, who in her pale blue floaty dress looked like Ginger Rogers out on the dance floor, even though there was no way Len could be mistaken for Fred Astaire. "All I'm say-ing is she should have found a way to do something that she loved to do."

Unable to argue with that, I nodded.

"Look at Beth," said Roger. **"Finally."**

"What do you mean?" I asked, but the math teacher chose this time to corral her alcohol-induced bravery and pull my uncle to the dance floor.

He looked at me, his expression wide-eyed, like a calf being roped and hog-tied, but to the math teacher he smiled as if the prospect of getting his feet trampled was one he could hardly wait for.

Looking past him and past my grandmother, who was now gamely following the lead-footed lead of one of Len's nephews, I saw my aunt Beth dancing with Linda, the friend she'd brought, and I immediately understood what Roger was talking about: Linda was Beth's girlfriend.

Once again, I'd been oblivious to the obvious. Immediately I tried to excuse my ignorance—it wasn't that unusual a thing for women to be dancing together at weddings, and in fact, on the floor right now were three female couples—but the weight of a dunce cap was heavy on my head. Or maybe it was the bottles of beer that made me a little woozy. Either way, I made my way through the throng of dancing couples, reaching my aunt just as the band finished playing "Begin the Beguine."

"May I have the next dance?" I asked.

My aunt held out her arms. "The next dance is all yours."

As her **friend** smiled and headed toward their table, the band began "Downtown."

"What a great little band," said Beth as we began dancing. "Do you suppose they'll stay together after tonight?"

"I don't know," I said. "Will you and Linda?"

I felt my aunt tense, but she followed my steps without missing a beat.

"I think I finally found the one I've always wanted," she said finally, and in her face there was not only happiness but gratitude and surprise.

Seeing that face, I felt like a chump, but couldn't

resist asking, "Why didn't you tell me before? Why am I always the last to know everything?"

Beth laughed and patted my shoulder. "As new as this is to you, Joe, it's pretty new to me too. I mean, it's **scary** to fall in love."

"You don't seemed scared," I said as she giggled again. "You seem **giddy**."

"Oh boy, if that's true, I'd better get it together. I don't want to wreck Carole's wedding by having everyone figure out that the bride's sister came with her lesbo girlfriend."

"She's too good-looking for people to think she's a lesbo," I said. "And so are you."

"Ha-ha," said my aunt, holding my hand as she spun in a circle toward me and then back out again. "As much as you think that's a compliment, it's not."

It was an excellent party. I was newly twenty-one and took full advantage of the open bar, getting loose but not smashed. I danced with my mother, my grandmother, my aunt, my aunt's girlfriend, assorted teachers (including the math teacher, whose feet **were** lethal weapons), assorted counselors and school administrators, Len's two sisters (my new stepaunts?), his three nieces, and a foreign exchange student from Barcelona.

I beat Roger in catching the garter Len threw and applauded wildly when Beth caught Mom's bouquet. I ate two pieces of cake and the contents of a half dozen little paper cups full of mints and cashews.

"That was our last song of the evening," announced the pianist at midnight. "'Cause our bass player's got to get up for his paper route."

"Gotta make a living," said the bassist, shrugging.

"So anyway, Mrs. A.—well, I guess you're not Mrs. A. anymore, but you'll always be our favorite teacher. And you too, Mr. Rusk, even though we all liked music better than we did civics." He cleared his throat, his ears reddening. "Anyway, we just played our last song, but the family of the bride would like to play another."

Amid applause that I encouraged by waving my hands, my grandma, Roger, Beth, and I climbed onto the stage.

In the middle of the dance floor, looking like figures on top of a wedding cake, stood the bride and groom, arms encircled around each other.

I sat at the piano as the others formed a semicircle around the microphone.

"Carole," said my grandmother, "you've got yourself a good man and I'm thrilled for you. Len, you've got yourself a wonderful woman."

Len nodded his agreement.

My grandmother turned toward me. "So go ahead," she said, still bossy even in her best mood.

I played a short intro and launched into a song my mom's dad—the grandfather I'd never met—had taught his kids to sing long ago.

It had been Beth's last-minute inspiration to serenade my mom with it, and we agreed—even my grandma—that it was a great idea and would make a great present to the bride.

We are the Lunds and this is what that means—
We like bacon in our baked beans
We like the funnies—Mark Trail and Mary Worth
We like the sky and we like the earth.

My uncle Roger stood in the middle of the trio, his arms around his mother and sister, and as my mother watched them, she alternately laughed and mouthed the words of the song, her eyes wet with tears. Whenever she had sung the song to me, she explained that it had been composed one night after Roger had said that a classmate of his had brought his family coat of arms to school for show-and-tell and why didn't **they** have a coat of arms?

"Because we don't," said his father, going to the piano, "but we could have a family song."

They composed it that night, with their father putting together the melody and the kids shouting out lyrics.

> We are the Lunds, we are a happy group
> Except when Mom makes her sauerkraut soup
> Except when Dad says to do our chores,
> Except when Roger falls asleep—he snores!
> Except when Beth tells her knock-knock jokes
> Except when Carole said that Santa was a hoax.

I was just so happy.

Have you ever seen the look on the faces of members of a really good choir, when they can't stop smiling over the fact that their voice is a part of a big, glorious whole? That's the look the trio wore—my aunt, my globe-trotting uncle, and my grandma. Man, I was so used to my grandma's face puckered in disappointment that I hardly recognized the woman standing with her two children, serenading her third.

> No coat of arms, but a family song to sing,
> Mairzy doats, babaloo, and ring-a-ding-ding.

I was so full of good feelings, I felt buoyant, bouncing up and down on the piano bench as I battered the keys. My mom was in love. Again. With that thought, I expected a shadow to pass over this yellow sunshine of emotion, but it did not come; instead, there was a bright little flash and an uptick of temperature. I felt the presence of my dad then, and I knew more deeply than I had known anything that my mother's happiness was cause for his own. Rolf Selmer Andreson wasn't here to spin Carole Lund Andreson Rusk on the dance floor or applaud Joseph Rolf Andreson for his Jerry Lee Lewis impersonation, but his love for us was. In that moment of music and happiness, I understood that while he might be in a place unfathomable to me, he was also **right here with us now.**

The thought filled me with such joy that I jumped up, pounding the keyboard as if it had caught fire and as the wedding guests clapped and shouted their approval, my mother and I looked at each other. She blew me a kiss and I pretended to catch it with my hand, tucking it into my vest pocket, next to my dad. Then I spun in one quick circle and thumbed a loud glissando going up the scale and another one coming back.

Twelve

Hey doofus—

Guess where I spent Thanksgiving break? In Cocoa Beach on a surfboard! Caught a bunch of waves, but they always caught me back before throwing me onto the ocean floor. Still, it was loads o'fun.

Having a great time wrestling alligators and girl watching—easy when they all wear bikinis to class. Suppose everyone's got their parkas on in Minnesota . . .

Hi to Ed,
Kirk

I pinned Kirk's postcard next to one from Darva, who was no longer living in Limoges as an au pair but was, as she had always wanted to be, **une étudiante aux beaux-arts** in Paris. The bulletin board above my desk held a class schedule, the name **Terri** scrawled on a Stub and Herb's matchbook cover along with a telephone number I hadn't successfully deciphered, and a **Minnesota Daily** article I'd written about a seventy-three-year-old nurse who was back in school working on a chemical engineering degree, but the majority of the corkboard was reserved for postcards. Florida and France were represented, but so were Scotland (Greg Hoppe was on a work-study program in Edinburgh) and Boston (where Blake Erlandsson was playing his last year of hockey for BU). As much as I enjoyed their messages, I usually pinned them picture side out, making a collage of the Eiffel Tower and the Arc de Triomphe, some guy in a kilt, Boston Common, a pyramid of water-skiers in leopard-print bikinis (I especially liked that postcard), and a sunning manatee. That my friends were having far-flung adventures bothered me not in the least because I happened to be having one of my own.

Kristi was back in my life again, bringing some pretty good dope, some excellent windowpane, and, joy of joys, sex. And this time the division of labor was fifty-fifty.

She had called me up out of the blue one October night when I was writing a paper on agricultural economics, using as my references a stack of books so dry I wouldn't have been surprised if they had spontaneously combusted. At least then they would have provided me a little entertainment.

"Joe," she said, sobbing, "Joe, my grandma died!"

I don't know why she sought comfort from me, but I was happy to provide it, and the day after the funeral, after I'd given Kirk and some other relatives a ride to the airport, she decided to reward me.

"Do you have any money, Joe?"

I shrugged, always a good answer to a loaded question.

"The reason I'm asking," she said, scooting a little closer to me in the car, "is because I thought it might be fun to get a motel room."

My dick was like a hand raised in agreement: **Yes, teacher, it would be really fun.**

And it was, or at least the sex was. Kristi was as un-inhibited and enthusiastic as I'd imagined (how many times had I imagined?) she'd be in bed. It was afterward, when we lay hot and sweaty and com-pletely sated on the rough, starchy-smelling sheets of the Hiawatha Motel, that things turned from fun to not so fun. I can understand a woman crying after sex—I mean, I understand it's a release—but Kristi didn't just cry; she wailed.

Holding a pillow to her stomach, she was curled up in a fetal position, rocking back and forth on the bed.

"I miss my grandma!"

I patted her shoulder (not the easiest thing to do with all her rocking), feeling totally ineffectual.

Then, not knowing what else to do, I shushed her softly, whispering that it was all right, and as she didn't tell me to shut up, I kept going,

"Nobody ever loved me like my grandma did," she said after downshifting from keening to soft crying to hiccups.

Instead of arguing with her and saying, **What about your mom or your dad?** I just held her. It was a nice feeling, cradling her in my arms; **vulnerable** wasn't a word you'd usually use to describe Kristi, but she was vulnerable now.

"She just loved me, you know?" Kristi lifted her head to look at me, her eyes swollen from crying, the tip of her nose pink.

I nodded. Seemingly happy with that, she nestled back down on my chest again.

"Anything I did she thought was great. I mean, she was proud of, you know, my **achievements,** but even if I hadn't been cheerleader captain, even if I hadn't been voted best-looking, even if I hadn't made the honor roll every single semester since junior high—well, she still would have thought I was great."

I smiled. Even in grief, Kristi found a way to promote herself.

Sensing my reaction, she lifted her head again. "I'm not bragging. I just meant that, well, I could have been the opposite—a thief, a drug addict, a dropout—and she still would have thought I was the greatest thing since Peter Lawford."

"Peter Lawford?"

"Her favorite movie star. An English guy. She said her two great disappointments were that she never met him and that her hair couldn't hold a curl."

I laughed, and Kristi hugged me—happy, it seemed, that I appreciated her grandmother's words.

I petted Kristi's hair, feeling the curve of her head.

"Mmm, that feels nice." A remnant of a sob staggered up her throat, and I petted her hair until her breathing settled back down.

"We just clicked, you know? There's something

about chemistry, and my grandma and I had it. It was like we got a joke no one else did."

She fell asleep in my arms, and I would have liked nothing more than to hold her all night, but my circulation was being cut off.

Hockey season started, and gloom descended like the gray winter weather—a gloom alleviated by Kristi's biweekly visits from Madison. We had made a little game of taking drives—we both loved road trips—and finding out-of-the-way motels.

"Hey," said Kristi, looking at the map as I drove out of the city one cold slushy afternoon, "did you know we've slept in four different counties?"

I laughed. "Let's make it our goal to sleep in all of them."

She was quiet for a moment, tapping the map, her lips moving.

"There's eighty-seven of them."

"All the better." And so "visit a new county" became our catchphrase for finding a place to have sex.

We had just finished our hot and sweaty business as tourists in the Flying Duck Motel in Isanti County when Kristi asked, "So if it bums you out so much not to play, why not try out again for the team?"

My fine postcoital mood was suddenly elbowed aside by my defensiveness.

"You don't understand, do you?"

"No, I don't," said Kristi cheerfully. "Explain it to me."

She was lying on her side, one hand supporting her head, her streaky blond hair now grown long and tumbling over one shoulder. It was the middle of winter, but the radiator in the Flying Duck chugged out so much heat that we had kicked off the bedding in the frenzy of our lovemaking. I had covered myself with the sheet, but Kristi suffered none of my modesty and lay there beautifully naked, her skin dark against the thick bleached sheets.

"How come you're so tanned in the middle of winter?"

Kristi smiled, her dimples asking the question they always asked: **Aren't I cute?**

"Don't change the subject," she said. "This is about you."

"Well, that's a switch."

Kristi laughed; I had learned she could appreciate a joke at her expense, so long as it was true.

"Come on," she said. "Tell me why you don't play anymore."

And so I did. I told her about how happy I'd been that my leg had healed and that I could still play, how everything had seemed to be going great at practices and during my first game back. Then I told her about getting that stick to the face, the knife cut of pain and the sudden gush of blood that fell like a curtain over my eye—the same eye that had gotten hurt a year earlier.

"I . . . I just chickened out. I didn't know I was such a wuss . . . but I guess I am."

Adding credence to my confession, I started crying, if you can believe that.

It wouldn't have surprised me if Kristi had laughed or made fun of me. In fact, I expected one or the other reaction from her. What I didn't expect was her taking me in her arms and comforting me.

"Oh, Joe, it's all right." Over and over, she whispered, "Shh," and told me it was all right—the same way I'd comforted her when she was mourning her grandmother, the same way people all over the world comfort one another: by promising that whatever it is, it's all right. Maybe that's why those words **are** so comforting, because they don't claim that things are going to be fantastic . . . just all right. And when you're crying, when you feel like shit, "all right" is a pretty good assurance.

"People quit things," she said after I'd stopped blubbering and told her what a loser I felt like. "I quit cheerleading."

"You did?"

"Sure," she said, reaching over to grab her pack of cigarettes off the nightstand. She squinted her eyes as she lit a Marlboro with a Zippo lighter. "It just wasn't fun anymore. I mean, I was never really in it for the rah-rahness; I just liked being in front of a crowd, you know?" She inhaled and watched the smoke waft up to the water-spotted ceiling. "It's nice to be in front of a big college crowd, but man . . . they still had me on the JV squad. Me—**on the JV squad!**"

If a peasant had invited Marie-Antoinette to join him for a glass of wine, the queen of France couldn't have given a more incredulous response than Kristi's, but I was smart enough not to laugh.

She inhaled and then puckered her lips to send her exhale upward, but her aim was off and she blew smoke right into my face.

"Oh, sorry," she said as I waved my hand in front of my nose. "Anyway, I don't know why quitting got such a bad rap. I mean, I quit cheerleading and now I've moved on to something else."

"What?"

Kristi took one more deep drag before stubbing out her cigarette in the black Bakelite ashtray.

"What have I moved on to?"

I nodded.

Clasping her hands, Kristi stretched her arms out in front of her. "Oh, lots of things. I might get into theater—this student-director guy asked me to try out for the one-act festival that's coming up in February—and I've been doing some stuff on our campus radio station."

"What kind of things?"

"Oh, right now I'm just helping out a friend of mine who hosts this program once a week—it's called **The Anti-Disco Hour or Two**—and I help him during the broadcast.

"But you," she said, rolling toward me and pushing her breasts against my chest. "We were talking about you. It really doesn't matter what your reasons were for quitting hockey; the fact is, you did. Now you can either cry about it—"

Seeing as I had just finished, it wasn't the most sensitive thing Kristi could have said, and something must have shown on my face, because she frowned and then came as close to blushing as Kristi Casey could come to blushing.

"Which I guess you just did." She gave me her brilliant all-forgiveness-is-possible smile. "But what I meant was if you quit something—**quit it!** Move on to something new!"

With her pressed up against me, I found it easy to take her advice.

"Okay," I said, as my hand slid up and down some of the most beautiful geography in the world: the slope and curves of a woman lying on her side.

I thought it was an April Fools' joke. I got the call on the second, but I figured Kristi was still getting mileage out of the holiday that gave her license to be a prick.

"Joe," she breathed, as if she'd just run a couple of laps. "Joe, I just wanted you to know that I'm pregnant."

I admit to holding the phone away from my ear and looking at it as if I was some bad comic.

"April Fool," I prompted, and then closed my eyes, willing her to repeat what I'd just said.

"Joe, I'm not kidding. I can't really say if you're the father or not, but I just thought you should know. Not that I'm going to keep it or anything . . . but I just thought you should know."

Leaning back in my chair, I exhaled a great blast of air. "Do you . . . Maybe we should talk about this."

Kristi barked a laugh. "What are we going to talk about, Joe? A marriage proposal? I doubt it. Like I said, I don't even know if you're the father."

"Thanks a lot," I said, my voice soft.

"Hey, it's not like we were going steady or anything. I do have a life here, you know."

"I'm sure you do."

"What's that supposed to mean?"

"It means what I said: I'm sure you do."

"I don't know if I like your tone, Joe."

"I'm sorry, Miss Casey." If she was going to talk to me like I was a kid, I'd answer like one.

"Well, thanks a lot for your concern."

"Kristi, I'm concerned. It's just that I wish—"

But Kristi didn't care what I wished; she'd hung up.

I don't know if I thought it was too proprietary to think of Kristi as a girlfriend—I don't really know what I considered her other than a **really** good time every other week—but this news floored me on all sorts of levels. I immediately called her back, but if she was still home, she chose not to answer. This was in the days when people could choose not to pick up a ringing phone, the days before answering machines, before caller ID, before cell phones . . . the days when you weren't so **reachable,** so **accountable.** I kept dialing her number and the only thing that dampened my growing anger was knowing that if she was home, the ringing and ringing must be really bugging her.

She showed up three weeks later, one rainy sloppy Friday afternoon, banging on my dorm door.

Having opened the door, I had expected to see the RA announcing a fire.

"**Kristi!**"

"I'm out front," she said. "And double-parked. So grab some warm clothes and meet me out there— I've got a cabin for us up north." She wiggled her eyebrows. "It'll be another county we can check off."

Ten minutes later we were on the freeway, on our way up past Duluth to Grand Marais.

"How'd you get into my dorm?"

"How'd I get into your **dorm**?" she said, her face showing that of all the questions I could ask her, this was one of the dumbest. "Some guy was walking in and I walked in with him." She punched the radio buttons until Linda Ronstadt came on.

I nodded. "Whose car is this anyway?"

"My European history professor's. It's his cabin we're staying at too."

I looked around the brand-new Pontiac Firebird. "Is he rich or something?"

"He's a **professor.** But his wife's got money."

"So why . . . why is he letting you use his car and his cabin?"

Kristi laughed. "Because I've been a very, **very** good student."

"Considering everything," I said as a pulse of anger surged through me, "that's a pretty cavalier thing to say."

Kristi's laugh now was more like a guffaw.

"God, you should listen to yourself sometimes, Joe. You talk more like an old lady than any guy I know."

"Yeah, well, you act more like a slut than anyone I know."

I think I was just as shocked as she was—probably more—over my words.

"That's a lousy thing to say," she said, turning on the windshield wipers.

I agreed with her that it **was** a lousy thing to say, but I still stood by the truth of it.

"I mean, I thought you were Mr. Feminist. Jesus Christ, you're the only guy I know who ever took a women's studies class."

"I told you, I took the class because I thought it'd be interesting to be surrounded by girls."

"Yeah, **right,** Mr. Margaret Mead. Except I would have expected you to learn in a women's studies class that **slut** is a sexist word. I mean, where's the male equivalent?"

"You didn't seem to care about the male equivalent when you used to call Sharon Winters a slut."

"Well, she **was** one!"

I was too annoyed to laugh. "Just for my own benefit, define **slut.**"

Sleet splatted against the windshield and Kristi turned the wipers on faster.

"Well, a slut is someone who sleeps with a lot of guys."

"And her doing that and you doing that is different because . . ."

"Because for a slut, it's all about the guy. A slut sleeps with someone because she thinks it's gonna make him like her better."

"Nothing wrong with that," I said.

"Well, do you sleep with girls hoping they'll like **you** better?"

I had two responses, but the first, **You're assuming I have a more active social life than I do,** I didn't say out loud. The second one I did. "I sleep with them because it's fun."

"Exactly," said Kristi. **"Bingo."**

She put in a new Grand Funk Railroad tape, and as nice as it would have been to sit and listen to music, I didn't want it to be her decision. Besides, I wasn't done talking.

"So you had the . . . the . . ."

"Abortion," said Kristi. "Yeah, I did."

"And how do you feel about it?"

"I feel like it's none of your business, that's how I feel about it."

"It is my business," I sputtered, "considering it might have been my baby."

"I'm pretty sure it wasn't," said Kristi. "And I don't want to talk about it anymore."

"Well, I do."

"Go ahead," she said. "It doesn't mean I have to listen." She turned up the volume so the car vibrated under the weight of the bass.

My impulse was to jump out of the car, but that wasn't the most practical idea, considering the rate of speed at which it was traveling. I could have turned down the volume, but I knew Kristi would have turned it up again, so I braced myself against the loud music, against the hate I felt for the driver, and looked out the window at the gray, wet world.

"Oh, bummer!" said Kristi, searching through her knapsack. "I left my stash in my other purse! Have you got anything?"

I indulged in a little pot at school but didn't make an effort to hunt down anything else because I knew Kristi always brought a supply of some upper, downer, psychedelic, or mood alterer.

"One dinky little joint," she said, holding up exactly what she described.

"Well, let's fire it up now," I said. "No time like the present."

I think it was stubbornness that had kept Kristi driving north and stubbornness that kept me from ordering her to turn around and take me back to my dorm. It was a five-hour drive that was spent in mostly sulky silence, but once we had passed Grand Marais, it was obvious Kristi needed a co-navigator to find the cabin. The windshield wipers were moving in frantic arcs trying to part the curtain of unrelenting rain.

"We're looking for a sign that says 'Hoffer's Hideaway,'" I'd said, reading from the directions Kristi had written on a lined piece of paper.

"If they'd use streetlights up here," Kristi had replied, her voice tense, "it might be a little easier to find the goddamned signs."

It was only six o'clock, but the rainstorm had darkened the skies, and since we had turned off Highway 61, we had missed two turnoffs and had spent nearly a half hour backtracking.

Finally, through the rain and darkness, I'd spotted a cockeyed sign nailed to a tree.

"There it is! Take a right, here, Kristi!"

She'd nearly gone into the ditch, taking the turn too wide, and after following a long road so narrow that evergreen branches brushed against the passenger side of the car, we came to the cabin. Both of us were so relieved to have reached our destination alive that all tension and acrimony was washed away by the rain as we raced to the cabin door.

"Aha!" Kristi had announced, peeling back the welcome mat on the lone step and finding a key. "Right where he said it'd be!"

Rain beat on us as she tried to fit the key into the lock, and when the door opened, we plunged through it, soaked to the skin, laughing hysterically.

Kristi had turned on a lamp on a side table by the door, and the contrast between the cozy interior and the wet exterior couldn't have been greater.

"Oh, it's darling!" she'd exclaimed. It was a rustic log cabin softened with frilled curtains on the windows, needlepoint pillows on the log-framed couch, and a table covered with a red gingham cloth. It was at the table we chose to sit, dropping our backpacks on the rag rug beneath it.

"Should I make some coffee?" Kristi had asked. "I'm freezing."

"We should really get out of these wet clothes," I'd said, and even though she could have accused me of talking like an old lady now, she didn't.

Instead, Kristi had wiggled her eyebrows. "Well, I guess we **have** made up."

After we had dressed in the robes hanging on the back of the bathroom door, we gathered at the table again, and it was there Kristi made her fruitless drug search.

The joint we smoked was weak, but our own good moods made it seem stronger and as we raided the cupboards and the old squat refrigerator, we laughed as if were high on the best sinsemilla.

"Is it okay to eat all this?" I asked, eating a second bowl of Cap'n Crunch.

"He said to help ourselves to anything," said Kristi, dipping a knife into a jar of peanut butter. She slathered it on a piece of toast with the care of a master bricklayer. "They hire a lady to come in and stock the kitchen before and after guests."

"Wow," I said, and even though I considered the guy a rival, I had to like him.

It rained through the night and half the next day, and we entertained ourselves by staying in the professor and his wife's very comfortable king-sized log bed. The appearance of the sun was no lure to me at all, but Kristi insisted we get out and take advantage of our surroundings.

"I mean, come on," she said, throwing me a T-shirt. "It's supposed to be beautiful up here."

"It is," I said, gazing at her as she wiggled into her jeans.

We drove a ways up the Gunflint Trail and took a long hike in the woods, the firs a brilliant green from their long shower. Kristi was not one to find the nearest rock and admire the view; I imagine her idea of a hike was very similar to a boot camp sergeant's, and I struggled behind her, silently cursing her speed and lung power.

We didn't get back until dark. Ravenous, we built a fire and roasted wieners and warmed a can of beans. The cabin was on a crest that overlooked Lake Superior, and as we ate we listened to the gentle slap of waves against the rocky shore. There were no marshmallows to roast for dessert ("I'm going to have to talk to my professor about **that**!" joked Kristi), but we found a bag of bridge mix in the cupboard, and as we drank coffee and ate chocolate-covered raisens and peanuts and malted-milk balls, I said, "Now, this is the life."

"How many times do you think people say that in front of a campfire?"

I stared up at the hazy night sky. "Billions. Maybe trillions."

"This is so nice," said Kristi, licking chocolate off her fingers before she snuggled up next to me, pulling the blanket up over our laps.

"It is," I agreed.

We leaned against the backrest fashioned out of wide splayed planks that faced the fire pit (other than the marshmallows, what **hadn't** the professor thought of?), and another cliché came to mind: **It doesn't get any better than this.** But it did.

I was staring at the shifting reds and oranges of the fire when Kristi gasped as if she had gotten stung by a nocturnal wasp.

She wasn't rubbing a swelling bite, but instead was staring up at the sky. I looked up and gasped myself.

"Oh!" cried Kristi. "Look at that!"

The sky was alive with a white light. Its western pulse was answered by one in the east, and then light jumped from all directions.

We reclined against our makeshift chairs, yelping with delight as a green light and then a pink one zigzagged across the white.

"It's the northern lights!" said Kristi. "I've wanted to see the northern lights all my life!"

"I saw them once as a kid," I said. "I was scared— I thought aliens were coming."

"I can see why you'd think that," said Kristi, her voice soft. "It's so . . . unearthly."

Like spectators watching fireworks, we expressed our delight by cries of "Wow!" or "Ooh!" but unlike fireworks, this display wasn't over in ten minutes. Just when it seemed the show was fading, another section of the sky would throb with a light that would ignite another pulse, a streak of purple, of green.

It was spectacular and humbling at the same time—there was nothing on TV, no movie, no Fourth of July extravaganza that could compete with the show in the skies above us.

"I feel like we're on top of the world," whispered Kristi. "On top of the world watching the sky explode."

"But in a good way," I added.

"You're right," said Kristi as a flame of pink licked across the white pulsations. "**Explode** is too . . . violent a word, and this sky means no violence—just wonder."

I had to kiss her after saying something like that, but it wasn't a lingering kiss; neither one of us wanted to miss what was happening in the sky.

Putting a hand on my knee, Kristi boosted herself to her feet and held her arms up to the sky. I joined her; it seemed an appropriate way to thank the sky.

"Here we are," said Kristi, "at . . ."

I filled in her pause. "At Hoffer's Hideaway."

Kristi laughed, her arms still outstretched. "No, we're somewhere else, Joe. Some magical place where the sky dances."

Okay, now she was getting poetic. I couldn't offer another pedestrian "wow" or "ooh"—if she wanted me to tell her where we were, I'd tell her.

"Here we are," I began, speaking slowly to give the wheels in my head time to turn, "on a hillside—"

"Not a hillside, Joe—a hillside is too small for where we're at."

Kristi was spinning around as if in slow motion, her arms still extended, and I turned around at the same rate, taking in the lavender flush the sky had added to its repertoire.

"Here we are," I began again, "on a mountaintop, on . . ."

The lavender deepened into purple and skipped like a rock on a river across the sky. We both yelped our approval, and I looked at Kristi. In her beaming face, I found my inspiration.

"Here we are," I said, "on beautiful, wondrous Mount Joy—"

"Yes!" shouted Kristi. "Yes—here we are on Mount Joy!"

"Mount Joy, where the skies dance—"

"And the humans do the funky chicken!"

We flapped our arms and hopped around in a circle, like crazed hillbillies. Then our dance was stopped by a great light pulsation that filled the sky like a fireworks finale, pounding, pounding in its whiteness, and if noise had accompanied the lights in the sky, it would be the thundering noise of Kristi playing the bass drum.

"Oh God!" she said, and it sounded more like an address than an exclamation.

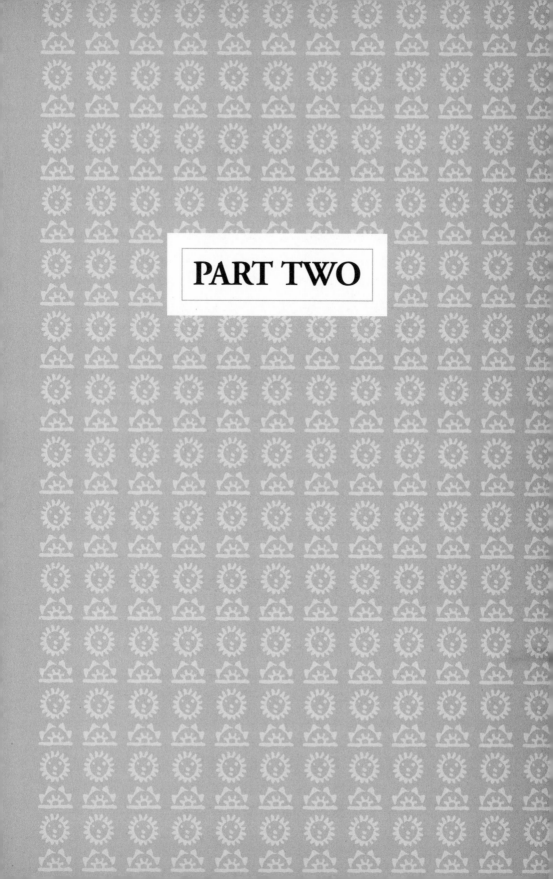

PART TWO

Thirteen

"I've stocked the freezer—that mint chip ice cream is really selling, by the way—so can I go now?"

I nodded. "Thanks, Birk. See you tomorrow."

After the teenager left, I sat in my swivel chair, rocking from side to side. Most of the tears that ran down my face were for Ed, but some were for me.

We had buried him yesterday. I say **we** because Ed's grocery store staff was more his family than Marian, the weathered platinum blonde who flew in from Del Mar, California, seemingly more aggrieved over missing a golf tournament than Ed.

"Our foursome came in second last year, thanks to my bogey on the seventeenth hole," she said in a deep smoker's voice. "Believe me, they were **not** happy to lose me this year."

"We weren't happy to lose Ed this year either," said Kirk from the backseat.

"Well, I don't mean . . . what I meant . . . ," stammered Marian.

I was glad Kirk had offered to come with me to the airport to pick up Ed's sister and glad he had called her on her stupid comment. I watched the road ahead of me but peripherally was aware of Marian wadding up a hanky and then smoothing it out on the surface of her purse.

"I . . . I know I could have been a better sister," she said, and I looked in the rearview mirror to see Kirk roll his eyes. "It's just that . . . well, I'm ten years older than Eddie and I've lived in California since I graduated from college and—" She crumpled her hanky up again. "And that was a long time ago!"

She dabbed at her eyes—the hanky finally serving its intended purpose—and the thought crossed my mind that she was mourning time's march more than her brother.

I had never set out to be more than an employee/friend/jamming partner to Ed Haugland, but his illness and resulting reliance on me had forged a deeper relationship—so deep that one day as I was wheeling him through the aisles of the store he said, in a voice barely a whisper, "You've been like a son to me, Joe."

I gripped the wheelchair handles, feeling my knees go a little weak. His aide brought him to the store two or three times a week, and Ed liked to tour his former domain aisle by aisle. He usually saved his commentary to harp about a particular product placement or sales display.

I didn't mind his criticism; I knew how much it meant to him to feel like he was still the boss of something.

"That's the worst part," he said when he'd made the sad transfer from walker to wheelchair, "when your own body gives up on you."

For a while his remissions would make us not so much hopeful as blithe; when he was healthy we assumed he'd stay that way, and we'd forget all about how he'd fallen in the cooler and practically frozen before a bag boy found him, or how his hands would grow so numb he couldn't hold on to a guitar pick, let alone groceries. (How many times had I mopped up a bottle of milk or a carton of eggs that had fallen out of his grasp, as if his fingers were oiled?)

After Kirk left for school, our jam sessions continued, our schedule set increasingly by his ability to play. As the months passed into years, the disease became the norm and the remissions the exception.

"It's the second time I've given up my music," said Ed when he became so weakened he couldn't even open the clasps on his guitar case. "This time hurts even more."

I was able to witness firsthand his slow demise because at age twenty-eight, instead of scoring goals for the North Stars or filing war reports from the Falklands, I was still working at Haugland Foods. Hell, not just working, I was the manager and now, upon Ed's death, I was not just the manager but the fucking owner.

"I'm leaving you the store," whispered Ed several weeks before he went into the hospital for the last time.

"What?" I said, my scalp prickling with heat.

"You heard me," said Ed, which was presumption

on his part because he talked so softly now most people had to ask him to repeat what he said.

The thing is, I had heard him; with regard to Ed, it was as if my ears had been fine-tuned to understand his barest whisper.

"Ed," I said, kneeling down so I could be eye level with him. "Ed, please. I do not need the store."

"Well," he said, closing his eyes as he made a face, "I need to give it to you."

"Ed—"

"Remember when I told you you were like a son to me? I wasn't exactly lying—I mean, more than anything I considered you a friend, even my best friend—but there wasn't a word for 'friend who feels like family,' so that's why I said son, even though I would have only been about fourteen when you were born."

"Eighteen," I said. "You're like an old movie star—always trying to pass yourself off as younger than you are."

Ed smiled weakly. He'd once said that one of the downers of getting sick was that no one dared joke around with him—"especially at my expense." Then he closed his eyes briefly, as if the smile had tired him.

"I've seen a lawyer and had all the papers taken care of."

"But I don't want a grocery store!" I said.

"Neither did I. But I got one. Trouble is, I kept it. But you, you can sell it. It'll give you a nice nest egg—a couple of nest eggs." He tried to smile again, but it turned into a wince. Pain was now a relentless predator with a ravenous appetite.

"I'm giving a couple of my favorite employees some money," he continued, "and Kirk a couple of grand to help him with his boat. But other than that, everything'll be yours."

"This stinks, Ed," I said, patting his leg. "You should be touring the Midwest in some bar band and I should—"

"Bar band? I should be jamming with Eric Clapton and Jimmy Page." Ed shook his head, or tried to, but it seemed too big a job for his neck muscles. "But life rarely makes the same plans you do."

"Aw, send it to **Reader's Digest**. They pay big money for quotes like that."

"You'd never forgive me if I published before you did."

"Ha-ha. You're so pitiful I forget how funny you are."

All his muscles worked hard to produce a smile that was one of pure enjoyment.

"I've got a good reason to be pitiful," he said. "What's yours?"

It was Saturday night and I'd wager there were millions of guys my age dancing at clubs, picking up girls, driving fast cars. How many twenty-eight-year-olds were wearing a white apron, sitting in the office that overlooked a dark grocery store, crying for his friends and other things he'd lost?

What had happened to me? The dreams that I'd had as a kid were as dead and brittle as a houseplant left outside in the middle of January. The guy I was now was not the guy I'd thought I would be when I made my first goal for the Gophers, when my first story for the university paper had been published. The map I had thought I'd follow—the one showing me on a fast-track career as a bold reporter or a professional hockey player—had long ago been crumpled up and tossed aside, in recognition of its fantasy destinations. Other people were capable of big plans, grand gestures, surprises, but not me.

Kirk had graduated with a degree in oceanography and lived in Florida, working with an exploratory team that was doing something with mollusks in the Caribbean. He was the tan pallbearer who was approached by all the girls at Ed's funeral reception.

Greg Hoppe lived in California and covered the state capitol for the **Sacramento Bee.** I asked him to send me his clippings, which I read with a mixture of envy (70 percent) and pride (30 percent).

Shannon Saxon was pregnant with her second child. She and her husband, a chiropractor from Dubuque, came into the store every now and then, and there was something about her husband and the proprietary way he held the small of her back (as if showing off both his wife **and** his profession) that pissed me off, so much so that once, as they inspected fruit in the produce section, I scolded him to not squeeze the melons. Shannon's face reddened, but the chiropractor thought I was riffing on the popular commercial and said, "Or the Charmin either."

Darva was in Paris, finishing an art degree ("For every year at school, I take one off to paint," she wrote me). And Kristi—I didn't exactly know what Kristi was up to, but based on a postcard I'd gotten a year ago from Mexico City (the only words I could decipher were "far out," "easy," and "honest woman")

I didn't need a codebreaker to figure out she was having a good time.

My own mother was living a life of adventure ten times more exciting than her son's. She and Len, after having visited my uncle Roger in Sweden (he had settled down, marrying a potter whose work, he said, was much admired by the royal family), were inspired to take a yearlong sabbatical and were now traveling through Europe.

"Even you and Linda," I complained when I was invited to my aunt's for dinner, "are living the wild lesbian life."

"And a wild life 'tis," said Beth in a serviceable Irish accent. "Divvying up chores, arguing about who didn't fill the gas tank—"

"And who forgot to plug in the Crock-Pot," said Linda.

"That's why we're having take-out," said Beth, passing me a carton of moo goo gai pan. "Plus both of us are working way too much. Did I tell you that Linda got a commission to design Ray Pryor's house?"

"Really?" I asked, willing to be distracted by some gossip about the Vikings quarterback. "What's he like?"

Linda shrugged. "I think he may have gotten tackled one too many times. He can't comprehend the specs, no matter how many times we go over them." She nodded toward the carton of ginger chicken and I passed it to her. "But really, Joe, your time will come."

"I have no doubt," said Beth, "that you'll do something amazing with your life."

"Yeah, right," I snorted. "Maybe I'll honor expired coupons."

Like a referee, the teakettle whistled, and for a while we respected the time-out, choosing our tea from the tins Beth kept (bagged tea was not allowed in her kitchen), filling our individual strainers with it, and then stirring in milk or sugar.

"To Ed," said Beth, holding up her teacup in a toast. She cringed as I clanked the bone china cups a little too forcefully. "Joe," she scolded, "these aren't beer steins."

"And how about his sister?" said Linda. "What a piece of work. Did you see her light up at the gravesite?"

"Well, at least she came to the funeral," I said. "Ed told me he wouldn't be surprised if she didn't."

That knocked over the fragile dam, and emotion flooded over. Suddenly I was crying, covering my eyes with the oblong napkin that read, "Lee's Chow Mein—Good 'n' Tasty."

With my paper blindfold, I couldn't see them, but I felt my aunt Beth on one side of me and Linda on the other, hugging and patting me. The tears I had cried the night before in the store's office were just the overture when compared to the full orchestral movement that was unleashed now, and when I was done, the napkin I had originally cried into had been replaced by two others.

"Why don't you spend the night, Joe?" asked Beth when the waterworks had been finally turned off. "You shouldn't be alone."

It was a fancy "guest suite" now, my old room, and even though it was sparkling clean, there was a sense of mustiness, as if all the dreams and plans I had made in it had turned to dust that hung invisible in the air and unseen under the bed.

Although the human reproductive system is about the only part of high school biology that truly engaged me (I loved the pictures), I do seem to remember that a person's cells regenerate every seven years. It sounds like a big deal—like a person would get a whole new lease on life—but in my limited experience, I can't say that turning seven felt a whole lot different from eight, or fourteen from fifteen or sixteen. Eighteen was a big deal, of course, because I was officially an adult, but I didn't feel more renewed at twenty-eight than I had in the years preceding. In truth, with Ed's death and my failure to launch the life I thought I was supposed to live, twenty-eight was stacking up to be a pretty depressing year. But suddenly the dead-end street I thought I was on changed into an expressway with all kinds of interesting on and off ramps, and all I could do was hang on for the ride. And man oh man, a lot more than my cells were regenerated.

"**Excusez-moi,** I would please like to know where are the **haricots verts.**"

"The what?" I said, turning around. A second later, I was knocked back a step, upending the little pyramid of grapefruit I had been arranging.

"Darva!" I said, my surprise pushed aside by astonishment. "And . . . ?"

"Flora," said Darva, tilting her head to look at the baby lashed to her chest in a patterned scarf.

"Flora," I repeated.

Darva laughed. "You sound a little . . . taken aback."

"I think I am. Is she yours?"

Darva cradled the baby in her arms. "My one and only."

"Do you have time for some coffee?"

"I've got time for anything with you, Joe."

Trying to translate the meaning of that, I led her to my office.

If I wasn't prepared for Darva to show up at Haugland Foods on a chilly fall day, I sure wasn't prepared for Darva to show up with a **baby,** and I **really** wasn't prepared for her lifting her breast out of her gauzy shirt and declaring, "**Déjeuner,** Flora!"

She got a big charge out of my discomfort, laughing so much that the baby was jiggled and peered up at her mother with a look that said, **Ma, cool it—I'm trying to eat lunch here!**

"Joe, I'm sorry," she said, and her apology made me redden even more. "It's just that . . . Well, you looked so startled."

"I am startled," I said. "And not just by your breast." I made a swooping gesture with my hand. "By all of you."

"I know. It was kind of mean of me, I guess. I should have warned you I was coming, and should have warned you I was coming with Flora."

"When . . . when did this happen? When did you get back?"

Those were only two of the questions I fired at her, and Darva answered every one and more.

"I know I hadn't written you lately," she said as the

baby nursed. She had covered herself with a cloth from her diaper bag so I didn't have to concentrate so hard on not looking at her breast. "But I had a lot going on."

I thought it redundant to say "obviously," so I busied myself at the coffeemaker.

"I was so swamped last year. I had this project going—it's basically an arborist explaining his love affair with trees, of all things, and not only did I illustrate the whole thing, I translated it! So when this opportunity for a holiday in Spain opened up, I jumped at it. It was going to be a long weekend of fun in the sun, and it was. But the fun included too much sangria and a very attentive Portuguese man and, well . . ." She looked down at the baby and smiled. "Well, that's how Flora got here."

The coffee machine clunked and made a hissing noise.

"Is the . . . is the father here too?"

"Oh, God, no. I hardly knew him. Don't even know his last name, although I do remember his first: Raoul."

"So your baby doesn't have a father?"

Darva's look held surprise and hurt.

"I'm sorry," I said, ashamed. "I didn't mean for that to sound so harsh. I just meant . . ." I shrugged helplessly.

"I know," she said, lifting the baby onto her shoulder and patting her back. "It's a lot to throw at you out of the blue."

The baby burped with more robustness than I would have thought her capable of, and Darva laughed, praising her.

"Is that coffee ready?" she asked.

"Just about."

"Well, then, here," she said, standing up. "You hold Flora and I'll get the coffee."

Before I had time to protest, the baby was passed off to me in a move as smooth as a quarterback makes with a running back, but this was no football, and I sat down gingerly in my office chair, scared of fumbling.

The baby gazed up at me with curiosity. Her eyes were brown and shiny, fringed with black lashes that matched the black curls on her head.

"She's so **pretty**," I said.

"Thanks," said Darva, tenderness making her word almost a plea. She set two cups of coffee on my desk.

"I drink it black." I nodded toward the window that overlooked the store. "But I've got cream and sugar. And cookies if you'd like, or donuts—we just put in a bakery section—or—"

"I'm good," said Darva, and looking at her, I could only agree.

She was still tall and thin, still sharp-featured, although there was a softness to her face and manner that I attributed to motherhood. From her ears dangled the elaborate, many-tiered earrings she liked to wear, and at least seven fingers were decorated with rings. But her long, straight hair was gone now, cut so short it looked like a black cap.

She sat in the chair on the other side of my desk, holding the coffee cup near her face, but not drinking from it.

"It is so good to see you, Joe," she said. "You're more handsome than ever."

"Your mother flatters me," I whispered to the baby, whose eyes were getting heavy. "Learn from her."

"Oh yes, that's big on my list of what to teach my daughter: how to use your feminine wiles to entrap and control men."

We sat there quietly, me using my office chair for a purpose it had never before been used for—to rock a baby to sleep—and Darva drinking her coffee and watching us.

"How old is she?" I whispered, sort of floored by how nice a baby in my arms felt.

"She'll be seven months tomorrow," said Darva and as her eyes welled up, she used the pads of her fingers as tear blotters. "Sorry."

As much as I enjoyed the weight of the baby in my arms, I realized then the real weight.

"It's hard, huh?"

Darva looked at me for a moment and then laughed. "Oh, Joe, not hard. Wonderful's more like it. I'm just . . . blown away by her."

The baby slept for two hours, and I would have held her the whole time, but when my assistant manager couldn't answer a question my meat supplier had, I had to surrender Flora to her mother for a few minutes to attend to business.

"Can I hold her again when I get back?" I asked.

"If you bring me back one of those donuts you were talking about."

I brought her back a chocolate donut and a glazed cruller, and she handed me the baby again, which I thought was more than a fair trade.

The afternoon was like a hot bath, one I settled back in and said, "Ahhh." It had been ten years since

I shared a lunch or art table with Darva, yet it seemed only last week that I'd traded her my apple for her chocolate milk or asked if the nose I was drawing was shaded right. I was so comfortable, so relieved to be in the company of such a good old friend.

"So how long are you staying?" I asked, and her answer heartened me more than I could say.

"I don't know. I gave up my apartment in Paris—that is, I told my roommates they could rent out my room if they wanted to. I don't know; I just thought I'd see how it goes here for a while."

"Here in Minneapolis?"

Darva shrugged. "My family's not doing too well—I'd like them to get to know Flora while they can."

In high school, Darva had described herself as a "P.S. in the letter of my parents' marriage," telling me that her mother had been forty-seven when she was born, her dad twelve years older. She had one brother twenty-three years older than her and a sister twenty years her senior. "The beauty part is that my parents are pretty tired and sort of let me do what I want."

Now she told me her father was in a nursing home and when she went to see him, he thought Flora was Darva and Darva was his wife.

"And my poor mom's so arthritic it actually hurts her to hold the baby," said Darva, and for the second time she wiped tears from her eyes. "On top of that, my sister-in-law is dying of cancer and my nephew has got a drug habit that put him in his third treatment facility."

"Wow," I said. "If I were you, I think I'd go back to France."

"I'd love to," said Darva. "God, not only did I love living there—I mean, it's **France!**—but family duty's pretty easy when it's confined to writing letters and making a monthly phone call."

The baby stirred, and finally I relinquished her to Darva's outstretched arms.

"But now," she said, her voice wistful, "now it's time to dig in and get my hands dirty. Right, Flora?"

The baby's eyes were open now, and looking up at her mother, she smiled. I did the same.

Fourteen

Hey, Buddy,

Check out the attached. I almost wish I could have seen it with my own eyes, but Florida's a big state, and fortunately I was down in Cocoa Beach while she was way up north. Good God—does she have to go by her real name? My old roommate lives up there and sent me the article. (Geez, I've got a lot of friends in this state—how many others are gonna make the connection that I'm related to her?) I'm choosing to find the whole thing funny, or else I'd be projectile vomiting, and since I'm going on a dive this weekend, that'd clog up my scuba mask. . . .

Other than my frickin' sister saving souls, things have been going well. Nance is a little bit nuts with all this wedding preparation crap, which I go out of my way to ignore. I mean, what answer can she possibly expect when she asks me stuff like, "Should we have the off-white chair covers at the reception or the eggshell?"

I'm glad you're coming down. It'll be great seeing you at a frickin' wedding (even if it's my own—ha!) instead of a funeral.

Nance is tapping her watch and giving me the fish eye—I gotta go get my tux fitted. Man, am I psyched! . . . Not.

Anyway, take some Pepto-Bismol before you read the article—believe me, you'll need it.

Kirk

The letter had been attached to a news clipping, and I unfolded it with a mixture of curiosity and what I could only describe as trepidation.

FROM THE Ft. Frederick Chronicle, MAY 20, 1983:

CAN I GET A WITNESS?

By T. M. Tomaczek

Hands were clapping and tambourines were shaking as Rev. George Darrel returned to his hometown, kicking off the beginning of his Hallelujah Revival traveling road show. A crowd of more than three hundred people gathered yesterday in the hot and dusty fairgrounds, cooling themselves with the complimentary fans ("Rev. George Luvs U!") that were passed out by two beaming young girls in puff-sleeved dresses.

The Rev. George Gospel Choir sang "Jesus Loves Me" and "Sweet Hour of Prayer," there were several testimonials, and Rev. George and his son, Ernie, both preached in fiery manners. In other words, the usual we've seen from the reverend, that is, until the audience was jolted in their seats by the loud bangs of a bass drum, a bass drum strapped to a comely young woman by the name of Kristi Casey, who proceeded to do a little preaching of her own.

Rev. George, in a homage to his hometown, claims Fort Frederick is known as "the town that God has smiled on," and certainly God was smiling all the brighter with the addition of the young woman who brought the crowd to its feet with her words of redemption and excellent rhythm.

This reporter spoke all too briefly with Miss Casey after the revival.

"I wasn't always on a righteous path," she remarked as chairs were being folded up and programs picked off the ground. "But until we've found the Lord, we really never are, are we?"

Queries as to her background were met with the simple phrase, "I'm here now, with God."

The Hallelujah Revival begins its five-state tour starting tomorrow, and with its new addition, the Lord has blessed it.

"Jesus Christ," I muttered after I read it. I wasn't trying to be funny, not even when the next words to fall out of my mouth were "Holy shit." I put the letter and article on top of the rest of the mail, so Darva would see it as soon as she got home.

"Oh, it's **beautiful**," said Nance as her eyes teared up.

"Wow," said Kirk, "I'm blown away. And what does it say down there?"

"Rapturia," Darva said.

"She says she wanted a name that described how you feel together," I put in.

"Oh my God," said Nance, and a tear spilled down her cheek as she looked at the artwork. "It's the best wedding present—no, the best **present** ever. Thank you so much."

The bridal couple had picked us up at the airport and, seeing the flat wrapped package, begged to open it early.

"You won't even be here when I open gifts at my parents'," Nance had said.

"Lucky," Kirk had muttered in an aside.

Darva had shrugged at me. "It's okay with me."

"Me too," I'd said. "How about you come up to our hotel room and you can open it there?"

After the present opening, the four of us hit it off so well that after the rehearsal dinner, Kirk and his bride-to-be continued the party with Darva and me. We were into our second pitcher of margaritas, and if there had been pain to feel, we weren't feeling it.

"So let me get this straight," said Kirk. "You guys are living together but you're not **together?**"

"Well, I couldn't resist his offer," said Darva. "He let me set up a studio in his attic—it's got great southern light."

"You should see the stuff she's doing," I said. "It's phenomenal."

"Thank you," said Darva, and blowing a kiss at me, she added, "You inspire me." She raised an eyebrow. "Anyone who changes diapers inspires me."

"The baby's," I said. "Just in case there's any confusion."

Darva pressed a finger against the rim of her glass and then sucked the salt off. "We love each other, but we don't **love** each other."

"I hate it when she talks like that," I said. Pretending to cry, I buried my head in my arms.

"So do you really wish it was something more?" asked Nance, putting her hand on my back.

"Yeah," said Kirk, "do you? Or is it just that Darva won't have you? And if that's the case," he said, raising his glass to Darva, "I commend you for your good taste."

"Speaking of good taste," I said, sitting up and looking pointedly at Nance, "did you abandon **all** of yours in the name of love?"

"Yup," said Nance as she tucked a strand of Kirk's bleached hair behind his ear. "There's not an ounce of good taste between us."

Kirk growled. "Now you're talking, honeybunch."

The couple, twelve hours away from legal matrimony, leaned toward each other and kissed. Darva and I, on the other hand, helped ourselves to more margaritas.

I thought Darva was beautiful, in her angular, pointy-featured way, and I appreciated her brain and her humor and her heart, but our relationship had never made that leap from the solid ground of friendship to the spongier marsh of love. At least that's how Darva explained it now.

"Spongier marsh!" said Nance. "Is that what we're jumping into?"

"Well, it **is** Florida," reminded Kirk. "Probably lots of alligators in there too."

Laughing, Darva shook her head, and her earrings

jangled in accompaniment. "That's just my point. When you fall in love, **because** you're in love, you're willing to sidestep the alligators, or sink in the muck a bit. Joe and I are best friends, but we don't have that passion shield that protects us from all the other stuff."

"Now, I'd think passion is less a shield than . . ." I thought for a moment. "Than a saber."

"Shield or saber," said Darva, "we don't have it."

I shrugged. "She's right. Whereas you guys"—I doled out the remaining contents of the margarita pitcher into our glasses—"are both shielded and sabered."

"I'll drink to that," said Kirk, raising his glass. "To shields and sabers."

"My **hero,**" said Nance, clinking his glass.

"**My** hero," said Darva, clinking my glass.

"Who's totally unarmed," I answered, clinking hers.

It was a beautiful wedding, although the sun shone a little too brightly for someone whose liver was pickling in tequila. France had added an elegance to Darva's style, so she looked now as if she was a cover girl for **French Hippie Gypsy** magazine. And the bride and groom—well, I have yet to see the bride and groom who've looked hung over at their wedding ceremony. Must be the excitement burns all traces of alcohol right out of them. Even behind my sunglasses, I could see Kirk and Nance were giving the sun a run for its money as far as dazzlement goes. They were both working on their master's degrees in marine biology and had been part of a research team studying manatees, which not only sounded cool but also bleached their hair the same sun-streaked way and gave them killer tans. Grocery store lighting doesn't do the same thing to a body.

Nance's family had a lot of money, which explained why the yacht the ceremony took place on belonged to Nance's father and why the reception was at the yacht club, whose Admirals' Hallway featured a picture of the selfsame father and the dates of his service as club president. (Twice—1958–59 and 1969–1970.)

Wealth hung in the air like a cologne sold at a counter I'd never get service at. Waiters did slow rumbas through the room, offering from their trays bites of seafood and flutes of champagne; diamonds weighted the fingers and scalloped the necks of blond thin women of a certain age whose husbands whose preferred ascots over ties; and a jazz trio I had actually seen on the **Tonight Show** played in the background.

The people representing Kirk's side of the guest list—mostly college and work friends—were without exception diamondless, at least honking-big-diamondless. One woman wore a wedding band with a stone that might have been a diamond, but it was so small I could hardly tell, and it was at this woman's table Darva and I found our place cards.

"Hey, Mrs. Casey," I said, sitting next to her, "pretty fancy party, huh?"

"I'd say **fancy**'s the word for it," said the bridegroom's mother after she'd exhaled a long plume of smoke. "Christ, how much do you think this whole shebang is setting them back?"

"Probably the gross national product of some small

country," said Darva, touching a petal of the orchid centerpiece.

"Like Trinidad or Tobago," I said, reaching for the little box wrapped in silver paper on my plate. "Come on, guys," I said, "what are you waiting for? Let's open 'em up."

The boxes held silver picture frames engraved with the names of the wedding couple and the date.

I whistled. "Make that Austria or Belgium."

Mrs. Casey smiled and turned to Darva. "So how are you doing? Have you talked to Flora yet?"

"Oh, just once . . . today."

"Our long-distance bill is going to be—" I held up the picture frame. "Well, at least as expensive as this."

"It's tough being away from your kids for the first time," said Mrs. Casey. "I remember when Jack and I went up north to go fishing and we left the kids with my mother. It was a piece of cake for Kristi— hell, she'd been having sleepovers with my mother since she was a baby. But Kirk—we could still hear Kirk wailing not only when we got into the car but as we drove down the block."

"She seems to be doing fine," said Darva with a little catch in her throat. "Of course, she **loves** Joe's mom. Carole's like a grandmother to her."

Another couple—of the diamond-drenched, ascotted variety—sat down, their tanned faces trying to hide their disappointment over having been exiled to our table. Introductions were made, and the fake smiles they wore blossomed into real ones when a couple of their kind joined us.

Fancy salads made with a dark lettuce that I, as a

grocer, couldn't identify were served, and I was suddenly lonesome for Flora, who had declared all green
food "yucky." She was a whirling dervish of a two-
year-old for whom I was "Horsey" (while giving her
a piggyback ride), "Monsto Man" (when I chased her
around like Frankenstein), and simply "**mon** Joe,"
when she wanted me to read to her, to play dollies
with her, or to drink imaginary tea with her.

I snuck a look at Mrs. Casey, who was eating her
salad with great care and occasionally checking,
with her pinkie, the corner of her mouth to see if
any bits of the dark and mysterious lettuce had
landed there. Mr. Casey had died a couple of years
ago, and the day after his funeral, according to Kirk,
she'd joined AA. Kirk had asked me to check on her
once, and that visit led to the occasional ones in
which I'd bring along Darva and Flora. She wasn't
hard to visit—she had a wicked sense of humor and
made good coffee—but she was lonely as hell and
seemed to think a two-year-old tearing through her
house was sort of a gift.

"I don't suppose Kristi's going to show up," I said
as our salad plates were being taken away.

Mrs. Casey looked like she was just about ready to
choke, but instead of a piece of lettuce, a laugh escaped from her.

"No, I don't think so," she said. Leaning toward
me, she whispered, "You heard how she's turned into
some kind of religious nut, haven't you?"

I nodded. "Kirk sent me the newspaper clipping."

She shook her head and laughed again, which caused
a little frisson of laughter between the three of us.

"Something funny?" asked one of the tan diamond ladies.

"Oh," said Mrs. Casey, "you have no idea."

What had happened? Kirk had no idea; distance and a general antipathy had done his relationship with his sister no favors.

"I thought we might, you know, get closer once we got older," he had told me. "But it didn't happen. She just wasn't interested."

I'd seen her a couple of times after that weekend northern lights extravaganza, but it seemed as if our relationship, or whatever it was, had peaked, and she didn't come back to Minneapolis after she graduated. In fact, I don't know where she went; the random phone calls and postcards had virtually stopped.

She did come home for her dad's funeral but left immediately afterward.

"I think she's avoiding me," I'd told Kirk.

"She's avoiding everybody," Kirk had said bitterly. "You'd think she'd stick around for a day or two—I mean, our dad did just **die.** But no, she's got more important things to do."

What those more important things were, she wasn't telling. Mrs. Casey told me every now and then that Kristi called her, but never offered many details.

"Honestly, I'd love to tell you, Joe, but I can't tell what I don't know. It's like she checks in to make sure I'm still breathing, and then says she's gotta run. The last phone call I got, she was in California."

"What part of California? What's she doing for work?"

"I don't know, and all she said was that she was temping."

As much fun as I'd had with Kristi, her absence in my life wasn't an aching one. She was sort of like a carnival—a lot of fun, but if I spent every day with her, I'd be exhausted. And probably have a stomachache.

As I watched Nance waltz with her father and Kirk dance with Mrs. Casey, I felt sorry for Kristi, who couldn't be bothered to quit drumming for Christ or whatever it was she was doing now to come to her only brother's wedding.

The big surprise in my life, besides getting Darva and Flora as roommates, was that I was warming up to my life as a grocer. It was like being mayor of a little town—a little town of food—and my goal was to keep everything running smoothly while pleasing my customers, who complained just like constituents. But they didn't just complain, they confided—man, they told me things that turned my ears red, and all during conversations that had started with a question about the best roast to serve their mother-in-law or whether there was a toilet bowl cleaner that **really** worked.

It was the tameness I had been so afraid of, the way the words "I run a grocery store" fell like lead weights when asked by women I met in bars what I did for a living. Not that I hung out in bars much; before Darva I went out once in a while with friends from high school or the U, but I seemed so busy with the store, with Ed in those last weeks, and with the house I had just bought (a mile from my mother, six blocks from my aunt, and three blocks from the store—man, I was knotted in apron strings from all directions), and after Darva and Flora moved in, my search for **the one** seemed propelled by an idling engine rather than one turbo-charged. I had had a couple girlfriends over the years, but our relationships always seemed to have the heft of a feather pillow and never became more, as my mother said, than passing fancies. Since Kelly the weirdo, I hadn't dated anyone who wanted to reenact a movie with me, although I'd had to break up with Marcia, a dental hygienist, when she flossed her teeth one too many times in front of me ("Don't come crying to me," she said when I gave her the it's-time-to-see-other-people speech, "when you're wearing dentures and I've still got all my beautiful **clean** teeth"), and Rhonda was as needy as a rescued dog, only you couldn't wrestle or play fetch with her. Sandy, who had scored a perfect mark on her math SATs and was a member of Mensa, liked to remind me of both, and dropped me after we played our third chess game.

"Hey, just because I beat you doesn't mean I cheat," I said. "Maybe you're not as smart as you tell me you are."

I was resigned. I still thought the perfect woman was waiting for me somewhere; I just hoped she wouldn't give up waiting, because I sure was having a hard time finding her.

I wasn't like Charlie Olsen, who claimed he only dated women willing to have sex at least three times a day. "And even if they meet my quota, sometimes

I go hunting for a little recreational pussy on the side." I'd see Charlie in the store with his bossy girl-friend ("Not that pizza, Charlie, the one we've got the double coupon for!") and I couldn't quite see her agreeing to his quota, let alone meeting it. Phil Lamereau, another guy I'd played hockey with in high school, came in one day asking if we had a pharmacy in the store. When I told him no, he swore.

"Damn, I need this prescription filled," he said, waving around a slip of paper. "I've got the clap again—for the second time." He wiggled his eyebrows. "Don't tell my wife."

Even Leonard Doerr, who had stopped in the store at Christmas, was getting a lot of action.

"This is my wife, Helga," he said, introducing me to the tall, attractive woman at his side. "We've been living in Munich for three years—this is her first visit to America."

"Well, I hope you're enjoying yourself," I said.

"Vell, ve're schleeping in Leonard's childhoot bet," she said, leaning on Leonard's arm. "It's been a bet zat's wery hard to leave."

I don't know who blushed more, me or Leonard. Then, as they pushed their cart past the butcher case, he turned and mouthed the words: "She's an animal!"

Darva got a big laugh out of that one.

"Good old Leonard Doerr," she said, helping herself to a cup of coffee.

"You should have seen his wife," I said. "She was hanging all over him, and you could tell she was just waiting to get him back in 'zat childhoot bet.'"

We were both looking out the office window to the store below, where Flora was being entertained up front by one of my cashiers. Darva walked her to the store nearly every afternoon, and Flora had become a favorite of my staff, who took turns pushing her around in a cart ("It's cheaper than Disneyland," Darva said) and playing with her.

"I love surprises like that. When the guy whose nickname was 'Class Nerd' turns into an international playboy—"

"Well," I interrupted, "I wouldn't go that far."

Darva laughed. "You sound jealous."

"Maybe. His Frau **was** good-looking." I shook my head. "What's happening to the world when a guy like me can be jealous of a guy like Leonard Doerr?"

"I'd think lots of people might be jealous of Leonard," said Darva with a little sniff. "He's living his dream."

"You're right," I said, thinking of Leonard back in homeroom making his German-club announcements.

"Hey, it must be Ole Bull reunion day," said Darva. "Look who just came in."

Shannon Saxon was folding one crying kid into the front of a grocery cart while trying to prevent another from breaking free of her grasp and tearing off through the aisles.

"Did you know her husband's having an affair with his receptionist?" said Darva.

I would have done a spit take had I had coffee in my mouth.

"Where'd you hear that?"

"From Shannon. In the park yesterday. I told you I see her there every now and then. Flora and Joshua play together."

A question flickered briefly in my head: **How do the receptionist's breasts stack up next to Shannon's?**

"**Il est un cochon,**" said Darva.

Startled for a moment, thinking she had just read my mind, I smiled weakly before offering, "**Mais oui.**"

Darva handed me her coffee cup. "I think I'll go down and say hello. Care to join me?"

I shook my head. I felt bad for Shannon but knew that nothing I might say was going to make her feel better. She confessed her marital problems to Darva, but that didn't mean she wanted me apprised of them.

Sitting behind my desk, I could still see what was happening on the floor, but customers looking up at the window couldn't so easily see me. I watched as Darva approached Shannon and gave her that double-cheeked French greeting kiss. Flora, who was "helping" rearrange a candy display with Eileen, my head cashier, saw her mother and ran over to her. I watched as Darva swooped her up, and Shannon, smiling, reached over to cup the little girl's head in her hand, even as one of her kids wailed and the other started jumping, as if he were spring-loaded, even as her marriage was falling apart. I was taken by these two women who hadn't had anything to do with each other in high school but who now as mothers understood each other in a way I never would. Shannon's big muscular chiropractor husband had once bragged to me that he liked to do push-ups with a ten-pound weight on his back, and I thought how he, how I, how **men** were big and strong on the outside but didn't know crap, how the women with their soft skin and curves could take us any day, in ways that really counted.

I thought of my own mother and how on the one-year anniversary of my dad's death she'd taken me to see **The Shakiest Gun in the West** because Don Knotts had been one of my dad's favorite actors and had said, "I think it would honor your dad if we had a good laugh." The movie, in fact, had been pretty hokey, and my mother asked me in the car going home if I'd thought it had been funny, and I said no, and that made us both sad enough to cry, which was the only thing that night that made us laugh.

Suddenly I switched on the microphone and spoke into it.

"Good afternoon, ladies," I said, with the practiced congeniality I used when announcing specials. "I hope everyone's enjoying shopping at Haugland Foods."

There were only three other shoppers besides Shannon and Darva, and they continued their hunting and gathering down the aisles.

"Now, most of you know that Mother's Day is in May."

I saw Mrs. Nelson, in aisle seven, look up at the window, as if by seeing me she might have a better answer to the question that was on her face: **What the hell are you talking about?**

"But here at Haugland Foods, we like to honor mothers any time of the year—"

Mrs. Kirkpatrick, whose hair I had never seen out of rollers, stopped pushing her cart to give me the same look Mrs. Nelson had.

"—by giving you a free two minutes of shopping. Yes, ladies, whatever groceries you've already got in your cart, shove them to one side, because you're going to have to pay for those. But when I ring the bell, all the groceries you're able to grab within two minutes are free. I'll ring the bell again when it's time to stop."

Everyone, including my cashiers and baggers, looked up at the window. For a moment it seemed as if I was looking at statues in some weird shoppers' wax museum. No one moved.

Glancing at my watch, I rang the bell—the kind found on a motel desk, and the one I always rang to announce a special—and the wax figures suddenly melted out of their torpor.

Darva pointed to herself and mouthed, "Me too?" and when I nodded, she raced toward the shopping carts, holding Flora under her arm like a rag doll.

Mrs. Nelson, who was conveniently at the butcher case, began throwing steaks and pounds of hamburger into her cart. Mrs. Kirkpatrick, who was in the cereal aisle, knocked boxes of Froot Loops and canisters of oatmeal into her cart. Another woman whom I didn't know grabbed soup and tuna and other canned goods before turning into the frozen foods aisle.

Shannon was in the bakery section, lobbing boxes of donuts and bags of cookies into her cart. Her son Joshua was helping, standing on his tiptoes and pulling coffee cakes off the shelf. The toddler in the cart had stopped crying and was clapping his hands, urging his brother on.

I found I was laughing maniacally, and my cackling only increased when I grabbed my guitar, turned it on, and started playing "Brown Sugar" into the mike. Darva looked up at me, laughing too.

Even though I was into the music and watching the frantic motion below, I was keeping an eye on my watch, and after two minutes had gone by, I strummed a final chord and tagged the bell. Like extras in a science fiction movie, everyone froze, as they waited for the visiting alien to speak.

"Excellent job, ladies," I said into the mike, lowering my voice like a late-night DJ. "Now remember, you're on the honor system, so please pay for the groceries you'd already gotten before our little Supermarket Sweep. All the others, of course, are free . . . and a tribute to the special mothers you are. Thank you for your patronage, and have a wonderful day."

I turned off the mike and disappeared into the back of my office, where I couldn't be seen. I was trying to figure out when I had felt the way I was feeling now, and then I remembered—it was when I'd scored my first goal for the Golden Gophers.

Fifteen

Good morning, you're on the air with God.

Hi, Kristi. Uh . . . hi, God.

Sounds like one of the flock's lambs is calling.

Well . . . I . . . um . . . do you mean I sound young?

That would be my meaning. Now, how can I help you . . . ?

Uh . . . Jane. My name's Jane.

How can God help you, Jane?

I just . . . well . . . is it really a bad thing if you have sex with your boyfriend before you're married?

Is that what you've done, Jane?

No! No, I . . . I was just wondering.

I'm glad you're still wondering, Jane. Now let me ask you—have you ever been on a diet, Jane?

Sure—millions of 'em!

And tell me—how does it feel if you've been doing really well on that diet and then you discover your mom's made a chocolate cake and you think, Boy, that chocolate cake sure looks good and so you try a piece and that tastes so good that you have another, and pretty soon you've eaten half the cake. How do you feel then, Jane?

Uh . . . pretty full, I guess.

And maybe a little sick to your stomach, Jane?

Yeah, I guess.

And how would you feel if you have avoided that cake, Jane?

Uh . . . that I wish I had had a piece?

Work with me here, Jane. When you honor your commitment to lose weight, doesn't it feel good, Jane?

Yeah, I guess.

Premarital sex is a temptation, Jane. If you give in to it, you might find that one piece doesn't satisfy you and that you want more and more, and ultimately you wind up sick to your stomach. Believe me, Jane, a commitment to Christ is a lot more important than a commitment to a diet, but the rewards are deeper than you can ever imagine. So be strong, Jane. There's really no comparison between the holy, lasting banquet that is marital love and the quick fix of junk sex.

Uh . . . okay. Um . . . thanks.

"Oh my God," said Darva as I clicked off the tape recorder.

"Darva, please," I said. "Don't take the name of the Lord in vain. What would Kristi think?"

A grin finally broke the look of astonished horror that had been on her face for the entire broadcast of **On the Air with God.** The grin grew into a giggle, which expanded into a laugh. The mirth increased until we both slouched in our chairs, done in by it.

"Oh man," she said, ripping off a square of paper towel to wipe her eyes with. "Kristi Casey, a radio evangelist. The world **must** be coming to an end!" A snort burbled up in her and, defeated, she sank back in her chair, laughing all over again.

"Kirk says she's on a bunch of AM stations in the South," I said, examining the tape he had sent me.

"Let's just hope sanity prevails up here." Darva looked at her watch. "Oh, I've got to get ready, What's your mom making for dinner?"

"Flora's favorite," I said. "Hamburger hotdish."

Getting up from the kitchen table, Darva leaned over to kiss my cheek. "I wish I could join you."

"As far as hamburger hotdishes goes, hers **is** pretty unmatched," I said. "What are you guys doing tonight anyway?"

"Reed's got tickets to the Guthrie. **A Midsummer Night's Dream.**"

"Well, have fun—just make sure you're home at a reasonable hour, young lady."

I had dinner at my mother's every Tuesday night, and Darva usually accompanied me. Flora **always** did; it was obvious she was the star attraction, the most coveted guest.

Darva's parents had gotten to know their grand-daughter, but not for long. Initially her dad thought Flora was Darva, but it didn't take long before he stopped confusing his generations, because he didn't remember them at all. He died several months after Darva got back, her mom joining him three months after that.

"Now I'm an orphan," she had said, calling from her mother's deathbed. The wistfulness in her voice quickly collapsed under a full-bodied wail.

She was so sad that she reminded me of those old, old women bent over from osteoporosis, even though her burden was guilt, and physically she looked nothing like them.

"I should have been around more," she said as we ambled along the river. After her mother's funeral, we'd put Flora in the stroller and taken a long walk, and we'd been walking early every morning since. "I shouldn't have spent all those years abroad."

"Darva, I'll bet your mother **loved** that you lived in Paris. I'll bet she bragged to all her friends about her cosmopolitan, French-speaking, beret-wearing, wine-drinking artist daughter."

Darva managed a laugh. "Not wine drinking. Mom was a teetotaler."

"Then espresso drinking."

"I hope so. It's funny—when I lived away from them, I hardly thought of my parents, but now that they're gone, I think of them all the time. And all the things I should have done."

"Mama—bir!" said Flora, pointing to a bird flying from a maple tree to a fir.

"**Oui, c'est un oiseau.**" Darva spoke both English and French to her daughter.

"You know what your mother said to me the last time I went with you to see her?"

"What?" said Darva, her voice soft.

"Remember, it was one of her good days, when her pain seemed to be under control?" I said. Mrs. Pratt's fingers and joints were gnarled knobs that were painful even to **look** at. "You were in the kitchen getting her some tea, and she said, 'There's no one who makes tea like Darva. I tell everyone—steep the leaves at least five minutes, and warm the milk first—but nobody listens. Except Darva—she has always listened to me. Always took the time to listen.' "

Darva drew in a quick breath, then covered my hand, which was on the stroller handle, with her own. "Thanks, Joe."

Now Flora was four, and my mother and Len were only too happy to act as surrogate grandparents.

"Grand-mère, Mme. Chou Chou couldn't come tonight. She has the measles."

"Oh my," said my mother of Flora's imaginary friend. "Maybe she'll feel better if we make a cupcake for her."

"Yes, but you do it—my face looks so mad. I want it to look pretty."

My mother leaned toward Flora. "It looks very pretty, honey, but here, try another piece of licorice for the mouth."

We were sitting around the kitchen table decorating cupcakes. There was always one part of our Tuesday night meal we had to actively participate in, by either its cooking or its decoration. Grand-mère, as Flora called her, thought it was a fun idea, and she was right, it was. Tonight she had set little bowls of chocolate chips, gumdrops, sprinkles, licorice bits, and nuts in front of us, with the objective of making faces on our frosted cupcakes.

"Tante Beth," said Flora, "yours looks just like Tante Linda's."

"Quit copying me," said Beth, shielding her cupcake with her hand.

"As if," said Linda, laughing.

"Look, mine looks like Gorbachev," said Grand-père.

I squinted, cocked my head, and squinted again, but the resemblance to the newly installed Soviet general secretary eluded me.

"Let me have that," I said, and after he handed it to me, I tapped red sprinkles onto Gorbachev's forehead, giving him his trademark birthmark.

"There," said Flora, and after showing all of us the much prettier smile she had made of licorice, she addressed her cupcake. "Why, you look so good, I could eat you up!"

Which she did promptly, charming us all, as usual.

"You look so bad," I said to my cupcake, which had a face only a very drunk Picasso could love, "I could eat you up!"

"And you," said Len to his cupcake, "you look so prime ministerial, I could eat you up!"

He unpeeled the paper wrapping and took a big bite, but Gorbachev was not one to go down without a fight. A blob of frosting, with half a birthmark, dropped on Len's shirt.

This delighted Flora, whose laugh was a chortle too deep to come from such a little girl. The fact that it did always made everyone else laugh.

That's what our Tuesday night dinners were like. Inevitably, we'd all sink to the four-year-old's level (or maybe it was Flora who sank to ours), throwing things at one another, playing with our food, and laughing so hard we might, as Beth did one night, pee in our pants.

Flora might have incited the frosting smearing, but she was always helpful in the cleanup, clearing the table, standing on a footstool drying dishes, or sweeping up crumbs with the little broom and dustpan my mother kept in the kitchen closet.

After she declared that everything looked **très bon** (my mother let Flora decide when we were done with our chores, and she took her job seriously, never letting us leave if there was a counter that still needed to be wiped down or a dish put away), we went into the living room and I sidled up to the piano bench as naturally as a cowboy jumps on his horse.

Len couldn't sing, but he had an adequate sense of rhythm, which he loudly shared by slapping his palms on his knees. Linda's voice didn't like to confine itself to either melody or harmony, but if someone looked in the window at one of our sing-alongs, they might think Norman Rockwell had come back to life and was now directing music videos.

Flora had a clear little voice and a memory that allowed her to learn songs quickly, so that if we sang "A Spoonful of Sugar" one week, she'd come back the next knowing the entire thing. (It didn't hurt that I had my own piano at home and always obliged her requests to **jouez et chantez**.) My mother was going to start giving her piano lessons, which thrilled Darva, who claimed not to have a musical bone in her body.

"Well, bones aren't by nature musical," I told her. "Unless they're used as drumsticks."

I was worried about this Reed guy—Darva, who taught French, had led a group of students on a tour through "Les Artistes' Francais" exhibit at the Institute of Arts, and Reed, visiting the museum himself, followed the group from the Matisses to the Monets, even though he didn't understand a word Darva was saying.

"I didn't even know if she understood English," he told me, "but I asked her out for coffee anyway."

My reason for worry wasn't that he was a jerk who treated Darva badly; it was the opposite. Darva seemed to like him a lot, and I could imagine them eventually marrying, which of course would mean she and Flora would move out. At the ripe old age of thirty-one, the most important relationships in my life were a platonic love with a high school pal and an avuncular one with a little girl who, in fact, called me not **Oncle** Joe but **mon** Joe—my Joe. I hadn't been swept up into a great inferno of passion, but that was okay; these little campfires of love were keeping me plenty warm. And then Jenny Baldacci, in the middle of baking a lemon meringue pie, happened to run out of eggs.

Ever since I had given Shannon, Darva, and those three housewives an opportunity to run amok in the store for their two-minute Supermarket Sweep, I had held other surprise contests. One Wednesday evening, I couldn't help noticing that none of the kids seemed happy to be there; the aisles were filled with so many whines and cries you would have thought the shopping carts they rode or clung to or ran ahead of were an element of torture. There were a few fathers braving SWC (shopping with children), but by and large the beleaguered parents making threats, pleas, or bribes were mothers.

I went up into my office and rang the bell.

"Good evening, shoppers," I said into the microphone. "Have you checked out the sale in aisle seven? All Good Home canned goods, four for a dollar. But here's a special that isn't advertised, and it's just for kids, so boys and girls, listen up." I rang the bell again, for dramatic effect. Many of the shoppers had stopped, as if the act of pushing their cart distracted them from listening. Most of the kids were looking up at the office window. I waved, and they waved back.

"Yes, kids, this is the Haugland Foods Quiet as a Mouse contest. Whoever can stay"—I lowered my voice to a whisper—"quiet as a mouse for ten minutes will get to choose any prize they like from the toy department."

My office wasn't soundproofed; noise came up through the vents and the thin glass window, and I could hear the whines and cries evaporate, replaced by an excited chatter.

"All right, kids," I said in my smooth announcer voice, "we'll start when I ring the bell, and you'll know we're done when I ring the bell again."

A strange quiet filled the store as soon as I struck the bell, and its effect was a thing to behold. Kyle, a toddler who loved to terrorize his baby sister, was now sitting quietly in the back of the cart, holding Tiffany in his lap. Anna and Evan, six-year-old twins who held the store breakage record for a single shopping trip (two jars of pickles and a bottle of chocolate milk) tiptoed solemnly, hand in hand, next to their father. The unruly Grinas, who liked to play tag in the aisles, reached for the groceries their mother pointed at. The looks on the parents' faces were beatific, as if they were spectators to a miracle.

After keeping careful track on my watch, I rang the bell.

"Congratulations, kids," I said. "Every single one of you is a winner. Now as quietly as you can, tiptoe to the toy aisle—it's across from the magazines—and pick out your toy."

The kids didn't seem to care that they weren't shopping at FAO Schwarz; they seemed happy to select a cheap plastic water pistol, a coloring book, a deck of Old Maid cards. Mrs. Ghizoni told me later that her son said it'd been just like Halloween, "instead of tricks, we had to be quiet, and instead of treats, we got toys."

One slow morning, I noticed Marlys Pitt pushing her cart as if it were filled with rocks instead of the boxes of macaroni and cheese she seemed to subsist on since her husband ran off with her sister. She looked terrible, swollen-eyed and stringy-haired, and so thin she kept having to hoist up her slacks to prevent them from sliding down her butt.

I rang my bell.

"Ladies and gentlemen," I said to the half dozen or so shoppers, "a prize will be awarded to anyone who right now has a box of Good Home macaroni and cheese in their shopping cart."

Marlys was apparently too deep in her funk to participate in the contest, and it wasn't until Estelle Brady, for whom everyone's business was her business, noticed Marlys and banged into her cart with her own.

"You won," she shouted, and then looking up at the window, shouted, "Joe! Joe—she's got a whole cartful!"

"All right, we've got a winner!" I said, as if surprised. "And you win . . ." Trying to think of a good prize, I revved up my brain. Inspiration came as I looked at Marlys and her unkempt hair. "You win a gift certificate to Patty Jane's House of Curl and . . . and dinner for two at the Canteen!"

Marlys gave me a rare smile, and thus began my cosponsorship with neighborhood businesses.

Once I asked if there was anyone shopping who could recite the entire Gettysburg Address. Surprisingly I had two winners—Jan Olafson, a waitress who always needing reminding that there was no smoking in the store, and Mr. Snowbeck, my Twinkies shoplifter. They each got gift certificates to a new bookstore that had opened on Cedar Avenue. Another time I asked shoppers if anyone had a picture of their grandmother in their wallet. No one did, but a little boy holding a gray-haired woman's hand said, "But I've got mine right here!" He took home a gift certificate from the Abdullah Candy Store.

Usually the contests were random and I didn't know who the winner would be (who'd have thought Irv Busch, a customer whose moods swung a short arc from bad to really bad, would know all the lyrics to "Some Enchanted Evening" and sing them, in a sweet tenor, in the middle of the feminine products aisle?). Other times I rigged the outcome, selecting the winner in advance according to the prize being offered. For instance, my mother offered six free piano lessons, and I awarded the prize to Cindy Waldron, who paid for her groceries with food stamps and whose son was a dreamy boy who always sang or whistled when he shopped with her. Another time I asked, "Who's got disposable diapers in their cart?" knowing that Helen Hanson, whose baby was three months old, had just told Shelly Ericson she was pregnant again and not exactly thrilled about it. Helen, who waved two packages of Dry-Didies in the air, won a weekend getaway at the Thunderbird Hotel (one of my customers was its vice president).

"It's romance that got me in trouble in the first place," said Helen, accepting her prize, but afterward she breathlessly reported, "They had a pool, and my husband and I actually met when we were lifeguards, so we spent the whole time in the water!"

The prizes often came from other stores (I had taken a beating during that first Supermarket Sweep I'd held—Kay Nelson had cleaned me out of porterhouse and T-bone steaks), but I donated my fair share and was just about to announce a contest when I saw an attractive, vaguely familiar brunette in the dairy section.

"You're drooling," said Darva.

"I know that person," I said, "I think."

"Maman, we made faces on our cupcakes!" said Flora, who had spent the night at my mother's after our Tuesday night dinner. This was a common occurrence; in fact, so common that she considered the guest room **chez grand-mère et grand-père** her second bedroom. Having slept on my mother's couch in the den, I had taken Flora to work with me, and Darva had come to pick her up.

"And Grand-mère read me seven books—I counted! And **mon** Joe let me help stack up the oranges!"

"I think she's got a career in produce," I said.

"So who do you think it is?" asked Darva, following my gaze out the office window.

After I shrugged, Darva took the bell off my desk.

"So figure it out," she said, holding it to the microphone and ringing it.

"Good morning, shoppers," I said, scrambling to the mike. "Today's prize will go to anyone"—I watched the brunette reach into the egg case—"who has a carton of eggs in their cart."

The dark-haired woman froze, holding the carton in her hand.

"I've got eggs!" shouted Red Carlson, who owned the hardware store down the block.

"We have a winner, then," I said. "Actually two, because even if you haven't put the eggs in your cart, you're still a winner."

I heard Darva laugh. "Smooth," she said, "real smooth."

"And today's prize"—my mind raced through new inventory items that might appeal to the brunette beauty—"is a free Mrs. Wilkerson's Fruit Pie, available for pickup in the bakery section."

"This is how you're going to charm her?" asked Darva. "With pie?"

"I'd like to win a pie," offered Flora.

"I guess I'll go down and make my prize presentation," I said, running a hand through my hair.

"You look good," said Darva, cheering me on.

I raced down the stairs, worried that the brunette might have left without claiming her prize, but when I reached the bakery section, she was standing with Red Carlson by the Mrs. Wilkerson pie display.

"Joe!" said Red. "What do you think—the cherry or the apple?"

"I don't think you could go wrong with either," I said.

"Then I'll take the cherry," he said, loading a red box into his cart. "And Joe, I've got a prize to donate for you—free duplicate keys made and a gallon of paint."

"Write up a gift certificate," I said, "and I'll use it."

The hardware store owner left, whistling "We're in the Money," and I stood next to the woman, who was even lovelier up close.

"Congratulations," I said.

"Thanks," she said, and when she smiled, a little cartilage softened in my knees. "It's so weird—I came here to buy eggs because I was making pie, and now I win one!"

"That **is** weird," I said, although I didn't think it was weird at all, having already decided that Fate was at work in bringing us together. "By the way . . . I'm Joe. Joe Andreson."

From her response, you would have thought I'd introduced myself as Mick Jagger.

"Oh my God!" she said, hugging me. Not wanting to be rude, I hugged her back, but it was all too brief.

"You're Mrs. A.'s son!" she said, pulling away.

"I am," I said, dipping my head in a nod. "Only now she's Mrs. Rusk, so then she'd be Mrs. R." I crossed and uncrossed my arms before putting my hands in my pockets. I no longer felt like the lead singer of the Rolling Stones as much as a member of the New Christy Minstrels.

"Oh yeah, I heard she had gotten married."

"Yup," I said and dawn rose in the horizon of my mind. "Hey, I remember you. From my mother's first spring concert at Nokomis Junior High. You played the flute. You played the theme from **Alfie.**"

"Wow," she said, blushing. "**Alfie.** I forgot all about that song. You've got some memory."

"Well, I . . ." I was worried I was coming across as some weirdo who memorized his mother's band concert playlist. "Well, that's all I remember: how well you played. I mean, I don't remember your name or anything."

"Jenny," she said, offering her hand, "Jenny Baldacci. And your mom . . . well, Mrs. A. was one of my all-time favorite teachers."

"I'll be sure to tell her."

"Please do."

"So what kind of pie were you making?"

"What?"

We hadn't broken our handshake, and it was as if the more we talked the more excuse we had for holding hands.

"You said you were getting eggs for a pie."

"Oh yeah. Lemon meringue. Meringue takes a lot of egg whites."

"Really."

"It's one of the few things I make well—meringue. I use a store-bought crust, but my meringue's delicious."

"I'd love to try it sometime."

Something shifted in Jenny's lovely, lively face.

"It's my husband's favorite pie."

Everything wilted: my blood pressure plummeted, my heart rate lowered, my hopeful erection deflated, and my testicles shrank to the size of marbles.

"So your husband likes meringue, does he?" I said, my voice loud and blustery enough to let her know I was the strong type, that I'd be able to survive this crushing blow.

"Yes, he's . . . ," she began, her blush deepening. "We're visiting my folks. It's their thirtieth wedding anniversary. So I'm making them a pie. . . . We live in New York."

"That's great," I said. "New York, that is. Although I'm not saying that with much firsthand knowledge. I mean, I was only there once. I was ten. I went with my mom and dad, and we went to the top of the Empire State Building. Oh yeah, I had a hot dog from one of those stands too."

As I blathered on, I screamed at myself, **Shut up! Can you possibly be more inane?**

"Well, so nice to have met you," said Jenny, grabbing the handle of her cart. "Please say hello to your mother for me and . . . and thanks for the pie."

"It's not lemon meringue," I said, "but it's free."

As I watched her approach the cash register, I noticed her pretty legs and the nice curve of her rump, but the knowledge that she was married was a cold bucket of water thrown on my appreciation.

Back in my office, Flora raised her arms, asking to be lifted. Letting someone hold her was her remedy for cheering someone up.

"**Mon** Joe, you look so sad!"

I exaggerated a grunt as I picked her up.

"Was that lady mean to you?" she asked seriously, pressing her palm against my cheek.

"Yeah, Joe," said Darva. "Was she?"

"Worse. She's married."

Sixteen

From the Minneapolis Star Tribune,
October 4, 1987:

HOMEGROWN EVANGELIST
WOWS LOCAL CROWD

by Robyn MacDonald

Billy Graham chose to headquarter his Evangelistic Association in Minneapolis, and now it looks as if a Minnesota native may be another force to be reckoned with in the evangelical world. At thirty-two, Kristi Casey still has the fit and toned body of a head cheerleader, which she was (Ole Bull High, Class of '72) and the pretty, open face of a homecoming queen.

"Unfortunately, I can't put that title on my résumé," she told this reporter, "but I think the voting was rigged."

In interviewing one of the stars of the Shout

Hallelujah! revival that took place at the Merina Auditorium this weekend, Ms. Casey exhibited the same playful sense of humor that is evident in the radio broadcasts the citizens of Minneapolis/St. Paul will be able to listen to beginning in January.

"I'm thrilled that I'll be bringing the good news over AM radio K-LUV Tuesday nights at seven o'clock to all my friends and family in the beautiful state of Minnesota," she said, and then, catching herself sounding like a press release, added: "I've got some old friends who could **use** some good news!"

After our short interview in Ms. Casey's dressing room, this reporter took her seat along with a crowd estimated at more than four thousand.

There was a lot of fire and brimstone interspersed with rousing renditions of "Onward Christian Soldiers" and "God Bless America," sung by the Shout Hallelujah! Chorus, and if the crowd was enthusiastic listening to Reverend Timmy Johns or Brother Quincy Byerly, they were positively rabid when the beat of a bass drum thundered through the auditorium.

Everyone stood up and clapped a reply to the beat as Kristi Casey marched inside a spotlight, wearing a white sparkling dress and a big bass drum. She beat out another rhythm, which was answered, and this interplay lasted, by this reporter's watch, for three minutes, until the crowd was clapping in one solid steady beat and shouting, "Kristi, Kristi, Kristi!"

Her message didn't offer anything new and revelatory to these ears, but as far as delivery went, she was peerless. Ms. Casey could recite "Three Blind Mice" and her fans—or as they call themselves, the Kristi Corps—would clamor for more.

She told the audience before leaving the stage,

"You don't have to go looking for God—because He's right here now!" and the shouts of "Amen!" rattled the rafters.

I can't say going to a revival had ever made it onto my top 100 list of things to do, but I would have braved the legions of the lost and the saved to see Kristi. By the time the article came out, however, she was already on her way to Detroit. I know, because I drove her to the airport.

Darva had taken Flora to Detroit for her nephew's wedding, and I had just popped a beer and settled back to watch Johnny Carson do his Art Fern bit when the telephone rang. Before answering machines became indispensable appliances, like toasters or coffeemakers, screening calls meant deciding to pick up the phone or let it ring. I let it ring—Ed McMahon was snorting with laughter, and while I didn't quite have Ed's apoplectic reaction, I was entertained enough to choose Johnny over the ringing phone. But this caller was persistent, and finally, thinking it was the kind of call you don't want to answer but should, I picked up the receiver.

"Jeepers, Joe—don't tell me you were in bed!"

I recognized the voice immediately. "**Kristi?**"

"The one and only. Now, if you're in your jammies, get dressed. We're going for a ride."

"But . . . what . . ."

"Still a sweet-talker. I'll see you in ten minutes."

I threw on some clothes and sat on the arm of the recliner, peeking out the window like the neighborhood busybody. A Cadillac pulled up in front of my house **exactly** ten minutes later and sat there, purring like a big black cat, and I scurried out toward it like a little mouse.

She sat behind the steering wheel, her hair all big and shellacky, her eyes weighted with fake lashes, her mouth glistening with deep pink lipstick . . . and she looked great.

"Hey," I said, and swallowed hard.

Laughing, Kristi leaned over in the seat to kiss me full on the mouth.

"So how long's it been, Joe?" she asked.

With her face inches from mine, with her perfume going up my nose and into some receptor part of my brain that shouted, **Yahoo!**, all I could answer was, "Too long."

"Nice house," she said, ducking her head to look out the passenger window.

"Thanks, I bought it when—"

"I've got an eight-thirty flight tomorrow morning," said Kristi, pulling away from the curb. "So let's have some fun while there's fun to be had. Some **real** fun."

Her implication was obvious.

"Are you talking about **visiting another county?**" I asked, using our old sexual shorthand.

Kristi made her voice husky. "I hear it's beautiful in Ottertail County this time of year."

"But Ottertail's way up north!"

"I'm kidding, Joe," said Kristi with a laugh. "I told you I've got a morning flight."

She turned the car on the parkway, heading east.

"We're going to St. Paul. At least it's in a different county than Minneapolis."

Val, my latest girlfriend, had been a new teacher at my mother's school, and while she initially seemed pretty nice, she began showing odd personality quirks. Anytime we had sex, she'd giggle and say things like, "Now don't tell your mother—that'd be telling tales out of school!" or "After that perform-ance, young man, I'd put you at the head of the class!" Once when I picked her up, she looked me over and said, "What, no apple for the teacher?"

Val started calling me more than I was comfortable with, and began sending me "report cards" (I got an A in foreplay and a D in remembering our first-month anniversary), so you can imagine my relief when she told me she was transferring to a school in Duluth and I'd no longer have to deal with her. She was beginning to rival Kelly, my old **Love Story** girl-friend, in the nut department, and nuts were not what I was looking for in a woman.

So you'd think I'd be wary of strange women, but Kristi's strangeness was an old friend to me, and the invitation to revisit our carnal knowledge of the past was too tempting to ignore.

"Do you always wear so much makeup?" I asked, noticing the pillowcase smeared with color.

"Very gallant of you to ask," she said. Laughing, she pulled the sheet off me and wrapped it around her. "But no, only when I'm onstage."

I watched as she went into the bathroom. "When **aren't** you onstage?"

This elicited another laugh. "That's what I love about you, Joe—you always tell it like it is."

"I noticed you're not denying it," I said, raising my voice as I heard the sound of water.

A minute later she emerged from the bathroom, tying the belt of the hotel bathrobe around her waist, her face scrubbed.

"Why should I?" she asked, opening the minibar. " 'All the world's a stage, and all the men and women merely players.' You want a beer?"

"Please," I said. We were staying in Kristi's downtown St. Paul hotel, in a fancier room than any of our motels had offered.

"You know what else?" I said, watching as she opened the beer. "We just had sex and your hair looks exactly the same as it did when you picked me up."

"Are you familiar with the adage 'If you don't have anything nice to say, don't say anything?' " asked Kristi, climbing back into bed.

I took the bottle she offered with my right hand and touched her hair, an elaborate blond cascade that was stiff to the touch.

"Do you know they've discovered hairspray's bad for the ozone layer?"

Kristi managed to smirk at me, even though she was in the middle of taking a long draw of beer.

"So," I said, "you're still allowed to have nonmarital sex and drink beer, huh?"

"Oh, goody," she said, clinking my bottle with her own. "The insults about my appearance are over and now it's time to start making fun of my life's work."

On the way to the hotel, she had told me why she was in town, bragging about how attendance had risen more than 17 percent since she'd joined the

Shout Hallelujah! revival, and complaining about her position following Mother Olive ("Really, there are only two women in the whole show, and what do they do? They put us on right next to each other!"), but when we passed Shannon Saxon's parents' house on River Road, we laughed about the stupid bull costume Shannon had had to wear, and our conversation veered back to high school.

But now I wanted to know just where the hell she'd been and what the hell had gotten into her.

"Your life's work," I said, sitting up against the headboard. "Am I allowed now to ask about how a girl who used to give me blow jobs in school is now on tour with the fucking Shout Hallelujah! revival?"

"Don't talk like that," she said quickly, a blush tinting her face.

"What's it you object to? Blow jobs or fucking? 'Cause you're pretty good at both."

Kristi took a swig of beer. "Do you want to hear about my life or don't you?"

I shrugged. "Fire away."

"Okay," she said, pulling the covers up and wriggling closer to me. She was going to talk about her favorite subject—herself—and her excitement was palpable.

"Okay, remember when we saw those northern lights up in Grand Marais?"

"Sure."

"Well, I think that's when I first saw God."

"**What?**"

She nodded, as if the tone of my voice suggested agreement rather than incredulity.

"I didn't know it right then—it took me a couple of weeks to figure out what it was I saw."

"Kristi, we saw the northern lights. It's a scientific phenomenon. Something about sunspots or something."

"I was sitting in the student union," she continued, as if she hadn't heard me, "when all of a sudden this big chill—you know, the kind you get if you drink a Slushie too fast—rushed through my body and I knew, I just **knew** that what I'd seen was a message from God."

"No, I remember," I said. "It's solar particles smacking into gas molecules."

"I knew right then that somehow, some way, I was going to dedicate my life to Christ." She took another sip of beer, nodding at the memory. "And then, I swear to God, I got another chill, thinking, **My name is Kristi.**"

It wasn't exactly a spit take, but some beer that had been heading down my throat came up through my nose.

"I know it sounds weird," she said, acknowledging my reaction, "but if you think about it, **Kristi**'s the female of **Christ.** I mean, I know it's a popular name for girls right now, but I believe it was all in His plan, that I should know He touched me because I was named Kristi."

The schoolteacher girlfriend I'd just broken up with was starting to seem a little more sane. I searched Kristi's face, expecting to find something in the tension of her mouth or a look in her eyes that let me know she was joking, but the face that stared back at mine was guileless, on her an expression I wasn't used to seeing. I finished my beer and set the bottle on the nightstand.

"What about everyone who's named Jesus?" I asked. "Or Christian? And there's gotta be some Amish guys named Jehovah. Should they all start thinking they're somehow **touched**?"

"I'm only explaining my experience," said Kristi impatiently. "Now are you going to make fun of me, or are you going to listen?"

I'm going to make fun of you, I thought, **just not out loud.**

"So why didn't you tell me any of this while it was happening?" I said instead. "I mean, considering I was a witness to you witnessing God."

"Are you kidding me? And put myself up to your ridicule?"

"What do you think you're putting yourself up to now?"

"Ha-ha," said Kristi. "And I thought time might have the odd effect of **maturing** you." She drained her beer and let out a loud, protracted burp.

"You should talk."

"Okay," I said after we'd shared a laugh, "keep going. Tell me how you got from A to . . . Z."

"Well, you can figure, if I couldn't tell **you**—'cause I can tell you just about everything—I couldn't tell anyone. And then, remember, I only saw you a couple times after that, before I graduated and left."

"Yeah, where **did** you go? It was like you vanished into thin air."

"I'm hungry," said Kristi, getting up and opening the minibar again. She took out a bag of M&Ms.

"This stuff is so expensive, and if you think Shout Hallelujah! pays for it, the answer is **n-o**."

"Okay, enough about your expense account," I said as she settled back into bed and poured a little mound of M&Ms into my hand. "Where'd you go after school?"

"Where does anyone like me go after school? California. North Hollywood, to be exact. It was cheaper to live in the valley than in L.A. proper."

"Were you trying to get into acting?"

"I didn't know. I was trying to get into something . . . public. I mean, I knew I was supposed to be famous, I just wasn't exactly sure if I should be a movie star or have my own TV show or be a news anchor or what. And then on top of everything else, I had to deal with that religious experience. I mean, as much as I was **awed** by what happened to me, I was scared too, you know? After all, I was only twenty-one years old when it happened! What twenty-one-year-old wants to devote herself to God? Well, what **normal** twenty-one-year-old? I began thinking maybe I'd just dreamt the whole thing, or maybe it was a reaction to all the drugs I'd taken—you know, some strange . . . well if not **flashback**, then **flash**." She eyed me carefully. "I haven't done drugs for years, by the way."

"Bummer," I said.

"It was like I knew I had seen the light, but I kept having to pull the shades. You know, when God points His finger at you, it's a big responsibility."

"Which finger?"

Kristi pulled a pillow out from behind her and swatted me with it.

"Are you going to heckle me all night or are you going to listen?"

I pretended to consider my choices for a moment, but she ignored me, plunging back into her story.

"So I'm struggling with everything, and you know me—I am **not** used to struggling. I tried to get an agent and eventually did, this old guy who said he was going to make me a big star, but I don't think he could make a peanut butter sandwich, let alone a star. I got sent out to crap auditions that I didn't get—sure, I might get a callback, I might get **this** close to some under-five part on a lousy sitcom, but did I ever get a job?" She shook her head, but not her immovable hair.

I could understand her disbelief. "Well, maybe you gave up too early. Maybe your big break was right around the corner."

Kristi's eyes blazed. "I **never** give up, Joe. I just explore other options."

She reached for her purse on the night table and fumbled around inside. She stuck a cigarette in her mouth and lit it.

"You're still smoking?" I said, waving away the smoke. "That's nasty."

After exhaling, she said, "Father, forgive them, for they know not what they do."

"Some preacher," I said.

"Judge not lest ye be judged."

I snorted. "I bet you have a biblical quote to excuse any kind of behavior."

Kristi smiled. "Just about. Now before I go on, you've got to promise me something, Joe."

"What, to tithe at least ten percent to Shout Hallelujah! every year?"

"I'm serious, Joe." She took a long drag of her cigarette but, sensing how it bothered me, turned her head to exhale and stubbed the cigarette out.

She changed position on the bed so that she was sitting facing me, her legs tucked under her. "Joe, I think more than anyone else in the world, I trust you the most."

"Kristi," I said, taken aback, "I haven't seen you for over ten years. We—"

Holding her finger to her lips, she shushed me. "Time or distance hasn't changed how I feel about you, Joe. Now, I'm going to tell you something I've never told anyone, but you've got to promise me it will be our secret, okay?"

"What am I, a priest?" I said, uncomfortable with the gravity in her eyes.

She was unmoved by my joke. "Because everyone needs a confidant, Joe, and you're mine."

Well, of course there was no way I was going to deny being Kristi Casey's confidant. I was curious as hell to hear what she was about to tell me, even as I felt a shadow of queasiness.

"I tried for three years," she said, "three long years, and I didn't get one job. **Not one job**—can you believe that, Joe? For the first time in my life, people weren't begging to do me favors, weren't bowing every time I passed. I didn't know who I was—but it sure wasn't Kristi Casey. So that meant to pay the rent in my crappy little apartment on Lankershim, I had to waitress, I had to temp—I mean, I was going into a serious depression! This wasn't how my life was supposed to be!

"So one day, I'm waiting tables at this semifancy steakhouse in Toluca Lake and this guy leaves me a fifty-dollar tip with his card paper-clipped to it. It wasn't the first time I'd been hit on at work, but this guy's card said he was a movie producer. So I called him."

"And did he give you a job?" I asked, for some reason wanting this story to have a happy ending. "Were you in anything I might have seen?"

"Not unless you hang out at triple-X theaters," she said, and laughed at my reaction. "No, I'm just kidding—they weren't really triple X. Per called them 'art films.' "

"**Per?**" I said, practically spitting out the name.

Kristi laughed again. "He was Danish. He was about fifty when I met him—yeah, I know that sounds gross, but he had all his hair and wore a long scarf and was very dashing in a European way."

"So what did you do when you found out what he did?" I asked, hoping her answer would be something along the lines of **Adiós, schmuck.**

"I said, 'If you think I'm ever going to be in one of your "art movies," think again.' "

I blew out a blast of air, more relieved than I could explain. "And so that was that?"

"Well, not exactly. I mean, I never was in one of his movies—I might be wild, but I was never a pervert—but I did wind up . . . living with him. He was my boyfriend."

"Kristi—ugh!"

"My little-old-lady friend Joe," said Kristi, kissing

me on the nose. "I can always count on you to be more uptight than my own grandma ever was."

She sighed and made a move as if to inspect the minibar again, but on second thought sank back against the headboard.

"I didn't have to work—Per paid for everything—but there was only so much entertainment to be gotten by lying around the pool all day or shopping on Rodeo Drive. Eventually luxury gets a little boring if that's all you've got going on. So when he offered a certain little **excursion**, I agreed to it."

My head moved back and forth, back and forth. I did not like where this was going.

"See, he had a couple of sideline businesses, and one was importing a little cocaine."

I opened my mouth, but formulating words was a task beyond me at the moment.

"You . . . you were a **drug runner**?" I said when I remembered how to talk.

Kristi's look of shame didn't last long before a big smile broke through it.

"Just twice. Once to Central America and once to Denmark."

"My God—you were doing cocaine?"

"Me?" Kristi laughed. "Nah. Well, I had to try it to see if I liked it, but I never really got its appeal. And besides, I knew there were people who'd blown out the insides of their noses with cocaine and I . . . Well, I have such a pretty nose, I didn't want anything to mess it up. I wasn't a user—just a pickup and delivery girl."

"What if you had gotten caught?"

"Well, see," said Kristi, smiling, "I didn't. But you

know what they say, a good poker player knows when to fold, and even though it was a little **exciting**, I knew it wasn't worth sharing a cell with a five-hundred-pound welfare cheat from Compton."

I had to laugh, thinking that of all the things I had imagined Kristi up to during the years she was MIA, making international drug runs for a porn king was not among them.

"Are you making this up? This is all a joke, right?"

"I wish," said Kristi. "I wish none of it had ever happened."

There was enough of a quaver to her voice to make me invite her into my arms. She was happy for the invitation and laid her head against my chest as I held her close.

"See, Joe, it was all right that I didn't want to be in his movies—I mean, I think he thought I was sort of **classy**—but when I told him I couldn't help him anymore with the drug stuff . . . Well, I guess he started thinking that I felt I was better than him. Which I did, by the way, but I was smart enough to pretend otherwise. But you know how it is—if you don't participate in something, you're condemning it, you're saying you're better than it. At least that's how Per thought. And he started getting mean. Name-calling, threats, and when he got really frustrated that he couldn't control me—"

She made a fist and slammed it into her open palm.

"He hit you?"

"Worse than that, Joe." She pulled back some of her shellacked bangs to show me the very fine scar that ran just under her hairline from the middle of her forehead to her temple.

"It took about a billion stitches to close that up," said Kristi. She bared her pretty white teeth at me and tapped the front ones. "And these are fake. At least the jerk had a great dentist."

"Kristi," I said, and it hurt to push her name up my throat. "How did you . . . Why didn't you leave him?"

Tears welled up in her green eyes. "Oh, Joe, I was so scared. I didn't know how. I had lost all belief in myself. . . . You wouldn't have recognized me. I felt . . . well, it got to the point where I didn't even feel. I couldn't. It was too painful."

She burrowed back into my arms, and soon my thirteen chest hairs were wet with her tears. For the second time since I had known her, I tried to comfort her as she cried, rubbing her back and rocking her until her sobs and the spasms that jumped through her body had stopped. I pressed my face into her hair, intending to kiss her head, but I sneezed from all the hairspray.

This made Kristi giggle.

"Sorry," she said, looking up at me, her eyes swollen. "I do like my Aqua Net."

The clock radio read 2:50 A.M., but sleep was the farthest thing from my mind. I hadn't planned going into the store until midmorning anyway, giving my manager the early morning shift.

"So how did you finally wind up where you are?" I asked.

Kristi stifled her yawn against my chest. "The housekeeper, Mercedes. She knew what was going on, even though Per never hit me in front of anyone. The day after I got my stitches in, I was sitting on the patio, just **empty**, staring out at the gardeners working in the backyard, and Mercedes brought me an iced tea and very softly said, 'That's my cousin. The one who's trimming the hedge.' I nodded, thinking, **What do I care about your cousin?** Then she leaned toward me, as if making sure I heard what she was going to say next.

" 'His van is the green one in the driveway. The one with its door facing the garage. He's leaving in an hour. No one could see anyone getting in or out of it. If you get into it, he will drive you to Barstow. To someplace safe. I wouldn't know a thing. No one would.'

"Joe, I don't know how fast my heart was beating, but it was faster than I'd ever felt before or since. I didn't say anything; I just got up, went to my bedroom, and packed a bag. Then I walked past Mercedes in the kitchen, out the side door, and into the back of the van. When the gardener opened the door, he saw me sitting there, terrified, but he didn't say anything; he just loaded up his equipment and slammed the door. A couple of hours later I was in Barstow, California, in a little house that overlooks a BMX track."

"Whose was it?"

A soft look passed on a face that seldom revealed tenderness.

"A woman named Marguerite. Mercedes's sister. She didn't speak much English and I didn't speak any Spanish, but she was the best friend I ever had. She fed me and sheltered me and helped me find God again, the God that I'd thought wanted nothing more to do with me."

Kristi yawned again.

"How long did you stay there?"

"I don't really remember," she said. "As long as I needed, which was when Kristi Casey came back."

"So how did you get hooked up in this evangelical thing? When did that—"

Kristi's yawn was an audible "Uhhhhhh."

"Joe, I'm sorry, I've got to go to sleep. I am **bushed**." She kissed my chest. "I already set the alarm—you will drive me to the airport, won't you? And return the Caddy to the rental place—it's right there at the terminal."

It seemed she was softly snoring before I could give her answer—but we both already knew it couldn't be anything but yes.

Seventeen

Good evening, caller from Council Bluffs, you're on the air with God.

Hi . . . yeah . . .

Go ahead.

(Sounds of sniffling)

It's all right; what's your name, dear?

I . . . I'd rather be anonymous.

Hmmm, that's an unusual name. Is it Greek? (Beat) That was a joke, caller.

Oh. Listen, Kristi, I . . . I need help staying on the program.

I decide whether or not you need . . . oh, the program. (Laughs) I thought you meant my radio show, but now I assume you're talking about a drug or alcohol program?

That's right.

Why do you need help, Ann?

Ann? . . . Oh, I get it—Ann for anonymous, huh?

Um . . . I just get so depressed. Life seems a little more fun if I'm high.

A life with God is as high as you can get, Ann.

I don't know—yesterday I had some really good dope and—

Are you on the level, Ann, or is this a prank call?

Please don't call me Ann. You can call me . . . Jean.

Okay, Jean, if you're serious, I'll be serious. You need to purge the dope, the liquor, anything that obscures your path to Christ.

But I've . . . haven't you ever had a few too many drinks or smoked a little doobie?

Ann—uh, Jean, I wouldn't know a marijuana plant from a ficus. And as far as liquor goes . . . well, yes, back in my college days, I did have the occasional beer or two. But since my sophomore year . . . well, I just haven't been interested.

You're lucky.

I'll tell you what, Ann. You pray extra hard tonight, until you fall asleep from exhaustion, and when you wake up again, start praying. The minute you feel like a drink or a doobie, back on your knees.

But I—

Extra hard, Ann. Thanks for calling.

I don't exactly know why, but I had kept the particulars of Kristi's and my high school relationship a secret from everyone, even Darva, and now I was glad, seeing as she **howled** when I told her Kristi's tale of redemption.

"Oh, of course she was with a porn czar named Per!" she said, slapping her knee.

"Oh, of course she ran drugs for him!" she said, clapping her hands.

"Oh, of course he beat her up!" she said, holding her stomach as if she feared splitting some internal seams. "And of course she was rescued by a Mexican housekeeper named Mercedes!"

I know I had promised Kristi to keep whatever she told me secret, but that had been **before** she told me. Her story was too mind-blowing to keep all to myself, and besides, I knew Darva could keep a secret, even if I couldn't. But I hadn't expected her reaction to be so . . . over the top.

"Darva, why are you laughing? Kristi went through a lot of shit, and that she **survived** tells a lot about her character."

Shaking her head, Darva held up her hand, a signal for me to please stop; she might laugh so hard she'd hurt herself.

I was angry and humiliated, not a pleasant combination. How could she be so dismissive of Kristi's real hardships, and furthermore, how could she be so dismissive of me?

"I'm glad you're so amused," I said hotly, "but she went through **hell.** And to tell you the truth, I'm a little shocked that you can't get past all your high school jealousies and have, well, have a little **empathy.**"

Darva's eyes bulged as a paroxysm of laughter overtook her.

"You disappoint me," I said, my voice haughty, as if I was a teacher scolding a prize student whom I'd caught drawing an unflattering portrait of me. "I thought if there's one person who can help me understand the complications of Kristi, it's you. I

thought you had an insight into people. I guess I was wrong."

Darva leaned forward, cradling her head in her arms, her shoulders jerking. When she had laughed herself out, she raised her head, wiping her eyes with the heels of her hands.

"Okay," she said, a little breathless. "I'm done. I won't laugh anymore." Breaking her promise, her face crumpled, but she quickly composed her features and took a deep breath.

Under her gaze, I sat there, fiddling with the handle of my mug. Flora had just gotten on her school bus and we **had** been enjoying our coffee before we went to work. When enough time passed without her laughing, I deigned to speak.

"God knows—no pun intended—I know her ministry thing is weird. I mean, I couldn't figure it out. But when she told me her story, it made more sense. That's why I'm so surprised by your reaction."

"Do you really think she's telling the truth?"

I nodded furiously. "Why would she lie?"

"I'm sure she thinks she has her reasons," said Darva. "All I know is I don't believe a word of it."

"You didn't hear her," I said. "Darva, she was **sobbing.** The only time I've ever seen her so shook up is when her grandma died. She wouldn't—she **couldn't** fake it to that degree."

With a shrug, Darva gathered our cups and took them to the sink.

"Pathological liars learn to fake it to any degree that'll get them believed."

"Darva, dramatic things happen to people all the time!" I don't know why it was so important for me to convince Darva that Kristi was telling the truth, nor did I know why it was so important that I believe Kristi. "Think about it. Why would she drop out like she did? There are all those years when no knew what she was up to—and Kristi **loves** people knowing what she's up to."

Darva rinsed the cups and set them on the drying rack. "I've got to go. The Neilson sisters are leaving for Paris next month and they don't even know their present tense yet, let alone the future." Turning toward me, she wiped her hands on the dish towel. "Listen, Joe, I really do try to see the best in people, but as far as Kristi goes, there's a shadow of deceit that sort of obscures my vision." She waggled her head, as if pleased by her words. "I don't know if her becoming the Aimee Semple McPherson of the eighties is a total hoax or ninety-five percent hoax or ninety percent hoax, but believe me, hoax is a big part of the equation. You know that yourself—you remember how hard you laughed when we listened to that tape of her show?"

I tried to shrug away the fact that I really didn't have any answer.

"She's so fake she makes regular fakes look sincere." Shaking her head, Darva folded the damp towel, draped it over the oven handle, and grabbed her purse off the table. "Listen, I'll see you tonight—that is, if you don't buy a tambourine and run off with Shout Hallelujah!"

She gave me a big smile along with a kiss on the cheek, but I wasn't about to return either.

"Shoppers," I said after ringing the bell, "for those of you who knew Mr. Emmet Nordlund, you probably know he recently died. It was quick and he was ninety-four, so as far as deaths go, his was pretty good." I noticed a woman I hadn't previously seen in the store looking around as if trying to find out where this disembodied obituary was coming from. When she saw me in the window, she looked at me as if I was nuts. I waved to her and continued.

"Mr. Nordlund's daughter Janine stopped by with a box of his favorite books and instructed me to give them away to a book lover."

There were about two dozen shoppers in the store, and except for the new one who thought I was crazy, they all stood at attention, waiting for instructions.

"I've reached into the box and I've got a . . ." I looked to see what I had pulled out. "I've got **Leaves of Grass** by Walt Whitman. So the contest is, anyone who can recite a Walt Whitman poem—or part of one—gets the entire box of books. Anybody out there interested?"

Two housewives in the produce aisle looked at each other, shrugged, and got back to their lettuce and green bean selection.

The new shopper, shaking her head, reached into the ice cream freezer. Two women and a man in the cereal aisle huddled together briefly but separated with no answer.

Several regulars let me know they were out of the competition by shaking their heads. I continued scanning the aisles for just one Whitman-memorizing customer.

There! A man was waving at me by the dish detergents, and . . . Wait a second, wait a second. Another contender had come into view, holding up a finger as if she was bidding at an auction. It was Mrs. Casey.

"Ladies and gentlemen, it looks as if we have two prize contenders! Will those contenders, and anyone interested in a poetry recital, please meet at Banana Square. Thank you."

"Hey, Joe," said Mrs. Casey as I met her and Clarence Selwin by the six-foot inflatable banana hanging in a little niche by the produce section. It had been given to me as a promotional item from the banana company, and it looked so stupid I just had to display it. It hung behind two easy chairs—people liked to sit in them and arrange their coupons or check over their lists before they began shopping—and was at the right height for most people to reach, which meant it had collected a lot of autographs. (I find that people always enjoy putting their name to something, even a six-foot banana.) Now nearly every shopper in the store gathered at Banana Square, as they did whenever a contest was announced.

"So," I said, setting down the box of books, "who wants to start?"

Clarence Selwin swept the air with his hand. "Ladies' choice."

"Go ahead," said Mrs. Casey.

Mr. Selwin, the neighborhood barber, stood with his hands on his hips.

" 'O Captain! O Captain! our fearful trip is done; the ship has weather'd every rack, the prize we sought is won.' "

He scratched the back of his head and moved his lips soundlessly for a moment before continuing.

" 'The port is near, the bells I hear, the people all exulting. While . . . while . . .' "

He scratched the back of his head with his other hand now, but it didn't appear any memory was jogged.

" 'While . . .' "

" 'While follow eyes the steady keel,' " prompted Mrs. Casey.

Nodding, Mr. Selwin repeated the phrase and added, " 'The vessel grim and daring; but—' "

Mrs. Casey jumped in, and together they recited, " 'But O heart! heart! heart! O the bleeding drops of red, where on the deck my Captain lies, fallen cold and dead.' "

The shoppers paused before applauding.

"There's more," said Mr. Selwin. "Not that I remember the rest, but I bet you do."

"I love Walt Whitman," said Mrs. Casey demurely.

"Recite your poem," said a customer through cupped hands.

"Well, all right," said Kristi's mother, and with a little toss of her head, she began. " 'It is time to explain myself—let us stand up. What is known I strip away, I launch all men and women forward with me into the Unknown.' "

You could have heard a grapefruit drop—which I did, when someone leaned against the citrus display. Still, the thud on the floor didn't distract everyone from listening closely as Mrs. Casey recited the poem, applauding wildly after she spoke the line " 'Now on this spot I stand with my robust soul.' "

"Wow," I said, impressed. "That was quite a treat. But I admit, I'm in a bit of a conundrum. I promised the box of books to anyone who could recite a Walt Whitman poem, and we seem to have two winners."

"Oh, give it to her," said Mr. Selwin. "She helped me remember my poem **plus** she recited her own." He turned to her. "Flawlessly I might add."

"Well, thank you," said Mrs. Casey, "but how about we split the box? Does that sound fair, Joe?"

"Sounds fair to me. I'll go get an empty box and you two can decide who gets what."

The other customers turned their carts around to get back to the business of shopping, and when I returned to my prize winners with another box, they were seated in the two chairs, spreading the books out on the floor in front of them and taking turns choosing which ones they wanted.

"Look at this, Joe, we'll each get a dozen books!" said Mr. Selwin, paging through a collection by Theodore Roethke.

I squatted next to them. "Say," I said to Mrs. Casey as I watched her choose **The Complete Poems of Emily Dickinson,** "what'd you think of Kristi? I thought she looked just like she did in high school— except with more hair, of course."

"You saw Kristi?" said Mrs. Casey, her voice rushed.

"Yes," I said, and realizing my gaffe, I clumsily tried to change the subject. "So, you're more partial to modern poets, eh, Mr. Selwin?"

"I knew she was in town," said Mrs. Casey, beginning to pack up her books, "but after the fact. I can't tell you how many people called me after that newspaper article came out!" She struggled to her feet.

"But she didn't call me and she didn't stop by to see me, which makes me—" She quickly swiped away a tear with her pointer finger. "Well, it doesn't make me feel so hot, as you can imagine."

Mr. Selwin had been making a big production of piling his books in the box but finally, unable to keep it to himself, muttered, "**Kids.**"

"Exactly," said Mrs. Casey with a laugh.

I offered to carry her books out to her car, but she said she still had shopping to do and thought she could manage.

"Come over sometime and tell me about Kristi," she said. "But for now . . . now I'm in the mood for poetry. So maybe my opponent . . . ," she said, nodding toward the former barber.

"Clarence," he offered. "Clarence Selwin."

"Maybe Clarence and I will recite some more Whitman," she said.

"That'll be easy," said Mr. Selwin, holding up the copy of **Leaves of Grass.** "Now that I have my cheat sheet with me."

I stood under the banana listening to them take turns reading poems, until a new cashier signaled me that her register was out of tape.

Good evening, Pat from Ann Arbor. You're on the air with God.

Hi, Kristi. Hi, God.

God says hi back.

I sure hope so—in fact, that's sorta why I'm calling. (Long pause)

Go ahead, Pat, this is radio. We leave the deep silences to philosophy class.

Oh, okay. (Nervous laugh) **Anyways, Kristi, I was wondering, when God answers your prayers, what does He sound like?**

Hmmm. That's a good question, Pat. What does He sound like to you?

Well, that's just it. I'm not sure I hear Him. Every time I try to talk to Him, it's a pretty one-sided conversation.

God's language is beyond words, Pat. When I'm "in conference" with God, I don't hear Him, but I sense Him. And not the usual sense organs, but with my heart. When you listen to God with your heart, you hear what He's saying loud and clear.

Oh. Okay . . . so I shouldn't worry that I don't hear a big booming voice?

(Chuckles) There isn't a voice big enough or booming enough to speak for all that God is, Pat. Now find yourself a quiet place, pray, and listen for God's answer in your heart.

Well, I had a bypass last year, Kristi—I sure hope that doesn't affect the reception! (Beat) That was a joke.

Thanks for the caveat.

A new feature had been added to the Tuesday night dinners at my mother's house—we all sat around digesting our meal as we listened to Kristi Casey on the radio.

"The name of the show is **On the Air with God**?" said my mother the first time we heard it. "That sounds so . . . presumptuous."

We had been listening since the show debuted in January, but we missed a lot of what was said, owing to our habit of talking back to her outrageousness. When a caller said her brother was in a gay relationship and her husband no longer allowed her to go his house, Kristi said, "As Paul says in his letter to the Colossians, a wife must submit to her husband. I think that's your answer there. Why would you choose your brother over your husband—especially a brother who has not respected God's laws?

"God's laws!" Aunt Beth said, so forcefully that she rose from her seat. "I thought God's biggest law was to love one another!"

"She seemed so . . . I don't know, **modern** in high school," said my mother. "Now she thinks a wife should submit to her husband?"

"Try it," said Len agreeably. "You might like it."

"Remember," said Kristi another time to a caller contemplating divorce, "in Mark we are reminded that 'anyone who divorces his wife and marries another woman commits adultery against her.' "

"I don't get this show," said Linda. "Is she trying to be funny?"

"Yes," said Darva, "in a very sick way."

Everyone had been entertained by the novelty of listening to someone we knew on the radio, but after several broadcasts, Len would start dealing cards for a game of rook before the show was ended, or Beth might start the coffee for dessert. Finally, one April night, when I had turned up the volume to better hear Kristi over a spring rainstorm that was pummeling the roof, my mother said, "Why don't you just turn it off, Joe?"

"Amen," said Beth.

Looking to the others and seeing from their nods it was a majority opinion, I shrugged and turned the knob.

"How about we turn it off permanently?" suggested Darva, who along with Len had been helping Flora build a LEGO house for her imaginary friend. "Whatever the novelty of listening to her was, the novelty's **gone.**"

"I agree," said Linda, sitting on the couch with my mom and Beth. "I get a stomachache listening to her."

"Mme. Chou Chou got a stomachache at school today," said Flora, fitting a corner piece into the house. "Because Miss Greer yelled at Derek Peterson for picking his nose."

"I think Miss Greer yells entirely too much," said Darva, quickly examining a LEGO before throwing it back into the pile.

"The earlier a kid learns it's not cool to pick his nose in public," I said, "the better."

"Ha! A lot you know about appropriate behavior!" said Darva, pushing the LEGO pieces off her lap and standing up. "Come on, Flora, it's time to go home!"

The child was as startled as the adults.

"Mais, Maman, je veux finir la maison."

Darva didn't care about finishing the LEGO house.

"C'est tard. On y va!"

"Darva, what's the matter?" I asked, rising too.

"You don't need to go," said Darva, and in her voice she made clear her wish that I didn't. "Thanks for the dinner," she said to my mother, impatient as Flora made her rounds kissing everyone good-bye.

"Are you sure you don't want to wait out the rain?" asked Len.

Darva shrugged on her coat.

"Mme. Chou Chou does **not** want to get wet," said Flora, knitting her eyebrows together in a frown.

"Quel dommage," said Darva.

I caught my aunt's eye; she gave me the same look that was being exchanged between others. They didn't need to speak French to know that Darva had only said "Too bad." What made all of us uneasy was her tone of voice; it was as if she had slapped Flora with the words. Darva was a mother with infinite patience, and if she raised her voice to her daughter, something was seriously wrong.

"At least take an umbrella," said my mother, plucking one out of the stand by the door and handing it to Darva.

She took it and her daughter's hand and raced out the door as if she'd been dry too long and couldn't wait to get wet.

Later, after a halfhearted game of Scrabble, Beth and Linda gave me a ride home. The rain had faded to a mist, and if the night was a fabric, it would be a purple velvet.

"So what do you suppose is the matter with Darva?" asked Beth. The question had been asked several times already, but apparently my answers—different versions of "I don't know"—were unsatisfactory.

"How're things going with Bernard?" asked Linda of the man Darva had brought once or twice to Tuesday night dinners.

"Fine, as far as I know," I said.

I didn't pay much attention to her romantic life. Darva had been as noncommital in her relationships as I had; Reed had been replaced by Cliff, who'd recently been replaced by a fellow French teacher. We joked, in fact, that while we liked the people we went out with well enough to have sex with; we just didn't like them as well as we liked each other.

"Well, I know there's nothing wrong with her painting," said Beth. "She just showed the series she's working on—the season stuff? Wow."

"Maybe she's working too much," said Linda "You know, with the painting and the teaching."

"I don't know," I said. "She loves both. How hard can it be to love what you're doing?"

It wasn't that hard . . . but it was, as I learned that night.

"Joe, before you say anything," she said, greeting me at the door wearing a robe, her head wrapped in a towel turban, "let me just say I'm sorry. I've already apologized to Flora and Mme. Chou Chou, who, according to Flora, thought I was **très impolie.**"

I smiled and shrugged, awkward with the exchange—probably because we found the need to apologize to each other so rare.

"Come on in the kitchen, I'm making tea."

"You sure got wet," I said, noting her all-terry-cloth ensemble.

"Not from the rain. I took a shower."

At the kitchen table, the scene of so many of our conferences, she told me why she had lately been so on edge and distracted.

"Joe, I can't take it anymore."

"Whoa," I said, my heart taking a little elevator ride. "What do you mean?"

"My life."

I can't say what the look was on my face, but whatever it was, it inspired Darva to laugh.

"Oh God, what an idiot I am." She reached across the table and took my hand. "You look like I just told you I'm suicidal."

I nodded and swallowed hard. I was relieved, but only by degrees. I still knew there was something else coming.

"What I mean is, I can't take my life here anymore. My American life. I think I'm going to move back to Paris."

"You think or you know?"

Darva blew at her hot tea. "Know. I feel like my painting's become more of a hobby—"

"But you had that show last year!"

"And I know for a fact I paint better in France. I've already got a couple of job leads as far as translation goes, and I'm working on an apartment."

The elevator that had plunged with my heart on it took another drop.

A numbness spread through me, like a sheet of ice covering up the roiling waters underneath. "What . . . what . . . you mean is you can't take your American life with me?"

Tears, like little sequins, sparkled in Darva's dark eyes.

"Oh, Joe, you're the reason I lasted here so long. You're the reason it's going to be so hard to leave."

I looked at the handle of my mug, infinitely interesting to me at the moment.

"Don't let it be hard," I said, feeling as if my words were chunks of plaster I had to cough up. "Don't go."

"How about you come with us?" asked Darva brightly. "Live the life of an expatriate?"

"Sure, and maybe I can open up a Haugland Foods on the Champs-Elysées."

It wasn't a particularly funny response, but I felt I had to say something to distract me from the word **us,** because the full weight of losing not just Darva but Flora had knocked me off my chair, even though it looked as if I still sat in it.

"Joe, do you know I dream more in French than I do in English? I wake up sometimes thinking I'll run down to the **boulangerie** for croissants and I'll feel so happy . . . and then I'll remember where I am and that I'll probably have Cheerios for breakfast."

"We'll get croissants! I'll get them at the store!"

"Joe, I never felt more at home—more me—than when I lived in Paris . . . and living here with you."

"Then stay! We'll take trips there—two or three a year! We'll spend Flora's summer vacation there!"

"**Mon chèr, chèr** Joe," she said, her eyes glittery with tears again. "In a contest between home here and home there, it was always you who tipped the scales and made me want to stay. You're the best friend I've ever had. But now . . . well, Bernard is going back to Paris in September and . . . I'm getting serious about Bernard."

"Bernard!" I said, practically shouting. "But you and I make fun of Bernard and his little tiny shoes and his lousy taste in music!"

Darva smiled. "He can't really help the size of

his feet and . . . well, nobody can be as perfect as us, Joe."

I felt my whole body hunch over like an autumn leaf curling up to die, and Darva reached over to smooth the hair on the head that now needed the table for support.

Eighteen

Good evening, you're on the air with God.

Hi, Kristi. I feel kinda funny calling you, like I'm writing a letter to the Christian Dear Abby or something.

What's on your mind . . . ?

Uh, Burt.

What's on your mind, Burt?

Well, Kristi, it's really about my wife. She, uh, well, there's a casino just opened up near us and she's kinda having a hard time staying away.

Is she gambling a lot, Burt?

Uh, quite a bit, yeah. (Sob)

And you've prayed for God to help her stop?

All the time.

Well, here's what you do, Burt. You go public with your prayers. You go with her to the casino and you sit next to her, and you pray as loud as you can every time she puts a coin into the slot machine. You shout your prayers so loud that you drown out the noise of those slot machines!

Uh, I don't know if I could do that.

Why not, Burt?

Well, for one, I'd feel stupid. And two, she'd feel stupid.

So you're willing to lose your savings but not risk feeling stupid?

Uh, I don't—

A reminder to you, Burt: Prayer anywhere, at any time, is not stupid. It's effective. Thanks for calling, Burt, and try to have a little faith.

Like most kids, I thought the world had been created for my pleasure and amusement, but when my dad died, I learned that not only did the world **not** think I was its golden boy, but on a scale of its great concerns, I didn't even register. When I say the world, I suppose I mean God, although after a childhood of Sunday school at Granite Creek Lutheran, I still can't say I believe in the God that was taught there, the almighty Father. Especially not after the almighty Father let my real father crash in that soybean field with Miles Milnar.

My mother, who had been the church pianist and organist, continued going to Granite Creek Lutheran, even though she never again sat on a piano bench there.

"I still believe," she told the choir director, "but right now, I just can't celebrate. And that's what playing music is for me: a celebration."

In that first raw year of grief, I thought I **had** to be the strong one for my mother, but occasionally my mother wrestled me for the title, and so to me she said, "Joe, I can understand you thinking God let you down. But it wasn't God. It was bad weather and a stalled engine."

"Oh sure. Moses can part the seas, Lazarus can rise from the dead, but God couldn't figure out how to get a little more gas into a fuel line?"

My mother tried to beat back her cringe with a smile. "So something from Sunday school has stuck." She sighed, and took my hand in hers.

"Joe, I don't have all the answers—in fact, I hardly have **any** answers. But I do have a couple big ones: love, of course, and faith and hope."

"But what do those answer?" I asked, my voice dark with sarcasm.

"Lots of things," said my mother quietly. "Especially 'How do I keep going?' "

I hated to cry in front of my mother, and sensing I was battling back tears, my mom dropped my hands and wrapped her arms around me. It was a shelter I couldn't fight.

"See, Joe," she said as my body shook with little tremors, "I love you, and that makes me keep going. Faith that as much as this hurts, we're handling it—that makes me keep going. And hope that things will get better for us makes me keep going."

Gathering enough breath to talk, I said, "Faith and hope sound kind of the same."

The laugh in her chest felt like a purr.

"I think faith is more everyday—like jeans—and hope is more dress-up. You know, you have faith you can get through this next hour, and you hope that someday everything will be wonderful."

I was already confirmed, so she let me drop out of Sunday school, but I did go to church with her every

Sunday, because no matter how much I silently heckled Pastor Allen when I listened to the sermons, or no matter where my mind wandered to when I didn't, I knew that having her son sitting next to her was helping my mother dress up.

When we moved to Minneapolis, we fell out of regular church membership until my mother accepted an invitation from a fellow teacher to visit her church, which had great music. Apparently my mom thought so too, and that was enough to bring her back to church, and take Beth along with her. She let me choose whether or not I wanted to go or sleep in, and I chose sleeping in.

"It's a holy thing for me," I joked.

I was happy to rouse myself on those holidays that other non-churchgoers muster themselves up for, but as an adult, I was a member of no church. Eventually my faith settled around the beliefs I had as a boy, although it was a little less egocentric. I believed that the whole universe and every being in it was a part of God in a great and mysterious way—words like **Force** and **Spirit** come to mind—and I often found myself thanking this force and asking for its help. Yeah, I prayed. And the prayer I repeated over and over for Darva in August 1988 wasn't that she **not** live in France but that she **live.**

It can be a clear sunny day, it can be a dark stormy night, or it can be any of those variables in between when the world as you know it stops and another one starts.

It had been a mild spring Saturday morning when my mother woke me up to tell me about my father's death, shaking my shoulder so hard that I thought she was trying to be funny, and so I groan-laughed every time her hand pumped my back, in parcels of "Uh—uh—uh," until she shouted my name and the panic in her voice let me know right away something was terribly wrong.

On this particular late morning I was at the store, in Banana Square with a small crowd who was deciding who should win a gift certificate to the Nokomis Shoe Shop. The contest had called for songs that had something to do with feet, and by their applause, it looked as if talent was going to best beauty. The crowd had responded politely to "Running on Empty" as sung by Randi, a young woman decked out in the summer bikini-top-and-towel-sarong uniform of teenage girls, but had gone crazy when Millie Purcell, whose summer uniform (in fact, her year-round uniform) read "Beeker's Bowling Alley," sang a soulful version of "I Walk the Line." Mr. Snowbeck, resident Twinkies shoplifter, had offered, "These Boots Are Made for Walkin' " but only knew the refrain.

I presented the certificate to Millie, who certainly could use nice new shoes, partial as she was to wearing a pair of faded, tricolored bowling shoes whether she was working or not. As the shoppers ambled away, I was admiring the colors of the summer produce when Stan, my new assistant manager, told me I had a telephone call.

"It's your mother," he said, the type of guy who always wanted to give you as much information as possible. "I asked if I could take a message, but she said she wanted to speak to you. She probably wants you to pick up something." Stan's own mother called once or twice a day to place grocery orders with him.

Sitting down in my swivel chair, I picked up the receiver on my desk. I had no idea that this simple gesture was a bridge taking me from one world to another.

"Ma," I said, "what are you out of? Chocolate or—"

"Joe," she said, and her voice was like a tank barreling through the foliage of my greeting. "Joe, you've got to come home now."

Beads of cold sweat sprouted on my upper lip and under my arms. She had come to our house that morning to babysit Flora while Darva and I worked.

"Is Flora—"

"Flora's fine," she said. "It's Darva."

When I pulled up to the curb in front of my house, my mother raced ran down the steps and jumped into the car.

"I'll go with you to the hospital," she said, fastening her seat belt.

"What about Flora?"

"Len's with her."

"What happened?"

"Oh, Joe, they just said there was an accident. A car accident."

Sitting in the hospital waiting room, I realized the heavy white cloth my fingernail kept drawing circles on was my store apron. I stood up, reaching around to pull the neck loop over my head, but then I sat again, deciding to keep it on. If anything represented my normal world, it was my store apron, and I didn't want to jinx anything by taking it off.

I thought that because I had experienced tragedy at a young age, I had earned a pass, redeemable only at an age (about eighty, I figured) when I might be able to handle the loss of those I loved.

Ed's death had shaken me in that I suspected the bargain might not be as inviolate as I'd thought, but still, I could handle his departure from this world better than say, my mother's or my aunt's.

And now a doctor was denying the protective power of my grocer's apron by standing in front of my mother and me and telling us things didn't look good.

"**Things?**" I said, fighting back the desire to throw up. "What things?"

"Miss—" He looked at his clipboard. "Miss Pratt has suffered severe head trauma. In a situation like this, we have to prepare ourselves for the worst."

"How would you suggest we do that?" I asked, my voice belligerent.

My mother squeezed my hand, a signal to back off, and I was seized with a sudden flash of hate for her, the person who had been the one to bring me— twice—out of my old world and into a worse one.

I think she felt **some** vibe I was giving off, but, unable to interpret it, she continued to hold my hand as she asked the doctor, "Can we go see her?"

That morning, less than four hours ago in the real time of the world, but eons ago in the surreal time I now lived in, my mother, accompanied by Len, had arrived at our house with a streusel coffee cake and a fairy dress she said she hadn't been able to resist buying for Flora.

"It's got a net skirt out to here," she said, gesturing with her hands. "The last time we played dress-up, she said she didn't have a good fairy dress, so when I saw it at Dayton's, I thought what the heck, I'll splurge."

"Flora's still sleeping," said Darva, "but can I see it?"

My mother took a package out of a Haugland Foods grocery bag (her tote of choice) but, seeing it was gift-wrapped, Darva said never mind, she'd see it after Flora opened it.

We could have opted for having some of the coffee cake but decided instead, as long as Flora was covered, to take a quick walk around the lake. My gratitude for that decision has never dimmed.

It had been a summer of discontent between us; when I wasn't mad at her for wanting to break up our life, I was depressed. Whenever Bernard came over, I couldn't hurry out of the room fast enough. It was childish, but I was honestly afraid that if I saw him, the desire to punch him in the face might jump over the gates of fantasy into reality, and I knew bloodying the Frenchman's **nez** was not going to earn me any points with Darva.

I didn't hide in another room when Darva pressed for "dialogue" and "civil discourse," which wasn't to say I had an adult response to these requests either. Any mature and helpful conversation usually burnt out within minutes with accusations and name-calling. Yes, mostly on my part, but sometimes on Darva's too, allowing me to say satisfying things like "So much for our dialogue" or "Now **that** was a civil discourse."

One afternoon Darva had come into the store for some milk, and I told her that she'd have to be careful in France, because they didn't pasteurize their milk as well as we did.

"You're a real xenophobe, you know that?"

"Yeah, well, you're . . . ," I began, filled with a gaseous mix of anger and embarrassment. "You're gonna find out how hard it'll be once you get there."

The expression on Darva's face asked, **Are you nuts?** and then she burst into tears. Mrs. Rog, who had been waddling toward me, waving a handful of what were probably expired coupons she wanted me to accept, stopped in the middle of the aisle, her mouth a tiny O of surprise.

I let her think I was harassing a customer, or whatever the hell she thought, and I let Darva stand there, digging in her purse for a tissue, as I stomped off to my office lair.

It was only when Flora became affected, when she'd take turns clinging to her mother or clinging to me, when she left a note on my pillow asking why I was so mad at Maman and when she left a note on Darva's asking why she was so mad at **mon** Joe, that we both came to the conclusion that it's all right to act like children only if no **real** children are affected by the behavior. So we took Flora out for ice cream and explained that both of us had been under a lot of pressure lately and it had made us crabby, but we both were going to try to act better.

"Why **are** you so crabby?" Flora asked me between solemn licks of her rocky road ice cream cone.

The chocolate malt I had swallowed flash-froze in my throat. I shrugged, and when the cold lump finally melted, I said, "Sometimes people get crabby when they're sad."

"Are you sad because we're moving to France?"

I nodded.

"But Maman says it will be a wonderful learning experience."

"I'm sure it will be."

Flora squinted her deep brown eyes at her mother. "I go to school," she said. "I don't need any more wonderful learning experiences."

My ally! I thought, and I couldn't help laughing, and then we all had a good laugh, sitting around that sticky round marble table, and Flora was thrilled, not noticing that the dispenser napkins her mother pressed to her eyes were not dabbing away tears of happiness.

And then, oh happy day, Darva told me in late July that she and Bernard were having problems. The news kept getting better—by mid-August she had decided their problems were unsolvable ones and Bernard was going back home but **sans** her. While she still wanted to live in France, maybe it would be on a seasonal basis; maybe she and Flora would spend their summers there.

"I mean, it would work out school-wise," she said, thinking aloud. "Although I do hate to be there during tourist season."

"Well, tourists don't go there in the summer for no reason," I said. "I'll bet it's the most spectacular time of the year there."

Darva raised one eyebrow in a look of bemused pity, and I grabbed her face in my hands and kissed her full on those beautiful smirking lips.

It had been a hot humid week, but when we took our walk around the lake that morning, it was cool, still too early for the heavy stew the sun and the dew point average would mix up later. We held hands—not because we were lovers, but because we were friends again—and as we were about to pass the dock, we saw a man in a straw hat standing out on it, waving his fishing pole back and forth in the water. Suddenly, we both broke into the song "Draggin' the Line."

"I know great minds think alike," I said, "but that was freaky."

"I know," said Darva. "I haven't sung that song in years."

Delighted in our synergy, we sang the chorus, swinging hands.

"It's not really true what I said about my painting," said Darva after we'd finished singing. "I thought if anything would suffer by my not going back to Paris, it would be my art. I mean, **mon Dieu,** it is **the** artists' mecca, but then I looked at what I've gotten done here, up in my little attic studio." She squeezed my hand. "Thank you for that, by the way."

"You're welcome."

"I guess I was kind of a snob thinking my painting suffered because I wasn't working in some garret on the rue d'Orsay, but now I think my work's a little richer, because I painted here, at home."

"I am so happy you're not leaving."

"For now," reminded Darva. "Remember, I'm serious about spending summers there."

"Summers I can handle."

"But what about when you fall in love, Joe? And what about when I do?"

"I like how you say **when** instead of **if**."

"You don't think it'll happen for you?"

We were still holding hands, and I held them up and looked at our entwined fingers.

"Sure I do," I said after a long moment. "In fact, I bet we'll both be married by next Friday."

"Whew," said Darva, laughing. "That's **fast**. I wonder where I'll meet my husband?"

"Don't get too excited," I said as a man on roller skates staggered toward us, "but I think that's him."

He had squeezed a big belly into a tank top with a picture of the band ZZ Top on it, and what hair he had was pulled back into a limp ponytail.

"**All right**," said Darva, and after he lurched by, she made a motion as if to follow him. "But what about you?"

"Well, Miss Dawson's been making overtures in the store," I said, referring to the eighty-year-old retired gym teacher. "Why, just yesterday she asked me to get her a can of tomatoes she couldn't reach, and when I did, she said I had awfully nice upper body musculature."

"Well, you do," agreed Darva.

"Bodybuilders and grocers," I said, "best bodies in the world. From all the heavy lifting."

"You know, Bernard was jealous of you. He was sure we had had an affair."

"It's never too late."

"He couldn't understand how we could be smart enough to always know we'd make better friends than lovers."

"How did we ever get that smart?"

"Well, you always liked big breasts, Joe, and I'm never going to have those."

"True," I said, pointedly looking at her modest chest. "And you always liked guys with small . . . feet."

"Well, you know what they say: small feet, deep intellect."

"So now you're calling me stupid?"

So besides good exercise (we clipped along), our walk around the lake was full of teasing, some singing, some laughs. Our usual good time—only what would make this so unusual was that it was our last.

PART THREE

Nineteen

Good evening, you're on the air with God.

You're a maniac! You're nuts! You're—

(Sound of phone hanging up)

God loves you, caller, but then God's a lot more patient than me. Now, everyone knows I don't screen my calls because, after all, God never screened anyone. And if He could handle lepers and prostitutes and sinners, surely I can handle the occasional unhinged caller. But that doesn't mean I have to waste valuable airtime with people whose brains are large enough only to hold the naughty words they learned in junior high.

The radio was always on. I might turn it up if I wanted to listen to Kristi's show, but otherwise it played softly, like parents murmuring in the other room. I remember when I was in my bed, ready to go to sleep, my parents' conversation in the living room was a lullaby; that's how safe their voices made me feel. But no DJ, no song, no evangelist could ever be Rolf and Carole Andreson talking about how much to contribute to the library fund, or what a dumb show **Green Acres** was, or whether or not to remodel the kitchen. Still, I couldn't turn it off; to be in silence was to know I wouldn't hear Darva calling down from her studio for me to come up and look at her new painting, wouldn't hear her chattering to Flora in French, wouldn't hear her talk back to the TV when she watched the news. The trouble was, sometimes the radio played songs that punched you in the gut, that brought you to your knees.

When I heard the Bee Gees song that asked how could you mend a broken heart, I screamed back, "You don't, you fucking idiots!" and when I heard "You've Got a Friend," I knew the DJ was out to get me, playing all these songs from when I first met Darva, and when Billy Joel sang "Piano Man" I had to lay my head down and cry, because I hated the song and Darva loved it, saying it reminded her of a French bar song.

"Why is the radio always on?" Flora asked me, a week or so after her mother died.

"Does it bother you?"

"If you like it," she said carefully, "I like it."

She was my charge now, not just emotionally but legally, thanks to Darva's responsible nature. When she and Flora had moved in with me, Darva had asked if I would be Flora's guardian "in the event of my death."

"So your death's going to be an event?" I'd said, laughing, "like a birthday party or a fish fry?"

"S'il te plaît," Darva had said, papers spread out in front of her on the coffee table. "Just for my piece of mind, say yes."

"Yes," I'd told her. "But only if you leave me all your worldly possessions."

"Flora's not really a **possession**," Darva had said, "but she's the most valuable thing in my life. That's why you'll have to take such good care of her."

"I will," I had said, feeling uncomfortable, "but don't die."

Darva had looked up from her papers and made a **tuh** sound. "Don't worry, I won't."

But she did.

My mother and I drove home from the hospital in that state of disbelief that erases all memory of motion, so when you turn the key in the lock of your front door, you wonder: **How did I get here?**

Len and Flora were sitting at the kitchen table, putting together a puzzle, and when he looked at us, his features sagged. Flora immediately burst into tears.

"Hey," I said, taking her in my arms, but anything else I'd planned to say to her was gobbled up by the black monster that was grief.

After the funeral, there had been a reception at my house, arranged by my mom and Len and Beth and Linda, who were doing everything I couldn't do. In this case, everything was **everything**.

Kirk had flown in, leaving behind Nance, who was about to deliver their first child.

"I can't believe how glad I am to see you," I said as we swayed together in a bear hug.

"I can't believe how much this sucks," he said, his voice breaking. "I'm . . . just . . . having a hard time taking it all in."

A lot of people from high school showed up; people I saw in the store and people I hadn't seen for years.

"She was one of the most talented students I ever had," said Mr. Eggert, our old art teacher, his artist's hands now shaky with Parkinson's. "Did you know she sent me little drawings from Paris? Sketches of a waiter, the Tuileries, those little boys she babysat for a while . . ."

His voice trailed off, and he stared at me, his expression half angry and half pained.

"She was so nice to me," said Shannon Saxon, her former lushness replaced by a thin brittleness. "When I was having all those problems with Don, I'd bring my kids to the park, because I knew Darva would be there. I'd talk for hours and she'd sit there, sometimes holding my hand, listening to me."

"Did I hear right that you guys never got it on?" said Todd Randolph, who was now a city councilman (even if he'd run in my district, I never would have voted for him).

I hoped he could see that the look I gave him contained all the scorn I had ever felt for him.

"Just wondering," he said with a shrug of his meaty shoulders. "Either way, I am sorry for your loss."

It was after everyone had gone, when Kirk was helping Len pick up dirty plates in the living room and my mom was scraping leftovers into a plastic dish and Beth and Linda were wrapping up the brownies and cookies that hadn't been eaten, that

Flora took my hand and led me to the backyard, to the swing set I had installed when she was two.

"Do you want me to push you?" I asked, confused, as she sat on the swing.

"No." She sat looking at her feet. "I just wanted to tell you something . . . and this is the only place where it's not loud."

The other swing was too small for me to sit on, so I sat sideways on the bottom of the slide. Looking at my feet, I noticed how the lawn seemed more clover than grass.

"The thing I wanted to tell you," she said, and I forced myself to look up at her, even though it was easier to inspect the clover, "is Mme. Chou Chou is dead too."

The manly stoicism I had managed to spackle together for the funeral service and reception crumbled like the inferior plaster it was.

"Oh, Flora," I said, my voice catching on the trip wire of my emotion. "Oh, Flora."

"I'm eight years old now," said Flora. "And Mme. Chou Chou knew I was getting too old to have her hanging around anymore."

My arms were wrapped around my legs, and I had leaned so far forward that I felt my cheek on my knees. I wanted to say something soothing, but my throat was a dry well.

"She's with Maman now," said Flora. Drawing herself back on her tiptoes, she pushed forward and began to swing. "They're in Paris."

I felt a curtain of sadness being pulled over me, but I resisted—I had to resist—and pulled it back.

"Flora," I said, trying not to let my voice crack, "you know they're not really in Paris, don't you?"

"Not **Paris** Paris," said Flora, stiffening her legs as she swung forward. "A different Paris. A better Paris.

"Paris Heaven," I suggested.

"**Mais oui,**" she said as tears began to stream down her face. "**Maman et Mme. Chou Chou sont à Paris et au ciel.**"

The business of life forces you to stay afloat when grief would just as soon as let you drown. Flora was going to start the third grade, and I was plunged into a world of meetings with her teacher, the school nurse, and the principal, all people who assured me their goal was to create, under the circumstances, the safest, happiest environment they could for her.

I walked Flora to school the first day, and when I picked her up in the afternoon, she raced to me as if I was home plate and she was being chased by the third baseman. I carried her for a block and a half, until she stopped crying.

When she lifted her head from the crook in my shoulder, she looked around, dazed.

"Wow," she said in a small voice, "you got far." She rubbed her face against my shirt, and I managed a laugh, knowing I was being used as a human tissue.

"I can walk now," said Flora.

"I can still carry you," I said.

"That's okay, I'll walk."

My biceps said **thank you** as I set her on the side-walk, and she smoothed the skirt of her dress and adjusted the straps of her backpack, which were draped halfway down her arms. She reached out for my hand, and I took it. As we proceeded to walk home, she told me, in a voice occasionally broken by gasps, about her day.

"Miss Englund is real nice," she said, and I saw that as she looked ahead she squinted, just as Darva had done when she was trying to concentrate. "I saw her eating Life Savers when we were practicing our letters."

"Did you ask if you could have one?"

Flora chuckled. "No. But I wanted to say, **I thought you said there was no eating in class!**"

"She said that?"

"Mmm-hmmm. Almost right after the bell rang, after she had everyone say who they were. She said, 'These are the class rules and I expect you to follow them.' And 'no eating' was on the list."

"Maybe you should turn her in to the principal," I suggested. "You can't have a teacher breaking her own rules."

Flora laughed again, a high note in a score full of bass ones.

"Caitlyn Anderson is my new friend and so is Erin . . . I forget her last name—it's real long. I sit next to a boy named Tony who wears glasses, and another boy named Jason said he had four eyes at recess. What does that mean?"

It means Jason's an asshole, I thought, but instead I said, "It means Jason needs to learn better manners."

"That's what Miss Englund said when Caitlyn told on him. She said one of the most important rules of the class is to respect your neighbor."

"That's a good rule."

"I think it's funny that she says **neighbor,** though.

Mr. and Mrs. O'Keefe are our neighbors. And Mr. and Mrs. Kingsbeck. But not the kids in my class."

"Sometimes **neighbor** is a word for everyone around you."

A young woman walked toward us, trying to reign in a golden retriever puppy with little success.

"Oh, can I pet him?" asked Flora, kneeling down on the sidewalk.

"Sure," said the woman as the puppy leapt up on Flora, its tail moving like a propeller, its tongue slathering every inch of Flora's face.

It was a real tonic; after the owner pulled her dog away, Flora got off the sidewalk. She was weak from laughter.

"I love your dog!" she called after the woman.

"Thanks!" she replied as the dog yanked her down the street.

Flora took my hand as we continued our walk home.

"Caitlyn has a dog. She says he's really old, though, and not much fun. Caitlyn says her mom's old too but pretty fun. Erin goes to day care after school, because her mom works. She's a nurse." Flora sighed. "I think I'm the only one in my class who doesn't have a mom."

It was a beautiful day; the afternoon sun was buttery, not bright, the sky was a pure deep blue, and the trace of melancholia that I've always felt was tucked under September's balminess deepened.

"Do you want me to carry you again?" I asked.

"**S'il te plaît,**" she said, and I gathered her up in my arms again and walked home.

Thank God for my tightly woven, extra-strength

safety net. My mom and Len, Flora's **grand-mère et grand-père,** and Tantes Beth and Linda were over so much that the surprise was when they **weren't** in the kitchen cooking dinner or baking cookies, when they **weren't** in the living room watching **MacGyver** or **Murder, She Wrote** with Flora or helping her with her spelling, when one or two of them **weren't** there defrosting the refrigerator or doing my laundry when I got home from work.

Because I had to work, of course. Actually, I fled to the store like the lifeboat it was. It was the one place where things hadn't changed. The cornflakes and oatmeal were still in the cereal aisle; the coffee and tea were still positioned next to the juices; the chips and snack food were still across from the candy. I could walk down any aisle, past any counter, and know exactly where everything was. And I knew my cashiers, my bag and stock boys, my butchers, and my assistant manager, and I knew my customers.

"Here, I made this for Flora," said Eileen, my head cashier, giving me a quilt with a small French flag and an artist's palette appliquéd on it. "It's in memory of her mother and the things she loved."

"Here," said Mr. Snowbeck, giving me a package of Twinkies he had stolen just minutes earlier. "Give them to Flora."

"Here," said Millie Purcell, handing me a homemade sock monkey that smelled vaguely of cigarette smoke. "I made this for Flora."

Most of the time I was touched by all the gestures of goodwill and thoughtfulness, but occasionally the kindness of my customers and staff was almost a burden, a weight I felt I couldn't bear, and I'd race to my office and sit in my swivel chair, rocking until my composure returned.

I had done just that—run to the shelter of my office—after Mrs. Rog gave me yet another plate of her "world-famous fudge." Both Flora and I, upon trying the first batch, decided it deserved its title, but it was the words that accompanied the gift that made me choke back tears.

"It's not a magic pill," said Mrs. Rog, who at eighty-seven still drove to the store every Monday afternoon for her weekly shopping. "But they do say that chocolate releases some kind of feel-good hormone in the body, and if anyone deserves to feel good, it's you and Flora."

There used to be a "cry room" in movie theaters—a small room off the balcony where mothers could take their babies or small children and watch the movie behind a glass window. Sometimes it seemed to me my office had become my cry room.

The phone rang, but I left it to someone in the back room to answer and was going to ignore the red blinking light that signaled the call was for me.

Reluctantly, heavily, I leaned forward and picked up the phone.

"Hello?"

"Joe, it's a girl!"

"Kirk?"

"We finally got our baby! Eight pounds, six ounces. Twenty-one inches, in case you're one for stats."

My mood climbed out of the basement as I fully comprehended what he was telling me.

"A girl! That's great! How's Nance? What's she look like? How're you? What'd you name her?"

Kirk filled me in with all the details. Nance was fine; it was hard to tell who the baby looked like—"their faces are kinda squished up, you know"; he was fine; they'd named her Coral—"you know, because we both think the reefs are about the most beautiful things we've ever seen."

The happy news buoyed our conversation for a good long while, until Kirk apologized.

"Nance feels so bad she wasn't at the funeral, Joe—but who'd have thought Coral would come three weeks late? Anyway, she just wanted me to let you know Coral's middle name."

Sometimes it hurt to hear Darva's name, and I tensed, preparing myself for him to say it.

"It's Rapturia—after that painting she gave us for our wedding. We thought it might be nice to name a work of our art after Darva's." Kirk laughed. "Shit, that sounds pretentious, doesn't it? What I mean is, we thought it was a nice way to honor Darva . . . and also because it sounded a lot better than Coral Darva."

His laugh was still self-conscious but eased up when I joined in.

"I think it's an all-around excellent choice," I said. "Darva would be thrilled—I just hope Coral is when the kids at school learn what her middle name is."

"Are you kidding me? Have you heard the names parents are giving their kids these days? Rapturia's like Mary or Ann compared to them."

He filled me in on the birth ("Man, I've seen

dophins and manatees get born, but this was something else"), on Nance ("At one point she told me to eat shit," he said happily. "I guess it's common at a certain point in labor to attack the father"), and his mother's reaction ("I can't remember when I've seen her so happy").

"Sorry," he said finally. "I guess I'm being an ass going on and on about all these great things in my life."

"Believe me, I could use some good news for a change."

There was a short pause. "It still doesn't seem real."

"What?" I asked. "Having the baby?"

"No . . . Darva."

My sigh could have blown out an octogenarian's birthday cake.

"It's just in the last couple days that I don't expect her to come through the door," I said. "Listen, Kirk, I should get back to work. Give Nance a big kiss for me, and Coral too. I'm really happy for you."

"Thanks, Joe. I know you are."

After I hung up the receiver, I picked it up again and did something I had done dozens of times since Darva died: I called my mom. She, more than anyone, understood the mind-bending, soul-numbing state I was in.

I told her Kirk's good news, and while she was happy to hear it, she knew I had something else on my mind. That's why it was so easy to call her; she could read my moods like a seer.

"So what is it today?" she asked, her voice gentle in the way only a concerned mother's can be.

"I can't stop thinking," I began, "how none of us is safe from anything. I could be hit by a guy on his way to sign divorce papers, **you** could be hit by a guy on his way to sign divorce papers, **Flora** could be hit by a guy on his way to sign divorce papers."

"But it was Darva," my mother said softly. "It was Darva who got hit by a guy on his way to sign divorce papers. Just like it was your dad who went up in that airplane that crashed."

"So what's your point exactly?" I said, bothered that she had failed to console me, the thing I'd counted on her to do.

"My point is that a guy who had an appointment with a divorce attorney ran a red light and hit Darva's car. That's what happened to **her**. It doesn't mean it's going to happen to any of us."

"I'm just so . . . afraid," I whispered, even though I was all alone in my office. "Afraid that anytime, anywhere, something terrible can happen."

"It can," said my mother, a response that made me hold the receiver out and look at it, as if I could see the flip and thoughtless person who'd intercepted my call from my mother. "But odds aren't it won't."

"Odds didn't work for Darva."

"No, they didn't, Joe."

"I feel . . . I feel like I blew it. I loved her so much, Mom—she was my best friend. I should have protected her more. I should have driven her to work that day."

"Joe, you know how I beat myself up when your dad died. Why did I let him go up in that plane with Miles? Why didn't I make him stay home and go drapery shopping with me? Why didn't I, why didn't I, why didn't I? As many times as you ask those questions, you're never going to get an answer."

"Life stinks."

"You're right, Joe. Sometimes it does." After a moment she said, her voice a tone brighter, "Are you and Flora coming tonight?"

"It's Tuesday, isn't it?"

"Good. Can you bring a pint of cream?"

"Yes, Mother," I said, like the good mama's boy I was.

Twenty

Hello, listeners. Before we get into your calls, I'd just like to take this opportunity to tell you about a wonderful new product I've been invited to endorse. As you can imagine, I get a lot of these invitations, but trust me, the Kristi Casey stamp of approval only goes on products that bless your life.

Like the Perfect Rose skin care line. Now, I happen to think that the gifts God gives us are gifts we need to take care of. And ladies, we can do that with the Perfect Rose astringent. And Perfect Rose cleanser. And lastly—but not leastly—Perfect Rose moisturizer. God doesn't make mistakes, but we do. And if you haven't taken care of your skin, if you've overtanned, overeaten, or undercleansed—what I'm saying, ladies, is if you've sinned against your skin—Perfect Rose will help you restore the bloom, the petal softness of the gift that is your perfect skin. Try it today—it's available at drugstores everywhere!

The scandals of televangelists in the late 1980s didn't touch Kristi; in fact, her appearance on the newly revamped **Hour of Christian Love** was said to have helped herald the new age of **HCL,** as it was called by its legions of followers.

I watched her, enthralled as an entomologist looking inside the hive at the queen bee.

"**Elle est belle,**" said Flora as Kristi strode out onto the sparkly set, wearing a long flowing gown and carrying, like a pageant winner, an armful of roses.

"She **is** pretty," I conceded.

"For you," said Kristi, and the new host (whose hair was so perfect it looked like he wore a toupee of plastic) who had replaced the ousted and jailed one held out his arms.

"Not **you,**" said Kristi with a laugh, "For your better half."

The host's wife, whose hair had its own teased and lacquered magnificence, accepted the flowers, drawling, "Bless your heart, Krissie."

I was probably the only viewer who saw Kristi's radar go up, saw that glint in her eye that said, **Well, let the games begin.**

"Did I just lose my **t**?" she asked comically, then lifted up several cushions of the guest's couch, finally waving at the camera to let everyone know, "I'm just joshin'."

The studio audience laughed and their applause turned into a chant: "Kristi. Kristi. Kristi."

"I believe those are your fans, the Kristi Corps, speaking," said the host, Johnny "How could you not be a man of God with a last name like mine?" Priestly.

"Yup, they'll correct your pronunciation every time!"

Jean Ann Priestly held up her hand. Looking at her lethal red fingernails, I thought, **I wonder if Johnny lets her pick the pimples on his back with those things.**

"As God is my witness, Kristi, I'll never forget one of your consonants again!"

This got a big laugh and more applause, so I turned to Flora to get a normal person's reaction. She looked less amused than puzzled.

"So if Maman and you went to school with her," she said, "how come she looks so young?"

I couldn't be offended, it was true; at thirty-seven, Kristi still had that smooth-faced, bright-eyed what's-next look of youth, whereas I, well, at least I had all my hair.

"And Uncle Kirk says she's mean, too," said Flora. "She doesn't look mean at all."

"You don't have to look mean to be mean," I said. "Remember Breanna what's-her-name?"

"Breanna **Brell**," said Flora disdainfully, referring to the cherub-faced girl who'd formed the Fourth-Grade Five, a club that liked to remind everyone who hadn't been invited to join—especially Flora—of its exclusiveness. I had been thrilled when Breanna's mother told me at a PTA meeting that her husband had been transferred and the whole family would be moving to Denver during the Thanksgiving holiday.

"Now isn't it true that the Kristi Corps will clap back a beat that you play on the drum?"

"That's right," said Kristi, and the fabric of her white gown pleated as she crossed her legs. "We all like causin' a ruckus for God!"

"Why didn't you bring your drum tonight?" asked Jean Ann, whose accent Kristi had subtly been mocking.

"Well, I would have brought it out, but I didn't want to crush your flowers! I do happen to have one right here, though."

To the audience's delight, Kristi bent over the back of the couch, giving us a view of her backside, chastely draped in white.

When she revealed the snare drum and sticks, the crowd went wild. Sitting back down, she smiled at the **HCL** hosts and said, "I think of drumming as my external heartbeat. My external heart that beats for God."

Oh, brother, I thought.

She played a simple rhythm, and the audience clapped back.

"**Our** external hearts that beat for God," she amended.

"Can I quit the clarinet?" asked Flora.

"Hmmm?" I said, taken with the frenzied interplay between Kristi and the audience.

"I think I'd rather play the flute. Mr. Benson says it's okay with him, because we have way too many clarinet players already."

"Sure," I said. "I like the flute. But what made you want to switch? Last year you were all excited."

"Mr. Benson played a record in band yesterday. It was this guy, Jean-Pierre Rampal is his name, and I don't know"—her voice grew soft—"maybe because he was French and his music was so pretty . . . it reminded me of Maman. And Mom. That's why."

"Good reason," I said, squeezing my daughter's

shoulder, and just as Kristi was telling a story that had Johnny Priestly genuinely laughing and had Jean Ann Priestly looking defensive, my wife walked in.

You heard it right: **my daughter, my wife.** Or should I say, my **pregnant** wife. Nearly three years after Darva's death threw me in life's ditch, I had not only climbed out, but I was practically on top of the mountain. Do not think, however, that I took my placement there for granted; I knew at any moment I could go tumbling back down into the abyss. But not wanting to sour the sweetness of my life, I was trying, as a book Beth had given me suggested, to "be here now."

My wife, of course, was thrilled that Flora wanted to play the flute, seeing as that was the instrument she played.

"I'd love to give you lessons," she said as she maneuvered herself and her big belly onto the couch, "but I'll understand if you'd rather take from someone else."

"**Toi,**" said Flora. "**Je veux que tu me l'enseignes.**"

"**Merci,**" said Jenny, patting the hand Flora had slipped through her arm. "**Nous bons passerons des moments.**"

But she was wrong—we were **already** having a good time.

Fifteen months after Darva's death (I had kept track of the weeks since Darva died, but somewhere around thirty, I switched to months) I was in my office, looking over my order from a vendor who specialized in foreign chocolates and cookies. Thanks to Beth, who'd been ahead of the curve as far as her international pantry went, I had a very popular section (half an aisle and a refrigerator case) stocked with foods from all over the world. The previous week there'd been a run on Swiss chocolate, and I was trying to figure out if it represented a trend or some school or language club had bought them for prizes. Thinking I'd ask Eileen if she'd had any single purchaser of a large amount of Lindt and Toblerone bars, I got up and went to look out the window to see if she was busy. She wasn't at her register, and, figuring she was probably taking her break, I was ready to go back to my order when I saw Jenny Baldacci in aisle 7. My heart quickened as if my desk was fifty yards from the window and I had sprinted the whole way. I switched on the mike, my mind racing as much as my heart.

"Welcome, shoppers," I said, and there was an immediate buzz on the floor.

After Darva's death, there hadn't been any contest giveaways until my customers, after waiting what they thought was a respectful time, politely enquired as to the possibility of their return. Still not having the heart for it, I had turned the job over to Stan, who might have had the heart but not the talent; he was not one to improvise, and he got nervous behind the mike, sometimes blurting out contests inspired by whatever his eyes landed on in the store. Once he announced that if anyone had feminine hygiene products in their cart, they'd win half a case of beans (we were having a hard time moving a new generic brand). Despite the presence of at least twenty female shoppers, no one fessed up.

"A special contest today for anyone shopping on this

beautiful morning in November. Anyone who can sing the song 'Alfie' will win"—I thought quickly what Jenny might like—"an arrangement of her choice from our new floral stand. Meet me at Banana Square."

"All right," said Eileen, as I cut through the break room. She was reading **Woman's Day** and eating a little packet of crackers. "It's about time."

The store hadn't been very busy, and there were only seven people standing by the six-foot banana. I was pierced with a flare of disappointment when I didn't see Jenny—had she left?

"Hi, Joe," said a voice, and my heart, which had just returned to its normal pace, stepped on the gas.

I turned around and pretended to be surprised.

"Jenny Baldacci!" I said. "Did you come back to Minneapolis to bake another lemon meringue pie?"

I took a mental picture of the smile she offered.

"Wow, you've got a good memory. Actually I'm just picking up a few things for my mom."

"Hey," said Swanny Swanson, a big barrel-chested guy whose grocery basket contained a couple of bottles of Geritol and a head of iceberg lettuce. "Let's get this show on the road. I know all the words to 'Alfie.'"

"All right," I said to the small gathering. "Who else?" I raised an eyebrow at Jenny.

"Don't look at me," she said.

"But you played it in the junior high concert!"

"It was an instrumental, Joe," she said. "I didn't learn the words."

"Okay," I said, turning toward the others. I was disappointed I wouldn't be giving Jenny a bouquet of flowers. "Just Swanny?"

No one else took the bait, and so the old Ford

plant foreman began to sing "Alfie," his hands splayed out at his sides. It wasn't Dionne Warwick, but it wasn't bad.

"All right," I said after he accepted his applause. "Get yourself over to the Floral Cart, Swanny, and pick out your flowers."

"You said the winner would pick out an arrangement of **her** choice," he said with a hard little chuckle. "Didn't think a guy would win, huh?"

"Guess not," I admitted. He and the other shoppers dispersed, and I was more relieved than I could say to see them go.

I put my hands in the pockets of my apron so I wouldn't be tempted to put them around her.

"So," I said, suddenly shy. "Jenny Baldacci."

"You seem to like to say my name," she noted.

A schoolboy blush stained my thirty-five-year-old face.

"It's a pretty name. I'm glad you didn't take your husband's." Saying the words **your husband**, I felt some of my buoyancy deflate, and I smiled extra hard, trying to raise it again.

"I . . . I'm not married anymore."

If the buoyancy I thought was waning had ballooned any more, I would have been floating around the ceiling light fixtures.

"You're not . . . married anymore?"

The lovely Jenny Baldacci shook her head. "He decided he needed his 'freedom.' "

"What is he, **nuts?**"

She smiled at the fervor of my question, but the happiness on her face muted quickly.

"No . . . just not in love anymore."

"Then **for sure** he's nuts." I picked an apple off the display cart, and after polishing it on my shirt, I gave it to her. "We just got these in from Washington. They're an especially good crop."

"Thanks," she said, and bit right into it. As she chewed, she nodded, and after she swallowed (me watching her throat move, entranced), she asked, "How'd you know apples are my favorite fruit?"

I felt like I'd broken the plate with the first ball at a state fair game booth.

"Because I'm an intuitive sumbitch," I said, and she laughed. "Also sensitive like you wouldn't believe. So how long are you here for? When can I take you out for dinner?"

"I'm here—" The merriment in her eyes pooled into seriousness. "I'm here to stay. At least for a while. I just moved back. I'm at my parents' house now, but I'll be moving into my sister's apartment when my stuff gets here."

"That answers one question," I said.

"Hey, Joe," said Mrs. Kirkpatrick, adjusting a hair curler above her ear. "How come those mixed vegetables you've got on sale aren't in aisle seven?"

"They're not canned," I said. "They're frozen."

"That would explain why I couldn't find them," muttered Mrs. Kirkpatrick, turning back to her cart.

"The other question—"

"About dinner?" asked Jenny. "I'd love to."

"Good. How about tomorrow night?"

"Is this a consolation prize for not knowing the words to 'Alfie'?"

"No, it's the grand prize for looking the prettiest while eating an apple."

She took another bite, managing the multidextrous task of chewing and smiling at the same time.

We went downtown, to the Café di Napoli, an Italian restaurant with a run-down charm. We split a plate of eggplant parmigiana and a bigger plate of spaghetti and meatballs.

"Once Darva and I skipped school to see a matinee of **The Godfather,**" I said after we had pushed away our plates. "Then we ate here. It was a very Italian kind of day."

Surprising me, Jenny reached across the table and took my hand. "I bet you two had a lot of fun."

Surprising myself, I teared up. Jeez, I was going to bawl in front of this woman whom, more than anything, I wanted to impress.

"Sorry," I said, opening my eyes wide, as if to air-dry my eyeballs. "Sometimes . . ." I blinked, the air-dry method not working so well.

"I know," said Jenny, and in solidarity, her own eyes welled up. "I still have a hard time with my divorce— even though it's been more than a year since it was final."

"So you . . . you've been living in New York by yourself since then?"

Jenny nodded and finished the wine in her glass. When I asked her if she wanted to order more, she held her palm toward me and waved it.

"I'm **full.**"

"How about some coffee?"

"Coffee'd be good."

Our waitress, who had treated us as if we were malnourished children, scolding us to eat more and use more butter on our bread, now tried to get us to order dessert.

"You gotta have something sweet when you're celebrating," she said, handing us menus.

Jenny and I looked at each other and laughed.

"But we're not celebrating anything," I said.

The waitress smiled, nodding slightly.

"Oh yes you are."

Of course, Jenny said later, she was right; we were celebrating the beginning of **us**.

We did allow the waitress to bring us a cannoli to split, but it sat there like a dessert cigar on the plate, untouched as we told more of our stories.

Jenny had met her husband outside the Eastman School of Music, where she had studied the flute.

"Is he a musician too?" I asked.

"Eric?" she asked. "God, no. He's a stockbroker. He'd come to hear a concert his sister was in. Melanie plays the cello.

"Anyway, it was snowing, and I was going to the same concert, and running, because I was late, and the heel of my boot—I was wearing these fancy high-heeled boots, of all the dumb things—gets stuck in the street grate and my foot slides right out of my boot and I go flying in the sleet and snow and fall onto the sidewalk hard enough that I ripped two big holes in the knees of my tights. Anyway, Eric picked me up. Literally. He told me to put my arms around his neck and I did, and he picked me up right there in the street and brought me into the concert hall. Then he ran back out and got my boot."

She sighed and smiled, and poked at the cannoli with her fork.

"And that, as they say, was that. We started dating and after I graduated, I moved to Manhattan to be near him. We got married three years later . . . and after seven years we got divorced."

"I'm sorry," I said, because I could hear in her voice how it still pained her.

"Don't be," she said. "I mean, it's a shock when the person you love doesn't love you back the same way, but as more time goes by, I realize he wasn't so hot. Of course, I thought he was for the longest time; I mean, that's why you marry someone, right? You wouldn't marry someone you didn't think was the most amazing person in the world—" She put down her fork and folded her hands in her lap. "I'm babbling."

"No you're not," I said, and reached across the table, coaxing her hands off her lap and into mine. "What did you do for work out there?" I asked, sensing that while she had a lot to say about her ex-husband, she didn't necessarily want to say it now.

"Oh Joe," she said, and as she straightened up, she let go of my hands to flick back her thick dark hair. "I got work playing almost right away. Studio work, mostly jazz, although some classical—I played on Ryer Tilden's first album and then Donita Belmonte's."

"My mom loves Donita Belmonte."

"Well, Mrs. A.'s always had excellent musical taste, as I recall. Then I got in this little combo—the Winds in the Willows. I know, kinda corny, but we had so much fun playing together and we got a lot of engagements. But here's the funny thing—the happier I got in my career, the more Eric seemed to resent it. I know it's a classic story, but really, who thinks her own husband is going to be jealous of her work, her happiness?" Jenny shook her head. "It was **incomprehensible** to me. So the more he pouted about me having this gig or that, the more I tried to please him, as if I was the one at fault, you know? Then I was hired to play in the orchestra for the show **Susie Loves Harold.** There I am, playing eight shows a week on Broadway and doing some work in the daytime with the Winds, and . . . well, that's when I think he started his first affair. At least, that's the first time I found out about an affair he was having. For all I know, it had been going on long before I caught him at it."

"Give me his address and I'll go break his face," I said, in an okay imitation of Marlon Brando as the Godfather.

"Oh, you've got better things to do," she said, finally sawing off a chunk of the cannoli with the side of her fork. When she was done, she blotted the powdered sugar on her lips with a napkin and said, "Better things to do with me. That is, if you want to."

A squad of cheerleaders somersaulted into my chest, shouting, **Score one for the home team!**

Jenny had two sisters and two brothers, and I met them all at Thanksgiving, along with two in-laws, two nieces, and one nephew. Her parents hosted the dinner, a noisy affair with people shouting over one another to be heard, but it was all good-natured, except when a brother who was of one political persuasion began arguing with a sister who was of another.

Fortunately this argument came just as we were finishing our pumpkin pie and were all ready to leave the table anyway.

Jenny met my family at one of my mother's Tuesday night dinners, which was considerably quieter than her family's but, I hoped, just as entertaining.

My mother was delighted to host a favorite student—"Really, Jenny, I remember feeling **giddy** the first time I heard you play"—and even more delighted to see that we were, as she called it, an item.

Flora was shy, clinging to my arm as if it was a vine and she was Tarzan, but when she heard Jenny was a musician, she whispered in my ear, asking if I thought she should play the piano for her.

"I bet she'd really like that," I whispered back, and very solemnly, with the proud, straight-backed posture she inherited from her mother, Flora walked to the piano, pretended to flip back the tails of her tuxedo, sat down, and played "Clouds." Emboldened by our applause, she proceeded to play "The Circle Song."

"Maman **loved** Joni Mitchell," she explained, looking over her shoulder.

Like an old pro, she played enough but not too much, taking a deep bow after "Both Sides Now" and trying modestly to suppress the smile that wanted to pop off her face.

"That was really lovely," said Jenny. "Just **lovely.**"

"**Merci,**" said Flora, deciding, I guess, that the wall would remain up.

"**Il n'y a pas de quoi,**" answered Jenny, telling her it was no big deal.

"**Vous parlez français?**" asked Flora, surprised.

"**Un peu,**" said Jenny. "If you went to Ole Bull High at a certain time and you were a girl, you took

French, because we had the coolest teacher ever, Mme. Dumont."

"That was my mom's French teacher!" said Flora.

"I know," said Jenny with a kind smile. "And you know what teacher you and I have in common?"

Flora nodded. "Grand-mère."

"That's right: Mrs. A. Although she's Mrs. R. now."

"I told her she could keep her own name," said Len, "but she was taken by the shimmering beauty of the name Rusk."

"Shimmering beauty," said my mother with a laugh.

Shimmering beauty, I thought, looking at my date.

"So where are you living now, Jenny?" asked Linda.

"For now, with my sister. She lives in a duplex near Lake Hiawatha."

"Carole and I lived together when she and Joe moved to Minneapolis," said my aunt Beth, "until the man with the shimmeringly beautiful name took her away."

"We like women who live with their sisters," said my mother.

If a poll had been taken among the adults, Jenny's approval rating would be through the roof. But it was Flora I was most concerned about; I wanted desperately for my daughter to like this new woman in my life.

Daughter. Saying, even thinking that word was still a surprise, like a handful of Pop Rocks going off in my mouth. It actually had been one of the easiest decisions of my life.

"I don't want to be Flora's **guardian**," I said in my lawyer's office, "I want to be her **father**."

"It's not like you haven't been," said Gary Conroy, my old defense partner from Granite Creek who'd gone to Minneapolis for law school and stayed. He handled all my store—and now that I had more of it—business. "I mean, she's lived with you since she was a baby."

It was true, but I had let the uncrossed boundaries of my relationship with Darva define the geography of my relationship to Flora, too. I was **mon** Joe, and even if I had changed her diapers; helped her with her homework; played Mousetrap and Operation and Old Maid and a million other games; built enough structures out of LEGO blocks and Lincoln Logs to populate a major metropolis; read **Goodnight Moon** and all the Curious George, Dr. Seuss, and Winnie the Pooh books a gazillion times; brought her to work and given her little chores (her reward being permission to go wild with the price gun); and brought her to the dentist and doctor—sometimes with Darva and sometimes without—even though I had done everything a dad does, I had never thought of myself as Papa. But now I did. Now I had to.

Flora had burst into tears when I told her I was completing the paperwork to officially become her father.

"Flora," I said, taking the girl on my lap, "I thought you'd like this."

"I do!"

"Then why are you crying, honey?"

"I don't like paperwork!"

This struck me as funny, but I didn't show it on my face, instead busying myself by smoothing her dark curls with my palm. "What do you mean?"

"Paper is so . . . papery! What if it gets thrown away? What if it burns up? What if someone rips it up? Then you won't be my papa and then I won't have a mom or a dad!"

"Someone could rip up all the paper in the world—all the licenses, all the certificates, all the documents, all the legal briefs—and I would still be your dad."

The sigh Flora exhaled had more air than I thought her lungs capable of holding.

"I'm glad," she said, hugging me, and then she asked, "What's a legal brief?"

She continued calling me **mon** Joe, and then, occasionally, shyly, Papa, but to both of us, it sounded unfinished, and she settled on Papa **mon** Joe, which I thought perfectly described what I was to her, even though it did sound like the name of a Caribbean restaurant.

On that Tuesday night at my mother's, I could see Flora was intrigued with Jenny, but when we sat on the couch together, she planted herself as close to me as she could without sitting on my lap. I knew she was calculating how much time this new woman might take away from her, how much affection. But as the months passed, the math that Flora had figured out was all about addition; nothing was taken away from her. In fact, Jenny added to her life, my life, our life, and when we sat together on the couch it was to Jenny's side Flora was drawn.

A year after she had come into the store to pick up milk and bread for her mother ("Okay," she later admitted, "I wasn't out of milk **or** bread. I was just hoping to see you"), Jenny and I got married.

It was the kind of no-hassle, no-fuss affair I can't recommend highly enough. The bride wore corduroys and a red sweater textured with lint balls. The groom wore blue flannel (a shirt, not a suit) and jeans. For all we knew, we were dressed only for the simple chore of picking Flora up after school, the day before Thanksgiving vacation was about to start.

A lazy snowfall had started when Flora climbed into the backseat, slamming the door behind her, and when I turned to greet her, I saw her stick her tongue out at a boy crossing the street.

"Is that your boyfriend?" I teased, even as I thought: **Don't tell me it's starting already!**

"Boyfriend?" said Flora, spitting out the word. "That's Tyler Renfield. That's the new kid I told you about—the grossest boy in the class."

"What makes him so gross?" asked Jenny, watching the boy pull a stocking cap out of his jacket pocket and tug it over his red hair.

Flora tsked loudly, as if asking, **Isn't it obvious?**

"Well, first of all, he's a big show-off. If he's not called on during math, he throws a little fit, and then he says back where he used to live, he went to a private school with only boys in it and he says he wishes he could go back to it, because all-boy classes are just naturally smarter, and then he plays the saxophone in band, and the way he plays—I'm not kidding— sounds like a really bad baby crying."

Jenny laughed into the collar of her pea coat.

"And today when Miss March asked what people were doing over Thanksgiving, he raised his hand and blurted out—even before Miss Marsh called on him—that his mom and dad and little brother are going to Hawaii 'for a little Honolulu getaway.' Isn't that show-offy **and** stupid, saying 'a little Honolulu getaway'?"

As I pulled into the street, I was about to respond, but Flora wasn't done talking yet.

"He said, 'My parents like to do things spontaneous,' and then Miss Marsh corrected him—ha!—and said 'do things **spontaneously**.'

"And then he said, 'We do **spontaneous** things all the time. It's the Renfield way.' "

Flora's voice was coated with scorn, and I could understand why; this kid sounded like a real jerk, who'd grow up to be the kind of adult who'd brag about being led through the casbah by a line of belly dancers during his latest vacation and then ask to see the photos of **your** recent trip to Duluth.

"Is he familiar with the Andreson-Pratt way?" I asked, pissed off at this little creep, who admittedly had made me question the last spur-of-the-moment thing I'd done.

"**Yeah**," said Jenny.

I smiled at my cheerleader on the passenger side of the car as a wave of spontaneity crashed over me and I switched the right-turn signal I had just turned on to the left.

"Where're we going, Papa **mon** Joe?" asked Flora, noticing the change of direction.

"Well," I said, reaching over to take Jenny's gloved

hand, "if this beautiful woman is agreeable, I think we should go get married."

The hinges of Jenny's mouth were unscrewed. We had in fact just taken the very big step of getting our marriage license the week before, in anticipation of a wedding whose time and place we thought—but hadn't yet planned—would occur in the spring.

Thankfully, the screws tightened quickly and her mouth widened into a smile. "We'll have to go home to get our license."

"In my wallet, dear lady."

"Hot diggety," she said, "today is my wedding day."

Flora cackled in the backseat.

"The Andreson-Pratt way," she said, the implication being **Take** that, **Tyler Renfield.**

Seeing a florist shop on Cedar Avenue, Jenny insisted we stop.

"Come on, Flora, help me pick out some flowers," she said as I pulled over to the curb. "You will be my flower girl, won't you?"

"**Certainement!** " she said, and as I watched both my girls run into the shop, a blue shadow fell across my happiness as I remembered the trip I had taken to a florist with Darva, shopping for a homecoming corsage for Shannon. The shadow flickered as I laughed, remembering the look on the clerk's face when Darva revealed her date was the football quarterback about to undergo transgender hormonal treatments.

"And now look where we are," I said out loud. "Your daughter—**our** daughter—is going to be the flower girl."

Three months after we stood in front of the clerk in a small courthouse room whose smell of burnt popcorn rode over the perfume and cologne left behind by the brides and grooms who had gone before us ("Sorry," said the clerk, "the break room's right down the hall and our microwave's kind of iffy"), Jenny found out she was pregnant. Counting back the weeks, I was certain that we had conceived on Christmas Eve, but she reminded me that the entire month of December had been one long extended honeymoon and we could hardly pinpoint one particular day.

"Say what you will," I said, pulling her toward me, "but I remember hearing something on the roof just as I was coming."

Jenny laughed, kissing me. "And that gives your argument credibility **how**?"

I drew my head back and frowned at her ignorance.

"Well, it was **obviously** Santa Claus I heard. Santa Claus dropping off our present."

Twenty-one

And we've got Charlene from Birmingham. Good evening, you're On the Air with God.

Finally! I kept getting a busy signal for over an hour!

How can I help you, Charlene?

Well, Kristi, what do you do as a Christian woman when your own child says he's not a believer?

Is that what happened to you, Charlene?

(Sniffling) Yes. My very own son who I raised in the Baptist Church now tells me religion is "the opiate of the masses."

Is your son new to college, Charlene?

Well, yes he is, ma'am. He's a freshman at 'Bama.

I wouldn't take him too seriously then, Charlene. College is a time of discovery, and it sounds like he's out there flexing his brand-new wings.

But I don't want him to flex his wings! I want him to love the Lord!

Which he probably will do, Charlene, once he gets this rebellion out of his system.

But he tells me things like, "religion is all a matter of geography—if we lived in India or Japan, we'd be Hindu or Buddhist!"

That's probably true, Charlene, but fortunately for you, you were born in America where it's easy to know the truth of Jesus.

You know what my son would say to that? He'd say, "Well, what about those Hindu people or those Buddhists? It's not their fault they were born in places where it's not so easy to know the truth of Jesus."

And that's why we have missionaries, Charlene. Now, in the meantime, just be patient with your son and pray for him. If he's been raised with a good Christian foundation, I guarantee he'll come back to it.

I hope you're right, Kristi.

The point is, Charlene: God is.

At the twentieth reunion of the Ole Bull High Class of '72, a guy named Keith Pugh had a heart attack. I knew him slightly—he hadn't been in any of my classes, but I'd asked him questions for one of my Roving Reporter interviews—and had spoken with him that night in the buffet line. He had told me he had his own athletic and exercise equipment store called Buff Stuff and that he'd give me a good price on a treadmill or weight machine if I was interested.

Jenny and I were out on the crammed little dance floor, bopping away to Three Dog Night's "One Is the Loneliest Number," when there was a flurry of motion below the little stage where the DJ spun his records and someone yelled, "Get Marcy!"

The former valedictorian, now a doctor, pushed through the crowd of people who twenty years ago had teased her for being a nerd.

She knelt down beside the prostrate alum and, after checking his pulse, ordered someone to call 911 and began CPR.

"Someone should call Kristi Casey," said Charlie Olsen as we watched the EMT crew load him on a stretcher. "That guy looks like he could use a miracle."

In her absence, Kristi was nearly as popular a topic as jobs and kids and divorces, and throughout the night I heard people talking about her.

"Did you know she's a regular on that **HCL** show?"

"It's a bunch of crap, but I tune it in for her. She's still a **fox**, but I can hardly believe what comes out of her mouth."

"Yeah," said Blake Erlandsson. "If she's never tried marijuana, I'd sure like to know what she was smoking all those times in my dad's car! I'll bet if she'd known I'd become a pharmaceutical salesman, she'd never have broken up with me!"

"How come she never comes back here?"

"Probably because she knows we're wise to her."

"Hey, people change." This was said by Shannon Saxon, who had traded in her philandering chiropractor for a TV weatherman. "Although I never saw anyone change as drastically as she did."

"I thought she was the most fantastic creature I'd ever seen," said Leonard Doerr, with his lovely German wife at his side, "until she opened her mouth and said something nasty to you. Which she did to me on average of . . . oh, every day."

Greg Hoppe, who had flown here from an assignment in Hong Kong, said, "You were pretty good friends with her, weren't you, Joe?"

"Yeah, but just to get in her pants," I said, and everyone laughed at the joke they were sure I was making. The smile Jenny offered to those standing in that little conversational circle looked innocuous enough, but I could read its message: **You have no idea.**

Remember, I'd shared a lot with Darva, but because she had always been smart enough to see through Kristi and because she could never understand my friendship with Kristi in high school ("How can you hang out with that self-absorbed little snot who thinks **cheerleading** is somehow relevant?"), I had never told her **everything.** There are just some things you need to protect your friends from (even stronger was my need to protect myself from my friends' reaction), and Kristi's and my strange sexual history was one of them.

But Jenny was my wife, and even though a lot of couples keep secrets from each other, we weren't among them. Our intimacy went far beyond the bedroom and into the past, into the mind, into the heart. I knew all about her ex-husband's inability to make love with her unless she had just showered.

"Can you imagine how that made me feel?" asked

my beautiful wife, whose sweat was an aphrodisiac to me. "Even on our honeymoon—and you know what honeymoons are like—he'd make me shower if we'd made love an hour earlier and were thinking about doing it again."

"He sounds pathological," I said.

"He was strange about his hygiene," said Jenny. "He would use only one particular laundry detergent—no substitutes—and every night when he'd get home from work, he'd brush his wing tips **and** put them on a shoe rack."

One night after we'd listened to **On the Air with God,** I told Jenny about Kristi and watched as her eyes and mouth opened wider and wider.

"She gave you blow jobs **in school**?"

"Well, twice in a car."

"Gee, and to think the wildest thing I ever did at Ole Bull was skip history to go to the donut shop." She snapped her fingers. "And there was that time we snuck out of the hotel during our band trip."

"See, we all have our sundry pasts."

She laughed, to my great relief. As I told her all the things I hadn't told anyone, I often had to look away from her face, so afraid was I of her reaction.

"So it's . . . okay? You don't think I'm a . . . ?"

"A high school boy? Because that's what you were—and what high school boy wouldn't be lining up to get what Kristi gave?" She shook her head. "Boy, to hear her on the radio . . . Anyway, even when the two of you got it on when she was here for that revival, that was what—five years ago? What's that got to do with you and me now? What do Eric and I have to do with you and me now? All I'm interested in is you and me here and now."

"Here and Now," I said. "Isn't that the name of a candy?"

Jenny leaned toward me and kissed me. "Man, you need to spend more time in your candy aisle. It's Now and Later."

It was my turn to kiss her now. "Here and Now, sweet and fruity." I kissed her again. "Now and Later. Tart and tangy." Another kiss. "It could be a never-ending candy cycle."

At the reunion, Jenny was visibly pregnant, and as the summer ripened, so did she.

She was **bella bella bella** in my book, but her constant assessment was, "I'm as big as a house!" and she voiced that same appraisal now as we lay in bed.

"**You're** not," I assured her. "Just your stomach is." I slipped my hands under her nightgown, rubbing my hands across the curved expanse of her belly and then upward. "And your breasts, they're pretty huge."

"You like that, don't you?"

I sighed. "I'll put up with them if I must."

Jenny shifted her position, and I thought she might be responding to the kisses I was planting on her big luscious breasts and her big luscious belly, but instead she reached for a music book on the nightstand.

"Honey, I'm too hot and too uncomfortable to do anything but figure out this stupid music."

"Fine," I said in the kind of petulant voice that means exactly the opposite, but I was only kidding;

really, at this stage of the game, her wish was my command. Turning over on my back, I put my hands behind my head, content to lie next to her. "Having any luck?"

Jenny had become a popular soloist, playing at weddings, parties, and receptions, and was trying to choose the music for a couple who had requested that she play nothing classical at their wedding. "We still want it serious, but fun," they'd explained.

"How about 'Moon River'?"

Staring up at the ceiling, I pondered this. "It's serious," I agreed. "But not serious **and** fun."

She turned a few more pages. "How about 'Fly Me to the Moon'?"

"Fun . . . but not serious."

She made a frustrated growl and then, after flipping through more pages, snapped her fingers. "I know—I'll give birth the day of their wedding!"

She had no labor pains the day of the wedding—a good thing, really, considering the baby wasn't due for another month—and so on a September afternoon, Jenny, in a rust-colored dress that was color-coordinated with the autumnal colors of the trees surrounding the property, found herself standing on a balcony amid pots of asters and marigolds, playing "Love Me Tender" as the bride passed the groom the tissue that he needed but she didn't.

The program said that the vows followed Jenny's song, but to me, the real action was up on that balcony. If I was available, I accompanied her to weddings; the food was usually good and I liked hearing her play music that led couples into their new lives as married people.

It was a spectacular day, with a mild sun shining in a deep aching blue sky and the soft resigned air of fall. The wedding guests were sneaking peeks behind them to look at the source of the lovely, serious, but **fun** music (I don't know how she did it), and I could have just about burst my shirt buttons with pride, thinking, **That's my Jenny.**

When she finished the song, she lowered her flute past her big belly and winked at me, and it was then that I got my idea.

"I'm going to build a balcony off the office at the store," I said as we drove the winding road that led away from the house by the lake. "That is, if we ever get home."

"We'll have to get home," said Jenny, "so I can go to the bathroom."

"You should have gone before we left."

"I did. But it won't be long before I have to go again."

This was true; her bladder of late had the holding capacity of a thimble. "Do you want me to turn back?"

Jenny lifted her heavy hair off her neck as she shook her head. "Like I said, I don't have to go yet. But I will. Now tell me about this balcony thing."

"Okay," I said, trying to read a street sign before I turned. "You know how much people like the little contests at Haugland Foods—"

"People **love** them," said Jenny. "I love them. I mean, if you hadn't let me win that apple pie years ago, who knows where we'd be now?"

"Damn," I said, realizing I was driving the same loop I thought I had just turned off of. "Whoever designed this road has a sick sense of humor."

"Turn there," ordered Jenny, pointing.

I obeyed and we were out on the main road.

"Don't worry, dear," she said, patting my knee. "You're still manly. Now go back to the balcony."

"I was thinking," I said, "how nice it would be to shop while listening to real live music played by real live musicians. Wouldn't you like to shop while a guitarist or a saxophonist or a flutist played music? Wouldn't that just be the ultimate in grocery shopping?"

"I don't know about the ultimate, but it'd be pretty cool," said Jenny. "Besides the flutist, where'll you get these musicians?"

Another idea bloomed in my head.

"From the customers. I'll advertise—maybe hold a little talent show. Hell, maybe I'll even start a little Haugland Foods band!"

Jenny laughed. "Catchy name."

I had wanted to build the balcony off my office, but Linda decided the space wouldn't work as well as the space by Banana Square.

"We can build it on this wall," she said, "about six feet from the floor. It'll have a railing around it and a staircase on this side."

I agreed, and she designed it and contracted the work—all for free.

"You know what this entitles you to, don't you?" I asked as we stood admiring the finished project, a six-by-eight-foot platform with a railing around it.

"A free cookie from the bakery every time you shop."

"Oh, Joe," said Linda, "I couldn't."

"Well, then how **can** I pay you?"

"You can let me hold Ben."

"Then consider us," I said, passing the sleeping baby to Linda, "paid in full."

I was throwing a party at the store both to celebrate the completion of the balcony and to introduce our son to the greater world.

He slept nonchalantly through nearly every introduction, except when Eileen held him—then he opened his eyes and smiled.

"I'm not saying I have a way with the men," said the cashier, returning Ben's smile with a big one of her own, "because it's so obvious."

Flora hovered around her baby brother, scowling when she thought we were letting someone hold him who wasn't up to the task. The look she gave us when we handed Ben to Mr. Snowbeck was priceless.

"You've got to support his head," she reminded the grandfather of seven.

For the baby's first three weeks, he slept in a bassinet in our bedroom, and when we moved him into the nursery, Flora dragged in a sleeping bag, announcing that she'd sleep next to his crib so he wouldn't be scared.

"When I was little, I thought Mme. Chou Chou was pretty neat," she confessed to me as she sat on the couch holding the baby. "But Ben is just the **best**."

"He is the best," I agreed. I sat next to her, my arm draped across her shoulder. "The best **boy**. You're the best **girl**."

Flora smiled and then made the kind of face people feel compelled to make while looking at a baby. "Wouldn't Maman have loved him?"

"Oh boy, would she," I said. "On the first day I met you, she told me she was **blown away** by you."

"She did?" whispered Flora.

"You were wrapped up in this big scarf—**très chic**—that she had tied around her. She told me she liked to feel your little heart beat."

Flora covered Ben's chest with her hand and after a moment said, "It does feel nice."

At the party, she dropped her vigilance only when some kids her own age showed up and she decided to join them at the refreshment table.

"But if you need me," she told me, "do not **hesitate.**"

With the baby safely in Len's arms, with my mother on deck to hold him next, Jenny and I slipped into the back of the store and up into the office.

"Don't turn on the lights," I said. "Let's just watch everything for a while."

I dragged my swivel chair close to the window and sat down, inviting Jenny to sit on my lap.

"Everyone's sure having fun," she said.

"Well, if you can't have fun in a grocery store," I said, "where can you?"

"Let's do a contest," said Jenny.

"Let's do something else," I said, letting my hands wander up my wife's thighs.

She twisted around to face me. "Come on, we can't have a party at Haugland Foods without having a contest."

"All right," I said, getting one final squeeze in. "What should we have them do?"

"How about a talent contest? You know, to inaugurate the new stage."

"But we already announced that you're going to play. Nobody's going to want to hear Red Carlson belt out 'This Land Is Your Land' in his two favorite notes."

"Well, come on," said Jenny. She got up, turning the microphone on. "Think of something."

She rang the little bell, and the partygoers instinctively looked up at the office window. Jenny turned on the light.

"Good evening," I said, taking the mike Jenny thrust at me. "We hope all of you are having a wonderful time. Let's give a big hand to Melissa and Dana in the deli department, who made all the great food you're snacking on!"

The crowd applauded, and I saw Ben, in his grandmother's arms, flail his arms and then settle back into sleep.

"Sorry, son," I whispered, and continuing in a low voice, I said, "Okay, people, we've got another contest going. And the contest is . . ." I looked at Jenny, but all she offered was a shrug. That proved good enough inspiration.

"The contest is to name our stage before our first performer takes her place on it! Ladies and gentlemen, meet me by the unnamed stage by Banana Square!"

Jenny and I held hands as we raced down the steps.

"My hero," she said. "I knew you'd think of something."

"How about the Haugland Foods Stage?" hollered Estelle Brady as Jenny and I made our way through the crowd and to the stage.

"How about the **Super** Market Stage?" said Marlys Pitt, and then blushed, as if embarrassed by her suggestion.

"The Banana Square Stage!" shouted Irv Busch. "That's perfect."

I had climbed up onto the stage, pulling Jenny along with me.

"Now, come on, people. My beautiful wife is going to perform in a matter of minutes, and you can't think of a better name?"

"Hey, what's the prize anyway?" asked Kay Nelson, who asked me nearly every time she was in the store when I was going to hold another Supermarket Sweep so she could load up on steaks.

"The prize is . . ." I looked at Kay. "Ten pounds of whatever you want from the butcher counter."

"But I'm a vegetarian!" said Helen Hanson's teenage daughter.

"Or ten pounds of fresh produce—your choice. Now to help you along, just think: this stage is going to be the home for performers who'll bring a little class to your grocery shopping—mostly musicians, but you never know when someone might want to recite a Shakespearean soliloquy."

"Why don't you just name it after yourself?" asked Millie Purcell. "Call it Joe's Place?"

"I appreciate the suggestion," I told Millie, "but I told you, I want a little class!"

I wasn't being modest—I thought Joe's Place

sounded like a hamburger joint. I fielded other suggestions and then felt an elbow in my side.

"I've got it!" said Jenny softly.

She told me later that the name came to her as she stood on that little stage with me and, looking out at all the customers, saw Flora.

"You could tell she was thinking hard, trying to come up with a good name," said Jenny. "I just felt this surge of love—could we have a sweeter girl? Could Ben have a better sister? And then I thought, let's honor her mother. I mean, she was an artist . . . and your best friend."

Talk about class.

And so the little stage my aunt's girlfriend designed and on which Jenny wowed the crowd by playing Handel and Bach was named the Darva Pratt Performance Center. Jan Olafson even made a plaque down in her basement woodshop, and every time Flora came into the store and passed by the stage, she ran her hand over it.

Twenty-two

FROM THE "Chat with Chip" INTERVIEW PUBLISHED IN Popular Life MAGAZINE, FEBRUARY 1995:

This month I'm talking to the talk of the town—if the town is Bethlehem, that is—Kristi Casey! For those of you who don't have radios or TVs—I guess I'm talking to you Amish folk—Kristi Casey has a devoted radio audience who tunes in five days a week to hear her **On the Air with God** show. Now the Kristi Corps, as her rabid fans call themselves, will have more of Kristi via her own television show, which begins next month on the Personal Prayer Power (PPP) Network. I caught up with Kristi at the very chic Tristano's in New York City, where she was enjoying a glass of pinot noir.

Chip: Whoa, Kristi—it's not often that I get to interview a real live evangelist!

Kristi: Nice to meet you, Chip.

Chip: So you're not one of these nuts who think liquor is taboo, eh?

Kristi: If Jesus changed water into wine for us to enjoy, who am I to refuse? **(She winks)** Actually, Chip my doctor advises me that a glass of red wine a day is good for my health.

Chip: So tell me, Kris, how'd a pretty woman like you decide to get into the preaching biz? Did you flip a coin or something—heads dental hygiene, tails evangelism?

Kristi: Honestly, Chip, I thought I was going to be a lawyer—a public defender representing the downtrodden! But one night, many years ago, God performed a little miracle for me. I was camping up in northern Minnesota—I've always liked to escape into the great outdoors—and suddenly the sky was filled with the northern lights. It was such a beautiful spectacle, and while I can't presume to think God put on this show just for me, I saw the miracle in it all. I was on a bluff overlooking Lake Superior and I was filled with His truth and presence and my heart was so gladdened, I truly thought, looking over the dark waters of the lake and into the changing colors of the sky, "Oh my goodness, I have been given the view from Mount Joy."

Chip: And that, in fact, will be the name of your new television show, isn't that right? What does "the view from Mount Joy" mean?

Kristi: Chip, I think anyone has the capability to climb their own Mount Joy—the place that makes them see the true miracles of God's world.

Chip: Yeah, yeah, yeah . . . Now listen, Kristi—you

do not look like your average evangelist. For a forty-year-old, honey, you're one hot mama.

Kristi (laughing): Now that was a segue if I ever heard one! And I thank you for the compliment, Chip, although I can't say I had much to do with the outside package—that's all God's work.

Chip: Seriously, Kris, don't you get bored by all this religion stuff? I mean, don't you ever want to kick off your shoes and have some fun?

Kristi (laughing): Believe it or not, Chip, bringing people to God can be fun. It can also be challenging, exhilarating, and frustrating, but yes, there is some fun there.

Chip: Sure, sure, it all sounds like BS to me. Anyway, ready to take my quiz?

Kristi: As ready as I'll ever be.

Chip: Okay, let's get down and dirty. I'm going to ask you questions and I want honest answers. No censoring.

Kristi: Fire away.

Chip: How old were you when you lost your virginity?

Kristi: You know what, Chip? I try to spread God's word, not salacious gossip.

Chip: But you're not really gossiping if you're talking about yourself, are you?

Kristi: I just think your readers aren't interested in inconsequential patter like this.

Chip: Obviously you don't know my readers. They don't think virginity—or the loss of it—is inconsequential at all. But I respect your need to play the proper church lady. Because really, all you guys are a bunch of hypocrites anyway, right?

Kristi (laughing): You know, Chip, I do read your column, so I am aware of how you like to put people on the spot. I understand it's your job and you do it well.

Chip: So as far as answering my question . . . you're not answering it, right?

Kristi: I will answer any serious questions put to me.

Chip: Oh, **serious** questions. Okay, I understand the First Lady is going to be the first guest on your television show. How'd you bag her?

Kristi: First of all, let me just say I'm very flattered the First Lady has agreed to grace my first show. I know she loves the Lord, and I imagine she's coming on my show to help spread the good news.

Chip: Lately you've had a lot of politicians on your show, but they all seem to be of one particular stripe. Doesn't God call you to welcome everyone in?

Kristi: I'd love to welcome everyone in, but not everyone takes me up on my invitations.

Chip: Riiiiiiiight. So does this TV show mark the end of your radio career?

Kristi: Goodness, no, I'll be on the radio even more. As you said, I'm on Monday through Friday. So I'll actually be spending more hours on the radio than on TV.

Chip: Is it true you and evangelist Johnny Priestly had a torrid affair?

Kristi: I always like to assume the best in people, Chip, so I'll assume you're going for humor with that question.

Chip: Well, the thought of an affair with Johnny Priestly **does** strike me as funny, but you didn't answer my question.

Kristi: I answered it, just not in the way you wanted me to.

Chip: You're no dummy, are you, Kristi?

Kristi: I like to think I use the brains the good Lord gave me.

Chip: I listened to a couple of your programs, and I haven't liked what you've said about gay people, seeing I'm pretty gay myself. What exactly do you have against me and my sisters?

Kristi: Chip, I think your sexuality is an unfortunate choice you made. I can't imagine the reasons— maybe because you could better use your naturally flamboyant personality as a gay man?

Chip: Kristi, you are so wrong you make my head spin. I didn't make a choice choosing my sexuality; I **am** gay.

Kristi: I'll pray for you, Chip.

Chip: And I'll pray for you, Kristi, because there's a lot of light you **haven't** seen. But it was brave of you to talk to me, and I thank you.

Kristi: Brave is Job standing up to all his trials. Brave is Daniel in the lion's den. I'm just delivering a message to people—like you—who desperately need to hear it.

Chip: Kristi, I'm going to shut off my tape recorder before I barf.

Fortunately, my time was taken up with my work and my family, so the temptation to waste time listening to Kristi lecture sinners was practically nil. Occasionally I might tune in, but it's my experience as a radio listener that the more time a host is given to talk, the less interesting the talk becomes. There was no denying she was a big deal, though—you could see her on the news, accepting a Christian Woman of the Year award; you could see her on a late-night talk show, sparring with the host in a such a way that he told her, blushing, "You make this old-time religion sexy." You could see her in newspapers and magazines, giving a cup of gruel to a starving child in Africa; sitting on the bed of a sick child in Chile; holding hands with the victim of a land mine. Kristi was spreading the Word throughout the world, and no matter what drought-ridden, virus-laden, war-torn place she found herself in, she always looked good.

"Your body really is your temple," she said in a story in **Vogue** magazine. "And I don't know about you, but I like a pulled-together-looking temple."

"Oh sure, now she shows up!" said Kirk, shooting the TV off with the remote control. Kristi had just been on the news, posing with Earl Ellis and Johnny Priestly before the three evangelists went into the Waldorf-Astoria for a political fund-raiser.

"She's everywhere!" said Nance.

"Everywhere but here," said Martha Casey.

Jenny and I were poolside, or close to it; we were sitting in Kirk and Nance's lanai, which was really an outdoor living room.

"Can you imagine having an outdoor living room back in Minnesota?" I asked Jenny, watching as Kirk mixed the daiquiris. "Watching TV and having drinks while the snow drifted up around us?"

"That's one thing I do **not** miss," said Clarence.

"I think moving down here was the smartest thing we ever did," said Martha.

We were in Florida for business and pleasure, the pleasure being another Casey wedding: the bride was Kirk's mother, the former Mrs. Casey (and who now insisted we call her Martha), and the groom was Clarence Selwin.

"Well, I suppose I ought to get dinner started," said Nance.

"Let me help," said Jenny.

"And me too," said Martha, but Nance told her to sit down; the bride was in no way expected to prepare her wedding supper.

"I suppose we shouldn't be expected to help either," said Kirk hopefully.

"I'll take a rain check," said Nance. "To be cashed in when it's time to wash the dishes."

There was a loud splash.

"You can't come on!"

"Why not?"

The kids were in the pool and eight-year-old Coral was exercising her right to torment her younger sister by barring her entry onto the small water slide.

"You gotta have a ticket!" demanded Coral.

"But I don't have one!" wailed Gina.

"Please tell me," said Kirk, pouring my drink, "that one day they'll grow up to be like yours."

I smiled. "She's something, isn't she?"

I had heard from enough parents at PTA meetings and along the sidelines at soccer games how their sweet and easygoing daughters had suddenly turned into, as one mother put it, teenzillas. It was as if fourteen was a foreign country with evil powers, changing those who entered into snotty, sullen girls who if they deigned to speak to you at all, would just as soon lie as tell the truth, But even though Flora was of age, her passport had not yet been stamped by fourteen. She still liked us, still conversed civilly with us, and still thought babysitting her three-year-old brother was actually fun.

"Daddy, she says I have to have a ticket to go down the slide I've gone down twenty hundred times for free!"

"Hey, you guys," said Flora from the center of the pool, where she and Ben floated on a giant inner tube. "See who can swim to us the weirdest!"

The smirk that had been on Coral's face and the rage on Gina's were replaced by expressions of glee, and the younger girls grabbed each other's hands. After they jumped into the water, Coral began flailing her arms and making faces, whereas Gina floated on her back as she kicked her legs up into the air.

"So contests are the key," said Kirk, nodding.

"They work in the store."

"We can vouch for that," said Martha, who had first met Clarence in Banana Square when they were reciting Walt Whitman poems.

"Amen!" said Clarence.

"Who won?" said Coral, who had reached the inner tube and hooked one arm around it.

"Yeah, who won?" asked Gina, scrambling onto the other side,

"You were the funniest!" said Ben, pointing at Gina, on whom he had a little crush.

"But you were the strangest," Flora quickly told Coral, and before an argument about who was the victor could begin, Flora said, "Now let's see who can swim the scariest!"

She pushed away from the inner tube, and Ben, wearing water wings, followed. He began paddling around the pool, pushing out his lower jaw and groaning, rolling his eyes back into his sockets.

"Genetically, I think he resembles you a lot more than Jenny," said Kirk.

Coral was walking around the shallow end, arms held rigidly in front of her, and Gina chose to once again float on her back, although this time she waved her arms and moaned.

"And it looks like both of your girls got all your DNA," I said.

Martha, watching the kids, laughed.

"Actually, Coral reminds me of Kristi at that age."

"Ma!" said Kirk. "Don't say that about my own daughter."

Martha winked at me. She was trim and tanned and the alcohol that had dragged down her features and spirit had been burned out of her system years ago, so at sixty-five she looked better than she had when I'd first met her, when I was in high school. "Kristi was a lot of fun when she was a little girl," she countered. She took a sip of her iced tea. "It was only after Daddy's accident that she changed."

"No," said Kirk, "she was mean way before that. At least to me."

"Well, she did always have that capability," agreed Martha. "Of being mean, that is." She sighed, and suddenly her eyes filled with tears. "I did really think she might want to see her own mother married."

Clarence took her hand and patted it. "It's all right, Martha. I'm sure she tried."

"Yeah, right," said Kirk bitterly. "She's seen my kids **twice**. Once in an airport in between flights and once when she allowed us to visit her hotel room in Miami for twenty minutes."

"She did shuffle us out of there awfully fast," agreed Martha.

Kirk drained his glass. "I hear she has a lot to say on the subject of 'family values.' Which is funny, since she treats her own like shit. Honey," he said, raising his voice, "don't go down the slide like that. You remember how you knocked out your tooth last time."

"But, Daddy," hollered Gina, "that'd be good because I've got another loose tooth that needs to come out!"

Kirk laughed. "Turn around anyway." Ever the good host, he looked at our glasses and refilled his mother's and Clarence's with iced tea and mine and his with daiquiri. "The fact that people—so many people—believe what she says," he said, continuing his Kristi rant, "makes my skin crawl. Seriously. It makes me fear for the fate of the world if there are that many ignorant people who think a person like Kristi Casey has God's ear. I mean, it's really pathetic."

There was a swish of aromas in the air—of perfume, spaghetti sauce, and garlic bread—as Nance and Jenny came through the inside living room and into the outside one, carrying trays.

"Oh, you've been talking about Kristi, haven't you?" said Nance, reading the look on her husband's face. "Let's promise not to bring her up at all during dinner. Coral, Gina, Flora, Ben!" she shouted as she and Jenny began unloading their trays on the kids' table. "Come and eat!"

Kristi was banned from further dinner conversation, leaving us to talk about a much brighter topic: the second reason we were here in Florida, the business reason.

"I like Don, he's a great guy," began Clarence after the business of plate passing and serving was finished.

"Thanks," I said, twirling pasta around my fork. "He's got a lot of experience in the grocery business, plus I think he's got the right personality."

"Oh, he'll be perfect," said Martha. "I can't wait to start working with him."

The new door that had opened in my life led directly into the second Haugland Foods, opening in three days in Cocoa Beach. Kirk had seen a For Sale sign on the grocery store and had been inspired to let me know about it, "because think of it, you're doing so well up there—this could be your vacation store. Or your retirement store. Or just a good investment. Anyway, it would get you down here more, which would be great."

I had been approached about expansion several times—Haugland Foods **was** successful, even meriting a front-page article in the business section of the **Minneapolis Star Tribune** entitled "Fun with Groceries." Content where I was, I always declined these offers, but the seed Kirk had planted sprouted, watered by Jenny's enthusiasm and the idea of doing something different.

"Will we live in Florida, Papa **mon** Joe?" asked Flora.

"Would you like to?"

She shook her head, her eyes flooding with tears.

"Me neither," I said. "I like Minnesota."

"Your dad will fly down there every month or so until he makes sure it's running like it should," explained Jenny. "And we'll go for little vacations."

"I like vacations," offered Ben, who thought any new place he went was "vacation."

For fun, and to help me out, both Clarence and Martha were going to work there, Martha as a cashier and Clarence as an assistant manager.

"I was ready to hang up my shears anyway," the barber said. "Now instead of cutting hair, I can cut prices."

"Not so fast," I said.

The wedding had been conveniently planned to take place just a few days before the grand opening of Haugland Foods.

"My parents are coming," said Nance, eying the

dinner table to see who needed what. "And they said they're bringing a bunch of their friends."

"But just watch," said Kirk. "All those rich farts and all they'll buy is whatever's on sale."

"Can we dress up for the grand opening?" asked Gina from the kids' table.

"What **is** the dress code, Joe?" asked Nance, passing the meatballs to Clarence.

"Let's just say if you **don't** dress up," I said, turning to face the kids, "I'll be very disappointed. I want all of you in the most extravagant of party dresses."

"**Dad**," complained Ben.

"Except you," I amended. "You, young man, can dress up as either a pirate or a cowboy,"

They took me literally. On the day of the grand opening, Coral wore a dress Nance said she had worn to a recent wedding, and Gina wore her fanciest dress from her tap dance recital. After a run to the local Goodwill, Jenny was able to make a pretty good pirate out of Ben, with a head scarf and eye patch and a parrot on his shoulder she fashioned out of an old Christmas ornament. And the old bridesmaids' dresses she found—ooh la la! Jenny's had tiers and tiers of pink dotted swiss, and Flora's was a deep purple velvet with a cabbage-sized velvet flower stitched to the hip. Still, somehow, they looked beautiful.

"And don't think you're getting off easy," said Jenny, handing me a hanger holding a plastic bag. "You're wearing this."

I tore open the plastic to find a suit jacket whose former owner was either a circus ringmaster or Edgar Allan Poe.

"What is this?" I asked, trying on the long black coat.

"It's a morning coat," said Jenny. "We couldn't believe it—it was only six dollars."

I could have used some of the coat's length—it came to my knees—in the sleeves, but for a shiny, mildewy jacket that smelled of rancid hair tonic, it fit me pretty well.

Ben laughed. "You look funny, Daddy."

With one hand on my stomach and one on my back, I bowed.

"I'm sure you mean in that in the best possible manner, matey."

Kirk and Nance were not about to let us leave their house looking like nuts without looking like nuts themselves. Kirk wore his best suit, along with an old multicolored afro he'd worn to a football game. Nance wore a lab coat with a scuba mask.

"Well, now I feel underdressed," I said.

The Haugland Foods in Cocoa Beach was about two-thirds the size of the Haugland Foods in Minneapolis, and so I had decided to make it a more gourmet grocery store. Our "fancy foods" (as my mother called it) section back home was very popular, so I thought I'd not only expand it in Florida but also make the general tone of the store very international.

You can get milk and bread anywhere, went the advertisement I ran in the local paper and on the radio station. **But you can only get lingonberry preserves and lefse at Haugland Foods.**

Sure enough, the question I got asked most during the grand opening was "What's lefse and where can I find it?" (It's like a Norwegian tortilla, made out of riced potatoes and rolled flat and thin, usually served with butter and brown sugar.)

The second question I got asked was "Who are those flute players?"

They were, of course, Jenny and Flora, playing in Palm Court, a little area by the produce section I had modeled after Banana Square. It was a much smaller space, but I still had managed to install a wooden cutout of a palm tree as well as a little stage, and it was on that small stage that my wife and daughter stood playing Telemann's Sonata in F.

"My Lord," said a tanned, bejeweled woman, "do you think I could get something like that going in the Palm Springs A&P?"

It was, I have to say, a grocery store opening like no other.

Ben manned a table with Clarence, offering free samples of lemon curd and scones with a hearty "Arghhh!" to every taker. Coral and Gina walked the aisles with trays of the German wafer cookies I had been introduced to at my aunt Beth's house. And Kirk and Nance took Polaroid pictures of customers posing with Nawoo of the Sea, a kid I had hired to dress up like a manatee.

"I'd rather have my picture taken with you," several old women told me, and Nance and Kirk happily obliged.

"Welcome to the grand opening of Haugland Foods," I said into a mike that had been rigged up by Palm Court (this store had no upstairs office). "I appreciate all of you coming, and I hope all of you will come back again . . . and again . . . and again."

There was polite laughter, but if they thought it was the usual thank-you speech, they were dead wrong.

"One of the things my store in Minneapolis has is contests. We don't just like people to shop, we like them to **compete.**"

This new, Floridian clientele looked at one another, their faces all asking, **What?**

"For instance, if I asked any of you to name a grocery store chain in, say, California, could any of you do so?"

"Albertsons!" shouted a white-haired woman in plaid shorts. She nodded, looking at the people around her. "I used to live there."

"Very good," I said, walking toward the palm tree cutout. "See, sometimes we have general-knowledge contests, sometimes we have what's-in-your-cart contests, and sometimes we have talent contests." I lifted up the gift basket I had hidden behind the cutout. "Prizes are always given; for example, whoever wins this contest wins this lovely gift basket chock full of grocery items certain to make your next party a hit."

It was a good present, filled with the kinds of cookies and biscuits and cheeses you'd find in a Paris or London or Munich grocery store.

A platinum-blond woman with skin the color of stained wood said to Nance's mother, "Oh, I could bring that to the Altmans' barbecue."

"Because my wife and children and I come from Minnesota, I think we need to learn a little more about your fair state. Kids?" This was a cue for Ben, Coral, and Gina to pass out little notepads and pencils that read **Haugland Foods.**

"The notepads and pencils are your complimentary gifts, but please use the first page to write your answers to our first contest. The beautiful gift basket you see right here will go to the person who can name Florida's state bird, its state motto, and its state flower. In the event of a tie, we will decide the winner on the basis of whoever answers this question best: Can you tell us something we probably don't know about Florida?"

I looked at Jenny and Flora, standing on the stage in their bridesmaids' dresses, holding their flutes at their sides like batons.

"My lovely wife and daughter—yes, folks, I am that lucky—will serve as our timekeepers. When they finish their song, your time will be up. So start your engines now. Oh yes—and remember to write your name down."

Jenny nodded to Flora, and they lifted their flutes to their lips and began playing a spirited duet. When they were finished, I said, "Kids, please collect all entries."

There were twenty little pieces of notepaper to read, but the judging went fast because nearly all of them had wrong answers. Everyone stood patiently, waiting for Don, the store manager, and me to read the entries, murmuring about their chances with their neighbor.

"All right!" I said finally. "We have two winners!"

"What's Florida's state bird?" asked the woman with the white hair and plaid shorts. "I know California's is the valley quail—does that count?"

"I'm sorry, ma'am, not for this contest. But the thing to remember about Haugland Foods is if you don't win one contest, there's always another. Now

I'd like to introduce you to Don Quinlan, the store manager, who'll be running most of these contests in the future."

Don waved his hand. "I've already got some local businesses lined up to donate prizes," he told the small crowd. "So make sure you stop in often."

"So what's the state bird?" asked the woman with the white hair and plaid shorts.

"That's what I like," I said, smiling, "an interested crowd. The Florida state bird is the mockingbird; the state flower is the orange blossom; and the state motto is 'In God we trust.' And two civic-minded people knew that: Gerta Mason and Lowell Cantwell."

"Oh, Lowell!" The diamond bracelets of the platinum-blond woman with the deep tan slid up her forearms as she clapped her hands. "We won, we won!"

"We have two people who got those answers right," I reminded the crowd. "And our tie breaker will determine the winner. What does Gerta Mason tell us about Florida, Dan?"

"Well, Joe, she tells us that flamingoes get their color from eating shrimp. The more shrimp they eat, the deeper pink they become."

"Why, that's very interesting, Dan. I did not know that before. And Lowell Cantwell tells us this about Florida," I said, reading from his entry. " 'The singer Pat Boone is from Jacksonville.' "

"Now, by applause, who thinks Gerta's fact is the most interesting?"

Enthusiastic applause caused the gray-haired woman with the walker to smile.

"And by applause, who thinks Lowell's fact is the most interesting?"

Poor Gerta never had a chance given that Lowell had shown up with Nance's parents and a half dozen of their friends. His wife, especially, whistled and hooted and stomped her feet until I wanted to eject her from the store with orders to take her rigged election and shove it. Judging from Gerta's rumpled clothing and demeanor, I imagined the old woman would use the gift basket contents to stretch out her meager food budget; I knew that Lowell and his wife were rich and yet would give the basket to the Altmans for their barbecue, saving themselves the trouble of buying a hostess gift. But I wasn't a social worker doling out benefits to the most deserving, and so the courtly man whose tan matched his wife's won the prize.

This is more fun than playing the stock market, I expected him to say, but he accepted the gift basket with a simple "Thank you. That was ever so much fun."

"That's what we want shopping at Haugland Foods to be," I said, even as I thought he and the platinum blonde no doubt had a household staff to do that sort of thing.

It was a long, full day and everyone retired early, except for me. I was too keyed up to go to sleep and so I swam the breaststroke (the quietest stroke), back and forth, back and forth in the small pool. When I pulled myself out, I was surprised to see an ember of a lit cigarette glowing.

"Martha," I whispered, "I hope I didn't wake you up."

"I've never been one for sleeping," said Martha. "I go to bed when Clarence does, but once he's asleep, I'm usually up and on the prowl for an hour or two."

I shrugged on the terry-cloth towel Nance had furnished to all her guests.

"So what do you do when you're on the prowl?"

Martha exhaled a line of smoke. "Oh, I think. Sometimes I read. And I always engage in my filthy habit." She nodded as she inhaled, in case I didn't know what filthy habit she was talking about.

I sat down on the chaise longue next to her. The night was balmy and starless.

"What do you usually think about?"

"Oh, you know—everything."

"What were you thinking about tonight?"

"Oh, you know—Kristi."

She inhaled again, and her exhale was a long sigh that generated smoke.

"I'm not proud to say this," she said, "but I'm so relieved that my name tag at the store just says 'Martha' on it. I'm so relieved that I have Selwin now for a last name instead of Casey so I don't have to deal with people asking me if I'm related to 'the evangelist.' You'd think a mother would be proud of her own daughter, but . . . " She took one more drag and then stubbed her cigarette out in the conch ashtray Nance brought out every time she visited.

I could tell by her voice how hard it was to say those words, and I reached for her hand. She took mine, squeezing it before releasing it, as if saying, **Thanks for the gesture, but I'm okay.**

"I have racked my brain over Kristi, wondering how she got the way she is. Oh, I know it was rough for her after Jack got hurt, rough for her when her own mother developed a closer relationship to the bottle than to her own kids, but still . . . look at Kirk. Look at how great he turned out." She nudged another cigarette out of her pack and lit it. "I'm sorry, Joe, I'm just going to have to smoke my way through this conversation." Blowing out the match, she took another long, deep drag. "Clarence, God bless him, worries about my health but doesn't mind that I reek of tobacco—he says it reminds him of how his dad used to smell."

"You're . . . you're feeling okay, aren't you?"

Martha laughed. "Joe, I just had a physical and you wouldn't believe it. I could have stayed on that treadmill for hours. My doctor says I'm one of those people who defy all odds."

Even as she repeated the good news, her voice was sad, and in the eerie glow the pool lights offered, I could see tears in her eyes.

"I just don't understand her," she said, shaking her head as if to deny herself any crying. "I know that's not such a bad thing—a lot of parents don't understand everything their children do—but I just don't understand her as a daughter. I don't understand her as a **person.**"

"I'm right with you there," I said.

"I know she has her fans—**legions** of them—and I know they think she helps them. But can't they see how phony she is, what a fraud she is? And don't you think being a fraud about God is just about the worst fraud you can be?"

I shrugged. "I don't know—maybe the means justify the ends. Maybe the fact that she provides people with hope is what matters, even if the hope she provides doesn't come from a real place.

"Hey, do you mind if I have one?" I asked, watching Martha aim smoke at the sky.

"You don't smoke," scolded Martha.

"Not regularly. But every couple of years or so, the urge grabs me."

Chuckling, she tapped a cigarette out of the pack and passed it and the matches to me.

A headache swarmed through my head at the first inhale, and so I adjusted, taking the smoke into my mouth but not down my throat. For a companionable minute or so, we were just two people out on a lanai having a late-night smoke.

"I don't know," said Martha finally. "It just baffles me, the way people look to such nuts to show them the way."

I had to laugh.

"You're calling Kristi a nut?"

Martha tilted her head and offered me an older, wiser version of the smile she had passed down to her daughter. "That's one of the nicer words I have for her."

Twenty-three

The Florida Haugland Foods was a hit. There was no shaky start-up, no growing pains; it immediately filled a niche that apparently was more than ready to be filled.

Don was an excellent manager and faxed me weekly sales reports, product and vendor suggestions, and contest results.

Yesterday a grandmother and an Australian surfer turned into Fred and Ginger. There were about thirty people in the store, and about three-quarters of them gathered in Palm Court when I announced the dance contest. You know how you told me you sometimes skew the contests because you hope a certain person will win? Well, that's what I did—I had a big-band tape and I told everyone we were going to have a jitterbug contest. A local landscaper had given the prize— a free garden consultation and $100 worth of plants and flowers—and I wanted Mrs. Babcock to win because she's sort of let her yard go to pot since her husband died. I knew the two of them had enjoyed dancing together, so I figured she had a good shot at this contest.

I turned on the music and told anyone who wanted to dance to choose a partner. Well, all but six people suddenly got shy, leaving me with a married couple on the floor, two teenage girls, and the surfer and Mrs. Babcock. Well, they danced everyone off the floor, and as they're wowing the crowd, I think how stupid I was—how can I give a prize to just one dancer in a partnered dance? So I gave the garden prize to Mrs. Babcock and, thinking fast, told the surfer that he could have $25 worth of groceries on the house.

Now get this—Mrs. Babcock asked if he'd mind trading prizes because she didn't think she was up to planting a whole new garden but she had wanted to try some of "those expensive cheeses that aren't in my budget," and the surfer says, "You're welcome to the groceries, and my girlfriend and I'd be very happy to put in your garden for you."

Well, Mrs. Babcock just beamed and said, "Oh, no I couldn't," and the surfer said, "I insist. Now go get those stinky cheeses, Granny, and let's get started on that garden."

As they were all leaving, I heard the girlfriend tell Mrs. Babcock that the surfer's mother teaches dance back in Sydney. "I can't dance a lick—but I expect I better learn so I can keep rivals like you away!"

As you know, Joe, my wife, Sue, is a

kindergarten teacher, and she always says she has
the most fun anyone can have while working.
Now I get to tell her, I beg to differ . . .

Dan

He also sent me enquiries from people interested
in franchise or expansion opportunities, and whereas
I hadn't been interested before, the success of the
Florida store was making me consider my position.

"What do you think, Jenny?"

"I'll say it again, Joe—what do **you** think? What do
we want to get and what are we willing to give up?"

"I know one thing I'm not willing to give up," I declared, taking her hand and pulling her to me. Kissing her was like falling into a well—a sweet, dark
well that posed no threat, only exhilaration.

"Joe, I've got to pick up Flora," said Jenny, pushing
herself with her big belly away—yes, she was pregnant again. "And don't forget to get the powdered
sugar for Carole."

"Did you know Ed told me he always wanted to
make love up in his office? He said his fantasy was
to turn on the store mike right in the middle of it so
that all his customers could hear Eileen screaming
about what a stud he was."

"**Head cashier** Eileen?"

"She was a twenty-three-year-old single mother
when he hired her," I said. "He always had a crush
on her."

"But he never acted on it?"

Wrapping my arms around her again, I shook my
head. "Nope. He never fulfilled that fantasy with
her—or anyone. So come on, in Ed's memory."

Jenny gave me one deep, promising kiss before she pushed me away for the second time.

"Really, I don't want Flora hanging around at school thinking I've forgotten about her." She gave me a quick sorry-but-there's-nothing-more-to-this kiss. "We'll see you at your mom's at eight."

"You alone?" asked my aunt Beth as she opened the door at my mother's house.

"Jenny went to pick Flora up at school. She's got play practice."

"Oh yeah," said Beth. "**Grease**, right?"

I handed her my coat. "If I hear that song about being 'lousy with virginity' one more time, I'm gonna puke."

"Oh, good, you brought the powdered sugar." Beth took the plastic bag I offered. "Now dessert's a definite go."

"Dad!" Ben raced toward me, and I scooped him up in my arms.

"Benjamin—**qué pasa?**"

"**No mucho,**" said my son, whose best friend in a pre-kindergarten program was Julio, a boy from Mexico. "Although Grandma's gonna let me help her make the frosting—if you remembered the power sugar."

"**Powdered** sugar," said Beth, holding up the bag on the way to the kitchen. "And he did remember."

The Tuesday night dinners were on again after another vacation taken by my mother and Len, who were both retired now and free to jet all over the place. They had already planned their next trip—this one to Great Britain—and both Beth and Linda and my uncle Roger and his wife were joining them. We'd been invited, but they were leaving three days after Jenny's due date.

"Dad, Mom let me drive all the way home!" announced Flora as she and Jenny came in. Flora had just gotten her learner's permit, but I was having a much harder time turning the wheel over to her than Jenny was.

"She did great," said Jenny.

"And it's really slippery out," said Flora, stomping the snow off her boots. "I hit this patch of ice and thought, Oh no, but—"

"Please," I said, holding up my hand. "Spare me the details."

"She did **great**," said Jenny again. "Didn't panic, just took it nice and easy."

"Thanks, Mom," said Jenny.

Right after she had delivered Ben, Jenny had told Flora that she'd love to adopt her, "just to make my love official."

Biting her lip, Flora had nodded. "Does that mean I can start calling you Mom?"

Jenny nodded, her eyes filling with tears.

"I could never call you Maman, no offense," said Flora.

"No offense taken."

"But I think Maman would like that I call you Mom."

"I hope that she would," said Jenny, taking Flora in her arms. "I know I sure will."

Sitting at the dinner table, I looked at them now, my dark-haired, brown-eyed loves. Physically, they looked like mother and daughter, although whereas my wife was curvy, Flora was lanky like Darva and already several inches taller than Jenny.

Ben resembled me—he was as blond as I had been when I was his age, but like me, his hair would probably darken as he gets older. I figured he'd be taller than his old man—I **hoped** he'd be taller than me, because I think a man should reach six feet. I do only if there's a little heel to my shoe.

I was so deep into my thoughts on hair color and height that I was startled when Flora called out, "Papa **mon** Joe!" It was a name no longer used for everyday but brought out only occasionally, this time to get my attention.

"What?" I said.

"I asked you a question . . . twice."

"I'm sorry, my dear darling forgiving daughter. Locked as I was in my reverie, I did not perchance to hear you."

Ben laughed and told me I was funny.

"Dad," said Flora, exasperation in her voice. "Mom says some guy in California wants to open a Haugland Foods—"

"'Tis true, 'tis true."

"Why's he talking like he's onstage at the Globe?" Linda asked Beth.

"Flora's got a Shakespeare class," explained Jenny. "She and Joe were reading **Merchant of Venice** to each other last night."

"You've gotten another offer?" asked my mother.

"Several," said Jenny. "I mean, he's had offers all along, but these are serious."

"**These?**" said Len, pouring hollandaise sauce over his asparagus. "How many are you talking about?"

"Well," I said, "there's California and Iowa and North Carolina and another offer from Florida."

"And what are you thinking?" asked my mother.

"That's what we're trying to figure out," said Jenny.

"I love my life," I said, feeling a lump rising in my throat. I swallowed it down, not wanting to start blubbering at the dinner table. "I don't have much to do with the Florida store—it practically runs itself—but if I start a chain . . . I don't want to get caught up in more work and a bunch of travel and . . . and . . ." I looked at the faces around the table. "And being away from all this."

I paused for a moment, squirming under a double whammy of feelings—embarrassment, and then embarrassment about feeling embarrassed. I didn't share any of Jenny's pregnancy food cravings (oyster crackers crushed on top of strawberry ice cream), but man, sometimes I found myself acting like some rogue estrogen had taken over my body.

"How much time do you think you'd have to be away?" asked Beth.

"I think Joe's in a position where he could decide that," said Jenny.

"You can do a lot by phone or computer," said Linda.

"Do you really think so, Jenny?" I said, turning to my wife. "Do you think I'm the one who'd get to decide when I'm away and when I'm at home? What if there's an emergency in one of the stores?"

"Dad," said Flora, "if you think you're the only one who can handle whatever emergency comes up, then you go and fix it. Otherwise, you let someone else handle it."

The little gravy boat of hollandaise sauce had finally wound its way back to me, but it was empty.

"Figures," I muttered, upturning it and palming the bottom.

"Dad, there's none left," observed Ben.

"So it sounds like you're all for this expansion," I said to Flora and Jenny. "What about you, Mom?" **Please, please, please, Mommy, tell me what to do.**

"Sorry about the hollandaise," she said. "I would have made more but I ran out of egg yolks. More potatoes?"

"Mom, I'm asking for advice, not second helpings."

"Joe, you know I support you in whatever you want to do. And Len and I are always here for the kids if you need babysitters, and I don't know—doesn't it make you proud that people like Haugland Foods so much that they want to bring it to other people?"

My mother didn't say anything Jenny and I hadn't already talked about it, but sometimes words spoken at a certain time by a certain person are a sharp scythe through the weeds.

"Would you be with me if I decided to franchise?" I asked Jenny. "What about the baby?"

"Joe, we'll grow our family and our business at the same time."

One of her hands rested over her big belly, and I covered it with my own.

"You think we can?"

"Papa **mon** Joe," said Flora with a dramatic sigh, "**please.** Why do you make everything such a big deal?"

"Yeah," parroted Ben. "Why, Papa **mon** Joe?"

I looked around the table, feeling weepy again. "I make everything such a big deal," I said, wishing my testosterone would quit cowering in the corner, "because it is."

The question I was asked by a business consortium in Santa Barbara was "Why Haugland Foods?" I knew my investors—including three brothers from Asheville, North Carolina, and the married couple from Des Moines—weren't suddenly doubting their interest in franchising the store, but simply asking about the name.

"Have you ever thought of changing it to something a little snappier?" asked a CPA from the business consortium.

"The store's just so unique," said one of the Asheville brothers. "Maybe a different name could reflect that."

"Why not Andreson Foods or Joe's Foods?" asked Mrs. Weime, one-half of the Des Moines couple.

I told each of them the same story, that Ed Haugland was a friend of mine who'd given me a store I hadn't even been sure I wanted. "But things worked out. Better than I imagined. And keeping Ed's name is sort of a thank-you, see?"

Our decision as to where to open stores was not dictated by market research but rather our own tastes: Would the store be in an area we'd like to vacation in?

The appeal of southern California and North Carolina is obvious, but my attorney was more surprised at our choice of Iowa.

"Why suburban Des Moines?" asked Gary. "There are more exotic suburbs, you know."

"Jenny's sister Joyce lives there and she's always looking for excuses to visit her," I said. "So when the Weimes expressed interest, it just made sense."

When we played hockey together as boys, Gary had always been a great teammate on the ice, but it was off the ice that he really outskated himself. He became a partner in Haugland Foods Unlimited and essentially became my point man, putting together a great team of advisors, taking the burden of travel from me, and making decisions when I was too dumb or too lazy to make them myself.

He was the one who suggested Steve Alquist, former BMOC at Granite Creek High, for the manager of the Des Moines store.

"He's had a rough time," said Gary. "He got laid off at the feed plant a week after his second wife served him with divorce papers."

"Steve Alquist was working at the feed plant?" I asked. That place was considered the last resort as far as employment in Granite Creek went.

"Yeah, and then he started drinking," said Gary. "You know, one domino of bad news knocked down the next and the next. Anyway, he's doing good now and definitely ready for a change. . . . I think he'd be a good man for the job."

"But the drinking?"

"I don't think it'll be a problem. He's been sober for almost a year. And you know his personality, Joe—everybody likes Steve."

It was true. Everyone liked Blake Erlandsson,

too—Ole Bull's version of Steve Alquist—and yet neither had gone on to do anything that their high school glory suggested they might. Blake was doing fine as a pharmaceutical rep, but I don't think his goal in life had been repping blood thinners and pain relievers.

Steve came down from Granite Creek for an interview, and despite the two wives and the stint at the feed plant and problems with the bottle, he had that old Alquist charm, albeit tempered with humility, and I hired him.

It was after helping him get settled into the West Des Moines Haugland Foods that I ran into another old acquaintance, the star of the PPP Network and saver of souls, Miss Kristi Casey herself.

After a full day at the new store, I was at a truck stop, eating a BLT with too much L and not enough B, reading the **Des Moines Register** and drinking coffee so bitter you would have thought the beans held a grudge. I choked, sputtering droplets of the bitter brew onto the newspaper, when I saw the headline: "Blind Local Artist Draws Kristi Casey."

The waitress, who'd seen me spewing my coffee, approached me, one hand on a padded hip and the other holding the coffeepot like a beer stein, and asked, "You okay?"

I nodded as she topped off my coffee. "Fine."

I folded the paper in half and began to read.

Herman Mitterweld, legally blind from macular degeneration, will paint Kristi Casey's picture this morning for an episode of **On TV with God**, her popular show on the Personal Prayer Power Network. Herman, a retired custodian at the Bank Hill Elementary School, says he was never artistic while sighted, "but once God took my regular sight away, he gave me the power to see the divine in people, the things most people can't see."

His paintings, rendered in pastels, have art critics calling them "amazing in their use of space and color," and "almost spiritual in their blasts of joy and light."

Kristi Casey, who occasionally goes on location to do shows with people whom she calls "called by God to do something special," will sit for Mr. Mitterweld in his garage studio.

Mrs. Mitterweld, a fan of Miss Casey's, is thrilled.

"She's the prettiest one on TV, that's for sure. Plus she's entertaining—some of those Power Network people just go on and on about the Bible and such and never crack jokes. Believe me, when you live with a blind husband who paints the divine in people, you need your jokes."

I looked at my watch—it was almost eight o'clock. I took a last gulp of coffee, shuddering as it went down, left the waitress a big tip, and went out to track Kristi down.

It was very likely that she had already left town, but if she was staying the night, she was probably staying at the Windemere, the fanciest hotel in Des Moines. I got back on the freeway and headed toward downtown.

The guy at the front desk was not going to be much help.

"Could you please tell me if Kristi Casey is staying here?" I asked.

"No," he said, "I could not tell you that. Our client list is confidential."

His hands were folded on top of a two-day-old **New York Times** Sunday crossword puzzle, one I had already done.

I leaned over the counter, turning my head to better see the puzzle.

"Hugh and Cary," I said.

"What?" said the clerk.

"Nine down. 'A couple of wishes.' In this case, they mean Grants. So the answer is Hugh and Cary."

The clerk lifted his hands and looked at the puzzle.

"Oh," he said, nodding. "I get it." He penciled in the answer. "I'm kind of new to these. My girlfriend says people who do crossword puzzles tend to be go-getters, and she likes go-getters."

"Who doesn't?" I offered.

The clerk looked at his co-worker at the end of the desk and said in a low voice, "I really can't tell you anything about Miss Casey. She doesn't want her privacy disturbed."

"I understand that perfectly," I said, taking out my wallet. I withdrew a twenty and pushed it toward him. He looked at the bill and then at me.

"All I'm asking is that you call her room and tell her Joe Andreson is down in the lobby and would like to see her."

He pressed his thin lips together and his wispy mustache sagged. Slowly he pinched the corner of the bill and slid it off the counter before punching a number on his telephone.

"Yes, Miss Kristi, ah, Miss Casey, this is the front desk," he said, his professional hotel voice cracking a

little. "There's a gentleman here, a Mr. Joe Anderson—"

"Andreson," I corrected.

"An-dray-son, who would . . . Oh, all right. Thank
you, Miss Casey."

He hung up the phone and stood taller, the way a
private will when an officer passes by. "She said to
send you right up. Room eight-ten."

I knew Jenny and the kids were having dinner at her
sister Jody's house, but I called her on my cell phone
on the way up and left a message that I didn't know
when I'd be home, but it would probably be late.

"Joe Andreson, as I live and breathe," said Kristi,
opening the door and welcoming me with a big hard
hug. "Jesus Christ, it's good to see you."

Laughing, I let myself be pulled into her suite.

"Didn't you just break a commandant?"

"I didn't take the Lord's name in vain," said Kristi,
not missing a beat. "I said 'Jesus Christ.' " She
stopped in the middle of the room and, still holding
my hands, swung my arms out and back again, as if
we were about to begin a minuet.

"Joe, you look great. A little grayer than when I last
saw you, but no paunch—that's good. I'll bet you're
still your college weight."

I couldn't help but be flattered, even as I knew
Kristi used flattery the way a spider uses its silk—
there was always a plan in mind.

"Give or take five pounds," I said. "And look at
you. I can't believe you're forty-four."

"Don't you dare tell anyone," she said, putting a
finger to her lips. "I stopped counting at thirty-three,
and I expect the world to do the same." She walked

to the bar, and I was afforded a pleasant backside view. More enjoyable to me than the slim curves underneath her dressing gown, however, was watching her walk—still the same light-footed, shoulders-back gait she'd had strolling the halls of Ole Bull High.

"What're you drinking? I'm having a rum and Diet Coke."

"Fine with me," I said, looking at my watch.

"It's eight fifty-three," said Kristi, as if she'd caught me doing something I shouldn't be doing. "Still early enough for this to be a completely respectable meeting."

"It **is** a completely respectable meeting," I said, taken aback.

"Dang," said Kristi. She walked across the room, her silk robe swishing and waving in ways that Jenny's quilted bathrobe never moved. She handed me my drink and sat next to me. "Because I was hoping we might have a nice fuck for old times' sake."

I was shocked but, not wanting her to know that, tried to deke her out.

"Is that how you talk to Johnny Priestly?"

Kristi hooted, clapping her hands. "I gave Johnny Priestly up long ago . . . for Lent, in fact." She laughed again. "Really, this is a guy so fastidious that he parts his pubic hair."

What can I say? She shocked me again, and this time my face must have shown it, because Kristi leaned back against the stack of ornate couch pillows and laughed.

"Oh, Joe, I'm just messing with you. That Johnny Priestly stuff was just . . . rumor." She lobbed two of the couch pillows across the room and resettled herself. "How **are** you, anyways? Married, I hear, with about eight kids."

"Three," I said with a jagged smile. "There's Flora—she's a senior in high school. And Ben—he's five. Conor is one."

Kristi's sip emptied half of her glass. "You've been busy."

"And so have you. I read the thing in the paper today—how'd that painting go?"

Kristi smirked, an expression I knew well. "Guy's kind of a nut—not that I don't get my share of nuts. He had me sit on this skanky old chair—he said it 'absorbed divinity, then bounced it back at him'— and then he starts scribbling on the paper and wiping the scribbles with his fingers. It gave me the creeps, actually, and the finished picture looked like something you'd find in any kindergarten anywhere." She tossed back the rest of her drink. "Waste of time, if you ask me. But we'll edit it so it looks like a miracle or something."

Sighing, she got up and went back to the bar, where she mixed herself another drink. When she returned, robe swishing and waving, she sat at the end of the couch and, stretching out her legs, put her feet on my lap. When I pushed them off, she laughed and put them on again. I gave up the fight, knowing no matter what I did, if she wanted her feet on my lap, her feet would be on my lap.

I kept one hand on my glass and the other I rested above my belt buckle, since there was no room on my lap. She nudged this hand with her toes, laughing.

"Come on, Joe, don't be so uptight. Give me a foot rub, will you?"

Setting my drink on the marble-topped end table, I took her feet in my hands and began kneading them.

"Oh, that feels good," said Kristi, closing her eyes. "But you always did know how to make me feel good, Joe."

I dug my thumbs into the ball of her foot, hard enough to get a yelp out of her.

"Ow! What the hell, Joe?"

"Kristi, please, just answer me one question."

She took her feet off my lap and sat up at the end of the couch, her face devoid of its usual sly merriment.

"What?"

I drew out the moment; she wasn't the only one who understood drama. I took a sip of my drink, then another, and then held the glass in front of me, as if its contents contained a rare wine and I was a vintner studying its complexities.

"Joe," she said, her voice like an **ahem,** "I believe you were going to ask me a question?"

I turned to her. Even in her hotel room, she was cognizant of lighting and only had table lamps on— nothing direct, nothing overhead, so that the face I looked at was protected by softness. Still, I could see age in her face, and because she tried so hard to hide it, it seemed like it should be hidden, like it was something shameful.

"Who **are** you?"

She blanched but arranged her features quickly into an expression of bemusement.

"Well, you, Joe, more than anyone, should know that."

"Are you kidding me? I have no idea who you are."

She rose, or began to, and I knew her destination was the bar, but seeing that I knew that, she sat back down. She shook her glass and the ice cubes clattered.

"Joe, please. It's been so long since I've been around a normal person—can't we just relax and have a little fun?"

"What do you mean, a normal person?"

She sat up, drawing her knees to her chest. One side of her robe dropped to the floor in soft pleats.

"I mean someone who's not so—" She made a face and stuck out her tongue, making a noise that sounded like **bya, bya, bya**.

"What the hell does that mean?"

"Someone who doesn't expect me to be so **Kristi**."

I looked a long moment at her. "Is there any part of you that's at all for real? Because everyone thinks you're a big fake."

"Who thinks I'm a fake?" she asked coldly. "Who's **everyone**?"

"Oh, Kirk, your mom—"

"As if Kirk and my mother even **know** me."

"You don't give them much of an opportunity."

She got up from the couch, but instead of going to the bar, she went to the big window that overlooked downtown Des Moines and stood looking out of it, her arms stretched out, her hands resting on the windowsill. Granted, the lights of downtown Des Moines aren't exactly Vegas, but still, it was a dramatic moment, especially when she turned around and I saw that there were tears in her eyes. The odds that they were summoned up by sincerity rather than thespian skills were probably about one in ten, so I crossed my arms and settled back to watch the show.

"What do you want?" she asked, her voice rusty with the fake emotion she was trying to pass off as real. "Why did you even come here?"

"I was curious, I guess. I have very fond memories of you, Kristi."

She smiled and began coming toward me, but I held up my hand.

"Please, I'm a married man. A very happily married man. Getting a Kristi Special is not what I'm after."

She stood about five feet away from me, hands on her hips, nodding as if she had been convinced of something. With a final sharp nod, she sat down in a chair across from me, helping herself to a cigarette from a silver box on the table next to her.

"Oh, you still smoke too?" I asked.

After lighting the cigarette, she shook the match as if she were punishing it. She answered in a deep, preacherly voice. "Yes, I am still full of the vices with which the devil still tempts me."

When I didn't answer she said, "Give me a break, Joe. I've got to have some releases. You cannot **begin** to imagine the stress I'm under."

"No, I can. I mean to have the world think you're one way, and then in truth be totally different . . . that **must** be hard."

She squinted her eyes at me as she exhaled.

"You really think you've got me all figured out, don't you?"

"Hardly."

"Well, then let me help you. What do you want to know, Joe? Ask me anything, anything at all."

Out of all the questions I had to ask Kristi, the one I blurted out was, "Why do you ignore your own mom and your own brother?"

"I don't ignore my mother," she said defensively. "I call her."

"You missed her wedding."

Kristi sighed. "Joe, I don't think you understand my obligations. I can't be in more than one place at a time. I can't be everything to everybody."

"Your own mother's wedding's a pretty big thing."

"My mother was not a mother to me when I needed her most," she said as coolly.

"Hmmm, I'd think someone who preaches about forgiveness would learn how to practice it."

She exhaled a perfect round smoke ring and watched its quivery ascent toward the ceiling. After a moment, I realized that was her answer.

"Well, what about Kirk? He's a great guy. My best friend, in fact."

She shrugged. "Sometimes I think it's just chemistry. Something between—or not between—people that makes them unable to get along."

"And that lets you off the hook for not even trying to be a sister, an aunt?"

She shrugged again and took a deep inhale of her cigarette. "Is this the kind of interview it's going to be, Joe? You just criticizing me for not being the perfect daughter, the perfect sister?"

"Okay," I said, "how come you lie about the Mount Joy thing? I was with you that night, Kristi. I coined the phrase, as I recall. And—"

Kristi laughed. "What, do you want royalties for thinking of the words 'Mount Joy'?"

"No, I just don't know why you had to lie about the whole thing. You make it sound like God came to you one night when you were camping and saw the northern lights, but remember: **I was with you.** We were bummed about being out of dope, but then we had a great time watching the sky, and that was it."

"Joe, a lot of things have to be shaped for dramatic effect. People don't want to listen to big long sagas these days, they want to listen to short, snappy stories. Stories with punch. I might fabricate the details, but the essence is there."

"That's bullshit," I said, watching as she stubbed out her cigarette. "God didn't come to you that night. My question is, has He ever really come to you at all?"

"I resent your tone of voice."

"You can't answer the question, can you?"

Kristi cocked her eyebrow. "I never expect people who haven't experienced grace to understand what happened to me."

"I experience grace every day."

We stared at each other, holding a duel with our eyes. Her hair—blonder now than it had been the last time I saw her—was piled on top of her head, and suddenly I became aware of something else about her that had changed.

"Oh my God," I said, breaking the stare to look at her chest. "You got breast implants, didn't you?"

Kristi gasped a little and then, because she was a fan of impertinence, she laughed.

"Took you long enough to notice."

"When did you . . . Why?"

She ran her hands over her silk-covered breasts and then, cupping them, gave them a little boost.

"Do you want to see them?"

"No!"

She laughed again. "They're real pretty. Not that they weren't before—they're just a little prettier and a little bigger now."

"But why?"

"People today want women to look womanly."

"Size doesn't determine femininity, just like size doesn't determine masculinity."

Kristi's smile was as sly as that of a cat burglar coming across an open back door.

"As I recall, Joe, you don't have to worry about your masculinity."

I fought hard to ignore the childish pleasure I felt at the compliment.

"What about your abortion?" I said, switching gears. "How come you've lied about that?"

"What do you mean?" she asked, tapping her fingers on the arm of the chair.

I rolled my eyes. "You're a big campaigner for Tuck Drake, Mr. 'I don't believe in contraceptives or in premarital or homosexual sex, and I definitely do not believe in abortions under any circumstances.' "

"You do a good impersonation of him," said Kristi, laughing. "But I'm not campaigning for him; he's just been a guest on my show is all."

"A guest—ha. It's like he's your new co-host." I shook my head; I wasn't going to let her sidetrack me. "You've had lots of opportunities to tell woman who are scared and in trouble of your experience."

"That's my business, Joe."

I shook my head. "Everybody's business is your business, but your own business is no one else's?"

"Something like that. Joe, these people need guidance. They need someone to tell them what to do because they can't figure it out for themselves."

"Man, you're cold."

"And how do you even know I ever had an abortion?"

My mouth opened and pushed out a little sound of surprise, a little "uh."

"Because you told me you did! You called me up and said I might be the father—of course, you couldn't tell for sure because you were having a high time sleeping around!"

She lit another cigarette and extinguished the match by striking the air with it.

"So now I'm a slut, huh?" Her cheekbones became more prominent as she sucked the cigarette. "The thing of it, Joe," she said, smoke cloaking her words, "is that whatever I told you doesn't mean anything. Maybe I was pregnant. Maybe I just said I was, to stir up things a little."

"Stir up things a little?"

"But you'll never know, will you, Joe? Because it's my body and ultimately what happens to it is my business."

My laugh was riddled with disgust. "Despite telling callers abortion is a sin, you've just made quite an argument for the other side."

She said nothing, staring at me as she smoked.

"So do you really believe in God, Kristi?" I asked as I stood to go. "I guess that's what I'd like to know the most. Do you really believe?"

"With all my heart and soul."

"That doesn't really tell me anything," I said, "because I doubt that you have either one."

As I walked across the suite she began to clap. "Is that your 'Frankly, Scarlett' line?"

I opened the door, but before I was able to slam shut, she shouted, "Too bad Rhett Butler said it better!"

Twenty-four

"Papa **mon** Joe," said Flora, laughing, "don't cry. I'll be fine!"

"I don't doubt that," I said, knuckling away a tear. "It's the rest of us I'm worried about."

Jenny smiled, hugging her daughter one last time. Leaving her dorm room had been harder than we thought; Flora seemed perfectly capable of cutting the apron strings that we kept trying to reel her back in with.

"Okay, Joe, I think we should go," said Jenny. "Flora's roommate is going to think we're strange."

"Oh, my parents were the same way," offered the young woman who sat on her bed, going through papers.

I held out my arms. "One for the road," I said as Flora walked into them. "Although for all we know, we might be on the Ventura Freeway and decide we have to come back for more."

"The Ventura turns into the Hollywood Freeway way before the airport," said Flora's roommate. "So I'd catch the 405 in the Valley."

"Thanks," I said, and then to Flora, I whispered, **"Tu est la meilleure fille dans le monde."**

"And you're the best dad," she whispered back. **"Merci pour tout."**

I had to pull myself away then or risk dissolving in a puddle at Flora's feet, which I was certain wouldn't win her any points with her know-it-all roommate.

"Call me as soon as you get home!" yelled Flora as we left the building. "And tell Ben and Conor I love them!"

Chicken pox had prevented her brothers from going with us to settle Flora in at UC Santa Barbara; they were staying with my mother and Len, their misery over their sister's leaving compounded by their blistered, itchy skin.

"Can you drive all right," asked Jenny as we got into the rental car, "or should I?"

I put the keys in the ignition but didn't switch it on.

"Maybe you'd better," I said, opening the driver's door.

"Let's go by the store," said Jenny as we left the campus. "That'll make us feel better."

"And then maybe we can come back and say goodbye to Flora again," I said.

Jenny laughed. "And then we'll go back to the store."

"And then go back and see Flora."

She reached across the console and took my hand.

"Did you think it would be this hard?"

"Yes. Did you?"

Jenny shook her head and pressed her lips together, blinking hard.

"Don't cry," I said softly, squeezing her hand. "We can't afford to get into a fiery crash—this is a rental."

Smiling, she nodded and put both hands on the wheel. She exhaled a puff of air, and after assuring me that she was okay, she said, "Darva would be so pleased."

I looked out the window, thinking how many times Flora had inspired us to say that.

"That was the **wrong** thing to say," I said, feeling myself tear up all over again. Trying to steer the emotion in a different direction, I laughed, but if laughter was medicine, there was no way the FDA would approve this weak dosage.

Jenny had been right: walking through Haugland Foods, Santa Barbara, was a tonic.

"You're back!" said Stella, the woman we'd hired as the store's general manager. "Just when I thought we could start goofing off."

"You'll be fired if you **don't** goof off," I said.

"Well, then I'll just go ask the vendor waiting in my office if he'd like to run off to Mexico with me. He's awfully cute."

"Send us a postcard," I said.

Jenny and I wandered through the aisles, admiring the displays. The produce section was big and bountiful, with the fruits and vegetables looking like props out of a movie set. The floral department had arrangements of the flashy flowers indigenous to California, and the health and fitness aisle had balms and lotions and elixirs that the rest of the country wouldn't catch onto for another year or two.

I waved to the bakery manager, who held up a danish he was putting on a tray.

"Shall we?" I asked Jenny.

"Well, it **is** the first day of school," I said, alluding to our tradition of celebrating the start of the school year with donuts.

After we seated ourselves in the little bakery section, with our complimentary coffee (all Haugland Foods offered free coffee) and chocolate donuts, Stella joined us.

"Oh no," I said. "The trip to Mexico fell through?"

Stella rolled her eyes. "The jerk. All he wanted was my signature on a couple of orders."

"Men," said Jenny, rolling her eyes in solidarity.

"So, you got Flora off with a minimum of tears?" asked the manager, pulling a chair up to our table.

"We got her off," I said.

Stella laughed. "Well, don't worry—we'll take good care of her."

"Please call us as soon as she's done," said Jenny. "We'll want to hear all about her first day here."

Flora was going to start working at Haugland Foods, cashiering **and** playing her flute in the small stage in the area they called Banyan Square. It was right next to us in the bakery section, and it made me happy to look at the stage, imagining Flora there, delighting shoppers with her runs and trills.

"I'll videotape it if you like," said Stella.

"Sure!" said Jenny, and after looking at each other, she and I burst out laughing.

"And then will you take a camera into each of her classes?" I asked. "And her dorm room?"

"And the cafeteria," said Jenny. "We want to make sure she's eating healthy."

By the time the rental car shuttle dropped us off at the airport terminal, we had convinced ourselves that Flora would be fine and that we'd be fine.

"If I can get through that," said Jenny as we walked to our gate, "Conor's first day of kindergarten will be a piece of cake."

"We probably won't even bother to take him to school," I said. "We'll let Ben do it."

Jenny turned toward a newsstand. "Let's get something to read."

I was at the newsstand, debating whether to buy the **LA Times** or the **Santa Barbara Messenger,** when my cell phone rang. The screen read "Kirk's cell."

"My man," I said into the phone. "How're our ocean floors looking?"

"Polluted," said Kirk, and even though his passion was the state of our waters, I could tell from his voice he was worried about something else. "Listen, Joe, something happened."

I braced myself for news I didn't want to hear while a large woman wearing a Mighty Ducks jersey reached across me to grab a **National Enquirer.**

"Are the girls okay? Nance?"

"They're fine. It's my mom. Joe, she had a stroke."

Jenny had sidled up to me and mouthed, "What is it?"

"Kirk," I mouthed back. "How is she doing?" I said into the phone.

"Not good," said Kirk, his voice breaking. I heard

two deep breaths over the phone, and then he continued. "She was only scheduled to work half a day
today and left at the usual time, telling Clarence to
bring home some deli food for dinner, because she
wasn't in the mood to cook. He told her he'd take her
out for dinner before they went to the library—
Thursday night was their library night—and she said
okay. When he got home about four hours later, he
found her on the kitchen floor. He called the ambu-
lance and then us. She's in surgery now but . . . I
don't think it looks good, Joe."

I wrapped my arm around Jenny and held her
close.

"Listen, Kirk, we're at LAX—we just took Flora to
school—"

"That went okay?"

"Okay enough," I said with a sad laugh. "Listen,
I'll call you as soon as we get back home."

"You've got my cell number?"

"Yup. You hang in there, Kirk. Give our love to
everyone."

"Okay, Joe. Love you, man."

This time it was my voice that cracked. "Me too."

**"And we're back from the break, but I'm not going
to take any more calls tonight, although you're still
on the air with God. For those of you who saw my
PPP program on Sunday, you know that my
beloved mother died. I announced it at the end of
the show, because I knew I'd break down and I
didn't want to be in front of the TV cameras with
the Mascara River running down my face."** There
was a pause and sounds of nose blowing.

"My mother would like that—the Mascara River. She was a big reader and liked a surprising turn of phrase. She also liked makeup—she loved all the Perfect Rose products I was able to send her—and swore that they helped her look younger."

"I can't believe it," said Kirk, "she's plugging her damn skin care crap."

"My mother, Martha Swenson Casey Selvin—"

"Selwin!" shouted Kirk, Nance, and I.

"—was only sixty-nine years old, but in that all-too short run, she went through a lot. My dad was in an accident and she cared for him until his death. She had her problems—she tried to find consolation in the bottle, although we all know that kind of consolation comes with price tags too high to pay—but she was able to pull herself out of her misery and move into a life of joy and purpose. She met Mr. Selvin—"

"Selwin!"

"—and they settled down to a happy life in Florida, near my brother and his family."

"Thank God she didn't say my name," said Kirk.

"Now, I can't say my mother's and my relationship wasn't fractious—"

"No," agreed Kirk, "you can't say that."

"—but what mother-daughter relationship isn't?"

Jenny looked at me, and I knew what she was thinking: Flora's and mine.

"I was a willful child—you have to be willful to get places—but I know it caused my mother pain, and for this I am sorry. Because I could take care of myself at a young age, I figured she just said, 'Fine, then I won't have to.' "

"Bitch," said Kirk, shaking his head.

"It served me from a very early age, knowing that I needed to rely on myself because they're weren't always others to rely on, and I consider that self-knowledge a gift, so thanks, Mom.

"Now, my mother's mother, my grandma, was a very special person to me. It has been said that often a grandchild will resemble its grandparent more than its own parent. Who knows—if I had been blessed to have children, maybe we would have fought like cats and dogs too. Maybe they would have run to my mother for solace, the way I ran to Grandma." Another pause, more nose blowing.

"What, is she doing coke or something?" asked Kirk.

"One thing I've realized in this great, complicated world of ours is that blessings are like seasonings; some are salty, some are sweet, some are bitter, and some are hot."

"Oh, brother," said Kirk.

"My grandma seasoned my life with sugar and cinnamon and vanilla—and my mother seasoned my life with paprika and curry and pepper. All those blessings—all those seasonings—helped make me the person I am today."

"Sugar isn't really a seasoning, is it?" asked Jenny.

"And I know that inside those great gates of Heaven, through which my mother has most recently passed, God has enveloped her in his arms and told her, 'Your gifts were great, Martha, and your daughter, Kristi, thanks you.'

"I hope all of you listening will pause to think of

your own mothers, who not only gave you life but sprinkled it with blessings, and I pray you'll be grateful for those seasonings—even the bitter ones. Let Jesus's forgiveness be a model to us and enable us to forgive those extra doses of pepper when we really wanted sugar.

"Remember, God's just not on the air, He's all around, He's everywhere. Good night."

I switched off the radio and the four of us sat there, mouths slightly open, as if we'd all been in the path of an underground electrical shock.

"If Kristi were here," said Kirk finally, "I'd kick her in the ass."

"Oh, Kirk," Nance scolded. "That wouldn't be a very nice seasoning."

"That'd be like horseradish," I said.

"Or wasabi," said Kirk.

"Those are condiments," said Nance. "Can't anybody tell the difference between a seasoning and a condiment?"

"Well, Kristi can't," said Jenny. "She think's sugar's a seasoning."

"When it's obviously a staple," said Nance.

"Dumb bitch," said Kirk.

There had been a small memorial service down in Florida—Martha had made enough friends down there who wanted to honor her passing—but the big service was held up in Minneapolis, where so many people knew her and Clarence. Poor Clarence had been hit hard—he was convinced that he should have known something was wrong with Martha.

"She just said 'okay' in kind of a tired voice when I told her we'd go to the library—and she **loved** our library nights. I should have known something from that tired little 'okay.' "

I had invited him to our house after the service luncheon, but he had said he was going to spend time with his sister, who was pretty broken up.

"Myrt **loved** Martha," said Clarence. "She stayed with us for three months last winter, and the two of them stayed up watching David Letterman and giggling like schoolgirls." He paused for a moment. "I prefer Koppel."

Kirk and Nance had come with us when we drove Flora back to the airport—our beautiful daughter had insisted on coming back even though we had just left her a week earlier in Santa Barbara.

"Dad," she had said over the phone, "I want to be there. I'll fly in Thursday night and leave after the funeral Friday. I'd stay the weekend, but there's this freshman welcome party I'd really like to make on Saturday."

Her brothers, still slightly speckled with chicken pox scabs but no longer itchy and miserable, were delighted to have their sister back and made use of her one night at home, dragging in their Star Wars sleeping bags and camping out in her bedroom.

They weren't pleased when she said another good-bye to them before we went to the funeral, and would have put up a big stink save for the fact that Jenny's sister, Jody, was coming to babysit and bringing along her own two boys, who were the kids' favorite cousins.

When Jody arrived, Ben and Conor squealed with delight, tackling their cousins before they got out of the entryway.

"I guess I'm pretty dispensable," said Flora with a shrug.

"No, you're not," I said, draping my arm around her.

Her presence had meant a lot to Kirk and Nance and Clarence; at her young age she knew the importance of showing up. But now she was gone again and, according to my watch, due to land in fourteen minutes, and the gloom that our laughter had blown away gathered itself and seeped back into the room.

"Anyone want a drink?" I asked.

"I could go for a walk," said Kirk. "A walk and **then** a drink."

"Ladies?" I asked.

"Do you mind if we stay?" Nance asked Jenny. "I'm sort of pooped."

"We'll start a fire," said Jenny, "and open a bottle of wine."

It was a cool September night, but not according to Kirk.

"Man, what's the wind chill factor?" he said before we were even down the front steps. "Twenty below?"

I stepped back into the house and grabbed a jacket from the closet.

"It's at least forty-five degrees," I said, handing Kirk the jacket. "Have you gone completely Floridian?"

"Totally," said Kirk, putting the jacket on over his sweatshirt. "If it's below seventy degrees, I start digging out the long underwear."

We walked down the sidewalk in silence for a while, a wind rustling through the leaves that would in a few weeks be on the ground. Kirk was right. It did feel cold, and I turned up my coat collar.

"You know, Coral did a reading at Mom's service in Cocoa Beach," said Kirk. "I couldn't believe it; she didn't break down or anything. Clarence had asked if I wanted to speak and I . . . I couldn't. I wish to hell I could have, but I couldn't."

"What did Coral read?"

"A Walt Whitman poem Clarence picked out. Clarence couldn't read either. But Kristi did. She didn't even ask Clarence, just told him that she'd be reading."

"What'd she read?"

"That's the thing. I thought she'd read something from the Bible in her big phony preacher's voice, but she read a poem she had written when she was a kid. It was a typical kid's poem, rhyming words like **ma** and **law**—in fact, the first line was 'I'm glad it's not against the law / To love my ma'—but I'm telling you, Joe, it was touching. It made me think maybe I was wrong about her, that maybe she did love Martha."

I nodded in the dark.

"And then after the service, she pulled me aside and said she hoped we could be better friends now and that she wanted to thank me for loving our mother and father even when they were at their most unlovable."

"She said that?"

"Uh-huh. And then she said she hated to leave, but she had a flight to catch and shows to tape—blah, blah, blah—but she'd stay in touch and then she hugged me—hard—and handed me an envelope and told me not to open it until I got home. Then she slipped out the back of the church and into the limousine that was waiting for her."

"What was in the envelope?"

"A check for five thousand dollars. On the memo line she wrote 'Mom.' And there was a copy of a picture."

"A picture of what?"

He stopped, the wind flipping up a side of his hair.

"Let's turn back," he said. "I'm too cold to go any further."

"Maybe I'm wrong about the temperature," I said as we turned around, both of us tucking our hands deep in our pockets.

"I had never seen the picture before," said Kirk, "but it was in perfect condition, which makes me think it was a copy. It was a picture of our family—I think it was taken down at the falls, in the pavilion. My mom and dad and I are sitting on top of a picnic table; I'm on my mom's lap and my mom's on my dad's lap and all of us have these big laughing smiles on our faces. And then there's Kristi—six or so, she's got braids—standing off to the side with her hands on her hips, her face turned up and away from us, her eyes closed, like she's shunning us."

"What do you suppose she meant by giving it to you?"

"I have no idea. On the back she had written, 'Members only.'"

"So who was the exclusive club? Kristi or the rest of your family?"

"Beats me, but it made me feel bad. And again, I thought maybe I'd been wrong about her all along. Then, hearing her on the radio tonight . . ."

"It did seem her eulogy had an agenda."

"That's just it. She doesn't wipe her butt without

an agenda. And I wonder why I'm such a sap to keep trying to find the good in her when I think it shriveled up and died a long time ago."

"That's pretty harsh."

"But pretty true, don't you think?"

A man standing in front of a picture window scratched his belly before pulling down the shade as we walked past his house.

"Yes," I said after a moment.

Up in my office, I had Conor ring the bell.

"Good morning, shoppers," I said into the microphone. "It's time for another contest here at Haugland Foods."

The dozen or so shoppers stopped in the aisles; Swanny Swanson waved up at me, and Jan Olafson pointed to herself as if letting me know she was going to win.

"Today's prize, courtesy of Lenny's Kitchen and Bath, is free, yes, free tile **and** installation for any bathroom in your house."

This was a rigged contest; Lenny had given me the gift certificate over a week ago, but I had waited to give it away until Belinda Long was in the store. She reminded me of my mother—a young widow, new in town—and I knew from Eileen that she had recently moved into a run-down house close to the airport. Eileen was our resident psychiatrist, learning all about people while ringing up their groceries, and had told me the young woman was originally from Toronto. This was information I used this for the contest.

"Anyone interested in this incredible value, meet me in Banana Square.

"Come on, Conor," I said, taking my five-year-old's hand. "We're going to go make someone's day."

I was a little frazzled to see that the group that awaited me at Banana Square did not include the young widow.

"Nice tie, Swanny," I said, stalling for time.

"It's the wife's idea," said Swanny. "Now I'm retired, she says I gotta make an extra effort with my appearance or I'll wind up in my bathrobe all day. Heck, I didn't wear a tie when I worked at the Ford plant!"

I saw Belinda shyly edging her cart toward the action.

"Say, young man," said Estelle Brady to Conor, "why aren't you in school?"

"I go to afternoon kinneygarten."

"**Kinneygarten,**" said Estelle, looking to her left and right. "Isn't that cute?"

"I think we're ready for the contest," I said. "For the free bathroom tile and installation, who can tell me what province Toronto is in and which provinces are to the east and west of it?"

Swanny opened his mouth but closed it again, and Jan Olafson looked up as if trying to visualize a map.

"If you know it, just shout it out," I said, looking directly at the young widow.

"Toronto's in the province of Ontario," she said, leaning over the cart handle. "Manitoba's to the west and Quebec is to the east."

"We have a winner!" I said. To tell you the truth, I wasn't exactly sure where each Canadian province was, but she was a Canadian and I was willing to take her word for it.

"Boy, can I use this," she said, accepting the gift certificate.

"Well, that's great," I said. "Bring us a picture when it's all done and we'll put it on the bulletin board."

"Okay," she said shyly, "I will. Thank you very much, Mr. . . ."

"Everyone calls me Joe."

"Thanks, Joe. Is this an American thing, these contests in grocery stores?"

"Well, it's our thing here at Haugland Foods, and we're American."

"Wait'll I tell my mother," said Belinda. "She thinks everyone carries a gun and can't wait to shoot one another. Wait'll I tell her I won a bathroom remodel in a grocery store!"

Up in my office, I showed Conor an A, G, and D chord. His brother Ben played both piano and guitar and Conor, whose competitiveness would either serve him well or do him in, had demanded that I start giving him lessons "because I wanna be the best guitar player in the whole wide world!"

I had kept a guitar in my office all these years and had gone over these same chords with Ben here and at home and now it thrilled me to think that the tradition of jam sessions up in this grocery store office might continue with my sons.

Still concentrating on watching my fingers roam the fret board, Conor said, "That lady who won the contest—why does her mommy think she'll be shot?"

"Oh," I said, wondering how to answer yet another

question I didn't really have an answer for. "Sometimes mommies worry about their children."

"If I were a cowboy, I might get shot. 'Cause cowboys have guns."

"Some do," I said. "Some just have lassos."

"I know what a lasso is," said Conor. "Ben drawed me one. It's a rope in a circle that you catch bears with."

I smiled, and played some twangy chords. "Well, cowboys usually catch cows with them. And bulls and horses."

"Yeah. And giraffes and monkeys."

"But the guys that catch those aren't called cowboys. They're called giraffeboys and monkeyboys."

Conor laughed. "And bullboys and horseboys."

"Hey, you know what, pardner?" I said, looking at my watch. "It's time we mosey on off to school."

"Oh," said Conor, disappointed.

"Come on," I said, putting my guitar back into its case. "Maybe you can play Bullboys and Monkeyboys at recess."

"Yeah! Let's hurry up, Dad!"

After I dropped Conor off at school, I walked across the playing field toward my car, trying to remember if I was supposed to do the shopping for tonight's dinner with Jenny's parents, or if she had wanted to. I decided to call her when my cell phone vibrated.

It was Kristi.

"Hey, Joe."

For the past couple years, since her mother died, she called me every few months. They were harmless enough conversations, never long or meaty; it seemed she just wanted to check in. Kirk got the same kind of phone calls; he said they never talked long enough to get into an argument, which seemed to suit both of them.

"It's not a real deep relationship," he told me once, "but at least it's a relationship . . . sort of."

Now Kristi was asking me what I was up to.

"Oh, I just brought Conor to school," I said. "Now I'm wondering if it's me or Jenny who's supposed to do the shopping for tonight's dinner."

"Well, you being the supermarket mogul," said Kristi, "I imagine it'd be you."

"So how're things in the soul-saving business?"

"The soul saving's going very well, thank you. Four billion at last count. But I'm calling you to share some personal news." Her laugh, for a change, was one of delight. "Joe, I want you to be one of the first to know. Tuck Drake—"

"Tuck Drake the nutty senator?"

Her laugh hardened. "Tuck Drake the highly regarded and esteemed senator has asked me to marry him."

I stepped into the street and a school bus honked its horn.

"So . . . what did you say?"

"Well, I said yes, of course. I've been waiting for a man like Tuck Drake all my life. Well, listen, Joe, I've got a million things to do. I just wanted to give you a heads-up so you could start shopping for the perfect gift."

"Kristi, I . . . don't know what to say."

"How about congratulations?"

"All right—congratulations."

Her laugh was back to its delight mode. "I really hit the jackpot with this one, Joe. Gotta run—and remember, diamonds are **always** an appropriate gift!"

"So are toasters," I replied, but she'd already hung up the phone.

Twenty-five

Tuck Drake was a big slab of a man, six feet five inches tall and as brawny as a blue-ribbon steer. He had played football for Clemson and was an all-American in 1973, but when he blew out a knee in a bowl game, he had to hang up his cleats for good.

"Ya gotta understand," he was quoted during his first Senate campaign, "football was my life. And when that life caved in, I pretty much let everything else. Yup, I drank, I caroused, I did everything my sweet mama told me not to, until after a night of par- tyin', when I was perched over the porcelain throne, throwing up all that was in me and a little bit more, I suddenly realized how far I'd strayed—the proud athlete God had made me was now just a vessel for alcohol and other poisons, a sinner who'd let his body and his mind be taken over by the Devil's temptations. That's when I rose up, rinsed my mouth out, and after I spit into the sink, I looked in the mirror and I said, 'Tuck Drake might not be a football all-star, but he can be an all-star on God's team.' Let me tell you, it's the best team I've ever been on, with the best coaching, and the thing is— everybody wins."

Tuck Drake had a big sheaf of blond hair and matching blond sideburns and was something of a folk hero in his home state. He also scared Beth and Linda half to death.

"I can't believe that even **Kristi Casey** could have married a guy like that," said Beth, who had seen the couple on a morning talk show, sharing pictures of their three-year anniversary party in the Caribbean. "I mean, she's **weird,** but not on the level of Tuck Drake."

My mother and aunt had entered their seventies (or "the age of advanced wisdom and subtle sexiness," as Beth preferred to call it) and they were both out on Lake Nokomis with me, skating the perimeter of the plowed-off rink, while Ben and Conor battled it out in a pickup game on the hockey rink.

The sun had given up its halfhearted battle to assert itself in the winter sky, skittering away behind a low bank of gray clouds. Occasionally we'd be drawn to watch what was happening on the hockey rink— Ben was a good player, but Conor was excellent, albeit hotheaded—a common enough pairing in the game of hockey.

"Don't you want to join them?" asked my mother, who skated linked to Beth at the elbow.

"No," I said, skating backward in front of them so I could talk, "I'd rather skate with my two favorite old ladies."

"So I'm taking that as a no. And now I'm going to hang up and wait for your call at some civil hour."

"Please, Joe," she said, an uncharacteristic vulnerability coating her voice. "I don't have anyone else I can talk to."

"Christ," I muttered, getting out of bed. Jenny groaned, as if she couldn't believe I was taking the call.

"Hold on a sec," I said into the cordless phone. "I've got to leave the room so I don't disturb my wife, whom you also woke up when you called."

"I'm sorry, Joe," said Kristi, and for a change, it sounded as if she were. Yanking my robe off the door hook, I padded out into the hallway.

Flora's room was closest, so I went inside and sank down on a furry beanbag chair.

"All right," I said, making sure she heard the sigh in my voice. "What's going on, Kristi?"

"I think Tuck's having an affair."

"Well, isn't that par for the course?" I said with a laugh.

"What's that supposed to mean?"

"Oh, come on, Kristi," I said, and her name bobbed along on a short wave of laughter. "It's always the guys who yell the loudest about other people's bad behavior who are usually in the middle of the bad behavior themselves."

"Why, you don't know a thing about—"

"But I really don't understand why you're so upset. You've never seemed to mind affairs, although you're usually on the cheating end rather than—"

The phone clicked off. I sat there in the dark for a moment before the phone rang again.

"I didn't call you for a lecture," said Kristi, her voice clogged with tears. "I called you because I needed a friend!"

"Sorry," I said, although I doubted my apology would nudge the needle on any sincerity meter.

"And if you're referring to Johnny Priestly, it's not like I broke up their marriage—FYI, they're still married. I just felt sorry for him, because his wife hadn't slept with him in two years and—"

"Okay, **okay**, Kristi. I don't need to hear all the sordid details. I'm sorry I lectured you. I guess I don't like being woken up in the middle of the night."

"We've already established that."

I sighed again, the chair scrunching as I repositioned myself.

"Okay, I'll just sit here—on a beanbag chair, no less—and listen to you as you tell me what's happening."

There was a long pause, as if Kristi was waiting for further complaints from me. Then she began to speak.

"Well, Tuck picked me up after the radio show tonight—you should see my D.C. studio, Joe, it's state-of-the-art. Anyway, I thought we were going to go out for dinner, but Tuck said he was beat and would I mind awfully if we went straight home? He did look tired—they've been going into special sessions trying to get this Families Foremost bill passed—and I wasn't about to make him sit through a fancy five-course dinner with a congressman who's not that important anyway. So we go home, he climbs into bed, and about twenty minutes later, the phone rings and a voice on the other line says, 'You might be interested to know that Senator Tuck Drake is having an affair with a Senate page.' " She paused—for dramatic effect, I assumed. "So you see, Joe, you're not the only one to get a call in the middle of the night."

"Not to be a stickler," I said, "but it doesn't sound like your call came at two-thirty in the morning."

"Yeah, well," said Kristi impatiently, "my news was a little more shocking."

I tried to laugh at the inanity of our argument, but I was too tired.

"Did you tell Tuck?"

"No! He's a bear if you wake him up out of a deep sleep."

"Are you going to tell him?"

"Should I?"

"I don't know, Kristi. I mean, how do you even know if it was real or not? Maybe it was just a prank."

"Do you think so?" asked Kristi, hope flooding into her voice. "Oh, Joe, I never even thought of that—I do get nuts calling the show and stuff, but not at home. I mean, this is a private number—"

"Kristi, you know there's no such thing as a private number. Really, I'm surprised at how quick you are to believe what some prankster tells you over the telephone."

Her laugh was weak but hopeful. "Do you really think it might have been a prankster? Because I couldn't stand it if I thought Tuck was cheating on me, Joe. I have poured **everything** into this relationship; God knows he doesn't need to go anywhere for sex, because he's getting all he wants here."

"Please, Kristi, spare me."

"It's just that . . . well, there's been some gossip."

"There's always gossip in Washington, Kristi. You know that."

"You're right, Joe. I'll bet Washington's even worse than Hollywood."

I heard the rasp of a match and an inhale.

"Don't tell me you're **still** smoking."

"Oh, I'm down to two a day."

"Packs or cigarettes?"

"Ha ha ha. **Cigarettes.** And most of the time it's just one, after breakfast. It's better than a laxative."

"Now you're starting to gross me out."

Kristi laughed. "Thanks for listening, Joe. I feel much better now."

She hung up then, unconcerned with good-byes.

"So what was **that** all about?" asked Jenny when I climbed back into bed. After I told her, she said, "I'll bet he is."

"Having an affair?"

"Sure," said Jenny. "He strikes me as the kind of man who needs more than his wife to tell him how great he is."

I pulled her close to me.

"It doesn't bother you when Kristi calls me, does it?" She had always told me she didn't mind, but I liked to check in case she had changed her mind.

"It does when she calls at two in the morning," said Jenny. She put a hand on the side of my face. "I used to find her calls kind of entertaining—or at least your retelling of them—but more and more, I just feel sorry for her."

"Don't ever tell her that."

"She just seems so lonely. Doesn't she have any other friends? Any girlfriends?"

"I think she thinks of women more as rivals than friends," I said, and then, tired from all the talk, I used my mouth to kiss my wife, my lips lingering on hers for a long while, as if they were weary and had found a place to rest.

We got another telephone call the next night, and it was about Flora—in fact, it was from Flora—but it came at a much earlier hour and was much better news. At least I hoped it was good news.

"Well, what's he like?" was my first question after Flora had shouted, "Guess what—I found the guy I'm going to marry!"

"What's he like?" she answered. "Oh, Papa **mon** Joe, he's **perfect.** He's kind and funny and smart and handsome—**mon dieu,** is he handsome. And he plays guitar—oh, you should hear him—and he's got a great singing voice too, and—"

"When did you meet him, honey?" asked Jenny, giggling over Flora's excitement.

"Last week, on the plane to Paris."

Flora was Haugland Foods' international buyer (yes, nepotism got her the job, but nepotism's an easy thing to practice when your daughter graduates summa cum laude from college—her degree was in French literature with a minor in business—and it didn't hurt that she was also fluent in Spanish and almost fluent in Japanese . . . I could go on and on, but I don't want to brag) and her job included travel to Europe and Asia, expanding our international foods and wine section.

"Is he French?" I asked.

"No," said Flora. "**English.** And his name's Nicholas—Nick. Isn't that the best name you've ever heard?"

"Does he live in England?" I asked, already lonesome, imagining Flora spending all her free time on the other side of the Atlantic.

"That's the funny thing, Dad—he lives in Monterey! And he's been to the Haugland Foods there!"

We now had two stores in California—Santa Barbara, where Flora still lived, and most recently Monterey.

"How'd he wind up in Monterey?"

"He got lucky," said Jenny, whose appreciation for the Monterey/Big Sur area was a factor in our choosing the location for the new store. I smiled at her; we were in the den, both sitting in recliners like old farts, talking on our individual cordless phones.

"Well, it was kind of lucky," said Flora. "He got a job here and decided to stay."

"What kind of job?" I asked. "What's he do for a living?"

"He's a songwriter. You know that song 'Beautiful Spots'?—remember, it was in the animated movie **Charlie and the Cheetah**? We all went to see it when I was home on Christmas break a couple years ago, because Conor wanted to see it so bad?"

I shrugged at Jenny and she shrugged back, although into the phone she said, "Oh, I love that song!"

Flora squealed with delight. "Oh, I do too, Mom! And that's how he landed up here—the director lives in Carmel, and Nick visited when he was working on the movie. Of course he fell in love with the place and has been living there for about five years."

"How old is this Nick?" I asked.

" 'This Nick,' " said Flora, "is twenty-nine. He's exactly four years and three days older than me. We're the same sign."

"Is that good?" I asked.

"How should I know?" said Flora with a laugh. "I don't follow that crap."

We talked for a few more minutes, and then Ben came home from his friend's, who conveniently lived right across the street, and I handed him the phone so he could hear all about his sister's new boyfriend.

"He plays guitar?" he said. "Cool! Maybe we can all jam together!"

"Yeah!" said Conor, who was supposed to be asleep but had a sixth sense that alerted him when something exciting was going on. "Tell Flora to tell him I know how to play 'Stairway to Heaven' now!"

Conor knew a chunk of the rhythm section, but it was a stretch to say he knew the classic song that all boys learning guitar want to play.

Ben cupped the receiver and said to his brother, "Flora says to tell you the guy she's going to marry wrote 'Beautiful Spots' from **Charlie and the Cheetah**."

"**Charlie and the Cheetah!**" screamed Conor, forgetting all about being the cool purveyor of Led Zeppelin music and reverting to the nine-year-old boy he was. "I love that movie!"

That's right, ladies, Perfect Rose skin cream, for your perfect skin . . . And now I've got some news I've been wanting to tell you, my dear listeners, for a long time. I've been a very lucky lady in my life, but you know that the luck of love wasn't mine for a long, long time. When I first had Tuck Drake on my television show, I thought, Hmmm, there's an interesting man, but of course he was married, and therefore I couldn't take the interest any further.

But God works in strange and wonderful ways, and although my heart bleeds for the pain of divorce, sometimes couples are not a godly match, and this was true for Tuck and his former wife, whose embrace of New Age religions surprised and then hurt him. Fortunately Tuck's two beautiful children, Jake and Jade, were already grown and off at college when Tuck and his former wife made the hard, yet ultimately correct, decision to go their separate ways. So when Tuck appeared again on my show, I knew the gates had been unlocked and I could enter.

Ladies and men (I'm on to you, fellas; my latest demographics show more and more of you are listening in), have you ever been struck dumb by love? That's what happened to yours truly when Tuck took the microphone from me and said, "I know we're supposed to talk about the day I accepted Christ, but I just can't get enough of that drumming of yours. It would just tickle me if you and the Kristi Corps did one of your drum battles."

I don't know how many of you listeners saw that episode, but as I beat my rhythms and the audience clapped back, I thought: Here is a man who rejoices in my talents; here is a man who's not afraid of a woman like me.

It was hard to give up my weekly show at the PPP network, but I wanted to spend weekends with the man I love, and I knew I could still spread the Lord's word through my radio program. But now, dear listeners, saints and sinners, this too will end. I have other fish to fry—and believe me, these are whoppers.

We'll be holding a press conference tomorrow—but I wanted my most devoted followers, my beloved Kristi Corps, to hear it first from me.

As you know, there has been talk of my husband, Senator Tuck Drake, running for president of our United most blessed of States. We have a solid base of supporters and a solid message that I believe the good folks of America are going to respond to. Tuck said, as a reward to my faithful listeners, "Why not tell them first?" So on behalf of my husband and myself, I'm announcing his candidacy. The good and godly Mr. Tuck Drake is running for president!

It's been more than an honor to be on the air with God and you, but there is a season for everything, and this is the time for me to work on my husband's campaign. I thank you for your time and attention, and I hope you'll support me in my new venture, just as I'm sure God is.

God bless you, and God bless America. And to keep track of the comings and goings of Drake for President, please check out our website.

Kirk called me as soon as he heard the news.

"Can she be serious? I know there are a lot of nuts in this country, but does she seriously think there are any nutty enough to support Tuck Drake for president?"

"Now I'm really scared," said Beth, "The day when

one lunatic can announce the candidacy of another lunatic and not be laughed out of the country is a terrifying day indeed."

Gary Conroy sent me a e-mail from Austin, where he was in negotiations to build a Haugland Foods.

It's all the buzz around here and I've been talking to a lot of people. Half seem excited—one woman said, "When a good Christian like Tuck Drake has a good Christian woman like Kristi Casey behind him, my vote's a guarantee!" On the other hand, an attorney I've been working with out here said, "He doesn't have a chance; with his wife, they're too off the wall—even for Texas!"

I saw Shannon Saxon whatever-her-name-was-now (she was on her third husband) in the store and she said, "I hope he gets the nomination and then I hope he wins the whole thing! I was kind of turned off by Kristi being a preacher and everything, but she'd be a great First Lady—I mean, they're so cute together!"

"God chose Tuck as my husband," Kristi was quoted in our local newspaper, "and I truly believe He's going to chose him for president."

"Maybe you should tell what you know, Joe," said Jenny after I folded the newspaper in half and sat on it, thinking it served a better purpose keeping my ass warm than being a forum for Kristi's craziness. Jenny and I were in the stands watching Conor's hockey team get creamed by a team from the suburbs. "You know, expose her for what she is."

I watched as Conor stole the puck and dashed

across the blue line, only to have a boy twice his size knock him down.

"Tripping!" I hollered, jumping up.

The play continued, the refs ignoring my calls to penalize the opposing goon.

"I actually have thought of that," I said, sitting down on Kristi and Tuck's smiling faces.

Jenny pulled the red plaid blanket she always brought to games over my knees.

"I don't think I could subject myself—could subject you and the kids—to all the scrutiny. Think of the headlines: 'Presidential Hopeful's Dreams Blindsided by Accusations of His Wife's High School Blow Jobs and College Acid Trips.' "

Jenny laughed, then shivered.

"Besides, it's old news. All that stuff happened more than thirty years ago. All she'd need to do is hold a press conference on the power of redemption."

"Still, it might show people what a hypocrite she is, and by association, Tuck Drake."

I shrugged, and then tensed as the other team's star center backhanded the puck. Our goalie stopped it, and I exhaled.

"She's had people try to call her on things before. Remember that guy who claimed he was married to her back in the early eighties? He said they lived down in Mexico and made their living selling fenced jewelry? Remember, they even printed a copy of a marriage certificate in the magazine, and all Kristi said was, 'I won't even dignify this sad man's fantasies and talents at forgery' or something like that, and it died down just like that?"

Jenny nodded. "I remember you saying, 'So that's what she was doing all those years.' "

"Right. Even though I've got two postcards from her that lend a lot more credence to that guy's story of her marriage than she'd like to admit. But that's just it." I unscrewed the Thermos of coffee and took a swallow. "Proof doesn't matter. Kristi will make you believe what she wants you to believe."

"Well, that's why someone's got to stop her, Joe. Stop her and her dangerous husband."

The clock ran out and the buzzer rang.

"Listen, Jenny, Americans are wising up. Even if his party gives him the nomination, he'll never get elected. No way. **Never.**"

"From your lips," said Jenny.

I laughed. "What? To God's ear? Well, let's hope— although we'll probably have to wrestle the Kristi Corps to get anywhere near."

Tuck, with Kristi at his side, continued to get more press coverage than other candidates—they were more than a novelty, after all; they were a force—but Jenny and I made it a point to turn the channel whenever their blond hair and pious faces came on the television; we had our own lives to live and could only take so much. Besides, we had a wedding—or we thought we had a wedding—to plan.

Flora brought her fiancé Nick home for Thanksgiving, and all the trepidation a father feels about his future son-in-law was for naught. I loved the guy. Immediately. And not just because he gave Conor an autographed CD of the **Charlie and the Cheetah** soundtrack or because he spent a half hour in Ben's room showing him chord progressions. It wasn't because he played a game of Scrabble with my mom, Len, and me and graciously lost, and it wasn't because he told Jenny he'd had the great fortune to be at a dinner party with Jean-Pierre Rampal a year before he died.

"I was composing some music for a movie that never saw the light of day," he said in his crisp British accent, "but the producer—who'd had much better luck with other films—had worked with Monsieur Rampal and he was giving a concert in London and one thing led to another . . . which ultimately was dinner."

"Oh, what was he like?" asked Jenny, her brown eyes shining.

"Everything you'd expect from his playing. Considerate. Funny. Passionate. And always listening, with a great eagerness, to what was going on."

But all that stuff was a bonus. Why I loved the guy immediately was because I could see how deeply and truly he loved Flora and how she returned that same deep and true love.

Still, I suppose I had to ask the standard questions, and I did so as we had our first Thanksgiving dinner together.

"Will you love and honor Flora the way she deserves to be loved and honored?"

"Dad!" said Flora in embarrassed protest.

"Yes, I will," said Nick solemnly.

Conor, watching all of this at the end of the table, giggled.

"Do you swear never to be a jerk, never to hurt her, never to become blind to all the wonder that is our Flora?"

Nick set his fork and knife down and folded his hands in his lap.

"I swear," he said.

Flora didn't protest and Conor didn't laugh. There was absolute silence around the dinner table.

"Can I trust you to always listen to her, to never shut her out, and to always tell her what's on your mind?"

"You can," said Nick, "although sometimes there are things on my mind that really aren't worth sharing."

"Point taken," I said, nodding. "Jenny, is there anything you'd like Nick to promise us?"

Jenny sat quietly for a moment, at the other end of the table.

"I really don't think he needs to promise us anything. It's Flora he should make the promises to."

At that moment, Flora leaned over her plate and began to cry, and for a moment, I thought all the good feelings I had for Nick were going to have to be chucked.

Her tears were brief, replaced quickly with a smile and then laughter.

"**Je suis desolée**," she said, dabbing at her face with her napkin. "I'm so sorry . . . but so glad."

I saw Ben and Conor exchange the same puzzled look that passed between all the adults at the table.

"See," continued Flora, "Nick has already made these promises. I mean to me. I'm sad because you weren't there to hear them being made . . . but so glad that I did and that . . . and that we're already married."

There was bedlam at the dinner table; shouts; questions thrown; answers; laughs; toasts; and then, tears. My own.

"Oh, Papa **mon** Joe," said Flora, getting up from her chair. She sat on the arm of my chair, her arm around me. "I'm so sorry, but we were just so—ready. And we didn't want to plan a big affair—we just wanted to do it. No fuss, no bother, and dinner at the deli section of Haugland Foods, Santa Barbara."

I sniffed. "I'm happy for you, honey, I really am." I brought my gaze up at Nick, who looked apologetic and miserable. "And for you too, Nick. It's just that I . . . I always wanted to walk you down the aisle, Flora."

There was a moment of pure silence and I sat in it, feeling like a fool, until Jenny broke it.

"Okay," she said, pushing back her chair. "Everybody get up. Dad's going to walk Flora down the aisle."

I asked the same question my boys asked: "Huh?" but I got up anyway.

"All right, Ben, you take Nick and Conor into your room and don't come out until I call you."

"Okay," said Ben, lifting his shoulders in a shrug but obeying his mother nevertheless. "Come on, guys," he said, leading them up the stairs to his room.

"And Flora, you come with me," said Jenny. "We'll get you ready. Carole, you sit at the piano. Beth, Linda, Len—I'm sure you'll come up with something."

Jenny wasn't the bossy type, so on the rare occasion that she issued orders, everyone listened.

Ten minutes later she emerged from the bedroom, hollering up the stairs for the boys to come out.

She had Conor and Ben stand by Nick at the fireplace, and she sat down next to Len on the couch. I was told to stand by the dining room and when she said, "Okay, Carole, hit it!" my mother began playing the wedding march, and Flora emerged from the hallway.

After seeing the fancy robe Kristi had worn in her Des Moines hotel room, I had been inspired to buy Jenny a white satin robe, but she never wore it, preferring her old pilled quilted one. While it might not be a suitable robe for my wife, it was the perfect wedding dress for my daughter, who wore it along with a veil made out of an old doily Jenny's grandmother had crocheted. She held a bouquet of silk flowers Jenny had heisted from an arrangement in the guest bathroom. I had never seen such a beautiful bride.

Flora took my arm and my knees turned to water.

"Come on, Dad," she whispered when it appeared I was unable to move. "Everybody's waiting for us."

Beth and Linda had dismantled some of the Thanksgiving centerpiece and threw yellow rose petals on the floor, and eventually I was able to move. Slowly, to my mother's enthusiastic rendering of "Here Comes the Bride," I escorted my daughter over the strewn petals, past the hallway table we kept our keys on, in front of the grandfather clock and behind the couch in the living room, past the wing chair, and to the fireplace.

Thinking fast, Len jumped up and said, "Who gives this bride?"

"I do," I said, surrendering her arm to Nick.

The ceremony consisted of anyone who had anything to say jumping in at any time. I started off by asking the same questions I had asked Nick at the dinner table.

Then Conor chirped in, "Do you swear to go to hockey games with her 'cause Flora loves hockey, even if you don't know much about the game yet?"

"I swear," said Nick.

"They say 'swear' in trials," Ben explained to his brother, "not at weddings."

To the groom, he asked, "Do you promise to introduce her to new bands because she has kind of squirrely taste when it comes to music?"

Nick said, "I promise," at the same time Flora said, "I don't have squirrely taste in music!"

"You like too many of those crybaby girl singer-songwriters," said Ben.

When everyone was done asking Nick what he promised to do in his marriage, we questioned Flora.

I asked her versions of the same questions I'd asked Nick; Jenny asked if she promised to show him how to do the laundry, because "marriage is strengthened when a man can do his own wash."

Nick maintained he already knew how and that not only did he not mind doing the laundry, he liked to iron.

My aunt and my mother looked at each other, their eyes wide.

"He's a keeper," said mom.

"Do you swear," said Conor, "I mean, promise to never be mean to Flora and buy her licorice ice cream, even though it's kind of hard to find, because it's her favorite?"

"I swear and promise," said Nick.

Flora leaned toward her little brother. "We carry it at the stores in California," she said. "I've made sure of it."

Finally, when all the promises were made, Jenny took her flute off the top of the piano and after a quick conference at the piano, and a fluttering of pages, she and my mother played "Ave Maria."

Nick Pullman, my new son-in-law and the professional songwriter, stood staring, his mouth agape, at my wife and mother. Underneath her little doily, Flora beamed, and I, the father of the bride, couldn't have known a bigger happiness. I had walked my daughter down the aisle and her beautiful wedding had cost me absolutely nothing.

Twenty-six

And we're back from the break on the Bud Farrell
Show. Today we've been talking to Senator Tuck Drake
and his wife, Kristi Casey Drake—the couple who next
year hopes to be calling themselves the president and
First Lady. We're going to open it up to callers now.
Line one, you're on the air.

Yes, thank you, Bud. Senator Drake, Mrs. Drake, I
just want to tell you how happy I am that godly people
such as yourselves have decided to get in there and
fight the good fight for our country!

Why, thank you, ma'am. If Mrs. Drake and I have
seen one thing as we travel this great country of ours,
it's how desperate people are to get our moral compass
pointed back to the right direction, the S by F direction—the direction that stands for safety and security,
as well as families, freedom, and faith.

Now, Senator, don't you think those are words that
butt up against our very Constitution and the separation of church and state?

I'm not saying we all need to worship in the same religion, Bud. I'm just saying that we all do better when we have God on our side.

Let's take another call. Line two, you're on the air.

Senator and Mrs. Drake—you're crazy! Well, let me tell you, I don't want to live the stupid "S by F" country you have planned—

Thank you, caller—

No, no, let him talk, Bud. The senator and I aren't afraid of our critics.

I'm more than a critic, I'm a citizen who values the rights I have in this country—and I want to keep those rights! I don't want your husband's and your lunatic religious views legislating how I'm supposed to live my life!

(Chuckling) Sir, ad hominens attacks aren't going to serve the debate at all. I can assure you that the senator reveres the Constitution and our Bill of Rights and will do everything in our power to maintain the glories of this democracy.

Your words mean nothing! You're a fraud! You're all frauds! You're a—

Thank you, caller. Does this happen to you a lot, Mrs. Drake?

Well, Bud, if you live in a country that guarantees freedom of speech, some of that speech isn't going to be what you want to hear. Believe me, after years on the radio, I've heard some hateful things and it didn't stop me from broadcasting. Nor will it stop my husband and me from campaigning.

So what's next, Senator?

I'll be in session next week, but we'll squeeze in a few visits in the upcoming months to talk to the good folks of this good country.

Thank you, Senator. Thank you, Mrs. Drake.

You're welcome, Bud. And let me just ask you one question, Bud: With looks like yours, why are you on the radio? You should be on television!

(Embarrassed laughter) Uh . . . thank you, Mrs. Drake.

Since I didn't have to spring for a wedding, I thought I'd throw a lollapalooza of a fiftieth-birthday party for Jenny.

As I told Flora about it on the phone, I got another bright idea. "And how about we combine it with a wedding reception for you?"

"Oh, Dad, **merci,** but then everyone would bring presents and Nick and I have everything we need, plus we'd have to figure out a way to cart everything back to California."

"Are you for real?" I asked her. "What happened to your consume-and-acquire gene?"

"I guess it's recessive." Flora laughed. "Besides, Nick's parents are throwing a party for us in London and we'll probably get tons of stuff from them. You'll come to that, right?"

"Yes, tell them the Yankees are most definitely coming. But about your mother's party—are you going to make it?"

"**Certainement,** Papa **mon** Joe!" said Flora. "We wouldn't miss it for the world!"

I had decided to throw a surprise party at the store, and the cashiers, customers, and bag boys were all in cahoots.

"We can have everyone hide in the basement," said Eileen, who had just celebrated her fortieth year cashiering at the store, "or we could have everyone just pretending to shop."

"That might be good," I said, "although she might be suspicious if there are a lot of people."

"We could say we're having a big sale," said Eileen. "A triple-coupon day or something."

I had already booked a caterer, and it wasn't hard to come up with musicians, considering so many had played on the Darva Pratt Performance Center's stage at Banana Square.

Ben and Conor and I were already working on a wild guitar version of "Happy Birthday," complete with wah-wah pedal and distortion.

"Are you planning something for my birthday?" Jenny asked one afternoon when I picked her up after a rehearsal. The woodwind quintet she had been a member of for years—All Busy Mothers—was rehearsing for one of their semiannual recitals. They practiced in the home of their oboist, and I had suggested a walk around Lake Harriet when they were done.

"You know, we should buy a house like this," I said as we walked down the wide flagstone path that led away from the oboist's home. "It's not like we couldn't afford it."

"Don't change the subject," said Jenny, opening the trunk of my car and putting her flute inside. "What are you planning for my birthday?"

"I wish I could tell you something," I said, taking her arm and steering her across the street. "But there's nothing to tell."

She looked at me coolly. "I don't believe a word you're saying."

"All right," I said, deciding to try another tack. "How does a trip to the Florida Keys with Kirk and Nance sound?"

"Great," said Jenny with a smile. "Anywhere warm and sunny in February is fine by me."

"Although we have to leave the day after your birthday, because Kirk's out on a dive and won't be back until then." I was pleased at how smoothly I was ad-libbing.

"With the kids too?"

"Sure," I said.

"Because we'll have to take them out of school then."

"We'll make it an educational trip," I said. "We'll have Kirk and Nance teach them about ocean currents or the breeding patterns of mollusks or something."

"I'm sure they'll appreciate that on their vacation," said Jenny.

"Hey, isn't that Helen Hanson?" I asked, wanting a subject change before my little lie got way too complicated.

"Where?" asked Jenny.

"Over there," I said, pointing at a woman who was jogging gingerly across the snow and onto the plowed walking path.

"Joe, that woman's about twenty years younger than Helen and at least fifty pounds lighter."

"Oh," I said, squinting my eyes at the woman. "I guess maybe I need my reading glasses for more than reading."

"Hey, Dad, there's your friend!" said Conor, pointing to the television with the remote.

I looked up from the magazine I'd been reading to see a picture of Kristi and Tuck Drake to the left of a newscaster. Scrolling below her were the words **Special Report.**

"Turn it up, Conor," I said.

"**—while Senator Drake is unharmed, it appears Mrs. Drake has been taken to Georgetown University Hospital—**"

"Turn it up!" I said as the phone rang.

Conor leapt up and after answering it, handed the receiver to me, his eyes wide.

"Joe," said Kirk, "have you heard about Kristi?"

"I've got the TV on right now. What happened?"

"She's been shot!"

"What?"

"Wait—they're saying something now!"

"**—while there were no witnesses, the assailant was apprehended by the parking lot's attendant, who gave chase when he saw a person running in between cars.**"

A man appeared on the screen with a title that identified him as George Ramirez.

"**I didn't know what was going on—all I knew was something was not right. I was sitting in the booth and didn't hear nothing—no gunshots, nothing. Then I saw someone running—the parking lot is lit up, but it was still kinda dark, I wasn't really sure what I was seeing, all I thought was: why is that person running so crazy? Next thing, I jumped out of my booth and that's when I started hearing someone yell for help, but I couldn't see them so I ran after the person I could see and tackled her. Then I called the police. My wife gave me my cell phone for Christmas—and I'm glad she did.**"

"Nance is on the phone with the hospital now," said Kirk. "I'll call you back when I know more."

Conor crawled onto my lap, his usual bluster evaporated.

"Daddy, I'm scared," he said.

I held him tight, feeling the same.

"Have you got everything?" asked Jenny.

"Everything but you," I said, leaning across the seat to give my wife one last kiss before I went into the airport. "I'll be back for your birthday."

"You better be," she said. "Give my best to Kirk and Nance and the girls." She hesitated a moment. "And Kristi."

"I will," I said, getting out of the car I'd rather have stayed in.

The hospital updates Kirk called in weren't much different from what we heard on TV but that changed when he was finally able to talk to her.

"She wants to see you, Joe."

While my inner voice protested, I offered a weak, "She does?"

"She says she needs all her friends right now and—" Kirk's voice broke and it took a moment before he went on. "And she said since you're her only one, she hopes you'll come and see her."

"How long is she going to be in the hospital?"

"They want her here one more night, then we're taking her home to Florida tomorrow morning."

"What about Tuck?"

"She wants him to stay in Washington." Kirk paused, then cleared his throat. "It would mean a lot to me too if you came down here, Joe."

"Talk about the burdens of friendship."

Kirk laughed. "So I'll see you tomorrow?"

"If I can get a flight."

I could, and Don, the manager of the Cocoa Beach Haugland Foods, picked me up at the airport.

"Strange times, huh?" he said, putting my suitcase in his trunk.

"You're telling me."

There were vans with television station logos parked in front of Kirk's house, and as soon as I got out of the car, a small crowd of reporters and cameramen surrounded me.

"Are you a friend of Mrs. Drake?"

"What's your connection to the family?"

"May we have your name?"

Keeping my head down, I made my way to the door, responding to none of their questions.

A moment after I knocked on the door, Kirk lifted a corner of the towel they had tacked over the rectangular door window. Seeing me, he smiled broadly and opened the door just wide enough for me to squeeze through. The cameramen jostled, hoping to get a shot of the interior of the house.

"Man, this is crazy!" I said after Kirk closed and locked the door behind me.

"You're telling me. We've got the girls staying at a friend's house, so at least the vultures aren't getting them on camera."

Nance hugged me. "We're so glad you're here, Joe."

"Where's the patient?"

"In the guest room," said Kirk, gesturing toward the hallway. "She's sleeping."

"How is she?"

"Subdued. Which isn't a bad thing for Kristi, I guess."

"Have you had dinner?" asked Nance.

I nodded. "They gave me a bag of peanuts on the plane."

"I'll make you a sandwich," said Nance, going into the kitchen.

"And I'll make you a drink," said Kirk.

I followed him to the bar.

"So tell me what you know," I said, sitting down.

"How about a key lime martini?" he asked, unscrewing the cap of a gin bottle.

"Sounds good."

"Well, you probably know as much as I do," he began, and as he made the martinis, he told me things I already knew: that the assailant was a woman in her thirties who claimed she loved Tuck Drake.

"Funny way of showing it," I said.

"Yeah, well, apparently she's been in and out of mental hospitals. Obviously delusional—although how anyone could be delusional enough to think they loved Tuck Drake is beyond me."

We both laughed.

"Nice way to talk about your sister who's just been shot," I said, and the word **shot** immediately snuffed out my laughter. "How is she, really? They said it was touch and go for a while."

"Well, she did lose a lot of blood," said Kirk, rubbing a twist of lime around the rim of the martini glass and handing it to me. "She got two transfusions. But I don't know if it was ever to the point of being touch and go. The bullet went right in here"—

he pointed to the side of his chest—"but it got lodged in the underwiring of her bra."

We looked at each other for a moment and laughed again.

"It's the wound to her arm that bled so much. She'll probably have some nerve damage."

Nance brought out my sandwich on a tray and set it on my lap.

"Free-range chicken," she said. "From Haugland Foods."

The phone rang, and Kirk answered it.

"No, she's still sleeping, Tuck. Yes . . . yes . . . yeah, I'll make sure she calls you when she wakes up. . . . Okay, Tuck, good night."

He shook his hand. "He's been calling every hour on the hour. He's pretty shook up."

"Who wouldn't be?" I said, taking another sip of my drink.

"Just for a change of subject," said Nance, "tell us about Jenny's party. I hope we can make it, but the way things are going . . ." She shrugged.

"Don't worry. I'll take lots of pictures." I finished the last inch of martini in my glass, and Kirk, whose true calling may well have been that of a master barkeep, took my glass to refill it.

"As far as I know," I continued, "she still doesn't know anything about it. Flora and Nick are flying in, but they'll stay at my mom and Len's house. Jenny has no **clue**."

"She'll be so thrilled."

"Her woodwind group is going to play, and so will the boys and I, and Flora said Nick's written her a special song he'll sing to her, with Flora accompanying him on the flute."

"Oh!" said Nance. "That sounds wonderful!"

A faint bell rang.

"What's that?" I asked, accepting my second martini of the last twenty minutes.

Both Kirk and Nance rose at the same time and said, "Kristi."

The hand of her bandaged arm rested on her lap and she patted the bed with her other hand.

"Joe," she said, "sit closer."

My heart raced as I sat gingerly next to her on the bed, wishing Kirk and Nance were still in the room, but she had banished them.

"Don't be afraid, Little Red Riding Hood," she said, smiling. "In fact, come closer and give Granny a kiss."

I leaned forward and brushed her forehead with my lips.

Sitting back up, I looked at her, thinking how frail she looked and then realizing she didn't look frail at all; she just looked different. Cleaner, somehow. Softer.

"It's the makeup," she said, reading my face. "I'm not wearing any."

"Oh," I said, and coughed.

She laughed. "I don't mean to scare you."

"Actually, you look good. I mean, for getting shot. Wow. That's a big deal. I'm so sorry."

Looking down at her fake, still plump breasts, she said, "You'd better believe I'm going to do a commer-

cial for the bra company that left these babies in-
tact." She laughed again, or started to, but then her
eyes teared up and she forgot what was so funny.

I took the hand on her lap and held it, repeating
how sorry I was.

Kristi shook her head. "I thought **I** had some de-
ranged fans," she said. "Never did I think it'd be one
of my husband's who'd get me."

I kneaded her hand, her big diamond digging into
the skin of my hand.

"Ouch."

"I'd take it off," said Kristi, "but I'm supposed to
keep my other arm still."

"Why would you want to take your wedding ring
off?" I asked.

The tears made a reappearance in her eyes.

"Because I don't think I'll have a husband much
longer."

I didn't understand. "Kristi, Tuck's fine—he didn't
get hurt."

"I know **that,**" said Kristi with some of the old fire
in her voice. "What, do you think I've got a head injury too?"

"It's just . . . I . . ."

Kristi's chest rose with one short laugh. "I'm sorry,
Joe, you're the last person I want to yell at." She exhaled sharply. "I know Tuck didn't get hurt. I know
I'm the one who told him to stay in Washington so
he could 'continue to do our good work.'" Her voice
sweetened in sarcasm as she said the last few words.
"I know **everything,** which in this case is way too
much."

I looked around the room; it was too hard to look

in her eyes. I was used to seeing many things in
them, but never such naked pain.

"Joe, he pushed me."

Her words hung in the air like a ripe fruit I didn't
want to pick.

She stared at me, scraping her teeth against her
bare lips.

"He didn't push me away from the shooter, he
pushed me toward her."

"Kristi, I—"

"Well, not really toward her, I guess. But to the
side near where she stood. As soon as she jumped up
from behind the car and we saw she had a gun, he
pushed me as he ducked behind a car."

Tears leaked out of the sides of her eyes.

"Oh, Kristi," I said, "I'm sure he tried to push you
out of the way. **Out of the way** from her."

Kristi shook her head. "I wish you were sure, Joe,
but you aren't. Because that's not what he did. He
acted purely on instinct, and his instinct told him to
get out of the way, however he could. Even if he put
me **in the way**."

"Have you . . . what does Tuck say?"

"Tuck knows what he did. I don't have to remind
him. And he's sick . . . sick with fear that I'm going
to tell someone."

"Well, you just did."

Kristi wiped her eyes with her fingers. "I told **you**,
Joe. Because I can always tell you anything. But nobody else is ever going to know."

My blood suddenly seemed hot inside my head.

"Now, wait a second, there's no way I'm not going
to tell what that bastard—that **coward** did."

Kristi smiled. Even without lipstick, or maybe because of the absence of it, her smile was radiant.

"You're not going to tell anyone, Joe. Please. I am going to divorce him, but this shooting's not going to be why. Or at least I'll make sure the public doesn't know it's why." Her sigh was so long it was almost comical. "I really loved him, Joe. It surprised me that I could love someone like that. He made me feel safe, if you can believe that." She shook her head. "The page I told you about?"

I nodded, pretty certain where the conversation was headed.

"He **was** sleeping with her. And one of his top fund-raisers. And a lobbyist for a company that makes artificial hearts, for God's sake—how's that for some lousy irony? There were probably more, but I stopped trying to find out."

"Kristi, I am so sorry."

"I know you are, Joe. I am too. Sorry about so many things, there aren't even numbers to count them with."

"What are you going to do now?"

"Find a new presidential candidate I can support."

We both gave her joke a little laugh and then she shrugged.

"I know my life is going to—**has to**—change drastically, but for my own sanity, I'm not thinking past anything but when I can use my right hand again." She waved her left hand. "Try as I might, I can't put my makeup on with this one."

There was a knock on the door and Kirk opened it a crack.

"Kristi, Tuck's on the phone again."

"Tell him I'll call him back in five minutes."

Like a discreet valet, Kirk closed the door noiselessly.

We locked eyes then, and Kristi's welled with tears.

"I . . . oh, I hurt so bad, Joe."

"Can I get you something?" I asked, reaching for the bottles on the bedside table. "Is it time for another pill?"

Kristi managed a smile. "None of those are going to heal the hurt I feel, Joe." With her good hand, she rubbed her chest. "It's way down here."

"Kristi, I'm sure everything will be fine."

Her smirk told me what she thought of this easy bromide, but after a moment, her face softened and she stared off at the window, as if she could see the poolside view even though the curtains were drawn.

"Maybe that's what it took to make me figure things out," she said after a long moment. "Although I think I could have handled a slightly less dramatic wake-up call."

I squeezed her hand. "So what are you going to tell Tuck?"

"Good-bye. Good riddance." She smiled. "That's the censored version."

"Thanks for sparing me."

She puckered her lips and, recognizing a signal to scram when I see it, I gave her a chaste little kiss and stood up.

"I'll come and see you tomorrow morning."

"Thanks, Joe. Thanks for everything. But remember, you can't tell anyone what I just told you."

My little bow made her laugh, but then she grimaced, cupping her still-intact silicone breast.

I was the only one having breakfast on the patio, the gusty winds that whipped napkins across tables and tossed the palm fronds side to side having driven in the other hotel guests. Determined to enjoy Florida in February, I dodged the pecan bits that flew off the top of my waffle as a section of my newspaper skittered across the tile. I tried to ignore the first few drops of rain, but seconds later they multiplied in volume and intensity, and the busboy and I practically knocked each other down in our race inside.

"The paper said there was a slight chance of **afternoon** showers," I said on the phone to Kirk. "It didn't say anything about a morning deluge."

"I'll admit to many talents, but unfortunately, there's not much I can do about the weather."

"Speaking of your many talents, I hope you're going to make up another batch of those martinis at lunch."

"Who invited you to lunch?"

"Since when have I needed an invitation?" I said with a laugh. "But I thought as long as I was coming to see Kristi, I might as well get a free lunch and liquor out of the deal."

"Kristi's gone."

In our little verbal spar, this was not a comment I was expecting.

"What? Where'd she go?"

"Back to Washington. Tuck and his entourage blew in at six o'clock this morning and they blew out by six-thirty."

Even though my mouth was open, there were no words coming out of it.

"Kristi didn't tell Nance and me much more than what we heard on the news, but we both got the impression that she wasn't at all happy with Tuck. It surprised the hell out of us that she went back to Washington with him. Did she tell you anything?"

I grimaced, grateful he couldn't see my face.

"No," I lied, trying to sound perplexed. "She told me about the shooting . . . but nothing more. I mean, not a lot of details. We mostly talked about old times; I thought I should just try to cheer her up."

Finally my mouth closed and the blathering stopped.

"Are you sure?" said Kirk after a moment.

My loyalties were at war; I had a belief in the sanctity of a secret, but it was a selective one. Still, I wasn't ready yet to tell Kristi's, so I lied again.

" 'Course I'm sure."

At lunch, Nance tried to pry more information out of me, but I played dumb.

"Well, you two know her better than I do, but I just got the sense there was something she wasn't telling us," she said as she poured me another cup of coffee to offset the martini.

"There's probably a lot Kristi doesn't tell us," I offered.

"It'd probably blow our minds if she did," said Kirk.

I nodded in agreement while thinking, **If only you knew.**

My flight was delayed due to the weather, and I sat in the terminal, slogging through a paperback—a supposed thriller. I had given it three chapters, but thoroughly unthrilled, I dog-eared the page and was about to browse through the magazine racks when the name Kristi Casey rose up over travelers' chatter, businessmen's conversations, and flight announcements.

I looked up at the television monitor to see Kristi leaning into Tuck Drake as they stepped up to a podium.

"Yeah, well, make sure it's defrosted, because if you put it in—"

My glare was successfully fierce, quieting the woman giving out cooking instructions over her cell phone.

"As you know," whispered a reporter, "Mrs. Drake has been in Florida, recuperating from her gunshot wounds, and it is a bit of a surprise to see her at this hastily called press conference. . . ."

Big blond Tuck Drake had one of his big beefy arms around Kristi, who looked like a yoked ox resigned to work the fields. Tuck leaned into the metal bouquet of microphones.

"Thank you all for comin'," drawled the cowardly sack of blond shit as flashbulbs flared and blazed, "but most of all, I'd like to publicly thank the beautiful brave woman next to me for being my wife . . . and hopefully your next vice president."

The collective gasp that was heard on the TV was echoed by one in the terminal.

"Now, I'm a little emotional, considerin' all that's happened, so I'd like to turn things over to my wife and running mate, and let her explain things to y'all."

Kristi turned on her beautiful, camera-ready smile

and then let it fall, as if it couldn't be sustained under the weight of emotion but then—there! yes!—she summoned the strength to show us that not only were her teeth white and sparkly but everything was all right.

"It's been a tumultuous week," she began, her voice so soft that everyone seated in the terminal leaned forward. Kristi began to speak again, but sat back, blinking back tears as she wrestled with the emotion that seemed determined to pin her. But Kristi, being Kristi, was able—of course—to persevere, and when she leaned in toward the microphones, her eyes glittering with tears, all of America knew what a strong woman we were dealing with.

"But I've always felt when God tests us, the only thing we can do is try to get an A plus!"

Her husband squeezed her shoulder, and I saw her wince. Unlike everyone else, I understood that wince, how she had to recoil from the touch of that big slab of cowardice, but she quickly recovered and, smiling bravely, touched her chest, as if it hurt to be jostled.

"After much prayer and meditation, Senator Drake and I decided that we were not going to let an act of violence ruin our lives. In fact, it was our duty, as Christians and patriots to rise above the violence, to use this act of violence for the greater good. And so when Tuck asked me to be his running mate I thought: **Yes, I will not serve the violence; instead, I will serve my country and serve my God.**"

As Kristi spoke, I have no memory of breathing, of blinking, of doing anything but stare at that television monitor, feeling as if there was life on Mars and I was witness to it.

"Oh, I know there will be outrage from some corners—'There can't be a husband and wife team running the country'—but surely you history fans know that the First Lady is often the first one the president goes to for counsel and advice. Drake and Casey Drake will just make it official. Others might holler about the separation of church and state, but let me tell you right here and now that the only thing I'll try to convert as VP is this country—convert it to the loving, moral, and righteous nation it can and should be! Others might scream, 'Are we ready for a woman second in command—especially one who has no experience in politics?' and my answer is, we're overdue. Women don't need degrees in political science or years shuffling paper as a city council member to know how the world turns. We're in trouble, people, and the old ways haven't been working. With your support, Tuck and I hope to pick up the hammer and the nails, the wrenches and the pliers, and get to work."

Tuck Drake's big meaty hand squeezed Kristi's shoulder, and then he offered his own white and shiny teeth for the cameras.

"All I'll say to that, ladies and gentlemen, is amen!"

The next day, on Jenny's birthday, I asked her to stop at the store.

"I left your present there," I said. "In my office."

"Oh, Joe, can't we pick it up after we eat? I don't want to lose our reservations."

"We'll dash in and dash out."

"We?" she said. "I'll wait outside. It'll make you hurry more."

My mind whirred. "Well," I said, "I'll need your help to carry the present."

"Can't you get someone in the store to help you?" she asked, but as soon as the words were out of her mouth, she smiled. "Oh, Joe, the present you're giving me doesn't happen to be a musical instrument, does it?"

I smiled enigmatically. She had mentioned recently that it might be fun to learn the cello, but I had paid no attention to it; she often said it would be fun to play an instrument other than her own.

She pulled into the lot. There were some cars parked there, but that wasn't unusual, as the store was still supposed to be open for another hour. To allay any suspicions a full parking lot might cause, we had arranged car pools and taxi rides for our friends and customers.

When we entered the store, Eileen looked up from her register and waved. This was our signal that Stan, standing behind a bakery display, saw, and he in turn waved to Ben, who was sitting up in my office with the lights off. His job was to send Conor down to the basement and tell everyone we had arrived.

"Okay," said Jenny, rushing by Banana Square. "Let's go get my present!"

"Hold on," I said, pulling her toward me. I kissed her. "Happy birthday."

"Thank you, honey, it is." She pushed herself away from me. "Come on, let's hurry."

"Look at these," I said, picking up a piece of fruit from a display. "Coconuts. Who'd ever think people would want to buy real coconuts—but they do. I mean, they taste nothing like the sweetened stuff in bags."

"Joe, what do I care about coconuts? Now come on, let's—"

"**Surprise!**"

Jenny stood frozen, staring at the flood of people that streamed up the aisles. It was only when Conor and Ben and Flora cut through the crowd and raced up to her that she seemed to realize what was going on. She covered her mouth with her hands and then opened her arms wide to let her children in.

It was a great party. Joe and Sons wowed the crowd with our electric-guitar version of "Happy Birthday." Jenny cried when "All Busy Mothers" played, and cried again when Flora accompanied Nick as he sang the song he wrote for his mother-in-law at the Darva Pratt Performance Center. Contests were held and all the answers had something to do with Jenny, and all the prizes were new Belgian chocolates that Flora had discovered on a buying trip.

When the caterers started circulating among the crowd with their trays, I stole up into my office. Ben had left on the radio and I sat in the dark, listening to the news program that was documenting Kristi's career.

"**After listening to that particular broadcast of** On the Air with God, **Kristi, I'd be interested in knowing how you would plan to govern a country made up of many different religions—and nonreligions for that matter.**"

"**First of all, it would be my husband, Tuck**

Drake, who as president would be governing, and second of all—"

I switched off the radio, which, along with the television, had been playing all Kristi all the time.

"Sorry, Kristi," I said out loud, "but you're not allowed to intrude upon this particular party. Or any future party, for that matter."

I took my chair and sat in the dark, looking out the window.

Seeing Ben flirting with one of the new cashiers, I could see Kirk at his age, doing the same thing with the college girls in their miniskirts. I saw my aunt Beth, laughing and talking with Linda and Swanny Swanson, and thought of how she had made the suggestion, all those years ago, that I go put in an application at Haugland Foods. I saw Len kiss my mother as Shelly Erickson fetched a plate for old Mrs. Brady. I saw Clarence Selwin in conference with Millie Purcell and remembered when he had first met Martha, his wife-to-be, while reciting Walt Whitman at Banana Square.

I saw Stan, my loyal assistant manager, sweeping up a spill, and thought of Ed and all he had given his own assistant manager.

I saw the newlyweds, Flora and Nick, showing their wedding rings to Eileen, the queen of cashiers. I saw Conor in the candy aisle, helping himself and another boy to less sophisticated chocolate than the Belgian stuff.

I looked in the bakery section.

"Joe?" whispered Jenny, coming toward me in the dark. She sat on my lap and the swivel chair creaked as it swayed. She put a hand to my face. "Why are you crying, honey?"

"Was I?" I said, feeling like an idiot as I sniffed and wiped my eyes with my fingers.

Jenny kissed me.

"It's the best birthday I ever had."

I nodded and we both sat for a moment, looking out the window.

"I love the view from up here," said Jenny. "Look, Conor's filling his pockets with candy!"

"Our modern-day Mr. Snowbeck," I said of our departed Twinkies shoplifter. I cleared my throat. "Do you know what else I was looking at?"

Jenny shook her head.

"I was looking at the bakery section, remembering the day you came in and you won the apple pie."

"You rigged the contest."

"Damn straight."

"I'm sure glad." She straightened her back. "Hey, Nick's getting back on the stage."

"We should go down and hear him," I said, but neither one of us moved.

The party, with its laughs and music and chatter, continued down below us, but for me, the party was holding my fifty-year-old wife in my arms, breathing in the smell of her fifty-year-old hair, her fifty-year-old skin.

"Joe," she said, "you're crying again."

"I know," I said. "It's just—well, I never could have imagined . . . all this. All this **life.** Everything I see out this window." She sat quietly in my arms, nodding as I added, "Our view from Mount Joy."

About the Author

Lorna Landvik is the bestselling author of Patty Jane's House of Curl, Your Oasis on Flame Lake, The Tall Pine Polka, Welcome to the Great Mysterious, Angry Housewives Eating Bon Bons, and Oh My Stars. Married and the mother of two daughters, she is also an actor, playwright, and dog park attendee with the handsome Julio.